PRAISE FOR JODI TAYLO
THE CHRONICLES OF ST. MA

"A carnival ride through laughter and tears with a bit of time travel thrown in for spice . . . readers will be impatient for later installments."

—*Publishers Weekly*, starred review

"What a mess. A *glorious, glorious* mess. Let no one ever say that *Just One Damned Thing After Another* is a book that fails to live up to its title . . . . These books are so perfectly bingeable."

—*B&N Sci-Fi Blog*

"Taylor does a great job of setting up an appealing cast of characters in this new series opener, most especially the intrepid Max. There is plenty of humor, lots of action, and even a touch of romance."

—*Library Journal*

"Taylor has written a madcap and very funny hodgepodge of a novel whose pacing and humor is reminiscent of a Simon Pegg–Edgar Wright film."

—*Booklist*

"Max is a thoroughly hilarious and confident narrator and the sense of real danger, interspersed with copious amounts of tea, pervades the story. This is the kind of book that you walk away from believing in time travel."

—*Manhattan Book Review*

"Danger, romance, history, financial and academic politics, hidden agendas, dangerous assignments, characters you care about, and the feeling that more is going on than you're actually reading about. I can hardly wait for book two. *Just One Damned Thing After Another* is a true page-turner."

—*SFRevu*

THE LONG AND SHORT OF IT

THE LONG AND SHORT OF IT

STORIES FROM THE CHRONICLES OF ST. MARY'S

JODI TAYLOR

Night Shade Books
New York

First Night Shade Books edition of *The Long and Short of It* published 2017

Night Shade books may be purchased in bulk at special discounts for sales promotion, corporate gifts, fund-raising, or educational purposes. Special editions can also be created to specifications. For details, contact the Special Sales Department, Night Shade Books, 307 West 36th Street, 11th Floor, New York, NY 10018 or info@skyhorsepublishing.com.

Night Shade Books™ is a trademark of Skyhorse Publishing, Inc.®, a Delaware corporation.

Visit our website at www.nightshadebooks.com.

10 9 8 7 6 5 4 3 2 1

Library of Congress Cataloging-in-Publication Data

Names: Taylor, Jodi, author.
Title: The long and short of it : stories from the chronicles of St. Mary's / Jodi Taylor.
Description: New York : Night Shade Books, [2017]
Identifiers: LCCN 2017025213 | ISBN 9781597809153 (softcover : acid-free paper)
Classification: LCC PR6120.A937 A6 2017 | DDC 823/.92--dc23
LC record available at https://lccn.loc.gov/2017025213

Printed in Canada

CONTENTS

INTRODUCTION

THIS BOOK CAME ABOUT because so many people told me how much they would like a print edition of the short stories, especially to give as a present. Since, at the time, there were only four St. Mary's short stories in existence, it seemed unlikely that Accent Press, magnificent though they are, would publish so short a book, so I put the idea to one side and got on with other stuff.

The requests, however, did not go away and now I finally have enough material to make a full-length paperback. I've also written a little introduction for each story, explaining where I got my ideas from and the often embarrassingly shameful series of circumstances that led to them being written. Please don't judge me.

The one I wanted to include, however—the twenty-thousand words I'd written for *What Could Possibly Go Wrong?* concerning the murder of the princes in the Tower of London—could not be found anywhere. I was cursing buckets, because it was good stuff and I only took it out of the novel because it made the book far too long. I searched and searched, but no luck. Every now and then, I still go back and have another trawl through the files. I think it was Einstein who said the definition of madness is doing the same thing over and over again and expecting a different result. So I'm well and truly bonkers then.

These stories—

When A Child is Born
Roman Holiday
Christmas Present
Ships and Stings and Wedding Rings
The Very First Damned Thing
The Great St. Mary's Day Out
My Name is Markham
A Perfect Storm

—have all already been published as e-books, but this is the first time they have appeared in print or collected in a single volume.

As always, huge thanks to everyone at Accent Press and even huger thanks to everyone who buys my books. You're obviously charming, intelligent, and perceptive people, all of you.

For God's sake, don't call it time travel.

WE WORK FOR THE Institute of Historical Research at St. Mary's Priory, just outside of Rushford. Our main task is to investigate major historical events in contemporary time. We don't ever call it time travel because our lives are difficult enough without incurring the wrath of our boss, Dr. Bairstow.

We ricochet around the timeline by means of our pods— small, flat-roofed, apparently stone-built shacks in which we jump to whichever time period we've been assigned. They're all slightly different; some are bigger than others, but the layout is more or less the same for all of them. The console is near the door, with the screen on the wall above it. There are specially designated areas for the important bits, such as the kettle, mugs, and biscuit tin, and you'll always find possibly one historian, but more probably two, firmly attached to their mug of steaming tea and dramatically describing their latest hair-raising escape.

Lockers run along the back wall, containing all the equipment we need for that particular jump, plus sleeping modules and my secret supply of chocolate. There is a tiny toilet but it never works properly and despite malicious accusations by the Technical Section, this is categorically not the fault of the History Department.

We live and work in these pods. We all have our favourites. Mine is Number Eight. They're cramped, squalid, the toilet explodes colourfully and regularly, and they always smell of cabbage, but they're our pods and we love them.

DRAMATIS THINGUMMY

Dr. Maxwell
Chief Operations Officer, historian, midwife, the only one covered in snake goo, instigator of all things illegal and slightly dishevelled fairy. Busy.

Dr. Bairstow
Director of St. Mary's. All-seeing, all-knowing; a bit like the Eye of Sauron but not so benign.

Mrs. Partridge
PA to Dr. Bairstow and Muse of History.

HISTORY DEPARTMENT

Dr. Peterson
Chief Training Officer and willing accomplice. Briefly Superman.

Miss Van Owen
Historian.

Mr. Roberts
Historian—not a eunuch.

Miss Grey
Set off for 12th Century Jerusalem and never returned, then did.

Mr. Bashford
Ditto. Concussed? Who can tell?

Mr. Atherton
Historian. Probably up to no good, because that's what historians do.

Miss Sykes
Ditto.

Mr. Baverstock
Historian.

Miss Lower
Historian.

Miss North
Historian. Can probably self-reproduce.

Mr. Clerk
Historian. Not Dr. Bairstow's father, despite statements to the contrary.

Miss Prentiss	One of the better-behaved historians.

TECHNICAL SECTION

Chief Farrell	Chief Technical Officer
Mr. Dieter	Senior Technician. Built like a brick . . . outhouse.
Mr. Lindstrom	Technician.

MEDICAL SECTION

Dr. Foster	Chief Medical Officer.
Nurse Hunter	Markham's beloved, but surprisingly normal.

SECURITY SECTION

Major Guthrie	Head of Security, stitcher-up of the woodcutter's leg
Mr. Markham	Security guard, cook, livestock tender, exotic carpet inhabitant, unlikely Shakespeare enthusiast, the back end of Rudolph the Red-Nosed Reindeer and everyone's favourite.
Mr. Cox	Security guard. Should have been more vigilant.
Mr. Gallacio	Ditto.
Mr. Evans	Security guard. Unaware of the true meaning of nursery rhymes.
Mr. Keller	Security guard.

RESEARCH AND DEVELOPMENT

Professor Rapson	Head of R&D.

Dr. Dowson	Librarian.
Miss Lingoss	Multi-coloured member of R&D. A steady hand with a recorder.

OTHERS

Mrs. Enderby	Head of Wardrobe and togally dextrous.
Mrs. Theresa Mack	Kitchen supremo and ex-urban guerrilla. Deadly with a skillet.
Dr. Black	Ex-historian. Thoroughly enjoying her reign of terror at the University of Thirsk.
Rupert	Markham's special little friend.
Snowman	With an oddly placed carrot.
Mr. Strong	A man with more memories than money.
Mr. Black and Mr. Brown	Two discreet government officials with varying levels of enthusiasm for "investigating major historical events in contemporary time".
Dr. Evelyn Chalfont	Chancellor of the University of Thirsk. Former leader of the resistance and still fighting.
The Man from SPOHB	Wears cardigans knitted by his mother. No more need be said.
Miss Spindle	A young woman for whom the sight of four naked security guards in more than a revelation.
Miss Lee	PA to Max.

Mr. Calvin Cutter	Co-founder and director of Cutter Cavendish Films. A man who doesn't quite see the point of History. But he will.
Angus	Don't ask. Just don't bloody ask.

<h2 style="text-align:center">HISTORICAL FIGURES</h2>

Aelfric	The woodcutter.
Alice	The woodcutter's wife.
Aline	The woodcutter's daughter.
Harold	The woodcutter's son.
Calpurnia Pisonis	Caesar's wife. Not quite as above reproach as previously believed.
Cleopatra VII Thea Philopaton	Caesar's mistress. Surprisingly nasally enhanced.
Julius Caesar	The man himself. Even more nasally enhanced than his bit on the side.
Greek Secretary	It's all his fault. He invited St. Mary's into the house; what was he thinking?
Boudicca	Another redhead. Say no more.
Mrs. Green	A lady who wants to go to the ball. Ancestor of someone special to Dr. Bairstow.
William Shakespeare	Playwright.
Alfred the Great	Fighting the good fight against the Danes. Founder of the Navy. Fire minder. Failed cake watcher.
A goodwife	Owner of the cakes. Broom wielder. Not happy.

Various Saxon sheep, an old hen, trampling Roman citizens, probably sober Roman chairmen, enraged Roman soldiers, maddened bullocks, Nubians, terrified citizens of Colchester, defiant veterans, unsavoury army deserters, Boudicca's enormous personal guards, an unspecified number of muscular, Egyptian labourers, various armies of various nationalities, urine-clutching students, bribed construction workers, the cast of *Hamlet*, vagabonds, cutpurses, prostitutes, sailors, market policemen, stinkards, and a very, very enraged pig.

WHEN A CHILD IS BORN

AUTHOR'S NOTE

"WHEN A CHILD IS BORN" is the first short story I ever wrote, apart from the stories I scribbled as a child, which were very short indeed and usually concerned the earth being invaded by giant robots and everyone dying horribly by the end of Chapter Two—an old habit I'm still struggling to rid myself of.

The story itself was no problem. These days I think it's a bit short, but everything has a natural length and the beauty of e-books is that a story can be any length it likes. I struggled to find an ending, though. Something that pulled it all together. A twist, maybe, or some sort of revelation. Why they'd found the woodman instead of attending the coronation. They couldn't just quietly go home. There had to be a point to the story.

I pummelled my brain for ages. I researched the key players of the day and their descendants, chasing them down through the centuries, but couldn't find anything that leaped out at me. I looked at major events. I pursued Hereward the Wake to the grave and beyond. I looked at meteorological disturbances, devastating catastrophes—other than William the Bastard himself, of course—I even briefly considered having the Saxons win at Hastings before friends and sanity prevailed.

Then, one night, staring at my laptop, I suddenly thought—I'm not looking at this the right way round. As Mrs. Partridge went on to say, I was looking at things like an historian. I was concentrating on the male side of the story and in fact, this story was all about the women. Once I'd discovered King Henry's inclination to bed any woman with a pulse, together with his determination to be the father of every child born over the next twenty years, I knew where to look. Discovering the wonderfully named Laurentia Henegouwen—of whom you may not have seen the last—I was off and running and so was the story.

The original title was "Don't Eat Yellow Snow", but a friend suggested this one instead. Thank you, Connie.

WHEN A CHILD IS BORN

I WAS IN TROUBLE again. No surprise there. It's my default state.

Dr. Bairstow raised his eyes from my report and regarded me steadily. Behind him, his PA, Mrs. Partridge, sat scratchpad in hand, making the Sphinx look like a collection of facial tics.

Yes, I was in trouble again.

He cleared his throat. Here we go.

"Dr. Maxwell, the assignment was—I believe I have I have the details here . . . ah, yes—jump to London, Westminster Abbey, 25th December 1066. Witness the coronation of King William I. Ascertain the cause of the disturbance that interrupted the ceremony and discover the extent of the subsequent fire and riots. I'm almost certain I impressed upon you the importance of our client and the need for a successful conclusion."

"Yes, sir. You were very clear."

"I also know that while brevity is admirable, I do require something a little more detailed than just 'It was very cold'."

He shut down the data stack and regarded me again. "You don't see the need to perhaps—flesh things out a little?"

I racked my brains for something that wouldn't make things worse.

"It was snowing, sir."

The silence in the room grew very loud.

"So, to recap. I despatch my two most senior historians—you, Dr. Maxwell and Dr. Peterson. I assign the head of security, Major Guthrie, to support you, together with—and the reason for this escapes me now—Mr. Markham. And your combined talents and expertise can produce nothing more remarkable than 'It was very cold'."

"And snowing," he added, seeing me open my mouth.

I shut it again.

"Where is the rest of your team, Dr. Maxwell?"

"In their quarters, sir."

"They did not feel the need to join us this morning?"

Of course they bloody didn't. They were in the bloody bar. We'd drawn lots. I'd lost.

He pointed.

"Sit down."

Half of me was glad to sit down. The other half was clamouring to join the others in the bar.

He settled back in his chair.

"Report."

I opened my mouth.

"In full, this time."

I discarded what I had been going to say and gave him the truth.

WE WORK FOR ST. Mary's Institute of Historical Research. We investigate major historical events in contemporary time. We do not call it time travel. The Boss, Dr. Bairstow, gets very annoyed about it. Actually, many things annoy him. Currently top of the list—me.

Using our pods, we jump back to whichever time period we've been allocated and observe. Just that. We do not interfere. It's supposed to be our prime directive.

That doesn't always turn out so well.

PETERSON BUMPED THE POD on landing. I don't know how he manages it.

When we got ourselves sorted out, we realised we were in the wrong place. Instead of being tucked away in a neat little alleyway only a stone's throw from Westminster Abbey, we were actually several miles away in a snowy wood on a hillside, looking down at smoky London town below us.

"I can't understand it," said Peterson, defensively, his breath clouding in the cold, frosty air. "The coordinates are spot on. Maybe IT made a mistake."

It was more likely the coordinates were right and we were wrong. It does happen occasionally, and at least we weren't perched precariously on the lip of an active volcano or at the bottom of the sea. It just meant we had a two-mile walk downhill through a Christmas-card landscape to get to our destination. It could have been worse. You can't outrun a pyroclastic flow.

We sent Markham on ahead as a kind of human snowplough and trudged along behind in single file. It wasn't unpleasant. Although the day was bitterly cold, the sun shone, the exercise kept us warm, and we had one of England's more exciting coronations to look forward to.

Just two months after his victory at Hastings, William the Conqueror, anxious to consolidate his hold on a sullen and resentful Saxon England, had ordered his coronation at Westminster Abbey. Peterson and I were keen to see the Abbey since we'd jumped there once before to watch its early construction. We hadn't seen a lot on that occasion because a huge block of stone had fallen out of the sky nearby and Peterson had peed on me.

Contemporary records say that at the part of the ceremony where William was crowned, the cries of acknowledgement were so enthusiastic that the soldiers stationed outside panicked and set fire to part of the building, thereby unleashing riots and generally disruptive behaviour.

"Typical military," said Peterson, wading through a snow-drift.

"Yes," said Major Guthrie sarcastically. "Because the history department's never set fire to anything in its entire life, has it?"

How this little discussion would have ended was anyone's guess, because at that moment, Markham halted, bent forward, and said quietly, "Blood."

"Stay here," said Guthrie, as he pushed past us on the narrow path and went to look. We ignored him and crowded round. Blood—a lot of blood—spotted the glistening snow. Indistinct scuffed tracks looked as if something had been dragged.

"He went this way," said Markham, pointing down the path.

"What did?" I said, peering between the trees.

"Not an animal," said Guthrie. "We need to go this way anyway, so everyone stick together and stay alert. For the benefit of all historians present, that means *do not wander off alone.*"

We followed the bloody tracks around the next bend. Guthrie was right. It was a man and he was badly hurt. He lay across the path, right in front of us. He wore thick, coarse trousers and a long tunic. His head and shoulders were covered with some kind of hood which was pushed back to show tangled, fair hair. His boots were sturdy, but he wore no gloves. A blood-stained axe lay nearby.

"He's a woodcutter," said Guthrie. "Had a bit of an accident by the looks of things." He paused. "Max?"

I sighed. I was mission controller. That meant they all did exactly as they pleased until an unpleasant decision needed to be made and then, suddenly, it was all down to me. I looked at the man, blue with cold, barely conscious and his left leg wet with bright, red blood.

We should leave him. If you want to put it in the harshest terms possible, we should step over him and continue on our way. Peterson and I had nearly been wiped out once when I just *thought* about intervening in a robbery. History really doesn't like us doing that sort of thing.

On the other hand, I'd saved lives when a wartime hospital blew up. And survived that. And I'd killed Jack the Ripper. And survived that. I'd even meddled with Mary Stuart. And survived that as well. This was just an ordinary woodcutter. In the scheme of things how important could he be? As I looked down at him, his eyelids fluttered.

Above us, a dark cloud passed across the sun. A few snowflakes drifted down.

I sold it to myself on the grounds that he was probably dying anyway. Even just moving him might be enough to kill him. We were just taking him somewhere to die in peace. And it was Christmas Day. Goodwill to all men . . .

They were all looking at me. I nodded and Peterson and Markham heaved him up. He never made a sound.

Guthrie picked up the axe and examined it.

"Was he attacked? Did he defend himself?"

"No. This is a workplace-related accident, I think. Swung at the tree and the axe rebounded. Hit his own leg. It happens."

"Will he die?"

"Probably."

Ahead of us, Markham halted again. "I smell wood smoke."

We inched our way forward to see. Ahead of us, in a small, snowy clearing stood a typical Saxon hut with several inches of snow on its sloping, straw-thatched roof. A tiny plume of smoke rose straight up in the still air. A lean-to literally leaned against the walls and several pens and enclosures were dotted around. Somewhere, a hungry sheep baa'd plaintively and others took up the bleat.

Hanging between Peterson and Markham, the woodcutter made a small noise.

"Wait here," said Guthrie. They lowered him to the ground and Guthrie and Markham crept forward. Peterson watched the clearing and I watched the path. The times were dangerous. All across the country, Norman overlords were taking ruthless possession. Saxon culture was being dismantled and destroyed. Desperate, landless Saxons roamed everywhere. Rebellions were bloodily obliterated before they even got going. William, aware of his still precarious hold on this country, was not messing around.

I shivered. With the sun gone, the temperature was plummeting.

There were no other footprints in the snow, but we were cautious all the same. Guthrie thumped on the wooden door and after a few seconds, carefully pushed it open. He disappeared inside. Markham remained on the threshold, covering him.

Guthrie reappeared suddenly. "Max! Quick!"

Responding to something in his voice, I was across the clearing and stepping down through the door almost without thinking.

The floor was further down than I thought and I stumbled slightly. Coming in from the blinding whiteness outside, I couldn't see a thing. The smells hit me immediately, however. Wood smoke, earth, old cooking, animals. And fear.

I stood still, waiting for my eyes to adjust themselves to the semi-darkness. When I could see properly again, I could make out a surprisingly spacious interior. The roof sloped down to become the walls. Thatch on the outside, planks with pitch on the inside. Two wide shelves held bowls and cooking utensils. Two small wooden stools sat by the fire and a high bench, which perhaps doubled as a table, was pushed against one wall. A few clothes hung from pegs around the walls. The beaten earth floor was swept clean. Everything looked to be in perfect order. Apart from the occupant.

A central fire, now burning very low, gave just enough light to see the woman on the hard earth floor, curled in rough blankets, her face twisted in pain. She brandished a broom handle threateningly, but even as I looked, her whole body convulsed and she let out a cry between clenched teeth.

I'd once done a stint as a nurse in an army A & E hospital and I knew that cry. I didn't need Guthrie to tell me what was happening here.

"Warm water," I said sharply. "Now."

Warm water was about the best I could hope for. Hot water was out of the question.

The dying fire gave off little light and even less heat, but I could see she was almost certainly younger than she appeared at that moment, with her pale face and shadowed eyes. She had light, flaxen hair, darkened by sweat. I found a cloth and wiped her face. She jerked away, eyes wide and fearful. We were well dressed. We spoke strangely. She had us pegged as Normans.

I have a few words of Old English. I did my best. I don't think she understood much of it, but she seemed reassured. I caught the word "*hus*" and "*dohtor.*" When she said, "Aelfric," the penny dropped.

"Bring him in," I called. "She's his wife."

Of course she was—who else would live in the woodcutter's house but the woodcutter's wife?

They lugged him in and lowered him gently to the ground on the other side of the fire. She cried out and tried to sit up but was gripped by another contraction. I gently pushed her back down again.

Peterson appeared at my side. I asked him if he knew what to do.

"A bit," he said tersely, "but this world is not yet ready for male midwives. I'll stay over the other side of the hut and shout advice and encouragement."

"I can't find the well under all this snow," said Markham, appearing at the door.

"Use the snow," said Guthrie. "Just pack some in that bowl and set it by the fire."

"Not the yellow stuff," instructed Peterson.

Markham grinned and disappeared.

"How's Aelfric?" I asked, rolling up her coarse, woollen dress to reveal her linen underdress.

"Is that his name? I'm cleaning the wound now while he's still unconscious. It's a bit gruesome and I don't have anything to sew it together with, but we can think about that later. How are things over there?"

"Oh, just peachy. Anyone know Old English for—'Put down the broom handle'?"

Sadly, no one did.

"I need a knife."

Guthrie pulled out something with which I could have skinned an elephant.

"Serious overcompensation there, Ian," said Peterson, sterilising it in the fire.

The next ten minutes were quite busy for all of us.

She was still fearful, so I touched my chest and said, "Max." She blinked a little at the unfamiliar sound, but said nothing. I tried again. "Max." I pointed to her husband and said, "Aelfric," and then pointed at her. At first, she stared at me and just as I was going to give it up, she said, "Alice." I persuaded her to relinquish her weapon and after that, she was as good as gold.

Peterson took her hand and then tried not to be girlie about having his fingers mangled.

Guthrie worked away on the woodcutter's leg.

"I can't believe he's still alive," he said on several occasions, "but he is."

I tried to tell myself this was good news but we were racking up demerits right, left, and centre. Without us—without me—he would probably already be dead. Without him to provide for her, and all alone out here in this biting cold weather, his wife might well have died too. And her baby with her.

It got worse. She kept pointing and saying *"dohter."* Peterson, who could see what I could not, looked thoughtfully over my shoulder and got to his feet.

An old blanket lay in the corner, apparently just carelessly dropped, which was suspicious enough in this immaculate interior, and when he carefully pulled it aside, a tiny face peered up at him. She must have scurried under there when she heard us coming.

"Hello there," he said gently, and squatted beside her. "My name's Tim. I'm very pleased to meet you."

If you ever want to charm a woman, Peterson's your man. From nine to ninety, they just drop out of the trees whenever he walks by. And if you want to reassure a terrified tiny tot, then you couldn't do better.

She reached out to him. He sat with her on his lap, carefully shielding her from what was happening to her parents and I could hear him singing snatches of nursery rhymes and childhood songs.

So, on the debit side—one woodcutter, one woodcutter's wife, one woodcutter's unborn child, and now, one woodcutter's daughter as well.

Markham appeared and dumped a final bowl of snow.

"I'm off to check on the livestock. Probably no one's fed them today."

Add one woodcutter's livestock to the charge list as well. We were more than doomed.

"Listen," I said. "All this is down to me. I'm responsible for all this. Seriously, if History turns up in any shape or form, you need to make it absolutely clear that this is all my fault."

"Don't worry," said Peterson, cheerfully. "If History turns up, you're completely on your own."

That was all right, then.

And so we worked away. St. Mary's competently and efficiently patching wounds, delivering babies, playing with the kid, feeding the sheep, and buggering up History like nobody's business.

Eventually, Guthrie stood up.

"I've done what I can for the time being. I'm going back to the pod for the first-aid kit and some bits and pieces."

"Me too," said Peterson, with relief.

"And me," said Markham from the door.

They marched out and the hide curtain fell across the door, which banged behind them.

Cowards!

But I could see their point. Neither the woodcutter nor the woodcutter's wife was likely to take kindly to a couple of men fumbling around her lady parts, however well intentioned.

"Now then," I said, to Alice, whose breathing was quickening alarmingly as she gathered herself for the final effort. "Push. Push. Push hard."

She got the message. She'd done this before.

It all happened far too quickly.

I saw the head appear and I wasn't ready. Wait, wait . . .

She gave the most enormous gut-wrenching cry, dropped her chin on her chest, and gave it everything she had.

I barely had time to collect myself before the baby was ejected with some force, and more by good luck than good judgement, I managed to field him before he bounced off the opposite wall.

I think both of us were speechless for a moment.

Sadly, so was the baby.

I should have let things be. How many more signs did I need today? But Alice was struggling to sit up and making distressed noises. I couldn't look at her. I stared at the tiny unmoving thing in my hands.

Oh, what the hell.

I gently worked my finger around his mouth to remove any yucky stuff and I know it's not the correct procedure, but I couldn't think of anything else, so I hung the poor little scrap upside down and smacked his bottom.

Nothing happened. Nothing bloody happened. So I did it again.

And then suddenly, gloriously, he waved his tiny arms and sneezed, sneezed again, and cried.

I nearly cried myself.

I cleaned up the baby, wrapped him in the cloth she had ready, handed him to smiling Alice, and left them together in a world of their own while I tidied up.

The other patient was awake and anxiously following my every move so I gently took the tiny bundle and carried it to where he could see it. He stared, making movements with his hands. Finally, I got the message and twitched aside the scrap of blanket. His face said everything. I'm sure he loved his daughter very much, but now he had a son. And a wife. And two legs.

It was hard to believe this was not a good day's work.

"Harald," he said faintly, and Alice nodded.

I cleared everything away, throwing what I could on the fire, and left the rest discreetly by the door for general disposal.

I built up the fire using the last of the logs. That was why he'd gone out and left them. He'd gone to get wood. Without the fire for warmth, light, and cooking, they would not have lasted long. Winter or summer, the fire must never be allowed to go out.

I sat playing quietly with the little girl, Aline, until Guthrie and the others should return. The woodcutter dozed and the woman suckled her baby. I sang "Away in a Manger" and Aline, who was the prettiest little girl I'd ever seen, la-la-la'd along with me. It was all very peaceful. Outside, the day darkened, the wind rose, and the snow came down harder.

I was just beginning to worry when they returned, banging in through the door, bringing a flurry of snowflakes and some much-needed supplies with them.

"There's a hell of a lot of shouting down in London," said Markham, cheerfully, dropping bundles by the fire. "Fires raging, people screaming and fighting. You can hear it all quite clearly from up here."

"Any chance of getting down there tonight?" I asked, hopefully.

"Out of the question," said Guthrie. "The snow's coming down hard. I won't even let anyone try and find their way back to the pod tonight, so we'll all be sleeping here."

"Will we all have to snuggle together to keep warm?" enquired Markham, hopefully.

"Only if the sheep will have you," said Peterson.

I closed my eyes. This was so bad.

I'd never actually failed on a mission before. True, they hadn't always gone as I planned. Actually, they rarely went as planned, but never this badly. Granted we'd once failed to find The Hanging Gardens of Babylon but that wasn't our fault because actually they were in Nineveh. Even Dr. Bairstow hadn't been able to blame us for that one. Although he had tried.

I was pretty sure I knew what Dr. Bairstow was going to say about this. In fact, if I listened hard, I could hear him saying it already.

Guthrie was taping Aelfric's leg back together. Peterson waited with the dressing. Markham was emptying a box of compo rations.

"I don't think they're yet ready for beef teriyaki or sticky toffee pudding," he said, "but I've brought porridge and some packs of stew—just add water. Here are some high-protein biscuits. You know, the brown ones no one ever eats. There are some glucose sweets and a bar of chocolate as a Christmas treat."

He bustled about, preparing a meal and I don't know what he did, but it was delicious. We served our hosts and settled down ourselves.

"This is really good," said Peterson, in surprise. "What's in it?"

"A little bit of everything. A couple of packets of beef and chicken stew, and some stock made with snow that definitely wasn't yellow, before anyone asks."

"Good work," said Guthrie. "Nice flavour."

"Oh, that'll be the liver."

His head snapped up. "Liver? What liver?"

"I chopped up that nice piece of liver I found by the door. Shame to let it go to waste."

Spoons paused in mid-air.

"What?"

Peterson was regarding his bowl with dawning horror. I wondered wildly whether this constituted cannibalism. Everyone stared at the suspiciously innocent Mr. Markham.

He couldn't keep it up, collapsing in a giggling heap. "Your faces," was all he managed to get out before Guthrie smacked him round the side of the head with his spoon.

Our hosts watched these strange Norman goings-on in polite silence.

WE SLEPT IN THE cottage that night and it was surprisingly warm and snug. Mind you, there were eight of us in there. And the fire. And a couple of rush lights. And the sheep on the other side of the wall. So from an olfactory point of view, quite lively.

The next morning, Markham fed the livestock. Guthrie chopped wood. Peterson stacked the logs outside the door. I stood in the clearing and stared down at the capital, as if, somehow, I could miraculously penetrate its smoky haze and observe the events of yesterday. The drama here might be over, but there would be hell to pay when we got back.

"Not your fault," said Peterson, coming up behind me. "Dr. Bairstow can assign someone else. For all we know, they're down there now, doing a cracking job."

"Tim . . ."

"Stop that. There are four people alive in there. To say nothing of the sheep. Who but Markham could bond overnight with three sheep and an old hen?"

We left at noon that day. They had everything they needed for another day or two and after that, Alice would be strong enough to fetch help if needed. They were pathetically grateful. We were a little light of kindness in a dark world that for them, was about to change for ever.

I silently wished them luck.

Nobody spoke much on the way back to the pod.

AND NOW, HERE I was in Dr. Bairstow's office. The May sunshine streamed in through his window. Christmas Day, 1066 seemed a very long time ago. In more ways than one.

He leaned back in his chair. Surprisingly, he seemed amused. Was I missing something?

"So, to sum up. On Christmas Day, long ago, you deliver a boy child to a woman in a rural establishment. Subsequently, three of you appear bearing strange gifts and a family of sheep apparently adopts Mr. Markham. Tell me, Dr. Maxwell, does any of this seem familiar to you?"

I shifted uneasily.

"In what way, sir?"

"Do these events remind you of anything? Anything at all?"

I shook my head, mystified.

"Are you sure? Perhaps if you consider carefully, you may find you have acquired a fresh insight into—a certain event?"

Always dispose of your placenta responsibly, was probably not the answer for which he was looking.

I wracked my brains.

"Yes sir," I said, glad to be able, finally, to pull something from the wreckage.

"Ah." He leaned forwards. "And that would be . . . ?"

"Don't eat yellow snow, sir."

I thought of the world's most unlikely Three Wise Men, currently having a quick quaff in the bar, apparently exhausted after having delivered their mystic gifts of casualty kit, kindling, and compo, and shook my head, unwilling to be dragged any further into these deep, theological waters.

He sighed. "That will be all, Dr. Maxwell."

I COULD JUST HAVE put the whole episode down to bad luck. You can't win them all. But for some reason, I just couldn't let it go. The coordinates were correct. So why had we missed one of the most important events of the decade. Why had we landed in the wood?

The answer to that, obviously, was so that we could find the woodcutter. But why? What impact could he possibly have had on History?

None at all, was the answer to that one. Even without his wounded leg, his future was uncertain. The land on which his hut stood might have belonged to him, but not for much longer. A Norman overlord would be installed at William's pleasure, and then their future would be uncertain indeed.

What about the son, Harald? That new-born baby, so limp and silent at his birth. Maybe he grew up—and what? Joined in Hereward's rebellion in the Fens? No. Far too young.

Dr. Dowson, our Librarian, and I searched and searched but there was nothing anywhere. I spent hours tracing family trees, chasing down obscure connections until late one night, alone in the dimly lit library, I let my head fall onto my arms and I must have dropped off because I was woken by Mrs. Partridge, another one who rarely slept. She had a load of files under one arm.

I blinked and focused.

"Working late, Dr. Maxwell?"

I shook my head. "Private research."

"Ah." She peered at my data stack for a moment. "Oh, I see." She turned away and then turned back again.

"Just a thought, Dr. Maxwell, but have you considered *not* thinking like a historian?" and she was gone before I could ask her what she meant.

I stared at the swirling stack of data. The woodcutter, Aelfric. The woodcutter's son, Harald. I had tried every combination, every spelling, every date, every event . . . Nothing.

I flicked a finger to disperse the data and accidentally brought up the woodcutter's wife and daughter. Alice and Aline. Alice Aline.

Something stirred.

I knew that name.

I rummaged amongst the data.

Alice Aline Fitzroy. Illegitimate daughter of Henry I and an unknown mistress. Alice. Aline.

With trembling fingers, I called up more data.

And there it was, all laid out in front of me. Generation after generation. Mrs. Partridge was right and I'd been wrong. I'd thought it was all about either the woodcutter or his son—and it wasn't. I'd been guilty of thinking like an historian. Something that doesn't happen very often, according to Dr. Bairstow.

Because it was *Aline* who was the important one. That big-eyed tot, peeping out from under the blanket. Who would become one of the most important women in English history. Pretty little Aline. Who would grow into a great beauty. So beautiful she would catch the eye of a king, Henry I. Although, admittedly, his eye did seem to have been caught by anything in a dress. Henry fathered a vast number of offspring, most of them illegitimate. But, he acknowledged them all, highborn and low.

The clue was in the name—and I'd nearly missed it because I was guilty of thinking like an historian and adopting the values of the time and disregarding the women.

Because in 1099, the adult Aline and Henry I produced an illegitimate daughter—Alice Aline Fitzroy, and she married Mathieu I de Montmorency and their child was Bouchard IV de Montmorency (who married the splendidly named Laurentia Henegouwen). And their child was Alice Montmorency who married the Earl of Leicester, and their child was—I could hardly believe it—Simon de Montfort.

The Simon de Montfort. The man himself. Sixth Earl of Leicester. The Father of the English Parliament. His successful rebellion against Henry III would enable him to call two Parliaments. Two of the most famous Parliaments in History. The first would curtail the absolute power of the king. The second would introduce the strange, new concept of selecting representatives from towns and villages. For the people to have their voices heard in Parliament.

Simon de Montfort, directly descended from little Aline, who, without a father to provide for her, would not have survived that bitter winter of 1066.

If we hadn't walked that particular path on that particular day . . .

Sometimes, it isn't all about kings or popes or battles or the big events. Sometimes, it's just about the little people.

And that was why the jump had failed. Why we'd landed where we did. Except that it hadn't failed. It had been a huge, an astounding, a dazzling success. Possibly one of the greatest successes St. Mary's had ever achieved. Although we hadn't done it all by ourselves. It was History who had sent us to the wrong location. History had known we wouldn't just step over the injured woodcutter and go on our way. As we should have done.

We'd been used before. History had used us to sort out the Mary Stuart muddle in 1567. And now Aline in 1066. Our actions then were part of History now. Bloody hell! This was serious stuff!

And what else was in store for us as History and St. Mary's inched their way towards a working relationship?

By making that one decision to save a life, we'd begun a series of events that culminated in the first hesitant steps towards the development of modern Parliament. St. Mary's had kick-started the beginnings of parliamentary democracy.

Our Christmas gift to the world.

Sadly, of course, with Parliament comes politicians.

Ah well, you can't win them all . . .

FROM EVERYONE AT ST. Mary's—*Glaed Geol and Gesaelig Niw Gear. Waes Hael!*

ROMAN HOLIDAY

AUTHOR'S NOTE

I WROTE THIS STORY because—and don't think I'm not embarrassed to admit this—I couldn't work out how to lock the front door of my offspring's flat in London. I was visiting, and the pressure of work meant I had to be left alone for a day.

"Not a problem," I said, inaccurately as it turned out. "I'll do an hour or so on my short story, and then go for a walk in the park over the road."

"Fine," they said. The front door slammed and away they went.

I wrote for an hour or so and then thought I'd get some fresh air. There was the usual exit routine—was I wearing matching shoes? (I did once go out with one white shoe and one blue shoe, and not one of my so-called friends thought to mention it to me.) Was everything that should be zipped up actually zipped up? Coat buttoned the right way? And so on.

Passing every test with flying colours, I let myself out of the front door and it had one of those funny hotel locks that I've never been able to get the hang of, and I couldn't lock the damned thing. I tried everything. Key turning, knob twisting, latch pressing, bad language—any and all combinations of all those—and got nowhere.

Defeated, I retreated back inside, and tried to lock myself in from the inside—something I inadvertently do all the time. That didn't work either. I wandered around the flat for a while, alternately embarrassed and annoyed with myself. I thought I'd watch a little TV, but there were around twenty-five remotes on the coffee table and I was terrified of accidentally switching on the oven, or reprogramming the central heating or causing aircraft to drop from the sky. So, lacking anything else to do, I picked up my short story again. I didn't have my laptop with me and so I wrote the whole thing longhand. It's about twelve thousand words, I think, although it seemed a lot more than that at the time. I was still writing some six hours later when they returned home and laughed at me for about forty-five minutes.

Anyway, that's *how* it came to be written. The why is much simpler. Sometimes, I have a picture or a sentence in my mind that forms the basis for the whole book. For instance, in *A Second Chance*, I had a very clear picture of Max standing at an easel, putting up her hair, turning around and saying, "Where's that cup of tea then?"

In *A Trail Through Time*, it was Leon tossing a coin and the two of them watching it rise into the air, winking in the sunlight.

In this story, "Roman Holiday", it was of Markham saying, "You utter bastards." Why he was saying that and to whom, I had no idea, so I had to sit and work out the whole story backwards. And then wrote it all out longhand. And then listened to my nearest and dearest laughing their heads off at me. It's really tough being a writer.

ROMAN HOLIDAY

T HE WORD ON THE street was that we had a project on Cleopatra. Everyone was talking about it. This would be part of the Ancient Rome assignment and everyone wanted to be involved.

The bar was packed. I'm not sure why I mention that, because here at St. Mary's, the bar is always packed.

We work for the Institute of Historical Research at St. Mary's Priory. We investigate major historical events in contemporary time. You might as well call it time travel. Everyone else does.

Anyway, the bar was packed. Everyone was discussing Cleopatra, including, regrettably, Dr. Dowson, our librarian and archivist, and Professor Rapson, head of Research and Development, both of whom can seldom agree on the date, let alone anything else. The discussion followed its inevitable course and they were eventually separated by their respective departments and led away to opposite ends of the room.

Peterson and I, who knew all about the Cleopatra assignment and had already made our recommendations, resumed our interrupted discussion over whether it was possible to smuggle a baby into a birthing chamber concealed inside a warming pan. Chief Farrell, that still, small voice of calm in the insanity that is St. Mary's, remarked that since St. Mary's didn't actually possess a baby, it was, at the moment, impossible to be certain one way or the other. And yes, borrowing one without the owner's consent was, as they say, contra-indicated. In the vigorous debate that followed, none of us saw Markham and Roberts exchange glances and slip quietly out of the bar.

I SUSPECTED SOMETHING WAS going on. People fell mysteriously silent as I walked past. Or rushed around clutching imperfectly concealed bundles of something or other. Data stacks were hurriedly flattened when I entered a room. Both Peterson, my fellow historian and partner in crime, and Major Guthrie, the head of our hard-worked security section, reported similar incidents, but as Guthrie remarked, although he was certain St. Mary's was up to something, behaviour here was so bizarre anyway, it was difficult to tell.

Three days later, Markham and Roberts unveiled their surprise.

They'd chosen their moment well. Almost everyone was assembled in the Great Hall, even our Director, Dr. Bairstow, who had Clerk's and Van Owen's report on the unfortunate death of the MP William Huskisson under his arm, and was enquiring why there wasn't an historian in his unit who could spell the word amonaly. Anonoly. Amono—irregularity.

Since I was stumped for an answer to this one, I was, initially, quite pleased to have a distraction. A blast of static-laden recorded music resolved itself into a fanfare of trumpets, followed by a mighty roll of drums. Startled, I turned to see Mr. Roberts, my youngest historian, standing on the half-landing, staggering slightly under the weight of a rolled carpet slung over one shoulder.

My first horrified thought was that he was naked and I hadn't had my lunch yet. A second glance, however, revealed a very inadequately secured loincloth. I gave private thanks to the god of historians that gravity seemed to have taken the day off. A magnificent torque, obviously made of tin foil, hung across his chest, and a thick, black wig swung around his face.

"Bloody hell," said someone. "Roberts is a eunuch."

"No, I'm not," he said, crossly. In what he fondly imagined was a deep and resonantly impressive voice, he squeaked, "I am Robertis, body servant of the Egyptian queen, great Cleopatra, come to pay her respects to mighty Caesar and entreat his favour in choosing the personnel for the upcoming Cleopatra assignment of which, of course, we know absolutely nothing."

He began, precariously, to make his way down the stairs towards a stunned Dr. Bairstow—or mighty Caesar, as he should probably be known for the purposes of this tale.

He—Robertis, not mighty Caesar, obviously—was sweating profusely under the weight of the carpet hefted over his shoulder. I recognised it as the moth-eaten old thing from Wardrobe. I shot an accusing glance at Mrs. Enderby, who refused to catch my eye.

He so nearly made it. He was only two steps from safety when his legs buckled. He fell to his knees, clutching at his loincloth, whose fastenings had, as predicted, proved unequal to their task. The carpet slipped from his shoulder, hit the oak stairs with considerable impact, and fell down into the Hall, unrolling as it went, to deposit Cleopatra, or Mr. Markham as he's sometimes known, at the feet of mighty Caesar.

I should state now: kids, don't try this at home, because it never happened. If you roll someone in a carpet then, thirty seconds later, they're unconscious through lack of oxygen. Or heatstroke. Or whiffy on carpet-cleaning fluid fumes. Trust me—I'm an historian.

I know that in the film, an immaculate Cleopatra lies appealingly on a priceless oriental rug, batting kohled eyelashes before seducing the most powerful man in the known world, but our Mr. Markham, lying semi-conscious and drenched in sweat, hadn't quite pulled it off.

You had to hand it to him though, he'd made a real effort.

All right, at some point, his wig had come off and was now glued to his sweaty face like one of those creatures from *Alien*, but hairier. His historically inaccurate diaphanous trousers had come horribly adrift, giving anyone who cared to look a first-class view of his Homer Simpson underpants. But it was his bosoms that were the star of the show.

God knew where he'd got the bra from. One of Nurse Hunter's, presumably. I hoped she hadn't been wearing it at the time, although with Markham, you never knew. She wouldn't want it back anyway, covered as it now was in sequins and glitter, and festooned with Christmas tinsel.

He'd obviously taken time and trouble over the composition of his bosoms, discarding the traditional favourites of rugby socks, tissues, or oranges, in favour of two half-lemons, which, as he later unacceptably explained to an unmoved and unmoving Dr. Bairstow, were just brilliant for that authentic nipple-look, sir.

That, however, was for later. At the moment, he was lying in a less-than-alluring heap, purple-faced and gasping for breath, covered in an unbelievable amount of greyish carpet fluff which had adhered itself to every available inch of sweaty, naked skin and showed no signs of letting go.

You want to look away, but you just can't do it. Even as I watched, one of his bosoms, obviously dislodged by the impact, fell from its holster and rolled gently across the floor, until Dr. Bairstow stopped it with his foot.

Silence fell.

St. Mary's held its breath.

Even Robertis seemed rooted to the spot.

Mr. Markham, however, was made of stern stuff.

He raised himself on one elbow, reached out a trembling hand, and exclaimed blearily, "Will you look at that. Some plonker is standing on my bosom."

"Yes," said Dr. Bairstow, icily. "That would be me."

And even as Retribution reached out for him, Markham had to have the last word.

"You're doing it beautifully, sir."

And wisely passed out.

I THINK IT MUST have been this unnerving manifestation of St. Mary's collective boredom that prompted Dr. Bairstow to move the schedule along a little. A few days later, Peterson and I were called to his office, handed the familiar file folders, and told to get on with it. And to take Mr. Markham with us. I didn't enquire, but I definitely got the impression that bringing him back was a bit of an optional extra.

Chief Farrell performed his usual miracles, announced Pod Three was fit for purpose, and that it was a shame the same couldn't be said of the crew.

I held a mini-briefing in my office. Present were Peterson and Van Owen, representing the History department. Major Guthrie and Markham represented—they said—the more stable element at St. Mary's, which came as a complete surprise to everyone else because we never knew we had one. Mrs. Enderby from Wardrobe was there to advise on costume and coach us on the wearing thereof, and Professor Rapson and Dr. Dowson prepared to argue each other to death in the interests of historical accuracy.

"Good morning," I said. "Thank you all for coming. This is the first stage of our Ancient Rome assignment and it's a good one. I'm sure it won't come as a complete surprise to anyone. Caesar and Cleopatra. 44BC. Ancient Rome."

A stir of anticipation ran around the room. Scratchpads were opened up and we got stuck in.

"In another of his moves to become, effectively, the sole ruler of the Roman Empire, Gaius Julius Caesar has invited his bit on the side, Cleopatra, Queen of Egypt, to stay with him Rome. He's the coming man. He's a cocky self-publicist. He's arrogant and insensitive. He's installed his mistress—that's Cleopatra, as so vividly brought to life by Mr. Markham just recently—in his own home. His wife, Calpurnia, who, famously, is above reproach, is still in residence, so only the gods know what his home life must be like at the moment.

"It doesn't matter much, however, because we're only six weeks or so away from the infamous Ides of March which is when he gets his comeuppance. Twenty-three times, actually, just as he's poised to take the final step to absolute power. Cleopatra will flee to Egypt, taking her son Caesarion with her. Later, she'll shack up with Mark Anthony, lose the Battle of Actium, and commit suicide with the probably unwilling participation of an asp or two.

"We won't be around for that, however. Our assignment is simply to observe the crucial run up to his assassination, gauge the mood of the people, and, if possible, catch a glimpse of the fabled Queen of the Nile."

"And return to St. Mary's, unscathed," muttered Guthrie.

"Yes. And that, of course," I said quickly, glossing over the fact that sometimes, that doesn't always happen. Quite rarely happens, actually. All right—not at all. However, there's always a first time and we live in hope.

"We intend to locate Caesar's villa, apparently just outside of Rome, in the Transtiberina area. You all have maps—please familiarise yourselves with the layout of the city.

"Now, I'll be going in as a Roman matron of impeccable antecedents. Roman society is heavily patriarchal, but a well-dressed lady, accompanied by an impressive retinue, will command immense respect. Sadly, however, instead of an impressive retinue, my escort will consist of Dr. Peterson and Miss Van Owen, with Major Guthrie and Mr. Markham to keep us safe."

A word about Roman names would perhaps be useful at this point. Roman men typically have three names: their personal name, their tribal name, and their family name, which is the equivalent of a surname. Hence, with Gaius Julius Caesar, Gaius is his first name, Julius is his tribal name—he belongs to the Julian tribe—and Caesar is his family name. Women have only two names. They're named for their tribe— hence Julius Caesar's daughter would be named Julia. I was Rupilia Euphemia—a name that, as well as sounding like a musical vegetable, simply oozed impeccable lineage. Van Owen was Sempronia Tertulla. Her protests had been ignored. Peterson as (nominal) head of the household rejoiced in Decimus Aelius Sura. The security section, being well below the salt, was making do with just one name apiece. Major Guthrie was Otho and Markham was Pullus. He'd already commented that since he appeared to have only one name at St. Mary's, it was appropriate that he should have only one name here as well. Major Guthrie, as usual, had nothing to say.

Dr. Dowson stirred. "I think most of you already speak Latin, but I've put together an Idiot's Guide for refresher purposes; plus, I'm available for private conjugation should anyone feel the need."

Markham blinked. "Is that even legal?"

I fixed them all with a stern eye. "Roman society sets great store by respectability and so it goes without saying that we will all be on our best behaviour."

There was a bit of a dubious silence.

Mrs. Enderby pulled her scratchpad towards her, smiled sweetly at Markham, and enquired brightly whether he would be togate.

"Certainly not," he said with great dignity. "Church of England."

MRS. ENDERBY TOOK A great deal of time and trouble over our wardrobe. Peterson wore a thick, cream tunic, heavily embroidered with a gold key pattern around the neckline and hem. He was also issued a piece of fabric about the same general size and weight as the county of Rushfordshire.

"Your toga," announced Mrs. Enderby a little breathlessly, depositing this thickly folded garment in his outstretched arms. He sagged a little. "You'll need to practise the folds. Make sure you drape it over the correct arm."

Muttering, he was led away for toga lessons.

Van Owen and I, as highborn Roman women, would wear elegantly draped tunics of pale green and pale blue respectively, ostensibly fastened with golden fibulae, but actually sewn firmly together for safety. As a married woman, I wore a coloured stola over the top of that, and we would both be wrapped in an all-encompassing palla to shield us from prying eyes. As with Peterson, there was a huge amount of fabric to manage. The palla should be draped over your left shoulder, around the back, under your right arm, and then back across the front of the body and carried over the left arm. Try it with a bed sheet sometime. Which is what we spent hours doing, practising climbing up and down stairs, getting through doors without mishap, and walking elegantly without falling flat on our faces.

Markham and Guthrie wore simple tunics and heavy-duty boots. I knew they would both be armed, but Roman tunics finish at knee level, so I really didn't want to speculate as to where they would be keeping their weapons.

WE ASSEMBLED OUTSIDE POD Three and gave each other the once-over for wristwatches, recently acquired tattoos, and the like. A crowd of people hung over the gallery, clapping and cheering.

We filed into the pod. Peterson and Leon Farrell checked over the coordinates, while the rest of us stowed our gear.

"Good luck, everyone," said Leon. He smiled at me and shook my hand as he always did when others were present.

His hand was very warm and strong. I took a moment to smile back. Everyone else looked at the ceiling, the floor, their feet, whatever. Then he was gone.

Peterson closed the door behind him, checked the console one last time, and looked at me for confirmation.

"In your own time, Dr. Peterson."

And the world went white.

WE LANDED ON THE northern side of a small square, which was surrounded by blank brick walls. The early morning sun cast long purple shadows across the dust. It would be warm later on, but at this time of year there was still a bit of a nip in the air. Early though it was, a few market traders were assembling, setting up their stalls and generally bustling around. No one paid us any attention.

Guthrie, Markham, and Peterson disappeared to hire a carrying-chair. No respectable Roman lady walked the streets. Since they were men, this simple task would take at least three of them. Peterson to do the talking, Guthrie to loom menacingly during the financial negotiations, and Markham to get himself into trouble.

Van Owen and I made ourselves a cup of tea, put our fashionably shod feet up on the console, and patiently awaited events.

They returned about an hour or so later with a huge, cumbersome, old-fashioned, wooden affair. To keep the weight down, the sides weren't solid, but swathed in yards of faded, dark red fabric, slightly worn through in parts. It looked like a recent reject from a gentleman's establishment (maybe his mother had died) and as such was perfect for our purpose. This was exactly the sort of conveyance in which a Roman matron would have herself carried around town. The four chairmen looked reasonably hale and hearty and, most importantly, sober.

We climbed awkwardly inside. We can research and practise and prepare until we're blue in the face, but the fact remains—

we never quite fit in. We're amonolous—anony—out of our own time—and in many small ways it always shows.

However, we were in and reasonably comfortable. We pulled the curtains closed to preserve our modesty and Peterson instructed the chairmen to take us to the residence of Gaius Julius Caesar. The chair was a doubly-good idea, not only giving credence to our story, but also taking us directly to our destination without us having to spend hours asking around and wandering the streets of Rome.

The chairmen lifted the chair almost simultaneously—presumably it was too early in the morning for them to be properly drunk—and with only a couple of lurches, we set off.

I swear, I could have crawled there more quickly. On one leg. Blindfolded. Or maybe they were taking us there via Carthage. I would have suspected they were padding their fee, but the streets were steep, rough, and increasingly crowded. The sun climbed higher. What would be a pleasant day to spend lolling in the shade of a fig tree, drinking wine and bullying your slaves, would be nowhere near as pleasant for the four sweating chairmen of the apocalypse. I personally would want to deliver my passengers as quickly as possible, collect my fee, and stagger into the nearest caupona to recover.

The truth was that Rome was a busy place and we moved at a snail's pace because of it. Our colleagues outside might have had to walk, but at least they could freely look around. Van Owen and I, bundled up inside our cloth-covered sweatbox, had to content ourselves with peering occasionally through a chink in the curtains and trying not to suffocate in the musty, hot gloom.

Eventually, however, after seemingly endless lurching, we arrived. Either that or one or more of our carriers had passed out. However, there was no shouting or screaming—always a good sign—and the chair was lowered to the ground with only a slight bump. Van Owen sighed and straightened her tiara—again.

I pulled my palla around me as protection against the bright sunshine and the contaminating glances of the hoi polloi, and with as much dignity as we could muster, we disembarked.

Peterson paid the chairmen a small sum and instructed them to wait. Because we never meant to go in. As we all strove to make clear to Dr. Bairstow in our subsequent reports—we never meant to go in, sir. We didn't think they'd let us in, even if we wanted to. Which we didn't. The plan was that we would stand around outside, mingling with those around us, identify those coming and going, hopefully catch a glimpse of mighty Caesar himself, judge the mood of the crowd, and return to the pod. Maybe doing it all again tomorrow until we had what we wanted. Honestly, Dr. Bairstow, we never meant to go in.

I stood in the warm sunshine and under the guise of adjusting the graceful folds of my costume, took surreptitious stock of our surroundings. Guthrie and Markham were checking out the crowds—and crowds there were, milling around all over the street, hoping to gain entrance eventually and present their petitions. Van Owen and Peterson were listening to what was being said and trying to put names to faces, and I was scanning the property.

It looked a nice little piece of real estate. I saw a smallish villa with its entrance set back a little way between two flanking shops—a leather worker on one side and a wine-seller on the other. Given the rough nature of the neighbourhood—this was far from being the best address in town—Caesar's affection for his first wife and her property must have been considerable.

The villa's wooden doors were thrown open as a gesture of hospitality, but two enormous, shaven-headed, surly-looking door wardens sat at each side, arms folded, ready to deal with potential troublemakers. They were big and they were solid and looked about as light-hearted as scrofula.

I knew the property had come to Caesar through his first wife, Cornelia Cinna. By all accounts, she was the love of his

life. He married again after her death—in fact, his current
wife, Calpurnia Pisonis was his third, but he'd never left this
villa, bringing all his wives here. Not simultaneously, obviously.
And now, obviously not a man who knew when to stop, he'd
installed his mistress as well.

I felt a certain sympathy for Calpurnia Pisonis, living in
the shadow of the first wife and now having to share her home
with the most flamboyant and famous woman in the ancient
world. Every man has a mistress, but they're usually installed
in a discreet set of rooms in a discreet part of town. He does not
brazenly hold court with her as all Rome traipses in and out,
ostensibly to pay their respects, but in reality, of course, to have
a good gawk, suss out what's going on, and report back to their
wives. Which, admittedly was exactly why we were here as well,
but we were carrying out important historical research, not just
being nosey. An important distinction. However, as is so often
the case with St. Mary's, events were about to spiral out of our
control.

Because we never meant to go in . . .

We stood in a tight little group, causing no trouble at all,
and not attracting attention in any way, when a body slipped
out from behind the door wardens and approached us. We
agreed afterwards that it was probably because we had women
in our party—the throng outside was exclusively male. And,
quite honestly, if you didn't know us, you would have agreed we
were the last word in Roman respectability.

Seeing a man draw near, I stepped behind Peterson. Never
speak if you can get a man to do it for you. It also serves as
a useful basis for recriminations afterwards when it all goes
pear-shaped.

Anyway, he was a shortish man and stockily built. Greek I
suspected, especially with that beard. He carried a tablet and
stylus and I decided he was a secretary, as many Greek slaves
often are.

He was enquiring, quite civilly, as to our business this morning.

Peterson took a chance.

"I am Decimus Aelius Sura. This is Rupilia Euphemia. We have recently returned to Rome from the country and wish to pay our respects to the lady of the house, Calpurnia Pisonis. However, should this not be convenient, we can call another day."

Plainly not expecting to be granted access, he was already stepping backwards, but the Greek had other ideas. He spoke briefly and gestured towards the open doorway. Apparently, we were being invited to step inside to pay our respects to the lady of the house, and which lady of the house that would be remained to be seen.

"Exciting, isn't it?" said Peterson, softly, offering me his arm as we were escorted past the door wardens, neither of whom looked particularly impressed by us. Scylla on one hand and Charybdis on the other.

Van Owen fell in quietly behind me and Guthrie and Markham brought up the rear. I made sure to walk slowly, leaning heavily on an ebony cane that could so easily become a weapon, should the need arise.

We advanced with dignity through the vestibule and paused in the entrance to the atrium. I remembered I was a highborn Roman matriarch and didn't gape, but it was a close thing.

Appearances, as I am continually learning, can be deceptive. This small villa, so nondescript from the outside, was beautifully appointed and decorated with taste and style.

Ahead of me, the traditional small pool with fountain bubbled cheerfully, to cool and refresh during the hot summer months. Around the edges of the atrium, doors opened into small offices—alae—in which I could see clerks and scribes bustling back and forth. Caesar was an important man—soon to be even more important if his plans succeeded (which they wouldn't), and his clerical infrastructure was already in place.

A small shrine venerating the household gods stood in a niche on the right-hand wall. Frescos of running lions decorated the walls. The paint looked fresh. I wondered if these decorations dated from his first wife's time and were simply renewed every couple of years.

The place was packed. Groups of men stood around, discussing politics, finance, and their favoured chariot teams: all the things men talk about. You could easily substitute football for gladiators and business suits for togas; nothing changes.

With a polite murmur, our guide disappeared. I squinted at the floor mosaics, trying to trace a line of superb leaping dolphins around the outside of the floor and then craned my neck to admire the view through the atrium across to the peristyle garden. Even this was crowded, with more groups of men sitting on benches and standing on flowerbeds, crushing the delicate plants even before they had time to flower.

I wondered how Calpurnia felt about this invasion of her privacy. Her house, the traditional setting for a Roman woman, was certainly no longer her home. The foreign woman had seen to that. Left to herself she might well have been happy playing hostess to her famous husband's parties, running his affairs during his long absences, working quietly behind the scenes for his good. This was a matron's accepted role, but now he stood, one foot poised, ready to rule the known world as Dictator Perpetuo of Rome. A king in everything but name. However, a king needs a queen and she must surely know that that queen would never be her. How did she feel?

I was about to find out.

The Greek was returning and he was not alone.

"Bloody hell," whispered Peterson. "Talk about stepping into the lions' den."

He was right. Dr. Bairstow was going to go ballistic. Except for one or two notable exceptions, we usually try to keep our heads down. We don't mix with the great and good. We linger discreetly in the background, observing, documenting, and surviving.

On the other hand, no one here was armed. The gathering was purely social with everyone busy eating and drinking at their host's expense. Caesar wasn't here. Cleopatra wasn't here. We'd meet Calpurnia, compliment her on her lovely home, and withdraw. What could go wrong?

Where to begin?

CALPURNIA PISONIS WAS VERY much younger than I'd expected. On the other hand, everyone is beginning to look young to me. She wore a beautiful peplos in a warm dove colour, embroidered with birds and flowers. The colour suited her perfectly, complementing her grey eyes and light brown hair. In fact, the word soft could have been invented just to describe her. Soft hair, soft eyes, soft lips, soft colouring. She stood before us, smiling gently, her head tilted to one side as her Greek secretary whispered our names behind her.

"Rupilia Euphemia! I heard you had returned to Rome after your stay in the country. How pleasant to see you again."

I inclined my head graciously. She couldn't possibly know me. Was she just exercising her undoubted social skills? I suspected something else. I suspected she was very fed up with being ignored in her own home. None of these people here today were anything to do with her. But now, suddenly, here we were, unexceptional guests of impeccable lineage who had called to see her—Calpurnia Pisonis—a person in her own right.

I couldn't blame her. She had ten or fifteen men trampling her garden, twice that number cluttering up the atrium, ten times that number besieging her front door, and her household slaves were going frantic trying to serve refreshments to everyone . . . I was suddenly thoughtful, but that was for later. Concentrate on the now.

And concentrate we did, because before I could say a word, two enormous black men, oiled, glistening, and clad in leopard skins, strode into the atrium and took up a position in the tabulinum—the open office area between the atrium and the garden. Another two Nubians transported a huge golden chair. No—not a chair—a throne. If the over-ornate and tasteless decorations themselves weren't a big enough clue, then the carved arms representing golden sphinxes gave the game way. The cushions were of gold and Egyptian lapis lazuli blue. There were a lot of them and they were probably needed. I've never sat on a throne myself, but they all look hideously uncomfortable to me. I'm obviously not cut out to be a princess. Stick a pea in my bed and far from having a bruised princess, you'd just have a squashed pea.

All around us, voices died in mid-sentence. Beside me, Peterson groped for my hand and squeezed. He was the calmest man I knew—not difficult at St. Mary's where the word volatile doesn't even begin to describe most of us—and for him, this was the equivalent of screaming hysterics.

Cleopatra was coming!

Glancing at our hostess, I could see she was less than entranced at the imminent arrival of supposedly the most beautiful woman in the world, and this was where it all started to go wrong.

In my defence, I can only say that I'm an historian. And human. Probably in that order. I could have kept my attention on my hostess for just a little longer. I could have exchanged a few words with her, perhaps. It would have been the polite and respectful thing to do, but I didn't.

I craned my neck to see Cleopatra's entrance. Just as everyone else was doing. I even took a few steps to one side for a better view. Then, too late, I remembered Calpurnia Pisonis and looked around. She was gone. I forgot her immediately.

I've always been in two minds about Cleopatra VII Thea Philopator. My first thought was—bloody hell, she's ugly!

Because she was. Her nose was out of all proportion to the rest of her face. I spared a thought for her son, Caesarion. By all accounts, Caesar had an enormous conk as well. The poor little kid probably had more nose than the rest of Egypt and Rome put together. I had a sudden vision of him being towed around the ancient world behind this immense nasal feature.

For God's sake, Maxwell. Focus!

My second thought was that you didn't notice how ugly she was. Cleopatra had "it." Whatever "it" was, she had it in spades. She had more "it" than the undoubtedly much prettier Calpurnia had or ever would have in her entire life.

After the shock of the nose, I was able to focus on her other features. She wore an elaborate wig, as did all Egyptian women, but I suspected her original hair was dark anyway. Neither did she did possess the milk-white skin for which she was famed— and at this point I should probably mention that Professor Rapson had done considerable research on how many asses needed to be milked for just one bath and had sent me a report claiming it would have taken a herd of between five hundred and seven hundred lady donkeys to provide enough milk for a daily bath. What he expected me to do with this information was never entirely clear, but his attempt to requisition said donkeys for further research was firmly rejected by Dr. Bairstow. But whether she wallowed in whey or not, Cleopatra's skin remained obstinately olive.

To remedy this, her face was covered in white makeup, emphasising the beautifully shaped but thick eyebrows that gave her face even more character. I suspected she kept the eyebrows to counter-balance the nose. Her eyes, so heavy-lidded as to be almost reptilian, were thickly outlined in kohl. Green eye shadow matched her eye colour, and her lips, in contrast to Calpurnia's, were full and a deep, dark crimson.

This was not a face to be forgotten. I'd never seen one like it before and I've not seen one like it since either. This was a face marked by Destiny. For good or ill, this was the face of a woman who would always be in control—who would take that Destiny and twist it to suit her own requirements. Maybe twist it until it snapped . . .

I pulled myself together and tried to concentrate. I wasn't the only one. Everyone present stared, their mouths hanging open.

Accompanied by some half-dozen handmaidens—what do handmaidens do? I asked Peterson once and he just laughed and said the clue was in the word "hand"—she paraded slowly around the atrium.

She was not wearing the white linen with which we always associate Egyptians. Perhaps it still wasn't warm enough. She wore a long, golden gown of some kind of shimmering silk that trailed along the ground behind her. A blue and gold torque hung around her neck. Gold bracelets climbed her forearms, and on her head she wore the golden uraeus of Egypt. Just in case we'd forgotten she was a queen.

She reached her throne, turned, and faced the room. You could have heard a pin drop. For what was she waiting?

And then it happened. First one, and then another, and then a small group, and then everyone, because no one wanted to be the last . . . In a room full of Romans, republicans to a man, they bowed their heads.

I would never have believed it if I hadn't been there. They bowed their heads. Caesar had chosen his queen well.

She allowed a small, triumphant smile to cross her face, and then, abruptly, she sat. Her dress settled in golden pools around her bare feet.

A sigh ran around the room.

I caught Van Owen's eye and she gestured at our menfolk, every single one of whom was staring, transfixed. She rolled her eyes.

It was too much to hope we would be presented. In fact, we should leave. The presence of royalty meant the presence of soldiers and our superficial disguise would never stand up to close investigation. The sensible thing to do would be to depart. Immediately.

Therefore, we stayed. Actually, I don't think wild horses could have dragged us out of that room. We're historians. When it comes to sensible thinking, someone else has to do the heavy lifting.

In our defence, we would have stayed quietly at the back, preferably somewhere near the side entrance in case we had to make a quick getaway. We were just beginning to ooze our way unobtrusively in that direction, when Calpurnia Pisonis reappeared.

She made a signal and immediately the house slaves began to scoop up the used beakers and dishes and to lay out new refreshments. This time, the platters were of gold and silver. She stood unobtrusively in the corner, quietly directing operations. As yet, the Egyptian queen had beckoned no one forward, talking instead only to members of her own household.

Calpurnia Pisonis approached the throne, inclined her head briefly—respectful but not obsequious—and spoke. An elderly Egyptian secretary translated, although I suspected Cleopatra spoke Latin as well as Calpurnia herself.

Having received a brief nod of assent, Calpurnia Pisonis beckoned to us. Oh my God, we were about to be presented to Cleopatra, Queen of Egypt.

It was Peterson who pulled himself together first. I knew I'd brought him along for a good reason.

He extended his arm to provide me with some much-needed support. We slowly skirted the pretty pool—I remember how loud the splashing water sounded in the sudden silence—and we presented ourselves to the glittering figure seated on the glittering throne.

Everyone regarded everyone else in complete silence. The Nubians stared over our heads. The handmaidens fiddled with their bracelets, bored. Cleopatra swept us with one brief look, which told her everything she needed to know about us, and turned her attention to her hostess.

Calpurnia's voice sounded clearly. I notice she did not address Cleopatra directly, thus obviating the need for any formal address.

"I beg leave to present Decimus Aelius Sura," and she melted away.

Peterson stepped forward, placed his hand on his heart, and nodded. A nice blend of formal and informal. Nice one, Tim. No Roman would kneel to a non-Roman, queen or not.

He half turned and opened his mouth to introduce Van Owen and me, but never got that far. There was a sudden commotion at the door and the room was suddenly full of soldiers.

I just had time to think, "Shit! Busted!" when Caesar himself marched into the room. I could hardly believe our luck. What a great day this was turning out to be.

Or not.

The effect on everyone was dramatic. The Egyptian queen immediately lost all interest in us, gazing expectantly over our shoulders as Caesar strode through the crowd, pausing to exchange greetings and forearm clasps with carefully selected people of influence, working the room like a modern politician. Ignoring his wife completely, he made a formal greeting to Cleopatra, who responded in kind.

And yes, he too had the most enormous nose, jutting from his face like a beak.

"Bloody hell," whispered Markham, behind me. "Imagine if they both sneezed simultaneously. It would be like a twenty-one gun nasal salute."

Caesar wasn't a tall man and I don't think he was as old as he looked. He had a sickly, yellow look that aged him prematurely. His hair was thin and greying and deep lines ran from his nose to the corner of his mouth. But he was a powerhouse.

Energy radiated off him in waves. His presence in the room changed everything within it.

A chair was brought for him. Not a throne, just a simple wooden affair, but several inches higher than Cleopatra's. I imagined their respective households sitting together, thrashing out these compromises.

He seated himself, pulling the folds of his purple toga around him as if he was cold. His short-sleeved tunic was of soft wool—understated, but of the finest quality.

His wife nodded her head and two slaves rushed forward with a marble-topped, claw-legged table. Another two began to lay out wine and snacks. The centrepiece was a great golden bowl of figs, drizzled with honey for extra sweetness. A true delicacy at this time of year.

We had been completely forgotten. Not unthankfully, we began to ease ourselves backwards, and we would have made it, too. We would have slipped away, climbed into our wooden edifice, been carried back to our pod, jumped away, and a large part of History might have been disastrously different.

But it wasn't, for which we have Markham to thank, and that's not a phrase that is often bandied around.

Caesar served the queen with wine and offered her the bowl of figs.

I remember it all very clearly—a frozen moment in time. Caesar holding the heavy bowl in both hands. Cleopatra, bracelets chinking, smiling up at him, and reaching gracefully to take a fig. And just as her hand hovered, just as she was making her choice, I heard a shout of warning; something thrust me violently to one side and Peterson to another. Markham lunged forwards and struck the bowl from Caesar's hands.

Figs flew through the air, flicking honey over everyone nearby.

And then everything speeded up again.

People shouted in anger. And fear. And confusion.

Two Nubians sprang forwards in one smoothly coordinated movement and formed an impenetrable barrier between the queen and us.

Not to be outdone, half-a-dozen Roman soldiers seized Guthrie and Peterson, but, thank God, hesitated before doing the same to Van Owen and me. Markham, however, being neither female nor highborn, was hurled to the floor with a sword at his throat.

No one had any idea what was happening and I was terrified they would kill us first and ask questions later. I was particularly anxious that Markham should be kept alive so I could kill him myself later.

And then, amongst the spilled figs, something moved.

Without stopping to think—again—I brought my sandal down on a small but very indignant snake.

An asp.

Markham very wisely didn't try to speak—just signalling with his eyes. Two more snakes lay curled in the bottom of the bowl. Another was wriggling across the floor as fast as he could go, looking for cover, but not anything like fast enough because Guthrie pulled an arm free, seized my stick from me, and brought it down hard on the snake, instantly breaking its backbone. A substantial amount of snake blood and guts splattered across my pretty tunic. Mrs. Enderby would be wanting a word with me. Again.

Another one was heading for the garden and freedom, but a quick-thinking slave brought a flagon down on its head, picked it up with a stick, and tossed it into the pool. I never saw what became of it afterwards.

A third Nubian had upended the bowl, trapping the two sleepier snakes beneath it. Their future looked nearly as bleak as ours did.

That we were suspects was very apparent.

Chaos cut in. Someone had attempted to assassinate either Caesar or Cleopatra or both of them. That it was deliberate, there could be no doubt. Six snakes do not accidentally find themselves in a bowl of honeyed figs. It seemed a safe bet that everyone here knew everyone else. In fact, there was only one set of strangers in the room and they were the idiots from St. Mary's who had chosen this one day of all others to observe Caesar and Cleopatra, and dropped themselves right in it.

I let everyone else mill about, exclaiming and speculating. I stared at the sad little pile of squashed snake under my sandal and then I lifted my eyes and found myself staring straight at Caesar's wife. Who stood quietly in the corner, as she always did. Unimportant. Unregarded. Unobserved. Unmoved.

As if she felt my gaze, she turned her head slightly. We exchanged looks and I knew.

Shouting men were stamping on already-dead snakes. Seeking to disassociate themselves from this shocking event, many more were stampeding towards the front doors. Scylla and Charybdis had disappeared, their place taken by a quartet of tough-looking soldiers. Another two guarded the side entrance. Calpurnia and I still stared at each other as if we were the only two people in the room. Which, at that moment, to all intents and purposes—we were.

She had attempted murder. But of whom? The hated foreign woman? Or the husband who had made her live in his first wife's house? Who had ordered her to give up her rooms to foreign guests? Who compelled her to serve his mistress? And when he became ruler of all the known world, he wouldn't want her any longer. He would want the woman who was already a queen. Who already had a son by him.

So which of them was the intended victim and did she even care?

I knew what she'd done and she knew I knew. We were in a very great deal of trouble here. I'm not sure whether she had deliberately sought to implicate us. That had not been her original plan, I was sure of it, but the sudden appearance of a bunch of strangers who might not be what they appeared to be . . . she had given instructions we were to be admitted. She had presented us to the queen to put us in the front line. Never mind that we'd had no opportunity. No one would care about that. As long as the blame didn't fall on them. Any minute now, Caesar's men would start taking names. Everyone present would be minutely examined. And not in a pleasant way. We'd given false names and an address that wouldn't stand up to any sort of close examination, let alone the stringent enquiries about to be made. The chances of us being allowed to depart were non-existent. We were in some very serious trouble. We would be arrested and taken away and once they split us up, there would be no hope of rescue. We'd be tortured and if we survived that, we'd be executed. Or crucified. Or sent to the arena. We had to get out of here.

It had happened in one of two ways. She'd either spotted us as impostors and recognised an opportunity to implement her plan and place the blame on legitimate targets, or—and I felt badly about this—I'd insulted her and this was her revenge. She genuinely thought we'd come to visit her—that someone was actually paying her some attention—and then I'd looked away as Cleopatra entered the room. Just as everyone else had done. And the insult had been just one too many.

And suppose she'd succeeded. Suppose Cleopatra died before Caesar. What then? No Mark Anthony. No Battle of Actium . . . No suicide by—ironically—asp bite.

And if Cleopatra had died today, what of Caesar? Suppose her death put him on his guard to such an extent that the assassination on the Ides of March either failed or never took place at all. Suppose Caesar was declared king of Rome. With his son Caesarion to succeed him. How much would that have changed History? The implications were breath-taking.

Were we meant to be here? To prevent a murder?

Possibly. And now it was a very good idea not to be here. But how we were to get out was anyone's guess. I didn't think we were under suspicion—yet. The little misunderstanding was being ironed out. Peterson was talking, his face calm and untroubled, and Markham was being pulled to his feet. But everyone in this room would be investigated and we needed to depart.

I caught Van Owen's eye. She nodded.

I gave a sudden, hoarse cry and clutched my chest.

"Quickly," called Van Owen. "Quickly. My aunt. Her heart. Please help her."

They did.

I was supported to a chair. Wine was pressed upon me. On the grounds that I deserved it, I drank the lot. Believe me, there are huge advantages to living in a society that believes women are delicate and fragile creatures, unable to withstand even the smallest shock. I rolled my eyes, groaned, panted, clutched my chest and everything else I could think of. It was a powerful performance, if I do say so myself.

By now, Caesar had assumed control of the situation. He murmured briefly to Cleopatra who gracefully but swiftly left the atrium, surrounded by her retinue. He issued a series of crisp instructions and the excited gabble subsided. Finally, he approached Peterson and I could see the two of them discussing what best to do. If they offered me a room here then we were sunk.

Never once did he glance at his wife or express any concern for her well-being. As far I as I was concerned, the bastard deserved everything he got.

Peterson, however, was adamant I would be more comfortable in my own home.

"Everyone knows where we live," he was declaring, confidently. "The Street of Six Vines behind the smaller Temple of Juno. Just ask for my house. Anyone can point it out."

Never buy a used car from an historian.

He became confidential.

"She often has these turns. They are getting worse. One day
. . ." he paused, significantly. "She's not getting any younger."

And he wasn't going to be getting any older. Directly after
we were safe, he was going to die. Slowly and painfully.

Caesar, however, appeared to have bought it. We were the
people who'd foiled the plot, after all.

Someone was sent to organise our chair. Since no more
wine appeared to be forthcoming, I allowed myself to be helped
to my feet.

Our old-fashioned conveyance awaited, exuding enough
respectability to satisfy anyone, together with a suddenly wide-
awake set of chairmen. I suspected rumours were already flying around Rome.

Both Caesar and his wife attended our departure, she
standing a little behind him, her face expressionless. I could
not help a little shiver. Whether he was aware of something or
not, Caesar turned around. For one long moment, he stared at
his wife. The man was no fool. I wasn't the only one who had
suspicions that Caesar's wife might not be as above reproach as
she should be. But was she above being caught?

What would he do?

I said, "We need to go. Now," and moaned a little more,
which gave Peterson a good reason for ordering them to get a
move on. And move they did. I swear we broke into a canter at
one point. The old chair creaked and swayed under the strain
and Van Owen, who has a delicate stomach, turned the same
colour as her dress.

I said to Van Owen, "Tell them to get a move on."

She stuck her head out of the curtains and a second later,
we moved up a gear.

We crossed the Tiber, muddy and swollen with winter
rainfall, and finally, two streets away from the pod, we pulled

over. We piled out and Peterson dismissed the chairmen. From the speed with which they disappeared, I suspected he'd massively over-tipped them, but should they subsequently be questioned, they could honestly say they dropped us in the middle of nowhere.

"This way," said Guthrie, getting his bearings and nudging us down a very unevenly paved street. We concentrated on not turning an ankle and Markham brought up the rear.

Nearly there.

WE WERE JUST ONE hundred yards from the pod. Just one hundred yards, when we heard a shout behind us. Mindful of Major Guthrie's oft-repeated instructions, we kept going.

"Never mind what's happening behind you. You'll find out soon enough if you turn to look."

Just about the first thing I learned at St. Mary's.

We kept our heads. Van Owen and I scooped up our skirts and did the hundred-yard dash, sandals slapping on the uneven cobbles. Peterson ran with us. Markham and Guthrie covered our rear. Really, we'd done this sort of thing so many times we barely even stopped to think about it.

It would appear we had considerably underestimated Gaius Julius Caesar, conqueror of Gaul, Dictator Perpetuo, etc., etc. He knew very well what his wife had done. He also knew he could not publicly accuse her. He needed scapegoats. His soldiers had followed us at a discreet distance and when it became apparent we weren't heading for the Street of Six Vines, they'd decided to move in.

Fat lot of good it would do them. We scrambled into the pod and heaved a sigh of relief. We were safe. They were outside the pod. We could just wait for them to give up and leave and then we could jump back to St. Mary's when it got dark.

They didn't give up and they didn't leave. Of course they didn't. Roman soldiers were the best in the world, Caesar's men would be the best of the best, and these would be the handpicked best of the best of the best.

They pounded on the door, which didn't do them the slightest bit of good. Nothing short of a thermo-nuclear blast would get through that door if we didn't want them to. They threw their weight against it and there were some big boys there, but they were wasting their time. After a while, someone turned up with the battering ram.

An interested crowd began to gather.

Soon afterwards, reinforcements turned up. You could see they didn't take it very seriously. The wandered around the pod, kicking the walls and laughing. It was just five fugitives in a small hut, for crying out loud. Come on, centurion, get that door down and we can all go back to the mess.

The attentive crowd shouted instructions and helpful advice.

We made some tea and Peterson handed the mugs around. "I have to ask," he said to Markham. "How did you spot what was going on?"

Markham, unexpectedly, said nothing.

Guthrie put down his mug. "Well, I'll tell you, since he won't."

I looked from one to the other. What was this all about?

He continued. "It's what we do. While you're caught up in the moment—and no criticism; you're historians and you don't see the world in the same way as normal people—anyway, while you're caught up in the moment, we watch what else is going on. We keep you safe. It's our job. Markham saw a movement where there shouldn't have been movement and he acted. Because it's his job and he's very good at it."

I looked at Markham and saw him—small, perpetually grubby, spiky hair, St. Mary's favourite disaster-magnet, but he wasn't, was he? He was tough, competent, and virtually indestructible. I suddenly realised that if I couldn't have Guthrie then I'd rather have Markham watching my back than anyone else I knew.

And what of Guthrie himself? Quiet, assured, solid as a rock. Keeping us all safe.

I took a breath. "We don't say this anything like often enough—but on behalf of everyone here—good job, guys. Thank you."

There was a moment of intense embarrassment, but fortunately the soldiers chose that moment to clamber onto the roof to try and batter their way through, so we were able to keep calm and carry on.

We drank our tea and laughed at them. Our plan was to wait for them to give up and jump away under cover of darkness.

We didn't laugh for long because they didn't give up.

Their next idea was to smoke us out. They dragged up great piles of brushwood and timber—God knows where from—doused it with oil, and set it alight.

Pods are built to withstand a great deal of punishment and I should know. I nearly melted one, once. However, solid and robust as they may be, there's some delicate stuff inside. I wasn't sure how it would respond to being engulfed in a fireball. And what on earth would I tell Leon? It's possible I might have a bit of a reputation for damaging pods and this wouldn't help.

The interior of the pod grew very hot. A couple of red lights flickered. I instructed Peterson to shut down non-essential systems.

We sat in near darkness and listened to them bringing up more firewood. There were five of us in a small space and things began to get stuffy.

"This is no good," said Guthrie, grimly. "We're going to have to jump soon."

"We can't," said Van Owen. "They're too close. This is why everyone stands behind the safety line in Hawking. So we don't inadvertently suck anyone into the vacuum."

"Ah," said Markham in tones of enlightenment. "Is that's what it's for? You'd think a far-seeing technical department would have fitted us with something to give the buggers some sort of electric shock, wouldn't you?"

There was a thoughtful pause and then Peterson said, "Actually . . ." and rummaged in a locker. "I've had a brilliant idea."

This was met with caution. Some of our brilliant ideas—aren't.

He pulled out a disk.

"Voilà! The Sonic Scream."

Van Owen and I stared at each other, baffled. Sweat ran down my back. I wiped my forehead on my palla.

"The what?"

"The Sonic Scream. Something Chief Farrell is putting together. Still experimental, of course."

Silence.

"Look. You've heard of that sonic device? The one that only affects teenagers?"

"What are you talking about?" said Van Owen. "Teenagers are inarticulate, acne-ridden lumps of inert matter. The only way you can ever induce movement is by trying to separate one from its mobile phone. And if you can do that then the only way you can stop it attacking is with rhinoceros tranquiliser."

Harsh words from someone who only ceased being a teenager herself a few years ago.

"No, no," he said, hastily. "You broadcast at low frequency and only they can hear it. Normal people aren't affected. It induces feelings of discomfort. And they're teenagers, so they're pretty uncomfortable already. They don't like it, so they move on. We have something similar here. Not low frequency, obviously, but the same sort of thing. I think Chief Farrell thought it might be useful for hostile animals and suchlike, but it might shift this lot."

I shook my head. "I really don't think broadcasting screams will make this lot go away. Half of Rome will turn up to see what's going on."

"No, that's the beauty of it. Nothing is actually audible. They'll just feel a bit odd—and then, without knowing why, they'll just go away."

"Just like that? These soldiers conquered Gaul. And fought in Egypt. And Spain. You're saying these battle-scarred veterans will feel a slight headache coming on and just wander off?"

"Pretty much. And it's painless. Probably. If it works on aurochs and mammoths and ostriches, it's bound to work on Roman soldiers."

"Ostriches?" said Guthrie, incredulously.

"Long story."

"If you're going to give it a go," interrupted Van Owen, who hadn't taken her eyes off the screen, "you should get a move on. They're coming down the street with chains and half-a-dozen oxen. I think we're about to be towed."

Well, that wasn't good. Obviously, they were fed up and had decided not to waste any more time. They were just going to drag us away. Pods are tough—and I should know after what historians have done to them over the years—but bumping us up and down the Seven Hills of Rome? We needed to get out of here.

"Go ahead," I said to Peterson. After all, it probably wouldn't even work.

He slapped in the disk and switched to audio.

It was embarrassing.

It was a disaster.

You can add Ancient Rome to the long list of places we can never go back to.

Inside the pod, of course, nothing happened.

Outside . . . Outside. . .

Words failed me.

WHEN OXEN STAMPEDE, THEY really don't mess about. Over the millennia, herds of bison have thundered majestically across the prairies, shaking the ground with the fury of their hooves. Six maddened oxen in a small Roman suburb channelled their ancestors and did even better.

The first casualty was a fruit-and-veg barrow. Two seconds later, we had vegetable purée and a lot of firewood. The owner sought refuge in a fig tree. Since he was only about four feet off the ground, it was hard to see what this would achieve, but this was advanced thinking for oxen and they lost interest.

All the Roman soldiers now scrambled up onto the roof— partly to escape the excited livestock and partly to get a better view. People in the square clutched their heads and then scattered as the oxen broke ranks and embarked on the bovine equivalent of asymmetric warfare.

Personally, I thought the fleeing hordes did more damage than the bullocks. The soldiers, shouting a variety of conflicting instructions and curses from the safety of the roof, also contributed more than their fair share to the confusion and disorder. Really, none of it was our fault.

There was only one exit from the square and with the exception of the man up the tree and the soldiers on the roof, everyone and everything headed in that direction. There was a massive bottleneck. Fights broke out. Women screamed. Soldiers shouted. Oxen bellowed.

We sipped our tea and watched the screen in awe.

Twenty minutes later, the square was deserted apart from a few disoriented souls who were rebounding from wall to wall as they attempted to find their way home.

Trampled vegetables lay in the gutters. The remains of market barrows and their goods were scattered over a surprisingly large area. The street was littered with odd sandals, discarded togas, several broken handcarts, abandoned shopping, and surely far more dung than was possible from only six oxen.

Every dog in Rome was still howling its head off. The purveyor of quality groceries was still up the tree and had been joined by large numbers of chickens and a stray goat. Markham wanted to go and help him down, but was restrained by Major Guthrie, who was staring at the screen as if he couldn't believe his eyes.

"Not our fault," I said, defensively.

He closed his eyes, briefly.

"Relax. No one's ever going to know," said Peterson. Wrongly.

One by one, the soldiers dropped off the roof.

"It's raining men," said Van Owen, which was something I'd always wanted to say.

Wrapping their cloaks around their heads, they went for more reinforcements.

"We could sell this device to Asterix," said Markham, the only one who appeared unaffected by Sonic Scream Trauma.

"Can we just go?" said Guthrie, between gritted teeth.

So we went.

IT WAS ONE OF Peterson's better landings. We hardly bumped at all.

"Rather in the manner of a stone skimming effortlessly across a limpid pool," he said.

What anyone would have said to that was never known because at this point it became apparent that our problems were not yet over.

All around Hawking, orange techies began to drop to the ground, arms curled protectively around their heads.

In the far corners of the hangar, the glass in both the IT and technical offices crazed suddenly, shattered, and fell to the ground.

"Shit!" said Peterson. "Did we do that?"

"You forgot to switch off the bloody Sonic Scream thing," I shouted. "Quick."

Peterson flicked a few switches and although nothing happened inside, outside the pod prone orange figures slowly began to unfurl.

"Like flowers at the beginning of a new day," I said, trying to look on the bright side and getting the look from Guthrie that I deserved.

"All this is your fault," said Guthrie to Markham. "If you'd kept your bosoms where they belonged, none of this would have happened. I hold you entirely responsible."

Markham blinked, indignantly. "Not my fault if I have unreliable bosoms. I've got nice bleached nipples, though. Do you want to see?"

"No!" shouted four voices, simultaneously.

Round the hangar, people started to pick themselves up.

Polly Perkins, head of IT and a sweet girl, was being forcibly restrained by members of her team.

Dieter, Chief Farrell's number two and built like a large brick shithouse, picked himself up, staggered a little, and then headed wrathfully for our pod. I had a moment of déjà vu. It was the oxen all over again. He picked up a fire bucket and hurled it with great accuracy and not a little force. It bounced off the pod with a dull thud.

We all stepped back.

"I don't actually care if I have to spend the rest of my life in here," said Van Owen. "I am never leaving this pod again."

I heard Leon's voice over the com link.

"What's going on in there?"

"I'm carrying out a complete systems check," said Peterson, swiftly. "Going to be some time, I'm afraid."

"And I'm checking the inventory," I said. "Don't wait up."

There was a pause and then he said, "You have five seconds. Get your arses out here. Now."

We sent Van Owen out first, because she has huge, pansy-purple eyes and you'd have to be a monster to yell at her, closely followed by me because I was covered in snake goo and people might feel sorry for me.

Dr. Bairstow, crunching his way across the glass fragments with magnificent disdain, met us just outside the pod.

"Dr. Maxwell. Are you injured?"

"Snake blood, sir. But good news, Cleopatra is still alive."

"Should she be otherwise?"

"An attempted murder, sir, magnificently foiled by St. Mary's in general and by Major Guthrie and Mr. Markham in particular."

I beckoned them forwards. They shuffled sideways instead.

"I'm almost certain the assignment was simply to observe and document. I distinctly remember saying so."

"Indeed you did, sir, but you know us. Always ready to go that extra mile."

"If you only knew how often I pray that some of you would go those extra miles."

I was unsure how to respond to that one and compromised by scrubbing uselessly at my snake goo.

"Good news," said Peterson, cheerfully. "The Sonic Scream thing seems to work."

"While I am certain the Technical Section rejoices in that knowledge," said Dr. Bairstow, "I suspect that thought is not uppermost in their minds at this moment. They appear to be anxious to discuss recent events with you. Should any of you survive, I look forward to reading your inadequate excuses for returning from your assignment in such an unexpectedly destructive manner."

He turned and limped away.

The Technical Section closed in for the kill.

"I BLAME MARKHAM," SAID Peterson, much later. We were in the bar, settling our nerves.

Markham, who had been eyeing Nurse Hunter in his usual besotted fashion, sat up indignantly, although I can't think why. It can't have been the first time he'd heard those words uttered.

"What baffles me," I said, in an attempt to head the argument off at the pass, "is why no one ever said how ugly she was. Cleopatra, I mean. You could have launched ships off that nose."

"Maybe," said Van Owen, "they just didn't want to admit their leading men fell for a woman who looked like a camel."

We nodded wisely.

"Am I right in thinking we did A Good Thing there?" asked Guthrie. "I'm assuming no one was supposed to die today. Except us, of course, and that happens so frequently, I've stopped worrying about it."

We nodded again, each of us running through the implications in our minds. Of course, if it hadn't been us, someone else might easily have spotted the asps amongst the figs. But if they hadn't . . . If one or both of them had died . . . It really didn't bear thinking about. Guthrie was right—just for once, we'd done a Really Good Thing today.

Mrs. Partridge appeared in the doorway, an ominously large number of "Deductions from Wages for Damages Incurred" forms in her hand.

Markham groaned. A doomed attempt to reproduce Native American smoke signals had resulted in an unexpectedly large conflagration, the destruction of a small copse, the incineration of a surprisingly large number of blankets, and a letter of protest from the parish council. These days, very little of his wages remained for damages incurred to be deducted from. Any day now, he would be paying Dr. Bairstow.

And behind Mrs. Partridge loomed a very large and still very irate Dieter.

We resisted the temptation to huddle together for mutual reassurance.

"Well, I'll be OK," I said, reaching for my drink. "I'm Chief Operations Officer. I outrank him."

"And I'm Chief Training Officer," said Peterson. "No problem here."

"I'm Head of Security," said Guthrie. "I'm safe."

"I'm a girl," said Van Owen, fluttering her eyelashes.

We all stared at Mr. Markham.

"You utter bastards," he said.

CHRISTMAS PRESENT

AUTHOR'S NOTE

*A*GAIN, THIS STORY WAS built around an image. I saw Ian Guthrie walking into a room and Helen Foster saying, "Merry Christmas, Ian." Why Ian Guthrie, I don't know. And if it was Dr. Foster then it had to be somewhere in Sick Bay. Was he sick? Or someone else? He wasn't in a relationship—or was he? All right, it had to be someone he cared about. But who? Running through the list of St. Mary's characters, I couldn't find anyone suitable, so I had to invent someone. And why wasn't she at St. Mary's any longer?

Ever since the first book, when Leon tells Max about the missing historians, I'd always intended to bring some of them back again. Suddenly this seemed the ideal opportunity, and Bashford and Grey were born.

I'm quite pleased with Grey, because she gave me an opportunity to show the slightly less gung-ho side of St. Mary's. I can't imagine anything more frightening than being abandoned in the wrong time. It's rather similar to being marooned on an alien planet. No matter how hard you struggle, how far you walk, how long you wait, you're never, ever going to be able to get home again. Something like that would, I think, be bound to affect anyone, and Grey has given me a chance to explore that, although, possible spoiler alert for the future, she comes through in the end. At least she will if I can work out that particular aspect of a future St. Mary's story.

Bashford, of course, is a typical historian, only semi-conscious at the best of times. It is possible that Miss Sykes might have her eye on him, although, of course, he is completely unaware of this.

Initially, I wasn't sure the story would be accepted—I worried that an account of the destruction of Roman Colchester wasn't particularly suitable for Christmas, but it seemed to go down quite well. Especially the scene with Max and Mrs. Partridge at the end.

While I'm at it, I'd like to take the opportunity to thank Jan Jones, another Accent Press author, whose Christmas short story had the same title. Strictly speaking, she submitted hers first, so it was her title, but she very generously agreed to change hers to "Christmas Gift," so that I could use "Christmas Present." Thanks very much, Jan.

CHRISTMAS PRESENT

 THOUGHT IT WAS a dream. To this day, I'm not convinced
it wasn't. It felt like a dream. There was the same lack of
reality. Although, at St. Mary's, a lack of reality doesn't
necessarily mean you're dreaming. And since I wasn't being
chased by giant scissors through a world suddenly turned to
custard, maybe it wasn't a dream.

But it probably was.

I wouldn't go so far as to describe Mrs. Partridge as a night-
mare—not if she was within earshot, anyway—but there she
was, standing at the bottom of my bed, regarding me with that
expressionless stare that never, ever, bodes well for me and I
should know. I've been the recipient of that stare on many occasions.

We looked at each other for a while. She was wearing the
full formal attire—Greek robes, silver diadem, sandals, and a
stern expression. Only Kleio, Muse of History, could brandish
a scroll as if it was a heat-seeking missile.

I, on the other hand, was not only in my PJs, but further
disadvantaged by the presence of a heavily slumbering Leon
Farrell beside me. The only good thing about this situation was
that she hadn't turned up twenty minutes earlier. By unspoken
but mutual consent, we ignored him.

I struggled to sit up. "Mrs. Partridge?"

As if there could be any doubt, but it was the middle of the night on Christmas Eve. It was freezing cold—I could see frost on the window—and St. Mary's was officially on holiday.

We work for the St. Mary's Institute of Historical Research. We investigate major historical events in contemporary time. We do *not* call it time travel. The Boss, Dr. Bairstow, detests that phrase. "This is not Science Fiction, Dr. Maxwell!"

I knew he was in Rushford tonight, dining with a bunch of civic dignitaries, and wouldn't return until tomorrow, just in time to preside over Christmas lunch. If he wasn't here and St. Mary's was on holiday, what could she possibly want? And how had she got in? Leon, wisely, always locked the door. I mentally kicked myself. She was Kleio, daughter of Zeus and immortal Muse of History. She could go anywhere she damned well pleased. And, apparently, she had.

She said, "Get up, please, Dr. Maxwell. I'll wait outside," and turned to go.

"Wait! What's happened? Is someone dead?"

But she'd gone.

I grabbed my dressing gown.

She was waiting for me on the dark landing. "Please, come with me." She took my hand.

"No. Wait. What's going on?"

Too late. She never likes to spoil the surprise with anything as mundane as an explanation. The ground disappeared beneath my feet and we whirled away into the air, as directionless and weightless as two tiny snowflakes in a blizzard. We landed, light as thistledown in her case, and like a small sack of coal in mine.

I picked myself up, dusted myself off, and started all over again.

"Mrs. Partridge, please, just tell me. What's this all about?"

She gestured ahead of us. We were in Hawking Hangar. But not the Hawking I knew. This one looked really rough. Primitive, even. For a start, the lighting was terrible. Eye-wateringly bright in some areas, but dangerously dim in others. A bit like our Technical Section, actually. The central area was taken up with long metal benches, smothered in tools, cables, and equipment. The floor and walls were of rough concrete and the whole place echoed like a cathedral. Huge, rubber-sheathed cables trailed across the floor, not tidily bundled against the walls as they should be, but snaking around the place in giant loops, seeking to trip the unwary.

Busy techies were moving around us, obviously completely unaware of our presence. Nobody actually walked through us though, which was a shame, because I would have liked to see how my dream coped with that.

Pods stood on plinths, ready to jump back to their allocated time, but instead of each plinth having its own set of controls built in, techies were trundling around a giant contraption of flashing lights, dials, levers, read-outs, and electronic beeping. Huge umbilicals sprouted from every orifice. They heaved it to plinth four—it took three of them—and started plugging things in. They all wore thick insulating gloves. They even wore protective goggles. For an organisation that tends to regard health and safety in the workplace as something that happens to someone else, this was a little worrying. It all looked very Heath Robinson to me. As if something new was being born and everyone was making it all up as they went along. A crisis would occur and someone would bolt on another piece of equipment, which would do until the next time something else went horribly wrong, and they had to come up with another solution.

Looking at the faces around me, I hardly recognised anyone until Dieter drifted past, wearing a stained, orange jumpsuit and looking as if he'd just escaped from college—which actually turned out to be the case. He was pounding his scratchpad and calling the results to someone inside Number Four. A disembodied but familiar voice replied and two seconds later, a very young looking Leon Farrell stuck his head out of the door, requesting clarification.

Yes, this was Hawking, but not as I knew it.

I looked around for a convenient calendar. Given the technical and mechanical nature of the place, the picture on the wall should be of some semi-naked nymph, sprawled elegantly across a high-end sports car, while a significant portion of her anatomy defied gravity. Since this was St. Mary's, a fluffy kitten and a fluffy duckling sat side by side above a date showing Christmas Eve. Ten years ago.

"Oh no," I said to Mrs. Partridge. "No, no, no. I am *not* doing the 'Ghost of Christmas Past' thing."

She sighed. "This is not about you, Dr. Maxwell. Please concentrate."

"You promise?"

"Please observe closely."

Three figures approached Number Four. Two, I didn't know at all, but I certainly recognised the third one. Major Ian Guthrie, head of our Security section.

Beside me, Mrs. Partridge said, "May I introduce two of St. Mary's Senior Historians. Mr. Bashford and Miss Grey."

I knew those names. I'd seen them up on our Board of Honour in the chapel, recording the names of those who didn't come back. Those who died in the service of St. Mary's.

It was before my time, but in the early days of St. Mary's, Bashford and Grey set out for 12th-century Jerusalem and never came back. Search parties failed to find any trace of them. They were killed by Clive Ronan, a renegade historian from the future. Killed for their pod, Number Four. We got it back, eventually, but Grey and Bashford were never found.

"Major Guthrie, of course, you know."

Well, I did, obviously, and he hadn't changed that much over the last ten years. Except that, at second glance, he had. I don't know how to put this, but sometimes, you don't know how unhappy someone is until you see them before the unhappiness. Before grief etches deep lines on their face and dulls the light in their eyes. He walked beside Miss Grey, looking down at her as she lifted her face to him, smiling. I never thought I'd say this, and certainly not about quiet, self-contained Ian Guthrie, but his very soul was in his eyes as he looked at her.

A half-forgotten memory flashed into my head. A naked Professor Rapson yodelling to himself on the top shelves of the archive. Dr. Foster draped all over Peterson telling him how much she loved him, and Ian Guthrie slumped against a wall, staring at something only he could see and whispering, "Elspeth, I looked for you. I looked everywhere for you."

I had wondered at the time who he was talking to. And yes, before anyone asks, they were all as high as kites on homemade, hallucinogenic, toxic honey. Long story. This must be that Elspeth Grey.

They paused outside Number Four. Bashford shook his head, laughed at them both, and disappeared inside with Chief Farrell.

Guthrie and Grey exchanged a few words. She was dressed for the 12th century in a long tunic of blue. Her hair was covered, but her eyebrows were fair. She looked up at Guthrie with large, dark, serious eyes. He said something. She laughed. They paused and then formally shook hands, as Leon and I did when we had to say goodbye in front of other people. A private moment in a public place. Guthrie retired back behind the safety line. She entered the pod. Leon came out and the door closed behind him. Thirty seconds later, they were gone. Gone forever, because they never came back. St. Mary's searched for them because we don't leave our people behind. But they were never found.

Mrs. Partridge turned to me.

"Well, Dr. Maxwell, what have we just seen?"

Obediently, I responded. "We have just seen Bashford and Grey depart on their last assignment. Twelfth-century Jerusalem. At some point, that bastard Clive Ronan will ambush them. He will kill them and steal their pod."

I stopped and waited. What did she want from me? It had already happened. I couldn't prevent it. Ronan stole Number Four and there was nothing anyone could do about it. She said nothing because I always have to work things out for myself. Seriously, would it have killed her to type up a briefing sheet every now and then?

I made myself think. All right, so not the pod. It would be stolen and it would be a long time before we saw it again, so it had to be the people. Bashford and Grey. I experienced the legendary Maxwell Leap of Revelation and nearly fell over a coil of cable at my feet.

"The historians!"

"Yes?"

Having made this promising beginning, I fell silent. She surely didn't want me to prevent the jump. I wouldn't do that. Even if I wanted to, I couldn't. It had already happened.

"I couldn't prevent them leaving."

"Of course not."

I racked my brains. For God's sake—what did she expect from me? It was the middle of the night. I'd been dragged from my bed and dumped, in a dream, in the middle of Hawking ten years ago and—And we were gone.

There was no gentle fading away. I blinked and found myself on the gallery, looking down into the Great Hall. I knew where we were now. And when. This was tomorrow. This was Christmas Present.

All our historian gear had been stored away. A slightly wonky Christmas tree stood by the stairs, tastelessly festooned with tinsel, lights, and ornaments of every shape and colour. There was no fashionable colour scheme. Every shade of the rainbow was more than represented. At the top, a lopsided star clung on for dear life.

As in the style of a medieval banquet, a long table ran down the middle of the room. This was rather more democratic, however. We're St. Mary's. We're all below the salt.

The noise levels were tremendous. Lunch had finished and crackers were being pulled. Such is the standard of sophisticated humour at St. Mary's, that the jokes inside were considered hilarious. Copious amounts of alcohol had obviously been consumed.

I leaned on the balustrade and looked down.

I saw Kalinda Black, temporarily returned from extorting money from the University of Thirsk, our hapless employers. She was laughing with Dieter and Polly Perkins from IT. Professor Rapson and Dr. Dowson were arguing amiably. Dr. Bairstow sat at the head of the table, benign and dormant—like a volcano taking the afternoon off.

Someone was missing. Someone's seat was empty. My finely honed historian senses told me something was wrong.

I turned suddenly to Mrs. Partridge—who wasn't there. And neither was I.

I was alone in a dark room. The curtains were pulled across the windows. A man sat, perfectly still, his sightless eyes staring at a muted TV screen. Light flickered across his face. The empty pill bottle stood at his elbow.

For Ian Guthrie, there would be no Christmas Future.

I heard my hiss of indrawn breath. Heard the blood pound in my temples. Felt the room sway around me. I stood still for a long time. Until I was sure I wasn't going to faint. My brain searched frantically for a reasonable explanation. A way to make sense of what I was seeing. The hope that I would open my eyes to find I'd made a terrible mistake. That it was some trick of the light. That it was a dream. Please, please, if there really is a merciful god somewhere, let this be a dream.

Ten years. Tonight was the ten-year anniversary of her death and I hadn't known. I'd never even had a clue. Had anyone else known? He was such a very private man. I thought of all his grief, building over the years, with nowhere to go, until suddenly . . . I've grieved for someone. I know what it's like. And he'd been grieving for years. And we hadn't known. . .

"Ian? No. No, no, no."

It came out as a dreadful, rasping whisper that hurt my throat, although no pain could be greater than the one in my heart.

I shouted. I tried to shake him. I don't know why. I tried to get the door open to call for help and found I could do none of these things. I was suffocating under that helpless feeling you have in dreams when something dreadful is happening and you can't move, can't speak, can't struggle, can't do anything . . . Oh God, let this be a dream. . .

I awoke with a jerk. Beside me, Leon muttered and turned over. I lay rigidly still for a moment, waiting for my heart rate to return to normal, while images I could well do without kaleidoscoped through my head.

I closed my eyes and had a bit of a think. I knew what I wanted to do. I knew what I had to do. What I must do. But first things first. I had to find someone to watch over Guthrie. Someone who would stay with him, no matter what. Someone not easily intimidated. Someone who wouldn't gossip. Someone I could trust.

I sat up and sacrificed Leon without hesitation.

"Wake up!"

"No more," he said, without opening his eyes. "I've told you before, your demands are beyond the limit of human endurance, and I need my sleep."

"You should be so lucky. Wake up."

He sighed. "What do you want?"

What did I say to him? Leon, I've had this weird dream which might not have been a dream at all actually, and Ian Guthrie is going to kill himself tonight, and I need you to keep an eye on him while I—while I what? What was I going to do? I'd come back to that.

"Leon, listen. I don't have time to explain now, but I will. You know I will."

He sat up, rubbed his hair, and said nothing.

"I need you to do something really, really important."

He didn't ask what was going on, or demand an explanation, or ask me what the hell I thought I was doing, and I remembered again just why he was so special.

"What do you want me to do?"

"I need you to stay with Ian Guthrie. All night if necessary. At least until I get back."

I waited for him to ask me where I was going at his time of night, and he didn't.

"Why?"

I was confused because he'd asked the wrong question. "Why what?"

"Why must I wake Ian Guthrie, who is almost certainly asleep by now, and stay with him all night at least until you get back?"

A reasonable question.

"That's a very reasonable question."

"And I can't wait to hear the very reasonable answer."

"There isn't one."

"That figures."

He folded his arms and waited. I had to tell him something.

"Leon. It's ten years tonight. She's been gone for ten years. I think he needs a friend."

I watched his expressions. Perplexity. Realisation. Shock. Guilt. Urgency. He swung his legs out of bed and reached for his clothes.

"How do you know this?"

I avoided the direct question. "It's ten years tonight, Leon. He shouldn't be alone."

"And if he's sleeping quietly in his bed? Which he probably is. I'm to wake him and spend the night with him? Have you any idea what he will be thinking?"

"No," I said, innocently. "What will he be thinking?"

He paused from dragging on his jeans. "We will be discussing this more fully tomorrow."

I blew him a kiss as he left the room and looked for my own clothes.

I CREPT DOWNSTAIRS TO the kitchen where I made myself a mug of tea and headed to the silent library for more thinking. The whole building was quiet, but there were a few people still around. Markham, doing a security sweep, came upon me at a data table.

"You too?" he said.

I blinked at him over my data stack. "Me too what?"

I'm really not good at anything until I've had at least two mugs of tea.

"Peterson. Prowling the gallery. Says he can't sleep."

"Really? Well, if you see him on your sweep, tell him to get me a bacon sarnie."

"Oh, I'm not working."

"It's the middle of the night, for crying out loud. Why are you wandering the corridors?"

He grinned at me. Short, disreputable, and indestructible.

"I'm waiting for Hunter. She's off duty now and I thought we could . . ." he trailed off and beamed at me.

I told him I couldn't understand why he hadn't gone blind.

"Me neither," he said, sunnily. "But I do eat a lot of carrots. Do you think that helps?"

"I thought I heard voices," said Peterson, appearing in the doorway. "At this hour I can only assume the two of you are up to no good. Whatever it is, I want to be included."

"I'm having a bad night," I said, and that was true enough. Historians have more than their fair share of nightmares. "And Mr. Markham is apparently roaming the building on the off-chance of a little casual sex."

"There's nothing casual about the way I do sex," he said, offended. "I have—what's that word? Begins with testi—testi something?"

"Dear God, please tell me you don't mean testicles?"

"No! Well, yes, obviously, but I meant the other things."

My mind boggled. What other things?

"Testimonials," said Peterson, enlightened.

"I'd like to see those sometime. The testimonials, I mean," I said, as they both opened their mouths. "Will you two clean up your act, please?"

Silence fell. The building creaked around us. I played with my empty mug.

"Tell me," I said to Markham. "How long have you worked here?"

"At St. Mary's? About ten years now. Just over."

"You knew Elspeth Grey, then?"

There was a long pause.

"A little."

Tim was rotating my data stack. "What are you doing?"

More silence.

"Max?"

"OK," I said. "Cards on the table. I've pulled the records from Number Four. The one that was stolen. I've had an idea. I thought maybe I could—" I stopped.

"What?" said Tim? "What did you think you could do?"

"I thought I could find Grey's jump to 12th-century Jerusalem and maybe—I don't know."

"We searched for ages afterwards," said Markham quietly. "Months. We never found either of them. Not the slightest trace. We took tag readers and combed the city. There was nothing."

Interesting. Even if they were dead, they should have found the tags.

"Maybe," I said slowly, testing my idea as I went along, "maybe that's because they weren't there at all. I was just thinking. Maybe they were seized along with the pod and instead of killing them there and then, that bastard Ronan jumped again—to somewhere else—and just pitched them out. That's just the sort of thing that would appeal to him. He tried it with me, once. Suppose he took a couple of historians who were geared up for the Crusades and dropped them in, say, a prehistoric Russian winter, or right slap bang in the middle of something nasty, such as Paris during the St. Bartholomew's Day massacre."

"Yes, but how would we ever know?" asked Markham.

"We wouldn't," I said. "But the pod might."

"That's what you're looking at, isn't it?" said Tim, stirring the data again.

I nodded. "This is the jump history from Number Four. There are two sets of coordinates for each jump. In and then out again. If I can find the jump after Jerusalem—that just might be where Ronan abandoned them. If that's what happened then I think . . . I think I might be able to find them."

"You keep saying 'I'," said Peterson. "Is this off the books?"

"Yes, I think so."

"Why? Why not go to Dr. Bairstow with this? He surely wouldn't refuse to try."

I hesitated, remembering my dream. "Dr. Bairstow's not here."

"Well, that doesn't matter. He's back for Christmas lunch tomorrow. Speak to him then."

Now what did I say? Ian Guthrie was an old and valued friend who had saved my life on more than one occasion. I wasn't going to give him away if I could help it. He deserved my loyalty.

I know it's hard to believe, but here at St. Mary's, we do undergo regular psychological monitoring. I believe Dr. Bairstow once discussed taking on an additional member of the medical team for very that purpose, until Dr. Foster told him there weren't enough mental health professionals in the entire world to sort out the staff at St. Mary's, and the plan came to nothing. While I'm prepared to concede the possibility that there might, occasionally, be outbursts of slightly odd behaviour that might lead the uninitiated to believe there's something seriously the matter with most of us, there was no way someone in Ian Guthrie's position could afford even the slightest hint that all might not be well. He was Head of Security—the rock on which we all leaned. I owed it to him to make every effort to safeguard his reputation. And if we could find them and bring them back safely, then no one would ever have to know how close he came.

I said, awkwardly, "I don't want to raise hopes I might not be able to fulfil."

"Sorry, I'm not with you."

I looked at Markham, who said nothing. If he'd been here ten years then he wasn't as young as he looked. And I knew he wasn't as scatterbrained as he would have everyone believe. And he obviously wasn't going to gossip about his boss, Ian Guthrie. I saw again that face in the flickering light of the TV and felt again the icy hand that stopped my heart. I said carefully, "I have some concerns."

I waited, but Markham still said nothing.

Peterson looked from one to the other of us. "What don't I know?"

Markham wouldn't say it.

"It was before our time, Tim, but Guthrie and Grey were . . ." I hesitated.

"He never saw anyone else if she was in the room," said Markham, quietly, and I'm not sure who he was talking to. "They didn't make a big thing of it, but it was special. And then, that Christmas, she didn't come back. He nearly drove himself into the ground. He barely spoke. He barely ate. He would have gone on every search party if he could. We searched and searched but the day came when the Boss had to call a halt." He sighed. "I suppose we all thought the Major had finally accepted she'd gone. He never said anything. Not to anyone. Not even to Chief Farrell. He was just as he was before and I suppose, after a while, people just forgot that they'd been . . ."

"It's ten years tonight," I said. And there would be that empty chair at the Christmas lunch tomorrow.

Unless. . .

More silence.

"So that's the three of us then," said Markham, briskly. "Are we going to steal Chief Farrell's pod and get ourselves into trouble again?"

"I certainly hope so," said Peterson. "Max, you and I will do the coordinates. Mr. Markham—you're in charge of refreshments."

I hesitated.

"What's the matter?" said Peterson. "You're not thinking of going without us, are you?"

"This is more than off the books, guys. If this goes wrong there will be hell to pay."

Peterson shook his head. "There isn't anyone at St. Mary's who doesn't owe Major Guthrie in one form or another. I know I do. Count me in."

"And me," said Markham.

I smiled sadly. "Guys, even if it all goes right, Dr. Bairstow will still come down on me like a ton of bricks. You should be aware."

"We'll wear hard hats," said Peterson.

"Yes," said Markham, cheerfully. "I've still got mine."

"What?" said Peterson. "Why have you . . . oh, never mind."

THE TASK WENT MUCH more quickly with two of us and we found the 12th-century coordinates easily enough. The computer identified the next set as AD 60. Camulodunum. Roman Colchester.

"Bastard," said Peterson, softly.

Markham swallowed the last of his bacon roll. "Why?"

"Boudicca's revolt," I said. "She levelled the town and slaughtered the inhabitants. Hardly anyone got out alive. He dropped them in the middle of a massacre."

"OK," said Peterson. "This needs careful planning. "We'll need to go in early, so we're already in place when Ronan turns up. Number Four will appear. The door will open. He'll throw them out. If they're still alive."

"They'll be alive," said Markham. "No point chucking them out dead. They might not be in good condition, but they'll be alive."

"True," said Peterson. "This all works in our favour. He won't want to hang around with anything up to a hundred thousand enraged Britons bearing down on him, so he'll push them out and jump away as quickly as possible. We grab them and get out ourselves."

I didn't say anything, but our window of opportunity would be tiny. We had a lot to do and not much time to do it in. Two historians to rescue from a vengeful Clive Ronan on one side, and Boudicca and her hordes to avoid on the other.

"Are we taking him with us?"

I came back to earth with a jolt. "Who?"

"Guthrie."

Peterson looked at me. "Are we?"

It was tempting. What a Christmas present that would be for him. But no. I shook my head. "If we get it wrong and he sees her die . . . or if she's already dead . . . We've no idea how this will pan out. We don't want to make things any worse for him."

Markham nodded. "All right. Can we go now?"

"A quick stop for some gear first," said Peterson, getting up. "Why, what's the rush?"

"He's meeting Nurse Hunter later on," I said. "He's under the impression this will be a treat for the poor girl."

"Hey," he said, wounded. "It was her idea. She sent me a note telling me what she has planned. Incidentally, do you know where I can get a tin of Swarfega and a wet suit?"

I SENT THEM ON ahead to gather what was needed, while I scribbled a few words for Leon. I folded the paper, and shoved it in his pigeonhole. Just in case. . .

I met Peterson and Markham outside Hawking. They had a flatbed loaded with equipment. We checked no one was around and let ourselves into the paint store where Leon kept his pod. We made our way to the back corner. I called for the door, and we entered Leon's pod. Here was the familiar smell of hot electrics, damp carpet, an overworked toilet, stale people, and cabbage. Our pod smell.

Pods are small, flat-roofed, apparently stone-built shacks in which we jump to whichever time period we've been assigned. We live and work in them. They're cramped, squalid, and thanks to the heroic efforts of the Technical Section, they never, ever let us down. There's no need to tell them I said that. The official attitude of the Technical Section is that the pods function *despite* the heroic efforts of historians. Leon and I have passed many a happy hour shamelessly slandering each other's departments.

We unloaded our gear. We weren't even considering trying to blend in with the local population. There was absolutely no point in looking wonderfully authentic if we were sprawled in a Colchester gutter with our throats cut. Or worse. So Markham had liberated body armour and helmets, and three big blasters. We couldn't shoot anyone, but we could put the blasters on a low charge and lightly singe everyone within range. And let's face it, no one was going to notice a few extra burns in a city already in flames. As a concession to historical accuracy, however, and to keep me quiet, Peterson had acquired three dark grey, woollen cloaks in which we could envelop our anomalous selves.

"Right," I said. "We're on the clock from this moment." By which I meant that time was ticking inexorably closer to the moment when Ian decided nothing was worth it any longer. Suppose we rescued the love of his life and returned to St. Mary's to find Guthrie already dead? How much of a tragedy would that be?

I crossed my fingers for Leon.

"We jump now. Tim, lay in the coordinates. We'll change and discuss tactics once we're on site."

"Understood," he said calmly and two minutes later, we were ready to go.

The world went white.

I HAVE NO IDEA what time of day it was. This was England. Heavy grey clouds obscured the sun. It could have been any time from nine in the morning to nine at night. On this jump, however, the time and the weather would be the least of our problems. For safety's sake, we usually land in a quiet back alley somewhere. In fact, should you ever find yourself in a quiet back alley somewhere, it's well worth checking around.

There's bound to be a pod and two bickering historians nearby. Wave, if you like.

In this case, however, we'd landed at the far edge of a large, wide-open space, the centre of which was occupied by a huge building with an imposing portico. I knew where we were. If I was right, then that was the Temple of Claudius and, with our usual luck, we'd landed right where the battle would be fiercest.

Having said that, the place was deserted. Tim angled the cameras, and apart from a small group of men standing on the Temple steps, there was no one around.

"Odd," said Tim.

"Perhaps the Brits have been and gone," said Markham, hopefully.

I looked at Tim, who made a "you tell him" gesture.

So I told him.

"This is Roman Colchester. Camulodunum. AD 60."

"Yes?"

"This is a Roman town, inhabited mainly by army veterans and their families. It's unfortified because, apparently, they thought they wouldn't need walls. So at the moment, the only thing encircling the town is about a hundred thousand enraged Iceni and Trinovantes tribesmen for whom Camulodunum encapsulates everything they've come to hate. Such is their loathing for everything Roman that Boudicca's army consists of not only every warrior she could lay her hands on, but women and children as well. I wouldn't be surprised if they've even brought their chickens along to fight. If they'd been and gone, there would be no town left. Trust me."

Markham nodded and then got his own back. "In that case, just a small correction to the original plan. We form a two-man snatch squad and one of us—Max—will stay with the pod to provide cover and get the door open.

"No," he said, as I opened my mouth. "Peterson will back me up on this. We'll need you—on the roof, probably—to give us an overview. We're either going to be up to our necks in hysterically-fleeing citizens or invading hordes of madmen and their chickens. Either way, we're going to need someone up high, to provide covering fire, tell us what's going on, and open the door for us. You don't need me to tell you that the few seconds it takes to get the door open could make all the difference. And if you don't like it then you shouldn't have brought me along."

There was a small silence. Peterson was suddenly very busy doing something to the console and no help at all.

I swallowed. "OK."

WE GEARED UP AND then turned our attention to what was going on outside.

"What's that big thing over there?" said Markham, pointing to the screen and displaying the Security Section's typical attitude towards the wonders of the past.

"That's the Temple of Claudius. Built with local forced labour. Symbol of everything they resent. The inhabitants thought they would be safe inside, but with hindsight, it's not the best place for them to take refuge."

Which was true, but they didn't have a lot of choice. It was easily the biggest and most substantial building around, set high above the ground with flights of steps leading to a magnificent portico. And yes, it would be successfully defended for two days, which was probably just long enough to give those cowering inside the hope that they might be rescued after all. Except that the legions would never come . . .

"How long before Ronan and Number Four turn up?" I said to Peterson.

"About fifteen minutes, I think."

"Let's get onto the roof. See what we're dealing with."

We scrambled up on top of the pod and stared around us.

The two parts of the city were clearly delineated. It's hard to tart-up thatched wattle and daub roundhouses, so the British part of the city was basically mud-coloured—with accents of mud thrown in.

The Romans, whether deliberately or not, had brought the colours and shapes of their homeland with them. Bathhouses, public buildings, temples, all were rectangular in shape, with terracotta-roof tiles and whitewashed walls. Sadly, of course, this was Britain, so these white walls were generously splashed with mud rather than sunshine. I know the grey day was sucking the colour out of everything, but the overall effect was dingy and dull. Still, give it an hour or so and we'd have lovely yellow and orange flames leaping merrily from one building to another, interspersed with those always cheerful puddles of red blood.

From the accounts I'd read, I'd always assumed that the Iceni swooped down on a comparatively unaware Colchester, slaughtering everything in their path, but looking around us now, I could see some defensive measures had been implemented. Of course they had. This was Colonia Victricensis, whose inhabitants were mainly army veterans and their families. Of course they would fight. Houses were bolted and barred. Barricades and other obstacles had been erected across the streets to hamper the Iceni chariots. Those who hadn't fled were taking refuge in the Temple.

More men hurried across the square. None of them was young. In fact, the youngest of them was middle-aged. Some were missing limbs or eyes. They were all grizzled and scarred. These were the Roman ex-legionaries and they were preparing to do what they did best. They all carried weapons of some kind. Some had obviously kept their short stabbing swords from their army days. Some had spears. Some had axes. Those who had no military gear had armed themselves with pitchforks or even heavy cudgels with vicious-looking nails protruding.

I turned my attention away from the Temple. Who would turn up first? Ronan or Boudicca? Would he literally throw them into the path of the oncoming army? To be trampled to death? Or worse? Or did he intend to drop them an hour or so beforehand? It would amuse him to have a pair of obvious foreigners—spies, possibly—running around Colchester, and in as much danger from the Romans as the Iceni. Yes, that would appeal to Clive Ronan. And that, of course, was the weakness in his plan. If you want someone dead then do it. I keep saying this. Don't gloat—just shoot.

I said to Peterson, "How much longer?"

"Now. It should be any moment now."

"Then go. Good luck to both of you."

"And you too, Max. Stay safe."

They jumped down.

I lay on the flat roof and kept watch.

A broad avenue led to the Temple. At a midpoint between the gates and the Temple itself, it split around some kind of ornate, four-sided public fountain that gave the illusion of cover, and there they crouched, waiting.

I checked again that my blaster was on its lowest setting and on wide beam.

The city was silent and for the first time, I became aware of a sound: the non-stop roar of Boudicca's army as they approached the city. Occasionally, the noise would swell to a terrifying crescendo as a thousand drums rolled and a hundred thousand voices called on their gods for revenge against the hated Romans.

I felt the hairs on my head lift. The veneer of civilisation is very thin. Deep inside all of us, the old instincts are still there. The instinct of the small, furry mammal when confronted with an enemy a hundred times larger is to flee. Flee for your life. Flee blindly, without thought, without plan—just get away. As far and as fast as possible.

Then the next instinct kicks in. The one that gives the small furry mammal the courage to turn at bay, bare its teeth, and fight. In defence of its young, its mate, its burrow. That was what we were watching now.

The men on the Temple steps were forming themselves into ranks. A stout, middle-aged man wearing a brown tunic and heavy boots pushed his way through them and turned to address his men.

Discipline dies hard. They fell silent. Other than the now very audible roar of the invaders, there was no sound.

His voice, battle-honed, echoed around the Temple precinct, bouncing off the walls of nearby buildings.

"Men of Rome. We are soldiers of the empire. We are the greatest soldiers in the world. From the Rhine to the Nile, there is no force that can withstand the might of Rome. The legions will come. Quintus Petillius Cerialis and the IX Hispania will come. Our task today is to hold the Temple of the Divine Claudius until they do. We will defend the Temple. We will defend our families. We will hold. We will hold for Rome!"

A roar went up from the assembled ranks. Weapons were brandished.

"Rome! Rome!"

For a moment, the sounds of invasion were lost under the thunder. "Rome! Rome!" Those who had shields clashed their weapons against them. For a moment, even I believed they would hold the Temple against overwhelming odds.

And then, as if in response, away, in the distance, primitive horns sounded. Drums rolled. There was a moment's complete silence. Here in the Temple precinct, all movement stopped. The world waited.

And then, a huge, ear-splitting roar. With a hundred thousand voices screaming their hatred, the British army began to move.

We could hear it. We could feel it under our feet.

How long did we have? And where was bloody Clive Ronan?

At the Temple, the big wooden doors slammed shut with a boom that echoed around the square. Outside, the veterans closed ranks and raised their weapons. The Temple would be defended at all costs.

Away in the distance, I could see a red glow. The Iceni had reached the outskirts.

The chariots would sweep through the city, clearing the way, bringing down everyone in their path and the foot soldiers would follow on behind, mopping up and torching everything in sight. Everything and everyone would be slaughtered. There are people who use the word "massacre" lightly, with no idea of its true meaning. They should have been in Colchester on that day.

Already, we could hear the far-off clatter of hooves on paved streets. The thunder of chariot wheels. The shouts of the warriors.

The glow of burning buildings grew brighter. I could smell smoke. Ash drifted on the wind. There were some public buildings made of stone—the Temple, for instance—but the majority were made of wood and with thatched roofs. They burned like torches.

Here in the Temple precinct, good order prevailed. The veterans stood in disciplined ranks, each one ready to do his duty.

Still no Clive Ronan. No Number Four. Why weren't they here? Had I got it wrong? Had I placed us in harm's way for nothing? Had it really been just a dream? I don't mind saying that those few minutes on the pod roof, looking down on a horribly exposed Peterson and Markham and waiting for something that I was becoming increasingly convinced might not happen, are not anything I ever want to do again.

I kept flicking my eyes from the fountain, to the grid pattern of streets around us, to the pathetically small army defending the Temple of Claudius, and back to the fountain again. I assumed the chariots would forge ahead into the square, desperate to get to this symbol of their oppressors. They would burst into view at any moment, and once they turned up, I

would pull us out. I would have no choice, even if Number
Four hadn't appeared. That moment hadn't yet arrived, but I
could prepare.

I said, "Peterson, Markham—when I say—on my mark—
you retreat back to the pod. That is an order. Understood?"

Silence.

"Understood?"

"Yes," said Peterson. No more—no less.

We waited.

Where the bloody hell was Number Four and Elspeth Grey?
The veterans stood still, solid and silent. They were waiting, too.

Peterson and Markham crouched, back to back in the shelter of the fountain.

I lay on the roof, wearing my eyes out watching for Number Four. I was as highly strung as a violin on steroids—which
would be a cello, I suppose. We were all set to go. The second
Ronan touched down, we would be on standby. The second the
door opened, we would be ready, and the second he jumped
away, we would move.

The clamour of Boudicca's approaching army drew ever
closer. The wind got up. Smoke mingled with the grey clouds,
darkening the day even further. More ash blew across the
square. I could smell burning wood. I even thought I could
make out individual voices and the rhythm of marching feet,
although that was unlikely. They weren't that close. Yet.

Still no sign of Ronan. I prepared to jump down and get the
two of them back in to safety.

Just as I bunched my muscles, everything happened all at
once.

Not twenty yards away from me, a small, battered stone hut
blinked into existence. My heart soared with relief. There they
were! I'd been right. We'd found them. Now all we had to do
was get them back.

I flattened myself on the roof. Peterson and Markham, who had been waiting for this moment, tensed themselves to move quickly.

At the far end of the square, some half dozen war chariots burst into view and headed towards to Temple, where they circled, out of reach of Roman weapons, hurling taunts and challenges in their own tongue.

Shit!

Time to move.

The veterans clashed their weapons, stamped their feet, and bellowed, "Rome! Rome!"

I said, "Run for the pod, guys. I'll get them."

It was the right thing to do. The pod had landed much nearer to me than to them. I could get there more quickly and without exposing myself to Boudicca's advance guard.

The pod door opened and someone was slung out with enough force to roll them across the paving stones, where they lay horribly still.

A second later, two struggling figures appeared in the doorway. It was Grey and she was battling with someone who might or might not have been Clive Ronan. I couldn't tell.

I wanted to shout to her. To tell her to stop. Rescue was at hand. Not to risk herself or Bashford, but I couldn't. If he knew we were here, he'd shoot them both stone dead and try for us as well. I really didn't know what to do, but Boudicca solved that little problem for me, because at that moment, another three or four chariots appeared from a different direction, also racing towards the Temple.

Grey was knocked to the ground. The door closed. The pod blinked out of existence.

"Now! Move! Now!"

I'd love to say that we moved with all the coordinated precision of a well-trained professional unit but that did not happen. In any way. The whole thing was just . . . typical.

I shouted and my voice was lost in the noise of the circling chariots and the taunts of the British. Grey and Bashford couldn't hear me. They did what historians are trained to do. Having no idea where or when they were, they sought shelter. She heaved Bashford to his feet and the two of them pelted across the square. In the wrong bloody direction.

I had a split second to make a decision, but it was no decision, really. We'd come here to rescue them. There was no point going back without them. The only thing that just might save me from the certain and terrible wrath of Dr. Bairstow was the production of Bashford and Grey. Preferably alive.

I scrambled down off the roof, landed awkwardly, and twisted my ankle. It wasn't serious, but I had to wait for the initial pain to subside before I could get after them.

Markham, seeing me sprawled on the paving stones, leaped to his feet, slipped in the very substantial evidence that a number of excited horses had passed this way quite recently, and crashed to the ground. Peterson fell over him.

I cursed, offered up a prayer to the god of historians, who, on the evidence so far, must be off on a comfort break, heaved myself up, and chased after our two fleeing historians.

Markham and Peterson set off after me.

I shouted at Bashford and Grey to wait.

Markham and Peterson shouted at me to wait.

Seriously, I swear trained chimps could do the job better than us.

The only thing that prevented the whole thing skidding along the famous St. Mary's catastrophe-curve and crashing straight into full-blown disaster was that there was nowhere for them to go. I've said before that Colchester was not unprepared and barricades had been set up at every corner. They ran straight into a blocked street.

They skidded to a halt, as did we, chests heaving.

I said, breathlessly, "Hey!"

Bashford spun around, his face covered in blood, and lashed out. If he'd connected then I'd have been on my back in the mud. And not for the first time. Typical bloody historians— you risk your life and career to save them and they respond by trying to punch your lights out.

I dragged up my visor and shouted, "It's me. The rescue party."

He responded by having another pop at me. He was way off target because, I realised belatedly, he couldn't see for the blood running down into his eyes. He wouldn't have a clue who I was.

"St. Mary's," I shouted, frantically dodging. "Guthrie sent us."

Grey seized his arm. "Tom. Wait. Stop. We're OK. It's St. Mary's."

He stopped swinging wildly.

She turned to me. "Is he here? Is Guthrie here?"

Markham, experienced in the ways of historians and their ability to stand chatting as a tsunami of disaster threatens to crash down upon them, strode forward. "No time to talk. We need to get out of here. Peterson, you take the lead. Max, Grey, and Bashford in the middle. I'll bring up the rear. The longer we stay, the less likely we are to get away. Move. Now."

We headed back towards the pod and I began to think we might make it after all.

Wrong.

Again.

IN ANY MAJOR DISTURBANCE, you will always find those who try to take advantage of the situation. A bit of freelance looting here—a bit of casual pillaging there. They're usually not bright, and just to prove my point, when everyone with more than one brain cell had either fled Colchester or sought safety, these men were trying to steal a pig.

I have no idea where they came from. I'd never seen such a villainous-looking crew. One was enormously fat. His mud-coloured tunic strained tightly over his belly and was stiff with what I really, really hoped were foodstains. One was small and skinny with terrible skin. He wore coarse brown trousers and a bright ochre tunic several sizes too big for him. I suspected it had been freshly liberated from its real owner. The other wore some kind of metal helmet that was far too big for him so again, I guessed it wasn't his. I have no idea what colour his clothes had originally been. They all stank. Huge sweat stains encircled each armpit. They were scruffy, scarred, and had opportunist thieves written all over them. Oh, and they were drunk. Very, very drunk. I could smell the fumes from here.

Hardly surprising, of course. They'd been going from house to house, looting what they could find. They all had bulging sacks of looted goods over their shoulders. I had no idea whether they were native Colchestrians or escaped slaves. They might even be freelancing Iceni soldiers. Boudicca had very little control over her army. She relied on numbers and savagery rather than tactics. Looking at these three, they'd been drunk for some time. Which was good, because they obviously weren't career soldiers. And bad, because they were unpredictable. With our luck, they'd be fighting drunks, rather than maudlin drunks. Or happy drunks. Or—and this was my favourite—unconscious drunks.

Markham shifted his stance slightly, ready for trouble.

"Wait," said Peterson, softly.

He was right. Drunk they might be, but they might also have about a hundred thousand friends out there, all of whom would be turning up any minute now.

We all stared at each other and while we were doing that, another two stuck their blond, tangle-haired heads out of a nearby ramshackle wooden shed. Both of them had beards in which you could lose a small car. Great. Now there were five of them. Maybe more, because in the depths of the shed, something else grunted and moved in the dark. We were trapped. They were between the pod and us.

I sighed. Now would be the time to have a really brilliant idea.

We couldn't kill them because we might, just might, be killing one of our own ancestors and History really doesn't like us doing that sort of thing.

We couldn't even seriously disable them because then someone else might go on to kill them and if they weren't supposed to die today then again, there would be Trouble.

Maybe we could intimidate them. All right, several of them were built like brick shithouses, but that's never a match for feminine guile. Or cheating, as Leon always calls it.

I was behind Bashford and Peterson. I whipped off my helmet and passed it to Grey. I pulled out my hairpins, shook my hair free, tossed back my cloak, set my blaster to full charge, and elbowed my way forwards to confront them.

I tried to see myself as they were seeing me.

A woman with red hair. Quite a lot of red hair. Actually, I have hair like Japanese knotweed. Cut it and it grows back ten times thicker. I'm still waiting for the hair-care industry to produce a shampoo that *reduces* volume and shine.

But, I was a red-haired woman wearing armour and if they were followers of Boudicca then this would not be an unfamiliar sight to them. And best of all, I was a woman who could do—this.

I raised my whining blaster and sent a stream of liquid fire onto the thatched roof of the ramshackle shed, which went up with a whoosh. There was a sudden blast of heat and red sparks flew skywards. Flames began to lick around the door.

They jumped a mile and stared at me, wide-eyed and swaying. Maybe we were going to get away unscathed, after all. I took advantage of their surprise and gestured in the direction

of the Temple, assembling words in my head. I don't speak
Brythonic and I only have a very little Old English. I hoped for
the best.

"Death! Death! Kill them all! Kill the Roman cats!"

I know, I know, but in the heat of the moment, I couldn't
remember the word for dogs and quite honestly, I think I
deserve some sort of credit here. Drunken looters were con-
fronting us and Boudicca's battalions were going to show up
any minute now. For God's sake, what do people expect from
me?

They stared at me blankly.

I sighed. Everything was going wrong. This was just not
our day. Today was the day we were all going to die in Roman
Colchester.

And then, typically, at this point the god of historians pulled
the chain, exited the comfort station, and returned to duty.

I really should have taken a second to wonder what the
other two were doing in the shed, although no one had much
chance to think about anything because the next moment, we
were all of us in fear for our lives.

An enormous, enraged pig erupted out of the burning
building, scattering squealing piglets around her feet. Two,
however, were made of sterner stuff than their siblings and
hung on, sucking grimly. She stood, head down, legs splayed,
piglets swinging.

She was massive. She was the biggest pig I'd ever seen in
my entire life, which, admittedly, has not been pig-filled, but
even so . . . Even when stationary, bits of her continued to
wobble and quiver of their own accord. Tiny, beady, piggy eyes
peered balefully at the world. She really wasn't happy at all. She
fixed those eyes on me, correctly identified the person who had
torched her sty, and began to lumber.

"Look out," shouted Peterson, and before I could protest,
he pushed me sideways. I landed in something pig-related and

unpleasant that I was given no chance to examine, because half a second later, he landed on top of me.

The pig uttered some sort of porcine battle cry, changed direction, and, trailing piglets, charged for the bearded buggers, who fell over themselves trying to get out of her way. They tried to scatter, but in a narrow street, it was more of an involuntary clump than a scatter. The fat one ran into a wall and rebounded, nearly bringing down the skinny one. One slipped over and scrabbled backwards on his bum to get up. Someone else tripped over Peterson and me. It had to have been one of our British friends. No pig could smell that bad. Dreadful oaths and bitter recriminations rent the air and not all of them were from St. Mary's. Piglets squealed and ran between people's legs. The pig barged into the still reeling fat bloke, knocking him into the burning shed. He shrieked and rolled back out again, beating at his smouldering clothing.

The pig, scenting victory, closed for the kill, followed by her equally enthusiastic offspring. The now ex-looters gave it up, hauled each other off the ground, and ran for it. The pig uttered a bellow of victory and followed on behind. They all vanished from view.

In our little street, silence fell.

"I don't believe any of this," said Grey, who had sensibly taken refuge behind Markham. "We've just been beaten up by a pig. Who *are* you people?"

Based on our performance to date, I would have thought that was obvious.

I DON'T KNOW ABOUT the others, but I don't have much memory of getting back to the pod. We hadn't been gone that long—although it seemed longer—but in our absence, the square had filled up with Boudicca's troops. Chariots still circled the Temple, but massive numbers of foot soldiers were pouring into the square from all directions. The noise was overwhelming.

We stayed well away from all that, working our way around the edge of the square and using such cover as we could find. We moved in a tight group. Peterson led the way; Grey and I steered a still rather wobbly Bashford, and Markham brought up the rear.

We kept our attention firmly on our route back to the pod because Markham had announced he would shoot the first historian who stopped and tried to identify Boudicca herself. Apparently it had been a long day and he just wanted to get home. Which was unfortunate, because without us even looking for her, there she was. I swear, it wasn't our fault. Although, as I tried to explain to him afterwards, if you thought about it logically, where else would she be?

Grey and I were struggling to manhandle the surprisingly difficult to steer Bashford, when he stopped, peered blearily over my shoulder, and said in surprise, "Boudicca?"

"No, no," said Grey, soothingly, trying to push him in the right direction. "St. Mary's."

"No," he said, "Oh my God, it is! It's Boudicca! Look! Cooee!" And he waved. He actually waved.

I just had time to think "Shit!" and we all turned slowly.

He was right.

No more than thirty feet away, leaning out of a mud-splattered chariot drawn by two wild-eyed, foaming horses—there she was. Even as we stared at her, she spotted us, straightened up, and stared right back.

I couldn't believe it. I was looking at Boudicca, Queen of the Iceni. The woman who took on the Romans and won. Who destroyed Colchester. And St. Albans. And London. Who would kill herself rather than be captured. And she was looking at us.

Some ten or twelve gigantic, heavily armed warriors, all on foot, surrounded her, their faces painted with identical, intricate blue patterns. They were looking at us as well. Everyone was looking at us. Even the bloody horses were looking at us.

There can't possibly have been silence anywhere in Colchester on that day, but I have no memory of any sound at all. No battle cries, no screams, no clash of weapons, not even the chink of harness or snorting breath from the horses. Just long, unmoving, complete silence.

She was tall and standing in the chariot meant that she easily towered over the heads of those around her. In contrast to her entourage who wore tunics and trousers of this year's latest colour, fashionable British Mud, she was dressed to catch the eye. To be instantly recognisable to friend and foe alike. A bright blue cloak covered her crimson dress. She wore a fabulous golden torc around her neck and her cloak was fastened at each shoulder with golden brooches in the shape of Celtic knots.

Contrary to popular depictions, her hair did not stream dramatically behind her. It was pulled back from her face and secured in a business-like knot at the nape of her neck. Her face was thin and hatchet-like and deep lines ran from her nose to her mouth. She was not beautiful. She was a warrior. She wore a plain, bronze breastplate and carried a spear. Backlit by the burning buildings, she was the living personification of Andred, the Iceni goddess of victory. No wonder they followed her.

Peterson said softly, "Max, you're up," and for a moment, I couldn't think what he was talking about and then I did. Boudicca had called on Andred before the battle, releasing a hare in her honour. I could use that.

I stepped in front of the others. Close to her, but not too close.

I tossed back my cloak so she could see my armour. This was not the time for fumbling in Old English. I spoke in Latin. As queen consort and then queen in her own right, I was certain she would have some Latin. I had to speak very slowly to give myself time to assemble the right words and it gave my voice an unfamiliar authority. I pitched it to carry across the distance between us.

"Boudicca of the Iceni. You called upon Andred and the goddess answered you. She sent the hare to run on the auspicious side. The goddess now demands repayment. I appeal to you, woman to woman, let these people go. It is her wish."

I paused for a moment. The Latin was possibly not a good move, given the circumstances, but it was vital that she understood me and I had deliberately used the phrase "woman to woman." The phrase she herself had used when calling on the goddess.

She stared down at us, her face expressionless. One word, that's all it would take. Just one word from her and it would all be over for us. Never mind Ian Guthrie, there would be no Christmas for Leon or Helen or Hunter, or anyone at St. Mary's. I swallowed. Dear God, what was I doing?

More and more Britons were pouring into the square. We really should go. The real battle for the Temple had not yet begun.

She hadn't taken her eyes off me.

"This is so cool," beamed Bashford, cross-eyed and blissfully unaware of the danger in which we stood. Obviously a natural historian.

She cut her eyes to him as he gently swayed, oblivious to nearly everything. He waved again. Just for one moment, I thought the corner of her mouth twitched, just very, very slightly. She said something to her driver. He whipped up the horses and the chariot rattled away towards the Temple.

What? What had she said? "Let them go?" That would be good. Or had she gone with the slightly less good, "Kill them all and throw their bodies to the dogs?"

Someone barked an order. I didn't see who. We braced ourselves. Her guard wheeled about and disappeared.

I became aware I hadn't breathed for quite a long time.

"Did you see?" said Grey grabbing Bashford's arm in excitement. "Did you see her clothes? And her armour?"

"Who?" he said, groggily. "Whose clothes?"

Markham could be heard calling on the god of Security Sections everywhere for patience and to make it bloody quick.

"About five foot seven or eight, I think," said Peterson, who was no better than the rest of us. "And where were her daughters? And the warriors around her must be some sort of personal guard. Do you think those facial markings were some sort of insignia or badge identifying them as such? And I couldn't quite see . . . Was she armed?"

"She had a sword and some sort of spear," I said, obeying my own instincts. "And did you see her chariot? Horsehide stretched over wood."

"And the placement of the axle . . ."

"*When* the history department has quite finished," said Markham, with commendable restraint, "the Security Section would like to inform them that anyone not on the move in two seconds will regret it."

"What?"

He kept it simple for historians. "Move or I'll shoot you."

So we did.

THOSE NOT FOLLOWING BOUDICCA were too busy torching the streets and looting to spare us any attention. We raced across the final few yards. I led the way, blaster whining, ready to zap anyone in my path, and keeping my eyes fixed firmly on the pod ahead of us. Peterson and Markham covered our rear.

I called for the door and we all crashed breathlessly into the pod.

We were safe. For the time being. Until Dr. Bairstow opened my report.

It was a bit of a squeeze once inside. Markham lowered Bashford to the floor and checked over his head wound. I sat

Grey down in the corner. Peterson passed over the First Aid kit, seated himself at the console, and activated the cameras.

"What are you doing?" said Markham, in disbelief. "You lot have absolutely no conception of priorities, do you?"

"Leave him alone," I said. "Presenting this information to Dr. Bairstow might be the one thing that saves our lives."

"I meant," he said with dignity, "isn't anyone going to put the kettle on?"

Somewhat groggily, Bashford began to laugh.

Grey said, "Who are you? I don't know any of you. How did you find us so quickly?"

The moment of truth. The three of us looked at each other. Here we go.

"Well, I'm Maxwell. He's Peterson. I think you may already know Markham here. And we didn't. Find you quickly, I mean."

I passed her some water, took a deep breath, and said quietly, "Elspeth, it's been ten years."

I'm not sure whether Bashford grasped what I'd said, but Grey did. She choked on the water and clutched my wrist.

"Ten—you're sure?"

"Yes, I'm sorry, Elspeth. Ten years."

She was silent for a moment. I could see exactly what she was thinking. This time yesterday she had been at St. Mary's, saying goodbye to Guthrie and setting off on her assignment. And now, ten years had passed.

She said hesitantly, "Ian? Ian Guthrie?"

"Safe and well," I said, hoping to God he was.

She looked around for him. Leon's pod is a single-seater and small. With five of us inside, it was smaller still. Did she think we had Guthrie folded up in a locker?

"He didn't come with you?"

"We didn't invite him. It seemed the more humane thing to do. Just in case . . . you know."

"Ten years," she said, disbelievingly. There was a pause as she wondered how to phrase it. "Has he . . . ? I mean . . ."

"No," I said cheerfully, pretending to misunderstand her. "No improvement at all. He's still the same grumpy, misogynistic, Caledonian bachelor he always was."

I could *hear* Peterson grinning.

Markham said, "There you go, mate," and helped a blood-smeared Bashford to sit up. His eyes swam around in his sockets like a couple of bewildered goldfish before he was finally able to focus.

"Markham? It *is* you."

"That's right," said Markham, sunnily. "How are you feeling now?"

"Absolutely fine," said Bashford, and threw up all over everything.

"Impressive," said Markham, staring down at his thoroughly pebble-dashed self.

Bashford smiled blearily. "Thank you."

I began to warm towards Mr. Bashford.

WE JUMPED BACK TO the paint store. I made Peterson call Dr. Foster on the grounds that of all of us, he was the least likely to be killed for disturbing her at this time of night. Or rather, the morning. Markham anxiously prompted him to remind her to bring Nurse Hunter, as well.

We surveyed the state of Leon's pod in silence.

"We'll see to it later," I said. "Or, with a bit of luck we'll be sacked for tonight's effort so it'll be someone else's problem."

"True," said Peterson cheerfully, shouldering Mr. Bashford. "Shall we go?"

The medical team was waiting. Ignoring us, they whisked away Grey and Bashford and we were left to fend for ourselves. Peterson and Markham made the tea and we sat down to wait.

Half an hour later, Helen Foster emerged. She folded her arms and surveyed us without speaking. I had to admit, we did look a bit on the sloppy side. Markham picked vaguely at his vomit-encrusted body armour. I was still dripping with pig product. There may have been a faint odour . . . Peterson, relatively unscathed, grinned at her.

She ignored him in a way that didn't augur well for the rest of his Christmas.

I asked her how they were.

"They will be fine. They're not fine at the moment, but they will be." She looked at me. "She's asking for Ian. Will you call him, or shall I?"

I stepped to one side, crossed my fingers, activated my com, and called Ian Guthrie. He answered immediately.

"Guthrie."

His voice was sharp and curt. He obviously wasn't in the best mood. However, at least he was still alive.

"Sorry to call you out, Major."

"Oh God—it's the other one."

"What other one?"

"I've had him here all bloody night, you know. He's been driving me insane. Apparently, he wants to discuss safety protocols. On Christmas Eve. In the middle of the night. I can't even go to the bathroom without him trying to follow me in. I'm about to shoot him."

"Really?" I said, sacrificing Leon for the second time that night. "How bizarre. Has he been drinking, do you think?"

I felt, rather than heard, Leon's indignant response.

Guthrie sighed.

"What do you want?"

"What? Oh. Yes. I'm in Sick Bay. We have intruders."

He remained unalarmed. "In Sick Bay? On Christmas Eve?"

"Yes."

"Who's we?"

"Um—well, reading from left to right—me, Dr. Foster, Peterson, Markham, oh, and Nurse Hunter."

"Sounds like a bloody army to me. Shoot them and go back to bed."

"We're not armed," I lied.

"I'll send Leon down. He can talk them to death. Why should I suffer alone?"

For crying out loud—we'd braved Boudicca's battalions to rescue the love of his life and he was instructing us to shoot her. This is typical of St. Mary's. You plan a romantic reunion for a pair of lovers who've been apart for ten years and one of them can't even be bothered to show up. If this were fiction, there would be a swelling soundtrack, tears of joy, people sobbing into tissues . . . What is the matter with us? Why can't we do things like normal people?

Markham uttered an impatient sound, unshouldered his blaster, screamed melodramatically, and fired two blasts into Helen's wall.

A large piece of burning plaster fell to the floor.

Helen screamed—in genuine rage this time—and Guthrie shouted, "On my way."

The link went dead.

We all regarded Markham.

"What?" he said, spreading his hands. "He's coming, isn't he?"

And indeed he was, crashing through the doors, weapon drawn. A one-man assault force.

We froze. Markham made sure to stand behind Hunter.

For a long time, nothing happened, then he clicked on the safety, tucked his gun away, activated his com and said, "Stand down. It's only the usual suspects."

I noticed Leon had not accompanied him, although he probably hadn't been offered the option.

Guthrie surveyed the still smouldering lump of plaster. "Exactly what is going on here?"

I don't think any of us knew what to say. I stepped up, put my arms around him, and hugged him tightly. Hunter did the same with the bits left over.

He patted us both, awkwardly. "Well, this is . . . not in line with normal Sick Bay protocols." His face changed. "I'm dying, aren't I? That's why you wanted me. To tell me I have some fatal disease. How long have I got?"

"If you continue hanging around with this bunch," said Helen, dryly, "who can tell? But no, that's not why you're here. Please put down those women and come with me."

He extricated himself, not without some difficulty, from our clutches. "What's this all about?"

"Would you come this way please, Major?"

She crossed to the female ward and opened the door for him.

He paused on the threshold. I caught the briefest glimpse of his face.

As he passed through the door, she said softly, "Merry Christmas, Ian," and closed the door behind him.

I couldn't hang around. I had things to do. There was Leon to placate and explain to. Then I had a very, very careful report to write for Dr. Bairstow and a breathtakingly monumental bollocking to prepare for. However, before all that, I had a gift to retrieve from my desk and deliver.

I bounced my way into Mrs. Partridge's office and all my careful plans collapsed because despite it being dawn on Christmas Day, she was sitting at her desk, elegant in her usual, beautifully tailored, black suit.

I skidded to a halt and said, awkwardly, "Oh. Good morning, Mrs. Partridge."

She inclined her head. "Good morning, Dr. Maxwell. How may I be of assistance?"

"Um . . . I came to wish you a Happy Christmas." And could have kicked myself.

"A different belief system, but nevertheless, thank you."

"Um . . ."

I'm not usually tongue-tied. Sex renders me speechless occasionally, but even then, not for long. I just hadn't banked on her being here. My plan had been to leave it on her desk and go.

Hesitantly, I pulled out the small parcel and handed it to her. "Season's greetings, then."

She stared at it for so long that I felt compelled to say, "It's a Christmas present." Just in case she was unfamiliar with the concept.

Slowly, she unwrapped the badly packaged rhomboid, not even defeated by the four-and-a-half miles of Sellotape holding it all together.

I'd done a pen-and-ink drawing of the Muses. They were all there, Calliope, Terpsichore, all of them grouped around a seated central figure, Kleio, the Muse of History, gracefully holding her scroll. I'd put a lot of time and effort into it, getting the faces just right and then applying a few gentle washes of colour. I was actually quite pleased with the likeness and that doesn't happen often.

She was still silent.

I kicked myself again. She didn't like it. I had stepped over our invisible but very clearly drawn line. Hot with embarrassment, I began to edge backwards to the door.

Finally, she looked up at me and smiled gently. "Thank you, Max. This is—quite beautiful."

I breathed a sigh of relief. No flaming sword for me today.

"You're welcome, Mrs. Partridge. See you later."

"One moment, please, I have a present for you, too," and to my astonishment, she handed me a small package, beautifully wrapped in tissue paper. No Sellotape in sight.

I gently pulled the paper aside to reveal a small but very heavy knife in a battered leather sheath.

"It's made of meteorite metal," she said. "It's extremely old and has quite a history." Just for a moment, I thought I saw a gleam of amusement. "You would not believe some of the people that's been in."

"Cool," I said, enthusiastically.

"I thought you would appreciate it."

We paused. She looked at her hands. I looked at my feet. Outside, the snow fell silently.

"Well, um . . . I must be going now."

"Yes."

Another long pause.

"So, um . . ."

She picked up some papers, stared at them, and then put them down again and looked out of the window, seemingly at a loss. "Yes . . . of course . . ."

"Um . . . Merry Christmas, Mrs. Partridge."

"And a very Merry Christmas to you, Dr. Maxwell."

SHIPS AND STINGS
AND WEDDING RINGS

AUTHOR'S NOTE

I HAD ALL SORTS of problems with this one. I made the mistake of writing it before I'd finished *What Could Possibly Go Wrong*, and found myself with all sorts of continuity problems, all of which were compounded further when I started *Lies, Damned Lies, and History*, as well.

Lesson learned, however. Get the story line of the first book straight before starting on the second. I also wanted to sow the seeds of Peterson and his Special Question that we learn more of in *Lies, Damned Lies, and History*. Short stories are quite useful for this sort of thing.

I never feel that bloody battlefields are particularly appropriate for Christmas stories, so I thought I'd do something a little gentler this time. Although just because there's no blood or violence doesn't mean the situation was any less serious.

It was an enjoyable book to write. Researching the effects of WD40 poisoning was fun, although one US site I contacted querying what would happen if you sprayed it on someone on a regular basis, emailed me back with panic-stricken disclaimers and warnings, making it very clear that they in no way condoned any intended improper use of this product, so they weren't a great deal of help. They're obviously a great deal more responsible with their lubricants in the US than we are in the UK.

Just digressing for a moment, I had a similar response when I emailed a gas appliance company about how to murder someone using a gas fire. Such fun!

I've had quite a few requests for the story of Leon and Max to have a happy ending—hmm. Still thinking about that one—but I thought the least I could do was give them a few moments together at the end.

Enjoy!

SHIPS AND STINGS
AND WEDDING RINGS

*Y*EARS AGO, WHEN I first came to St. Mary's, Chief Farrell said, "You get a feel for when things have gone wrong," and he was right. You do. So when Grey, Bashford, Cox, and Gallaccio stepped out of their pod, one look was all I needed to see that something had happened.

I stood quietly while they were ushered off to Sick Bay for the statutory checkup, waited for everyone else to disappear, and then followed on behind.

"Why are you here?" said Nurse Hunter to me, ushering Bashford into an examination room. "Is everything all right?"

"Absolutely fine," I said. "Why shouldn't it be?"

"You're here voluntarily, that's why."

"I'm just checking up on my people. They've returned from a vital and important assignment and I want to debrief them as soon as possible."

She consulted her scratchpad. "Are you sure? They've only been checking out shipbuilding in . . . Ancient Egypt."

"Quite sure," I said firmly. "Where's Grey?"

She nodded in the direction of the women's ward.

Elspeth Grey was sitting in the window seat, staring at the snow falling silently outside. She turned her head as I entered and I knew I was right. Something had gone wrong. From the look on her face, something had gone badly wrong.

This wasn't unknown. We're St. Mary's—something always goes wrong. To give us our full title, we're the Institute of Historical Research, based at St. Mary's Priory just outside Rushford. We investigate major historical events in contemporary time. We don't ever call it time travel because our lives are hazardous enough without deliberately calling down the wrath of our boss, Dr. Bairstow, upon ourselves.

Grey and her team had returned from Ancient Egypt and something had happened. I was at a bit of a loss. They all seemed relatively intact to me. Very sunburned, obviously and with hair like straw, but no one was missing a vital body part, or leaking vast amounts of body fluids everywhere. I had a horrible feeling this was more serious than simple physical injury.

I dragged up a chair. "What's happened?"

She was so pale that I was surprised Hunter hadn't shoved her back into the scanner again.

She said quietly, "I've done something terrible, Max," and stopped, unable to go on.

Many terrible things can happen to historians. It was obviously up to me to whittle them down a bit.

I said, "Is anyone dead?" and waited for her hasty denial.

It didn't come.

I felt myself grow cold. The team was all present and as correct as St. Mary's was ever able to achieve, which only left. . .

"Elspeth. Is someone dead?" I took a deep breath. "Did you—has someone—killed a contemporary?"

She shook her head, then nodded, and then said, "I don't know."

I'd had enough. If something catastrophic had happened, I needed to know immediately. Before the bloody Time Police came crashing through the door to arrest us all.

I pitched my voice to bring her back. "Report."

She pulled herself together. "The assignment went well. No one knew who we were. We've got masses of good footage."

"So what went wrong?"

"It was me. I did it."

"What did you do?"

She clenched her hands tightly in her lap. I'm not actually that terrifying. All right, I'm slightly pregnant, but that doesn't usually reduce people to a state of speechless terror. My husband Leon had actually been quite pleased. And Dr. Bairstow had immediately commanded Mrs. Partridge to prepare him a briefing on the duties of a godfather. Even I was coming round to the idea.

I said gently, "Elspeth. You must tell me so I can put it right."

She took a deep shuddering breath and braced herself. "I took a gun on the assignment."

I braced myself because I could see what was coming.

"And. . . ?"

"And I lost it."

"Where?"

She couldn't bring herself to say it. "Not . . . here."

"You took a gun on assignment?"

"Yes."

"To Ancient Egypt?"

She nodded, miserably.

"But why? You had two security guards."

Yes, she did. One more than normal, but there were special circumstances attached to Elspeth Grey and Tom Bashford. They'd gone missing in 12th-century Jerusalem and were eventually discovered in Roman Colchester, only minutes before Boudicca's army crashed down upon the town, hell-bent on obliterating everyone and everything within it. Something like that can take some time to recover from.

Bashford had apparently picked up the threads of his old life with no problems at all, but Grey, who had been the one who battled to keep them both alive while he'd been semi-conscious, had been having problems. It had taken her a year to pluck up the courage to re-enter a pod. I'd selected her for the shipbuilding assignment specifically because it would be quiet and uneventful. And I'd allocated her an extra security guard. To make her feel safe. There were no wars, no plagues, no famines, and no civil unrest at that point in Egypt's history. All they had to do was record the various stages of shipbuilding and anything else they thought might be useful, stay out of trouble, not die, and return to St. Mary's. All of which they appeared to have achieved, no problem at all. And now—this.

Keeping my voice steady, I said, "What did you take?"

She swallowed and whispered, "A Glock."

Shit. Glocks don't have a conventional safety catch. They have safe action designed to prevent the weapon from accidentally discharging, should it be dropped or banged, but if you pull the trigger, it will fire. Because that's what it's designed to do. And now we had one in Ancient Egypt. Just waiting for someone to pick it up, wave it around, and blow someone's head off.

We're not allowed to kill contemporaries. Think of all the thousands of people who must be descended from one single person living say, three thousand years ago. Now imagine that person never lived long enough to have children. What would happen? Would all those people disappear? Some would never be born. Others would be the product of different parents and all that would work its way down to the present day. Suppose Grey herself suddenly vanished, never having been born. And if she'd never been born then she couldn't go back to Ancient

Egypt to leave the gun that was the cause of all the trouble. What would happen then? At the very least the Time Police would come down on us like the proverbial ton of bricks and at the very worst, we'd be looking at the "P" word.

Paradox.

With two security guards to keep her safe, why on earth would she feel the need to take a weapon? At the very most, historians are allowed a stun gun to defend themselves. Our normal defence strategy is to run like mad away from any trouble. Obviously, it would be nice if we could rely on not getting into trouble in the first place, but we're St. Mary's and that's not really a reasonable expectation.

"Elspeth," I said carefully. "Tell me about your problem."

The door opened and Bashford entered.

Without turning my head, I said, "Go away."

He closed the door behind him. "With the greatest respect, Max, no."

I'd never actually had someone defy me before. They would stand in front of me and argue themselves to a standstill—that's the definition of an historian—but I don't think I've ever actually had someone look me in the eye and say no.

He said, "I can explain."

"No need. Miss Grey is about to do that. Continue, Miss Grey."

"No, Max . . ."

"Be silent, Mr. Bashford, or leave the room. Continue, Miss Grey."

She returned from wherever she had been and focused on me again.

"I took a gun on the assignment in case . . . in case . . . *he* was there."

She meant Clive Ronan. The man who'd snatched them out of Jerusalem and abandoned them in Colchester. Abandoned them to die.

She was continuing, clenching her hands so tightly I could see red crescents where her fingernails were digging into her palms. "I can't . . . I know . . . I know it's stupid to expect him to be everywhere I go. I do know that, but I just can't rid myself of the fear that I'll step out of the pod and he'll be there and I'll be whirled off to somewhere and this time . . . this time . . . there won't be anyone to pull me out and I'll die. And yes, I know you allocated an extra guard. And I know there is no reason to suspect anything like that would ever happen again. I know all that. But I keep thinking, Max . . . suppose you hadn't found us. Suppose you hadn't pulled us out in time. Suppose it happens again . . ."

Silence fell in the tiny ward. On the other side of the door, I could hear Dr. Foster giving Cox a hard time over something or other. She'd be in here in a moment to find out what was going on.

Bashford stirred. "Max, she's been through enough," he said, and put a protective hand on her shoulder.

It wasn't needed. I wasn't going to shout at her. Actually, I didn't know what I was going to do. I fell back on more questions.

"So, what happened to the gun?"

"I don't know. I was carrying it in my pack so I could get to it quickly if I needed to. And we stopped for water, and when I looked, it wasn't there."

"Could it have been stolen?"

"No. Not a chance."

"Did you take it out and leave it somewhere?"

"No. I think . . . I fell . . . and my pack came undone. I think it must have been then."

"Did you go back and look?"

"Yes. Three times."

"So Cox and Gallaccio know what happened?"

She nodded.

I had huge sympathy for her, but she'd committed a cardinal sin by taking a gun in the first place and an even bigger cardinal sin by leaving it. My blood ran cold just thinking about a child picking it up, staring down the barrel and wondering what would happen if you pulled this funny bit here. . .

"Did the others know you had this weapon?"

"No," she said, too quickly.

Another cardinal sin. They should have taken it off her.

"Get them in here, please. Now."

Bashford left the room.

Tears ran down her cheeks. "Max, I'm so sorry."

"Good, but don't cry yet. We'll think of something."

She shook her head.

I had several options open to me. The correct procedure would be to go to Dr. Bairstow who would probably place the matter in the hands of the Time Police. That was their function, after all. To police the timeline, hoovering up anomalies. He would also arrest Miss Grey—he'd have to—and she'd be handed over to the Time Police as well. I really didn't want that to happen. Their opinion of us is not high and the last thing we needed was to provide proof that we really were the bunch of irresponsible idiots they thought we were. Leaving something behind is unprofessional. Leaving behind a gun capable of killing a contemporary is a major crime. They would probably deal fairly leniently with Grey since she obviously had a problem, but we should have noticed this. I should have noticed it. She was in my department. I knew she'd been struggling, but I hadn't known it was this bad. Neither had Helen Foster, who had cleared her for duty. And it wasn't really Elspeth's fault. She'd done everything she could to avoid going back on the active list and I'd stupidly thought that once she got back on the horse—or into the pod—that everything would be fine. And it hadn't—been fine, I mean. A lot of this was my fault and I was buggered if I was going to hand over the problem to someone else without having a good go at fixing it first.

Bashford came back with a very sheepish-looking Cox and Gallaccio.

"We're going to fix this," I said. "Before Dr. Bairstow or the Time Police or Major Guthrie have even the slightest idea there's been a problem."

This was an effective threat. Dangling their boss, Ian Guthrie, in front of them focused their minds wonderfully. They would give a great deal for him not to know how badly things had gone wrong on this assignment.

I got up and opened the door. Dr. Foster was heading towards me. "What's going on in there?"

"How plausible do you want your deniability to be?"

"Oh for God's sake, Max."

"Give me an hour or so, and then you need to have a quiet talk with Grey."

She sighed. "One hour. No longer."

An hour was all I needed.

STILL UNSURE WHAT I was going to say, I sat down again with Elspeth, but my fears were unfounded.

"I know, Max. You don't have to say anything. I'll write out my notice and it'll be on Dr. Bairstow's desk the first morning after the Christmas holiday."

I sighed but she was right. She'd had a year to resume her old life and it was very obvious that she didn't wish to do so.

"Max, I'm so sorry—whatever you're going to do, I'm sure I shouldn't let you do it. Maybe I should confess to Dr. Bairstow now and take my medicine."

She was underestimating the seriousness of the matter. A loaded gun adrift in Ancient Egypt was far more than a disciplinary problem but there was no point in making things worse for her. Not at the moment, anyway. I tried for optimism.

"It needn't come to that. I'm going to take Markham, have a poke around, and see what we can find. Who knows—we might be able to pick it straight up and be back here before you've even had time to turn around—and if—when—we find it, Markham will have it back in the Armoury before anyone even knows it was missing."

"Ian won't be happy."

No, he wouldn't. As someone with a close personal interest in Miss Grey, he would be unhappy she hadn't confided in him. As Head of the Security Section, he would be incandescent with rage if he ever found out what she'd done.

"We'll sort that out later as well," I said, ignoring all these potential disasters piling up on the horizon like oncoming storm clouds. "You were in Pod Five?"

She nodded.

"Which you have, of course, thoroughly searched from top to bottom?"

"Four times."

I thought. "Do you have any idea when you could possibly have lost it?"

"There was a day—at the launching—when I dropped my pack and it fell open, but I'm not stupid, Max. I checked very, very thoroughly, and so did Cox who was with me at the time. It wasn't there."

"Did you ever leave the pod at night?"

She just looked at me. Yes all right—a stupid question. If she'd been terrified of Clive Ronan turning up during the day then she was hardly likely to leave the safety of the pod to blunder around in the dark.

I got up.

"OK, Dr. Foster will be in to see you in a moment. Listen to what she has to say, keep your mouth shut to everyone else, and leave everything to me."

I WENT TO FIND Markham and we stood in an empty training room where no one could see us or hear us and had a long talk.

When we'd hammered out the details, he said, "What about Peterson?"

"What about him?"

"Isn't this our Christmas tradition? We steal a pod—usually Chief Farrell's—make an illegal jump to put something right and everything ends happily. So far, we're well on track, but there's always the three of us. You, me, and Peterson."

I sighed. "We really shouldn't involve him. He's going to be Deputy Director. And he's not fit enough yet."

Peterson had sustained a terrible wound in 15th-century France. His arm was healed and he'd regained some movement—enough to come third in the Security Section's Annual All Comers One-Handed Bra Unfastening Competition (or SSAACOHBUC for short), but if things went south, he might not be able to defend himself. I saw the scene again—Peterson sprawled on the floor, soaked in blood, dying under my hands. . .

Markham said gently, "Surely it's his decision to make, Max."

"It's not one we should ask him to make. We'd be putting him in a difficult position."

He shrugged. "It's just you and me, then."

"Just you and me. Do you know what you have to do?"

He nodded.

"Right, we'll meet in the paint store in . . . thirty minutes."

I RACED AROUND THE building like a madwoman because I didn't have time to be discreet. I strode into Wardrobe and requisitioned what we needed. Confidence is the key. I'm the Chief Operations Officer and head of the History Department. If I can't march around helping myself to all the equipment needed for an illegal jump to save a colleague, preserve the reputation of St. Mary's, and protect the timeline, then who can?

I deposited everything at the back of the paint store, safely concealed behind the tins of Sunshine Yellow, and went off to see what had happened to Markham. I found him in what the Security Section likes to refer to as their nerve centre, which was a fancy name for a small, windowless room with a kettle, seven mugs, two tins of biscuits, a calendar picturing two fluffy kittens sitting in a slipper, and the petty cash box lying open on a shelf and bulging with IOUs. Half a dozen monitors showed various views from around the building. A giant fuse box with a zigzag lightning bolt painted across it was attached to the wall.

Markham was festooning strings of fairy lights around the security monitors. A cat's cradle of wires connected them to each other and the fuse box.

I opened my mouth to demand what the hell he thought he was playing at and then remembered to whom I was talking.

"Pretty," I said.

"You don't know the half of it," he said. "When this is over I'm going to rig them to flash on and off in time to 'White Christmas.' Now stand in the middle of the room and, for God's sake, don't touch anything metal. In fact, put your hands in your pockets."

"Why?"

He threw a switch. There was a white flash, followed by a bang, followed by the smell of burnt fish. I just had time to register that all the monitors had faded to black with only a little white dot in the centre, when all the lights went out. Then the fire alarms went off.

Hat trick.

"Deary, deary me," he said, in a voice of immense satisfaction. "I wonder how that could have happened."

In the distance, I could hear my husband Leon, the unit's Chief Technical Officer, demanding to know which idiot was responsible for . . . the last part of the sentence was lost as a door closed somewhere.

"How long have we got?"

"Well, speaking from personal experience, evacuating St. Mary's is a bit like herding cats. No one will be able to find Professor Rapson. Mrs. Mack won't move without Vortigern." (Vortigern is her beloved kitchen cat.) "And he won't move at all if he can help it. No one will be able to remember where the assembly point is. Someone will fall into the lake. All the historians will just stand around looking stupid and refusing to budge because it's snowing out there and they don't want to get their precious selves cold and wet. A good hour, I reckon."

"Brilliant," I said in awe. "Absolutely bloody brilliant."

"Yeah," he said modestly. "Aren't I?"

"On this occasion—yes."

He produced a torch and we slipped out of the door.

It was chaos out there. It's bedlam at St. Mary's when the lights are on. It's a hundred times worse when the lights are out.

All around us was a maelstrom of raised voices shouting conflicting instructions, supernova-bright torches blinding everyone they shone on, dreadful language, and the odd scream as someone fell over something. We crept cautiously along the corridors, but quite honestly, they wouldn't have noticed if Napoleon's army had swung through on their way to Moscow, singing the *1812 Overture* scored for full chorus, twenty-one cannons, and a tambourine.

We battled our way through the crowds. "Like salmon swimming upstream," said Markham at one point, eventually arriving at the paint store. We oozed inside and closed the door, shutting out the noise behind us. In the sudden silence, I heaved a sigh of relief. Difficult part over with.

No it wasn't. Peterson was waiting for us.

We stopped dead and everyone looked at everyone else.

When it became apparent he wasn't going to speak, I said, "How on earth did you know?"

He raised his eyebrows at me, his expression enigmatic. At that moment, he looked very like Dr. Bairstow. He was going to make a wonderful Deputy Director.

"Is that a serious question? It's Christmas. The two of you are whispering in corners looking mysterious. Grey's in tears. Then, mysteriously, the lights go out. Why didn't you just make a public announcement?"

Markham shuffled his feet and muttered something.

I sighed. "Does everyone know?"

"If you mean Chief Farrell and Major Guthrie—Leon's racing around trying to get the lights on and the fire alarms off, and Guthrie's gearing up for the invasion he's convinced is imminent. Of course, neither of them is going to be pleased when they discover the true cause of the emergency."

"I may have to live abroad for a while," said Markham gloomily.

"You should live so long. So, what's this all about?"

I was uneasy for him. "You oughtn't to be involved."

"Tell me or I grass the pair of you up to Dr. Bairstow right now."

"You tell him," I said to Markham, and pushed my way past them to retrieve our equipment and load up the pod.

Pods are our centre of operations. We use them to jump back to whichever time period we've been assigned. We live in them and work in them. Occasionally, we die in them. They're small, cramped, and smelly, and that's even before you add a couple of historians to the mix. Leon's pod is a single-seater, so this one was even smaller and more cramped than usual. I activated the screen and watched the two of them indulge in a heated discussion while I laid in the coordinates.

When I emerged, task done, Markham was just finishing. "And let's face it, it wouldn't be Christmas if we weren't stealing Chief Farrell's pod and breaking all the rules for a good cause."

"Once. We did that once."

"All traditions have to start somewhere."

Peterson sighed. "So how is this going to work, then? Don't tell me you haven't got a plan?"

"We jump to the original coordinates. Very carefully ensuring we are not seen by Bashford and his gang, we shadow them. We follow their every move. With luck, we can identify the exact moment the gun goes missing. As soon as they're clear, we swoop in, grab the bloody thing, and jump back to St. Mary's. Markham will get it back to the Armoury and no one ever knows a thing about it."

There was a brief silence as we contemplated all the many things that could go wrong with this simple plan.

"If they catch sight of us . . ." said Peterson doubtfully.

"They won't," I said with a confidence worthy of a much better scheme.

Peterson shook his head. "You'll go too far one day, Max."

"Very likely, but not today. Shall we go?"

That's the thing about time travel—or investigating major historical events in contemporary time, of course—once we were actually in Ancient Egypt, we were off the clock. We could take as long as we liked to find this bloody gun and still get back less than an hour after we jumped. We climbed into the pod.

"There are only rations for about a week," announced Peterson, rummaging through the lockers. "If we haven't found it by then we might have a problem."

"We'd have less of a problem if you stayed behind," I said, pointedly.

"And more food, too," added Markham.

"Drag your mind away from your stomach, will you?" said Peterson.

"Hey, I'm not the one jeopardising the entire mission with my unwanted presence," said Markham.

"Shut up, the pair of you," I said in my newly acquired role of mission facilitator and peacemaker. "Let's get out of here before anyone comes looking for us."

There was the usual quarrel about who was to drive. Peterson lost because he can't help bouncing his pod whenever and wherever he lands. We've never dared take him to Constantinople in case he skims, pebble-like, across the Bosphorus and we end up in the wrong continent. I left Markham to make this telling argument while I made myself comfortable and started flicking switches. Peterson's indignant response that, since we weren't actually going to Constantinople it hardly mattered, was ignored.

"Computer, initiate jump."

"Jump initiated."

The world went white.

AND HERE I WAS again. Ancient Egypt. I'd been here before. Several times, actually. If I had it right, we'd arrived during the reign of Hatshepsut, when Egypt was at the height of her power. One of this female Pharaoh's many achievements was her trading expedition to the legendary land of Punt in the ninth year of her reign. She built five ships—quite an achievement in a land where wood was scarce—and this was what Bashford's team were here to check out.

Bashford's pod, Number Five, should be arriving any moment now. We'd aimed to arrive just before them because we couldn't afford to miss a second.

"There," said Peterson, leaning over my shoulder as they materialised. "On the other side of that palm grove. Don't let them see us."

This was the real reason we'd brought Leon's pod. It has a camouflage device. And no—it's not cloaking. It's camouflage. Apparently, there's a difference. Leon will be happy to explain it to you, although that will be a week of your life you'll never get back again. I operated the system and, to all intents and purposes, we were invisible. We just had to hope a camel didn't walk into us.

I watched the screen, waiting for Bashford's team to emerge, while Markham and Peterson quarrelled over the gear I'd blagged from Wardrobe. Since I hadn't expected Peterson to join our happy band, unless one of them was prepared to wear a dress, it was obvious there wasn't enough to cover the pair of them adequately. Peterson solved the problem by pulling rank, leaving a complaining Markham to do something ingenious with an old bed sheet he found in a locker.

"There," he said, securing himself firmly with a length of material he was using as a belt. "What do you think?"

Markham looks unkempt and dishevelled in any century. There are people in the world who can make even the richest and most gorgeous clothes look scruffy and, if they had a professional organisation to represent them, Markham would be Chairman. And probably Secretary and Treasurer as well.

We contemplated him.

"You look like a girl," said Peterson.

"And not for the first time," I told him.

"I think he looks adorable," said Peterson.

"I think I look like someone wearing a bed sheet."

"Perhaps we could tell people he's on some sort of institutional day-release scheme," I said doubtfully.

"We'll tell people he's our slave," said Peterson.

"Why am I always the slave?"

"Demarcation. We're historians. You're not. It's not rocket science."

"They'll be out in a minute," I said, endeavouring to get things back on track. "We should get a move on. Keep an eye on things. I'll join you in a minute."

I scrambled into the long linen tunic-dress I'd brought with me. It was a little tight because of my expanding waistline, but my waistline is always expanding. It seems to have been a one-way process throughout my life and pregnancy wasn't helping. I tied up my hair, plonked the coarse black wig on top, and sighed. I was going to be very hot.

I had, however, brought a linen parasol and my makeup bag. Two minutes in front of a mirror with eye shadow and black eyeliner and I looked moderately respectable. As did Peterson. Markham looked like a grumpy transvestite who had escaped from a Care in the Community Programme. With mascara.

"Just stay at the back," advised Peterson.

"Here they come," I said.

I MIGHT AS WELL say now that their behaviour during this assignment was impeccable. Bashford—when not concussed—was an excellent historian, and his team, even Grey, was unobtrusive and professional. They walked as a quiet group, heads down, discreet.

They had a strict walking order. Bashford at the front, then Gallaccio, then Grey, and Cox brought up the rear. The men had wicker baskets heaved over their shoulders and Grey carried a soft, knotted pack. It had straps but she wouldn't wear it on her back, insisting on carrying it in her arms. So that she could get to the gun quickly, as I now realised, because hindsight is so marvellous and we all have it in spades.

They walked well-trodden paths, but even I couldn't have got lost here. All paths led to the bustling boatyard.

I know there are still places in the present world where boats are made by hand—I've seen one or two as a tourist—but this was amazing.

The boatyard was vast. All around us, I could see craft of every description in varying degrees of completion. Reed rafts for hunting game birds in the marshes; papyrus boats, commissioned by the Pharaoh or her priests for ceremonial purposes; and big wooden barges for military use or for transporting cargo. Some were already in the water. Some had been hauled onto dry land and propped upright on wooden spars, presumably for repair.

Great wooden hulls were silhouetted against the sky. The sound of hammering and sawing filled the air. I could smell the river, hot mud, new wood, and burning tar.

Stocky men, burned dark by the sun and wearing loincloths or short tunics swarmed everywhere, shouting to each other. Everyone was busy and full of purpose. There were no women anywhere. Any food and water was brought by young boys. I made sure to stay well back.

Surrounding the boatyard were a number of workshops housing carpenters, rope makers, caulkers, and other allied trades. Canvas awnings slung between them provided much-needed shade in which to work.

Because it was hot. It was very, very hot. As hot as hell. Dust rose everywhere in great clouds, sticking to my sweaty skin. It was in my hair, my eyes, even my mouth. I could feel it under my clothing. Within minutes, we were all covered in a film of gritty, reddish dust, just like everyone else, but the upside was that now we fitted right in. If Bashford and the others turned around at this very moment, they were unlikely to recognise us.

Sadly, this worked both ways. We had the same problem recognising them. In fact, if they hadn't had Grey with them, we might not have been able to pick them out at all. On the other hand, of course, if they hadn't had Grey with them then we wouldn't be here.

They settled themselves unobtrusively, sharing the shade of an acacia tree with several dogs who refused to budge. The best we could get was a clump of thorny bushes some way back behind a sort of lean-to where they appeared to be boiling papyrus. Probably to make caulk. That's the material with which they waterproof their boats. The demand seemed insatiable.

Piles of the harvested papyrus lay around and men arrived with fresh supplies almost hourly.

Huge vats of the stuff were being heated over open fires and I could see the heat haze rippling above each cauldron, because, of course, we weren't hot enough, were we? The men working here were practically naked and I didn't blame them in the slightest. Just watching them made my hair prickle and sweat run down my back. My tunic was drenched and limp.

Back at St. Mary's, they'd be having a pre-Christmas snowball fight in which many old scores would be settled by a handful of cold wet snow down the back of your neck. I'd give anything for a handful of cold wet snow down the back of my neck.

I've no idea what type of straggly bush was providing our only patch of shade—this is what happens when you're not properly prepped—but they were apparently made of razor blades. We struggled to the centre of the thicket, made ourselves as comfortable as possible, and watched.

And watched.

We never took our eyes off them and I honestly couldn't see how she'd ever managed to lose the bloody thing. Even when working, she usually kept one hand on her pack and she certainly never let it out of her reach. I noticed too that Bashford was never very far away from her. In fact, deliberately or otherwise, she was never left alone. Even from this distance, I could see how nervous she was, jumping at every sound. Continually alert for the unexpected. It was only this time last year that we were yanking her out of Colchester. I sighed. This was all my fault. I should never have assigned her.

When Bashford's team returned to their pod, we returned to ours, since Grey had never left it at night. A shower would have been wonderful but not having been prepped to go out, the tanks weren't full and we had to conserve water. We did briefly discuss a quick dip in the Nile but I was once chased by a herd (or whatever the collective noun is) of Nile crocodiles;

Leon and I barely escaped, and that sort of experience does tend to discourage the use of the Nile for casual bathing and recreational purposes. So we shook out our clothes, washed carefully, and conserved water.

Days passed. Our supplies grew low and I began to worry. Every morning, just before dawn, Bashford's team left their pod. We followed on as closely as we dared. Not too close, but not too far behind either. Following in their footsteps, eyes on the ground, always looking for that bloody gun.

They would settle themselves in for a long day's observing and we observed the observers. After they departed, one of us would nip over and give the area the once over in case she'd dropped it there. She never had.

As far as we could see, they were making general observations, but concentrating mainly on a ninety-foot long transportation barge, which was taking shape in front of our eyes. Four others lay alongside. Men swarmed all over them, up and down wooden ladders. Long ago, Herodotus had described how Egyptian boats were built, using methods that, with typical Egyptian resistance to change, had remained virtually unaltered over the centuries. Just wooden planking, cut to a precise shape that would fit tightly together in a brick pattern.

"Not a nail in sight," said Peterson admiringly.

Time passed slowly. It does in Egypt. I now knew more about Egyptian shipbuilding than was good for me. We couldn't even fall back on that standard English conversational device, the weather, because once we'd agreed it was hot, that was pretty well it. There were flies everywhere, most of whom fell in love with Markham. At one point, nearly every insect in the country seemed to regard him as a desirable place to take up residence, or lay their eggs and bring up their family, and he was covered in lumps, bumps, bites, and stings, and had developed a small but interesting rash on his elbow.

"Not a clue," said Peterson, peering at it. "Does it hurt?"

"Like buggery."

"Well, don't scratch it."

"Is that it? You're both field medics and the best you can come up with is 'Don't scratch it'?"

"We could amputate your arm if you like," I offered, out of the goodness of my heart. "That would certainly enable us to showcase our medical skills."

Peterson nodded enthusiastically.

Markham protectively clutched his diseased arm and glared at us.

"You know what," said Peterson, settling back as comfortably as he could, "one day we'll have a normal Christmas. We'll spend the run up decorating St. Mary's. There will be streamers and tinsel and a tree and, if I can manoeuvre Helen into the right position *vis-à-vis* the mistletoe, some serious snogging. There will be carols and eggnog and silly games. We'll listen to the King's Speech. We'll all consume a year's worth of calories in one meal and then, when she's too stuffed to put up any sort of resistance, I'll ask Helen a very important question. It will be a proper Christmas."

He sat, staring happily into his future. Markham and I eyed each other and said nothing.

To pass the time, we discussed names for the baby. Agamemnon got the most votes, followed by Iphigenia.

To assist him in his ongoing struggle against the insect world, we pumped Markham full of everything we could find in the med kit and each morning, at his request, I sprayed him thoroughly with a can of some sort of repellent he said was at the back of one of the lockers and which seemed to be doing the job, even if he did smell of rancid grease afterwards.

"WE'VE BEEN HERE NEARLY a week," said Markham one day, wiping sweat off his face. "Suppose we don't ever find it? Would it be safe to assume that if *we* can't find it—and we've been looking hard—then no one else will either? That it's been buried forever or at the bottom of an irrigation ditch or something?"

"Not with our luck," said Peterson. "I wish they'd hurry up and launch this bloody ship. We're running short of food and water."

He was right on both counts. With our luck, the gun would be picked up by some kid who, in the sort of freakish set of circumstances with which St. Mary's is so familiar, would manage to blow Hatshepsut's head off and change History for all time. And our supplies were dwindling fast.

I was beginning to lose my optimism. We huddled together, following our tiny patch of shade as best we could, dogging the other team's every step, and there was no sign anywhere of that bloody gun. For two pins, I'd have stormed across, grabbed the thing from her pack, and jumped back to St. Mary's as quickly as possible, but I couldn't. She never let it out of her reach.

We were hot, hungry, thirsty, sunburned, stung, and going nowhere. The barge, which appeared to be the focus of their observations, was nearing completion. They would pack up and jump back and we'd have no choice other than to follow them. Then I'd have to go and have a very difficult conversation with Dr. Bairstow.

For the first time, I began to wonder whether I should have gone straight to the Time Police and left them to sort it out. Every day we were here we risked being discovered, and that would be disastrous because it would influence events that had already happened. Doubt gnawed at me and there were several occasions when I hovered on the brink of pulling us out and heading home.

"No," said Markham, reading my mind. "Give it a little while longer."

I looked at our sunburned selves. "I don't know how I'm going to explain this away. We're going to be in such trouble."

"I wouldn't worry too much," he said, examining his rash again which had spread to his other elbow via his knees. "Everyone knows you can talk people into pulling the most outrageous stunts that seem perfectly logical at the time, and we always seem to get back more or less safely. It's me that has to explain to Major Guthrie just how I managed to get trampled by a war elephant/covered in boiling oil/locked in the oubliette/stung by the scorpion and so on. He's never impressed by any of it and somehow the mad redhead always gets off scot-free and everything turns out to be my fault."

"True," I said, feeling more cheerful.

On the sixth day, we wearily heaved ourselves out of the pod and trudged off to the boatyard, carefully following in Bashford's footsteps. Peterson checked the left-hand side of the path, Markham the right, and I came along behind, acting as sweeper.

So far, everything as usual. On this day, however, we would have some excitement. Today was the day the ship would be launched. It wasn't completed yet, but there would be a small ceremony as it was dragged down to the water. We assumed they had to float it now before it became too big and heavy to be moved.

"A bit like you in a few months, Max," said Markham to me.

I SUPPOSE THAT, FOR a race which casually dots massive pyramids willy-nilly around the landscape, launching a boat, however large, presents no problems at all.

There was the obligatory shouting, of course, even when addressing the man only two feet away, because if you don't shout, how will people know how important you are?

Thick, chocolate-coloured ropes were attached in what was almost a cat's cradle. The boat had a mast but no rigging or any of the horizontal bits—whatever they're called. There were no quarter rudders yet—that's the two big oars at the back.

Look, I'm not a sailor—OK? The big bit of wood, the sternpost, which helped compress the planking and keep it watertight, was carved in the image of a huge lotus. The work was obviously a labour of love—it was beautiful. The lotus is a sacred symbol in Egypt.

Lines of men arrived, apparently from nowhere, their bodies already glistening with sweat. Someone somewhere had a drum. Someone always has a drum. They lined up in their teams, complete with overseer, planted their feet, spat on their hands, and took up the slack.

The drumbeat began, slow and rhythmical. The lines of men threw themselves into a near horizontal position and heaved.

"Interesting," said Peterson. "They pull backwards—like a tug-of-war team."

They were just like a tug-of-war team. Shifting their weight from foot to foot, barely moving an inch at a time, grunting with the effort, they began to build up a momentum. The drum banged on, providing the rhythm. Crowds of people, men, women, and children cheered with enthusiasm and threw flowers. This was obviously a great day for those who had built her. The day she went down to the water. I wondered what her name was. There would be five of these beautiful boats making that epic voyage to the fabulous land of Punt, and all their names are lost in the mists of History.

Slowly, imperceptibly, the boat began to move down the slipway. I say slipway, but it was just a gentle slope down to the water, baked hard as concrete by sun and regular use. Two men ran down each side, knocking away the wooden props.

We stood up for a better view. No one was bothering to look at us, least of all Bashford and his crew. Even Grey was completely involved in what was happening, her pack clutched tightly to her chest.

To our left, a group of priests began to chant, raising their hands skywards, possibly invoking the blessing of the great god Re as he travelled across the heavens in his solar boat. Or if not his blessing then those of whichever deities considered themselves responsible for ships and sailors in this god-laden country.

As the boat slid majestically past them, their chanting rose to a crescendo and acolytes began flicking what I suspected was blood along the hull. There's always blood at a ship launch. I read somewhere that the Norsemen launched their boats over living sacrifices, to ensure the keel was well and truly saturated, because that always brought good fortune. Although not to the sacrifices, of course.

Small boys ran up and down the lines of toiling men, throwing buckets of water over them before anyone expired in the heat.

The noise was enormous. In addition to the drum, a small group of musicians had turned up with the priests. A pipe wailed mournfully, although this was probably a happy song. It's quite hard to tell sometimes. Cymbals clashed. Even the dogs woke up and ran around barking hysterically and getting in everyone's way.

"This is the way to launch a ship," shouted Markham, peering red-eyed at the scene.

"It's still done more or less this way," I said. "They just use champagne and a brass band these days. Not half so much fun, though."

"Yes," said Peterson thoughtfully. "Sadly, I have to say I can't see Princess Alice flinging a bucket of blood at a ship as it slides past. Which is a shame, really. She'd enjoy it."

Now, at a command from somewhere, a number of men at the front relinquished their ropes, trotted around to the back, and began to push. The boat picked up speed, reaching the point where it would be unstoppable. Anxious mothers called for their children. The dogs got out of the way. The long lines of men, beautifully coordinated, began to peel away. She was moving by herself now, eager to reach the water. Men were cheering and urging her on. This was obviously a good sign.

And before anyone asks, I hadn't forgotten about Grey. She still stood, eyes fixed on the launching, still holding on to her pack for dear life.

Ten feet to go.

Then six.

Then three.

She was there, gliding smoothly into the water. Pushing a bow wave before her. The lines at the back tightened. In a torrent of white water, she jerked to a halt, swaying (or whatever the nautical term is) from side to side. With a final triumphant shout, men took the strain, feet skidding in the dust. Someone lobbed a couple of sea anchors over the side and there she was. Unfinished, lacking a complete mast, sail, or oars, but beautiful nevertheless. And alive. This ship was a living thing. I can understand now why shipbuilders and sailors always refer to boats as she and endow them with living characteristics. I was so glad I'd had the opportunity to see this.

The ship's crew were unhitching the ropes and tossing them into the water, where they were pulled in, coiled, and stowed away.

The crowd broke ranks, running to the water's edge in excitement. Everyone was eager to see the new ship.

And then it happened. I was watching and I saw exactly what happened to the gun.

As you can imagine, there were crowds of excited kids running everywhere. Most of them were stark naked, covered in God knows what, with crusty nostrils, weeping eyes, and completely bald apart from their side knots. They made Markham look spotless and those are two words I never thought I'd get to use in the same sentence.

A group of shrieking youngsters, all tangled up with yelping dogs, raced down to the water's edge for a better view, and ran straight into Bashford's team. There was no harm done, but Grey was knocked down. She staggered, fell, and dropped her pack, which hit the ground and fell open, spilling its contents everywhere.

I took two paces to the left for a better view.

The kids raced on regardless, kicking her stuff in all directions and I saw it. I saw the gun hit the ground and spin sideways. A laughing little boy, completely unaware of what he was doing, accidentally kicked it under a vat of caulk.

No one noticed except me.

Grey was on her knees, scrabbling her stuff together and ramming it back into her pack. Bashford and Gallaccio were still watching the boat. Cox stood guard over her as she knotted her pack together again and scrambled to her feet.

I saw him say something to her, presumably asking if she had everything. I saw her look around. They both did. They both checked the area very, very thoroughly. It wasn't their fault the gun was about ten feet away under a cauldron of cold pitch. And that was about the only thing we could be grateful for. That today the fire had been extinguished and the ashes were cold.

Taking her arm, he helped her to run after the others at the shoreline.

I stood undecided. Go after it now and risk the other team turning around and seeing us? Or wait for them to move off and risk losing it again?

I hesitated and that hesitation was fatal. Even as I stood and stared, a tiny boy darted forwards, scooped up the gun, turned it over in his grubby paws, and before I could get to him, he ran off.

"Bollocks! Come on."

We set off after him. Very carefully, because there is never a time period when chasing after a kid is a good idea. The chances were that almost everyone in this boatyard was a relation of some kind or other. My plans for Christmas did not include being impaled.

He raced around the sailmakers' workshop and along the riverbank.

We trotted after him, doing our best to look inconspicuous.

He stopped after a while, looked around, and crouched in the dust to examine his prize.

Peterson pushed past me and sprinted. Never mind what anyone thought—if he pulled the trigger then we really would be in the shit. Even more deeply than usual.

Peterson was nearly there. A few more yards, grab the gun, ignore the inevitable protests and possible tears, then it was everyone back to the pod, jump back to St. Mary's, replace the gun, smile at everyone, and deny everything. We could do this.

And then another boy burst out of a reed bed. Older and bigger, he'd lost his side knot, so he wasn't a child any longer. Looking back, he might have been an older brother, and in the manner of older brothers everywhere, he clumped the smaller kid round the side of the head, relieved him of his treasure, and was away off down the path before anyone else had quite worked out what was happening.

I made a mental note to remember how inconveniently fast children could move.

Markham and I caught up and stared after the vanishing figure.

"Go," I said. "Both of you. I'll catch up. Now. Go now."

They didn't argue. A second later, the kid and I were alone. He knuckled his eyes and peered up at me, tears leaving tracks through the dirt on his face. I stared down at him. He looked like a giant germ. I should do something. I was going to be a mother. I should get some practice. Gingerly, I patted his head. Making a mental note that no kid of mine would ever be that sticky, I wiped my hand on my tunic and set off after my boys.

I trotted around a stand of corn and nearly fell over Markham, sprawled across the path.

"What are you doing? Are you hurt?"

"No," he said, primly rearranging his bed sheet for decency and looking sheepish. "I . . . just . . . fell over."

"You tripped?"

"Don't think so. I just . . . lost my balance and toppled over." He reached up a hand and I hauled him to his feet.

I peered at him as he swayed gently, squinting at me through swollen eyes.

"Are you sure you're OK? I think you might have been stung by something."

"I've been stung by bloody everything. This repellent you've been spraying's rubbish and the fumes are making me feel sick," he said.

"How long have you been feeling like this?"

"I've felt a bit iffy for a day or so. It's worse today. Come on."

We set off after Peterson, who was crouched behind a fig tree, peering at a group of children of indeterminate age.

"What's going on?"

"He's met some friends."

"Bollocks."

"Exactly."

"How many?"

"Too many for us to take on. Hang on—he's on the move again."

He was indeed, heading towards the town. Head down, he trotted purposefully along the track until the track became a path and then a small road.

I groaned in frustration. There were far too many people around for us to attempt a little gentle highway robbery. I had a horrible feeling our best chance had been and gone and we'd blown it.

Behind me, Markham was throwing up.

I turned. "I really think you should go back to the pod."

"I'm fine," he said, wiping his chin. "Everyone's sick when they go to Egypt. It's part of the tourist tradition. See the pyramids. Get ripped off in the markets. Throw up your breakfast."

He looked terrible. All right, the insect stings were clearing up but his rash was much worse. His eyes were swollen and red. His nose was running faster than an historian late for her tea break, and he was swaying gracefully in the breeze.

This assignment was just going from bad to worse. Not only had we significantly failed to retrieve the gun, but Markham had obviously contracted something dreadful and was dying by inches in front of my eyes.

I turned to Peterson, meaning to call the whole thing off there and then. We'd done our best but we'd just made things worse. Time to admit defeat, return home, and face the music.

"No," croaked Markham, leaning against a convenient bit of tree trunk. "He's gone to sell it on, I bet you. And once that happens we've lost it forever. We have to move now or we're sunk. Come on."

Moving like something from one of those zombie movies, he staggered off down the road. Peterson and I looked help-lessly at each other and then followed.

This wasn't a major city. This was barely a settlement. There certainly weren't any walls. Or guards. But there was a market. Quite a large market actually. Mostly livestock, but there were a few stalls off to one side.

We fought our way through belligerent goats, greasy sheep that left a long smear of grubby lanolin down my dress, and stroppy donkeys. We avoided the camels, tied up in the shade. Enough people had spat at us in our time. Besides, we had Markham with us and his relations with the animal kingdom are never cordial. My own theory is that somewhere, back in the mists of time, one of his ancestors and an unknown animal had an unfortunate experience which has somehow survived in the animal kingdom's race memory and the instruction has gone out that he's to be attacked at every opportunity. Over the years, he's been chased, bitten, kicked, trampled, half-eaten, and generally terrorised, so now he tends to give all wildlife a wide berth. Although looking at the state of him now, not wide enough.

We fought our way through the crowds, never taking our eyes off the boy. Fortunately for us, he was wearing a scrappy tunic of a particularly disgusting ochre colour. I guessed it had once been white but been badly stained and someone, probably his mum, had attempted to dye it to cover the damage. She'd have done better to have left the stain. The poor kid looked like the unpleasant aftermath of a bout of amoebic dysentery. Anyway, bad choice of wardrobe or not, he was easy to track. We drew closer and closer until we were right behind him.

He knew exactly where he was going. He headed straight for one particular stall near the end.

No. No, no, no. This was not good. Once money changed hands, the gun would acquire value and be so much more difficult to retrieve. To say nothing of being bought by someone else. I cursed. We should have overpowered him when we could and taken our chances.

No money changed hands. The stallholder acquired the gun from the boy in exactly the same manner as he had acquired it from his younger brother. He clumped him round the side of the head and took it.

The lad said something rude, got a clip around the other ear, melted back into the crowd, and was gone.

"Now," I said.

"But there are people everywhere."

"There's never going to be a right moment. Let's get out there and make our own opportunities."

We strolled casually towards the stall. Peterson in the lead. Me, one pace behind and (I hoped) the epitome of matronly respectability with my parasol, and Markham, looking every inch the abused and diseased slave brought along to carry the shopping.

The place was a real dump. This was not a bright, shining Egyptian metropolis with stelae and monuments to the gods, beautiful temples, and imposing public buildings. This place was full of mud-brick houses, many of them reverting to their natural state; a public well surrounded by gossiping women; the ever-present clouds of dust; a very funny smell; and more goats than were attractive—unless you were another goat, of course. The streets were narrow, unpaved, and deep in rubbish. The smell was robust and livestock based, with top notes of spices, cooking, and people. If this settlement had grown up to service the boatyard then it was failing. The boatyard was thriving—this place was not.

Deprived of the cooling breezes from the river, the narrow streets were hot and airless. Flies buzzed everywhere. I could feel them crawling on my arms and shoulders. They kept settling in my eyes, which was incredibly irritating. And painful. I could see how infection spread so easily here.

Speaking of which, I turned to check out Markham who gave me a feeble grin and a wave. He looked dreadful. I decided if we hadn't retrieved the bloody gun in the next thirty minutes then we were out of here. He needed medical treatment.

Peterson had paused at the stall. Assuming his "Let's hope I don't catch anything unpleasant" expression, he began to rummage through the bric-a-brac on the stall, ignoring the gun displayed on an old wooden tray, half concealed under a string of badly matched amber beads and worth more than everything on the stall put together, and probably even the stallholder himself.

I leaned forwards and fingered the shabby jewellery. No hurry. No rush. We were just a couple of browsing shoppers who might possibly buy something today. . .

Peterson picked up the gun by the barrel and turned it over curiously. He did it beautifully. He passed it to me. I took it, carefully held it upside down, and said, "Laugh."

We all laughed merrily at the funny metal object with no clearly discernible function.

I itched to remove the clip and break it open, but the last thing we needed was anyone seeing how it worked.

Peterson took it back off me, held it up, and made a gesture to the stallholder. How much?

He shrugged. I suspected he had no idea how much to ask. He'd never seen anything like it before. He'd assessed us, our clothing, our clearly sub-standard slave, and was waiting to see how much we would offer.

I briefly considered just grabbing the bloody thing and running away. If the pod was closer then we might have got away with it. But not today. The market was crowded and, with our luck, they would all be his friends and relations. Just for once, we needed to be legitimate.

While I was dithering, the stallholder suddenly grabbed it back off Peterson and embarked on his sales pitch. Holding it by the barrel, he began to bang the handle on the table. I suspected he was demonstrating its nut-cracking capabilities.

We all winced and stepped back. This was not a weapon ever designed for bludgeoning nuts. Of course, he was the one in the most danger. I imagined the scene, heard the bang, saw him drop to the ground, blood pooling around him . . . Or suppose the bullet ricocheted into the crowds of people around us. . .

We had to do something. I bet he had friends all around the place. Sooner or later, someone would show up and pretend to be interested. That might attract the attention of other bona fide buyers. A bidding war. Anything to force the price up. We had to act now.

I smiled at Peterson and indicated, through the medium of mime, that I just had to have it. My life would be ruined if I didn't.

Now we came to the sticking point because none of us had any money. Or anything of value. Even our slave was the equivalent of an old banger that had had its clock wound back twice. Now what did we do?

As it turned out, we didn't have to do anything. He'd seen my wedding ring.

We're not actually allowed to wear jewellery on assignment. I shouldn't be wearing it now, but in the rush to get away, I'd forgotten to take it off. In gold-rich Egypt it couldn't be worth that much but he'd seen it, assessed its worth, and small though it might be, it was definitely worth more than this bizarre metal object, purpose unknown, that probably wasn't very good at crushing nuts.

We're not allowed to leave anything behind, although in the scheme of things, a small golden ring was considerably less hazardous than a 9mm Glock. I was prepared to accept the lesser of two evils. That wasn't what was making me pause.

I stared at my ring. Half of me thought, *it's just a small piece of gold. It's just a thing.*

The other half said, *this is the ring that Leon gave you. You wear it because it's a symbol of his love. He gave you a ring. You gave him a ring. But you give each other more than that—and this ring is a symbol of that.*

I looked at Markham who'd unhesitatingly sabotaged the Security Section's monitors—an offence probably punishable by death under Major Guthrie's jurisdiction.

I looked at Peterson, who'd insisted on coming. Yes, he'd spouted a lot of claptrap about Christmas traditions but if things went wrong, he had more to lose than any of us.

I thought of Elspeth Grey who was almost certainly finished at St. Mary's but for whom a successful outcome today would mean the difference between leaving with dignity or in disgrace. Or with a possible prison sentence.

They were both looking at me. I knew neither of them would say anything. This was a personal decision.

I don't know why I hesitated. There really was no choice. It was the least I could do. I wriggled it off my finger and handed it to Markham to hand to the stallholder.

Peterson said quietly, "Max, are you sure?"

"Yes," I said, wondering what on earth I was going to say to Leon.

I saw it glint briefly, and then the stallholder magicked it away into some mysterious hiding place. Smiling hugely—I suspected we'd really been ripped off here—he handed Peterson the gun and, in a probably very unfamiliar fit of generosity, handed over the hideous amber beads as well. Peterson nodded his thanks, Markham shoved the gun down the front of his bed sheet—and it would be a brave as well as a foolish thief who followed it down there—and we left the market before anything else could go wrong.

ONCE OUT OF THE crowded streets, the air was a little fresher. I dropped the beads in the dust and we each took one of Markham's elbows and piloted him along the path back to the pod. Now that we had the bloody gun back, I just wanted to get him back to the pod as quickly as possible.

"I can see a rainbow," he said at one point.

"Jolly good," said Peterson.

He turned to look at me. "So beautiful."

"Thank you," I said, touched.

"No, not you."

I'm not sure why I didn't drop him there and then and just leave him to fester by the path.

"What's the matter with him?" said Peterson, trying to shoulder more of his uncoordinated weight.

"Not sure, but I think one or more of his stings may have become infected. He's certainly running a temperature. I can feel the heat coming off him."

Our burden began to sing a song about throwing snowballs at the moon.

"I'm not so sure," said Peterson. "Put him down a minute."

We dropped him in the dust and bent over him for a quick examination. The only thing more inflamed than his eyes were his nostrils. In addition to his fading insect bites, none of which looked particularly infected, his skin was red and raw. In some places, it appeared to be splitting open.

Peterson stared at him thoughtfully. "If I didn't know better I'd say he'd been poisoned."

"How? You and I are fine."

"No idea. Maybe he's allergic to papyrus or something."

"How likely is that?"

"Well, not very, but I can't think of anything else. Everything we've done, he's done. And vice versa."

"It must be a sting gone bad. He was covered in them. Maybe it's the cumulative effect. Maybe I should have sprayed him twice a day but the can was only half full so I had to be careful with it."

"What spray?"

"The insect repellent. In the blue and yellow can in the locker by the door."

He sat back on his heels and stared at me. "Blue and yellow can?"

"That's the one."

"The insect repellent is in the orange and white can. Max, you're not colour-blind, are you?"

"No. Definitely not. Not according to my eye test last year."

I try to keep quiet about eye tests. Sometimes, I can't always quite make out the small print. I usually nip into Sick Bay a couple of days beforehand and memorise the chart. It's not that I can't see—my eyesight is fine—it's just that they make the print on these stupid cans so small these days.

He stared thoughtfully at me for a moment and then said, "Max, I think you might have been spraying him with WD40 by mistake."

I stared at him. "Is that a problem? Leon swears by the stuff. That and duct tape are always his *tools du jour.*"

"I daresay, but not in this context. Did you spray him all over?"

I nodded.

"Help me get his clothes off. And for God's sake hang on to that bloody gun. There's no way I'm ever doing this again."

We stripped off Markham and lugged him down to the river. The mud felt warm and squishy between my toes. We sat him down up to his neck in the water and gently washed his face and hair. I know, leptospirosis, leeches, and all that, to say nothing of the Nile crocodiles, but as Peterson remarked, he smelled like an old engine and they probably weren't that desperate for a meal.

I left him with Peterson, went back for his bed sheet and rinsed that thoroughly as well, wondering how much it was going to cost me to keep Peterson quiet about his. I suspected his price would be high.

Still, we had the gun. Focus on the positive.

Markham lay happily on his back in the Nile, hands laced behind his head, feet waving in the gentle current, still singing away to himself. I wrung out his bed sheet; we heaved him out and endeavoured to make him decent again. Wet sheets aren't easy to handle. Wrapping a wet bed sheet around a damp and naked Markham was well-nigh impossible. Especially since I had my eyes closed a lot of the time.

"You stand still, Max," said Peterson eventually, exasperated. "I'll just walk it around him. Like cling-film."

There was a very minor argument as to whose fault it was that we forgot to leave his arms free, but we couldn't be bothered to do it again and, as Peterson said, it stopped him scratching.

"And he looks so clean, too," I said, endeavouring to smooth down his spiky hair.

He smiled happily at the pair of us and threw up again.

FORTUNATELY, THE SUN WAS setting as we made our way back to the pod. There's not much twilight at these latitudes. One minute it's light—the next minute it's nearly dark. Bashford's team had already returned to their pod. We snuck through the boatyard. Everyone seemed to be at the feast centred on the space where the barge had been. I stood for a moment, watching sparks from the fires flying up towards the stars, listening to the happy voices, smelling the savoury smells and then turned away into the night that now seemed even darker in comparison.

We whiled away the last hundred yards or so by making a list of things to do.

"Things to do," said Peterson.

"Buy Markham a beer," said a voice.

"Put the gun back," I said. "I'll do that since the young master can't even remember his own name at the moment. You get him up to Sick Bay, use your manly wiles on Helen, and impress upon her the need for complete secrecy. After I've been cleared, I'll go and talk to Dr. Bairstow about what's happened. With luck he'll be so full of the Christmas spirit he'll forgive us everything."

We both paused to contemplate this unlikely scenario.

"It'll be fine," I said. "I'll talk to him, emphasise the lack of Time Police in the whole affair, and try to persuade him to let us all live."

"And Leon?"

I sighed. "I won't lie to him. I would have told him anyway. And there'll be his pod to clean up—so guess how I'll be spending Christmas morning. It's Ian who's going to be the problem. He's head of the Security Section, and somehow Grey got the gun out of his Armoury. He's her boyfriend and she's obviously never discussed her problem with him. He's not going to be a happy man on either count."

"Neither am I. I'm the one who's going to have to tell Helen we've inadvertently poisoned Markham."

"You shouldn't have to do that."

"Fair division of labour, Max. You face Dr. Bairstow. I'll face Dr. Foster."

"And just for once, young buggerlugs here is going to get off scot-free."

"If you count petroleum distillate poisoning as scot-free."

"Oh my God, is that what he's got?"

"Almost certainly. Skin lesions, fever, headache, nausea, disorientation, loss of balance."

"Surely," I said, conscience stricken, "we didn't do all that. He had a lot of those symptoms before we set out."

"True but I don't think we're going to be able to pass this off as sunstroke."

"Door," I said as we approached the pod.

We lowered the damp bundle of Markham to the floor where he began a long and involved conversation with someone called Rupert.

"Let's get this over with," I said. "Computer, initiate jump."

"Jump initiated."

The world went white.

AFTER SIX DAYS IN the blazing hot sunshine, the murky chaos still reigning at St. Mary's came as a bit of a culture shock.

"You get off to the Armoury while everyone's still busy sorting all this out," said Peterson, heaving Markham to his feet again. "Say goodbye to Rupert, young man. He can come out to play again tomorrow."

I scrambled back into my original gear, stuffing the damp linen into a locker for future retrieval.

Judging by the racket coming from further down the building, the evacuation was over and people were pouring back in again.

I wiped the gun as best I could, entered the code for access into the Armoury, and squeezed through the door.

I'd just closed it behind me when the lights came on and there stood Leon and Major Guthrie.

Bollocks.

Everyone looked at everyone else and it was obviously all up to me.

I said, "Good afternoon," because there's no excuse for bad manners.

There wasn't a huge response. They barely blinked. I couldn't deal with both of them together, so after an awkward pause I said, "Major, I wonder if you could spare me a moment, please? Alone?"

There was another even more awkward pause, and then Leon unfolded his arms and silently left the room. I was in so much trouble.

"Before you start," I said, and handed Guthrie the gun.

He stared at it but not for long. Ian Guthrie puts two and two together faster than any man I know.

"Why?" he said. "Why did she take it? Why *would* she take it?"

"I think you need to talk to her, Ian. There are some problems there. It's my fault. I'm her department head. I should have realised what was happening."

"And I'm her . . ." he stopped. "At least I thought I was."

"I think you still are," I said quickly. "Her main fear was that you would find out."

"In which capacity, he said bitterly. "Head of Security or . . ." he stopped again.

"As Ian Guthrie," I said gently.

He locked the gun away, taking his time about it. When he turned back, his face was perfectly normal, if a little grim.

He said, "Max . . ."

"She can't stay here at St. Mary's, Ian. It would be cruel to try and make her."

"I know," he said, heavily. He smiled bitterly. "I think I had hoped for something of what you and Leon have but it doesn't look as if this particular story will have a happy ending."

He straightened his shoulders. "It looks as if we might have some decisions to make, doesn't it?"

"Something for you both to think about," I said, "but have Christmas first. New year—new beginnings."

He nodded. "Sound advice. And from an historian. Who'd have thought?"

I grinned at him. "You already know what you're going to do, don't you?"

"I do, yes." His rare smile lit up his face. "You know what?" he said.

"What?"

"I think I shall miss you most of all, Scarecrow."

RIGHT, THAT WAS SETTLED for the time being. Only several more problems to go.

"Very Christmassy," said Helen, staring at our red noses. The standard of wit in Sick Bay is not high but this probably wasn't a good time to mention that.

She indicated Markham. "What have you done to him this time?"

Silently, Peterson handed over the can.

She took it, read the label, and rolled her eyes.

"How long's he been like this?"

"Only today, really," said Peterson. "And we dunked him in the Nile as soon as we discovered what we'd . . . what had happened. So he's nice and clean, at least."

"Just to be clear, you've added immersion in a parasite-riddled, leech-infested open sewer to his original symptoms?"

Put like that, it didn't sound good.

She glared impartially at the two of us. "Two days' observation for both of you. Don't even think of trying to get out of it."

We watched her wheel away a still chattering Markham, presumably to have his symptoms alleviated but you never knew with her.

"She's pleased to see me," confided Peterson.

"How on earth can you tell?"

"I'm not dead."

"Will you be telling her I was the one who poisoned Markham?"

"Not unless she turns ugly for some reason and I have to save myself."

"You're a true friend, Tim."

GREY, BASHFORD, GALLACCIO, AND Cox were waiting for me.

"We've warmed the bed for you," said Bashford.

Grey said nothing, staring anxiously at me.

I put her out of her misery. "It's OK. Problem solved. Gun recovered and returned."

The collective sigh of relief nearly blew me off my feet.

"Thank you," said Grey. "Oh, thank you."

"What happens now?" said Bashford.

"I'll go and see Dr. Bairstow as soon as I can," she said.

"I'd have a word with Major Guthrie first," I said.

She paled. "How much trouble am I in?"

"Not anything like as much as me, so stop worrying."

"Max . . ."

I remembered I was supposed to be head of the History Department and drew myself up. I'd like to think I loomed. I certainly gave looming my best shot.

"Listen to me, you lot. It's all sorted now, but if any of you ever, *ever* do anything like this again, I *will* kill you all. One by one. Slowly. And painfully. And I *will* get away with it because there are thousands of years of History out there, and I know exactly where to bury the bodies. And what to say to Dr. Bairstow afterwards. Now, go away and give me a moment's peace, please."

THEY CLATTERED OUT, LEAVING me alone in the ward. I was too strung up to get into bed, so I showered, washed the dust of Egypt out of my hair, put some cream on my nose, and sat in the window seat, looking out over the white gardens. Dusk was falling and the uncurtained windows were making pretty patterns of light on the snow. Someone had built an enormous snowman on the South Lawn. I'm almost certain the carrot is supposed to go on the face.

In the distance, I could see Atherton and Sykes trudging off through the snow. God knows what they were up to, but if it was anything illegal someone would be in to complain about it soon enough.

I heard the door open and close. Silence. I knew it was Leon. I sighed and struggled to marshal the words to explain what I'd done. How important it had been to get the gun back. How the fact that I'd given away my wedding ring didn't mean I didn't value it.

He came to sit opposite me in the window seat. "Move your knees."

I moved my knees and we sat together.

He picked up my hand and looked at the white line on my finger. "Did you lose it?"

I shook my head. "Worse. I gave it away."

"Well," he said comfortably, "I expect it was for a good reason."

I nodded. "It was, but that doesn't mean I was happy to do it."

"Why not? I thought to an historian, the preservation of the timeline was paramount."

"It is, but these days I have other priorities as well."

"Such as?"

"You. The two of us. Soon to be the three of us. I want you to know I didn't let it go lightly. I'm not sure how much I can say at the moment. How much I should say. I need to talk to Dr. Bairstow, but I'm sorry Leon. I am really sorry."

To my amazement, I felt a tear slide down my cheek.

He squeezed my hand. "Don't cry."

"I'm not crying. Pregnancy makes my eyes run."

"Of course," he said. "I had stupidly forgotten that. Mention it to Dr. Foster at your next ante-natal session."

I sniffed, appreciating his efforts to comfort me. "I haven't got over the last one yet. Helen and I watched a short film about childbirth and it was so gruesome we had to turn it off. She had a stiff drink, I had a cup of tea, and we swore we'd never have sex again."

"You've had sex with Helen Foster?"

I managed a chuckle. "Not recently."

"That's better. Aren't you going to open your Christmas present?"

"I have a Christmas present?"

"An early one." He grubbed around in his pocket, pulling out a huge red and gold striped rugby sock, which he dangled in front of me.

"Thank you, I said, wondering why, out of the two of us, I was always the one who was reckoned to be slightly odd. "Am I supposed to wear it?"

"It's your Christmas stocking."

"It's an old rugby sock."

"Not today it isn't. Here. Merry Christmas. Sorry I didn't have time for tangerines or nuts."

I took the sock. "Thank you."

"You're welcome."

I regarded the sock.

"Get a move on," he said, grinning.

"What?"

"Open your present."

The sock wasn't as empty as I thought. There was something in the toe. I rummaged around, pulling out a small box, which, according to the picture on the front, should be full of paperclips. If he'd been an historian, I would have suspected a surfeit of Christmas punch. Or possible concussion.

"Well, go on. Open it."

"Now?"

"I don't think there will ever be a better time. I'm sorry it's not wrapped, but I didn't think you'd mind."

I opened the box carefully and stared.

"Well? Don't you like it?"

Nestling on a bed of cotton wool was a wedding ring. My wedding ring.

I'm not often stuck for words but on this occasion, I just sat and stared, too afraid even to reach out and take it. Eventually, I dragged my eyes away to his face.

"How did you know?"

"Because I'm the dog's bollocks," he said modestly. "Observing the big white mark on your finger, your guilty expression, and remembering Bashford and Grey's recent jump, I leaped, gazelle-like, to the correct conclusion. Easy for a man of my talents."

"You mean you checked your pod logs."

"And that as well."

"You went back for it?"

"I did. I simply retraced your jump and followed you follow-ing them. I made your stallholder an offer he couldn't refuse and retrieved your ring."

Wild thoughts ran through my mind. What had he done? Had we substituted the problem of the gun for something even worse? What had we left behind now?

"Oh my God. Leon, what did you offer him?"

He smirked. "Three rolls of toilet paper."

The afternoon began to take on a slightly surreal quality. "What?"

He repeated it patiently. "Three rolls of toilet paper. You know—'Property of St. Mary's' stamped on each sheet. Although God knows why. It's not as if anyone has ever que-ried ownership. Either before or after use. I don't know why on earth you didn't think of it. A clear demonstration of the superiority of the technical mind I think even you must admit. Anyway, he was delighted. When I left, he was pulling off the individual sheets, one by one, to the huge admiration of those around him."

Toilet rolls—enough of a novelty to be valuable and attrac-tive and very biodegradable.

"Leon, you are . . ." I stopped, unable to go on.

"Yes? Don't stop there."

I shook my head.

"You're not going to cry again, are you?"

I shook my head.

"Give me your hand."

I stretched out my hand.

He slid it on to my finger. "Max, I give you this ring—again—because I love you. You are all the world to me and there's nothing I wouldn't do for you."

"Leon, I take this ring—again—because I love you and . . ."

I couldn't go on. More pregnancy tears.

He cleared his own throat, dropped a kiss in my hair, and put his arm around me.

I rested my head on his shoulder and closed my eyes. Suddenly, things didn't seem so bad. Dr. Bairstow would frown at me but I'd survive that. Elspeth Grey and Ian Guthrie would work something out. With luck, Helen would never know it was me who had inadvertently poisoned Markham.

And it was Christmas. It was snowing. St. Mary's smelled of good food. All my historians were home safe and sound, and I was here with Leon.

Sometimes—every now and then—there are moments of stillness. When nothing moves. When there is a sudden realisation of absolute happiness. A small, still moment to be remembered and cherished.

I burrowed deeper into his arms, enjoying his solid warmth. "So, apart from all that, how was your day?"

"Well, someone hooked up the security monitors to every set of fairy lights in the northern hemisphere and rigged the whole lot to blow the main fuse and set off the fire alarms . . ."

I tutted at such misbehaviour.

"Someone else shoved half a ton of wet linen into a locker in my pod and it stinks to high heaven."

I chirped sympathetically.

"My pod is filthy and reeks of people who haven't showered for a very long time."

I indicated my astonishment.

"And some bugger's pinched my last can of WD40, but other than that . . ."

THE VERY FIRST DAMNED THING

AUTHOR'S NOTE

I HAD SUCH A strong urge to write this story. Phrases and images kept popping into my mind as I was trying to concentrate on whichever book I was writing at the time. In the end, it seemed easiest just to give in and get on with it. So I did.

Apart from the research I had to do for Waterloo—a nod in the direction of the anniversary, though I didn't want to make too big a thing of it because nearly everyone in the country could make a better job of it than me—it was one of the easiest stories I've ever written. Words just flowed. I could see everyone's backstory very clearly.

It wasn't supposed to be so long, but there were so many characters with such interesting stories to tell. I particularly enjoyed Markham stealing the furniture, Professor Rapson's flies, and the young lady from SPOHB.

I also wanted to say more about the Battersea Barricades, the civil unrest, and all the other bits and pieces I'd alluded to throughout the books, together with Dr. Bairstow's struggle to get the show up and running. I'd like to say more about Mrs. Mack and maybe Mrs. Enderby as well—perhaps that's for future stories.

Of course, the star of the show is Dr. Bairstow and most of it is seen through his eyes. And it was while I was writing this story that I had an idea about *a future* Mrs. Green . . . Yes, that could be interesting . . .

THE VERY FIRST DAMNED THING

O NE OF THE MOST important events in the history of mankind—after the discovery of fire, the development of the wheel, and the invention of chocolate, of course—occurred in London on an overcast chilly rainy afternoon, and it is entirely typical that it should have been witnessed only by two bedraggled pigeons and a scrawny cat.

The cat, slinking his way across that almost unheard of London phenomenon, a half-empty car park, paused and considered the sudden appearance of a small stone shack in the back right-hand corner. Since cats possess intelligence far superior to that of the human race, he found nothing untoward in this occurrence, picked up the pace, and vanished out of the car park and out of this story.

The pigeons, it can be assumed, considered their options and then continued with their own plans for the afternoon.

For long minutes, nothing happened and then, almost on the stroke of three forty-five, a tall gentleman, clad in a long dark overcoat and well muffled against the cold, stepped out of the hut. For a moment, he stared about him, his expression bearing a more than passing resemblance to a middle-aged vulture waiting impatiently for the soul of an imminent corpse to get a move on and start heading towards the light. His disap-

proval deepened further as the rain increased and he opened
his umbrella with something of a snap.

Nearly two years after the final victory at the Battersea Barricades, London was still a drab and dreary place. Damaged
buildings glistened wetly in the drizzle. There was no colour.
Many shop windows were empty. Cannibalised vehicles lined
the pavements. Everything was broken down or worn out or
just plain old and that included the people. In the aftermath of
any major conflict, the younger generation are usually conspicuous by their absence.

The gentleman, leaning rather heavily on his walking stick,
gingerly picked his way across the remains of the scaffolded
Chelsea Bridge, contemplated for a moment the miraculously
unscathed outline of Battersea Power Station, and descended
a flight of steps to the cluster of inconspicuous buildings huddled between that and the bridge itself. Passing a newsagent's,
he paused to contemplate the headline, "Where did all the
money go?" compressed his lips, and approached an anony-
mous, shabby, grey building amply decorated with pigeon
product. The modest sign over the door read "Britannic Enterprises." Just as he opened the front door, a nearby clock began
to strike four. The gentleman allowed himself the satisfied nod
of the habitually punctual.

In his tiny office to the left of the door, a grizzled, grey-
haired man looked up, an expression of welcome on his face.

"Dr. Bairstow, sir. Nice to see you back again."

"Glad to be back, Mr. Strong. I believe I have another
appointment with the panel in Room 29 at four this afternoon."

"You do indeed, sir. If you care to place your feet in the
marked area . . . That's it, sir . . . And look up, please . . ."

The biometric needs of the security system having been
taken care of, Dr. Bairstow consented to be wanded, while
agreeing that yes indeed, it was very chilly out, but that was
only to be expected at this time of year.

"There we are, sir, all done. I'll get the major to take you up." He pressed a hidden buzzer and another door farther down the shabby corridor instantly opened and a tall man with dark blond hair stepped out. Since Mr. Strong had already vanished back into his cubbyhole and no actual conversation had been exchanged, Dr. Bairstow concluded that the major had been watching proceedings via the discreetly concealed but always present CCTV cameras. Very shabby the building might be, but the security was top of the range.

"Dr. Bairstow?"

"Major Guthrie, isn't it?"

"That's right, sir. This way please."

"This way" proved to be along a dusty corridor to an old-fashioned, open cage lift at the end. Clashing the doors open, the major ushered his guest inside and pulled the doors to behind them. Ignoring the old-fashioned push buttons in front of him, none of which would have taken him to his destination, he said quietly, "Second floor. Room 29. Authority Guthrie, bravo echo two."

The lift purred surprisingly smoothly upwards.

Emerging, the two men turned left. Room 29 was at the end.

Major Guthrie tapped at the door and opened it, announcing, "Dr. Bairstow."

The three people sitting behind an empty desk rose politely to their feet. In keeping with the office, which had surely not been decorated since the relief of Mafeking, they too wore grey. Grey suits, white shirts. The men wore plain grey ties—the woman a scarlet scarf twisted around her neck. Other than a set of military prints depicting scenes from Waterloo, this was the only splash of colour in the room.

Greetings were exchanged, the major left the room, and everyone sat down. There was a long pause. Dr. Bairstow waited impassively.

The man sitting on the left, who had been introduced on previous occasions as Mr. Black, began. "Well, Dr. Bairstow, our experts have finally finished reading your proposals. Based on what you have given us so far, they say that what you propose could be done. The full details of how it could be done, of course, are the parts you have chosen to withhold."

He waited politely, but so did his guest. Eventually, when it was clear Dr. Bairstow was not going to speak, he continued. "However, since you have made it perfectly clear that nothing in History can be altered or removed, I have to ask you again: what is the point of—" he coughed and said with some embarrassment, "—time travel?"

Dr. Bairstow frowned. "You might find it easier to think in terms of an organisation that investigates major historical events in contemporary time, rather than actually undertaking—" his face wrinkled in distaste, "—what you refer to as time travel."

"Does it actually matter what we call it?"

"We have been over this several times already," interrupted his colleague—the one sitting on the right, and known as Mr. Brown. "I think that what Dr. Bairstow is saying—without actually being so presumptuous as to put words into your mouth of course, sir," he added, "is that if nothing else, the value arises from possession. If we have it then no one else does. I'm sure I am right in thinking that should we say no to this extraordinary proposal, there are many out there who would say yes."

Silence settled heavily. Whether it was the effect of the heavy curtains or thick carpet, sound died very easily in this room.

Dr. Bairstow smiled thinly. "You won't say no."

Mr. Black seemed to bridle. "You seem very sure of that. I have to tell you, that given the current state of the economy, those whom we have consulted are far from convinced of the prudence of committing large—no, I beg your pardon—*colossal* sums of money to this endeavour."

"I'm sorry. I should perhaps have said, 'You *don't* say no.'"

"You don't know that."

"My dear sir, I invite you to contemplate the nature of the . . . enterprise . . . I have placed before you. I *know* you don't say no."

There was a pause.

"Ah."

"Precisely."

Mr. Black tried again. "But the cost . . ."

"Astronomical, I should think," said Mr. Brown, cheerfully.

Dr. Bairstow appeared to choose his words very carefully.

"There is about to be a new renaissance. New ideas are sweeping aside the old. Political thinking in this country has changed forever. There is, at present, a power vacuum waiting to be filled. New leaders are emerging at every level. I believe a new young Chancellor has been appointed at the University of Thirsk. I intend to involve her fully in this project."

Mr. Black looked up sharply. "Do I understand that you support Dr. Chalfont's politics?"

Dr. Bairstow smiled slightly.

"I do not support anyone's politics. I generally find that governments are more than capable of making their own mess without any help from me. What I want to say is that for the protection of everyone, my organisation will be politically neutral. It will be written into our contracts. We will surrender our right to vote or partake in political activity of any kind. We will voluntarily disenfranchise ourselves. In return, no government will seek to influence us or our findings. We will not submit to such actions."

"What sort of people will you employ? How will you recruit them?"

"I shall look for people who took part in the recent upris-ings. Who fought for and value the peace and freedom we enjoy today. They will, I'm afraid, be people who will not appreciate the virtues of committees or debate. They will be people who get things done. They will be accustomed to overcoming dif-ficulties and obstacles. They will be brash. They will be loud. They will be very disrespectful of authority in all forms. How-ever, they will be dedicated. They will get the job done." He smiled at Mr. Black. "You will get your money's worth."

"But of what *use* will it be?"

Dr. Bairstow frowned. "The truth is always important. It may not be popular, or fashionable, or convenient, but it is always important. Somewhere there must always be a record of events as they actually occurred. Not the politically airbrushed record, or religious wishful thinking or the socially acceptable version, but the often inconvenient truth."

"My dear sir, you are describing a powder keg. What on earth would we do with this inconvenient truth?"

Dr. Bairstow shrugged. "That is entirely up to you, sir. For example, one day, the events of the last years will be considered History. How important is it for people to know what happened? Or why it happened? And why it should never happen again?"

Mrs. Green, the third part of the colourful trio, who had so far remained silent, turned her head. She had light, honey-co-loured hair and the eyes of one who has seen too much happen, too quickly. "*Will* it ever happen again?"

Her voice was quiet.

Dr. Bairstow regarded her for some time before replying.

"Madam, I cannot say."

"I think you could say very easily. So tell me, please—will it all happen again? Should we be taking measures to prevent such events ever reoccurring?"

"Madam, I cannot say because I am not allowed to say. If it helps, however, I can say that *if* you take sufficient steps to ensure that similar events never happen again within your life-time, then similar events *will* never again happen in your life-time."

"But the cost," persisted Mr. Black. "Where's the return?"

Dr. Bairstow regarded them silently for a few seconds and then rose to his feet. "I have made all my arguments. Perhaps, now, a small demonstration might be in order."

No one rose with him.

Mr. Brown said warily, "What sort of a demonstration?"

Dr. Bairstow gestured at the prints around the walls. "You have an interest in the events of June 1815? Or are these rather fine prints just office furniture?"

Mr. Black bridled slightly. "An ancestor of mine fought at Waterloo and these are from my own personal collection."

"Then, madam, gentlemen, I invite you, please, to come with me."

"Where are we going?"

"I think 'when?' might be a more appropriate question."

Mr. Brown, half-risen from his seat, stopped in mid-move-ment. "Are we . . . ? Are we actually . . . ?"

Dr. Bairstow nodded. "I can think of no quicker or easier way to ensure your enthusiastic support—and funding, obvi-ously—than a small demonstration. I have, therefore, pro-grammed in what I consider to be a most appropriate destina-tion."

"But . . ."

"Yes?"

Mr. Black moistened his suddenly dry lips. "Where to? I mean, when to?"

He paused and mentally reviewed the sentence.

Dr. Bairstow smiled faintly. "Yes, the rules of grammar do need to be bent occasionally. The phrase 'a long time ago in the future' can take some getting used to. Along with that old favourite, 'he will die a hundred years ago.' I thought you might enjoy a short but educational visit to Waterloo, 18th June 1815. The Stirrup Charge. When the Scots Greys broke Napoleon's square. Thirty minutes. No longer."

They gaped at him. "But you can't expect us to just—get up and go."

"Why ever not?"

"There are committees before which your proposal must be put. Working groups to be set up. Risks assessed. Benefits calculated. Safeguards installed. Security implemented."

"Dear me," commented Dr. Bairstow. "No wonder it takes so very long to get anything done here. Do you think they had time to set up committees on the Barricades?"

Silence followed as this remark was contemplated with incomprehension.

Dr. Bairstow relented. "If it makes you feel more comfortable, we can certainly include that rather formidable-looking young major who escorted me here. He seems very capable and I'm sure is more than equal to any threat I might—inadvertently, of course—represent. Shall we go?"

THE WEATHER HAD NOT improved. Such streetlights as were working had come on early and sleet could clearly be seen amongst the drizzle. No one else was on the streets.

Dr. Bairstow, stick tapping on the paving stones, led them across the car park to the shack still parked in the far right-hand corner. Both the cat and the pigeons had disappeared.

The small party halted outside the scruffy shack appropriately parked in the disabled space. There was an air of unspoken disappointment.

"You were, perhaps, expecting something a little more . . . science fiction based?"

"Well," said Mr. Brown. "Yes." He smiled, mischievously. "Perhaps it's bigger on the inside?"

"Alas . . ."

Major Guthrie pushed his way forwards. "If you don't mind, sir, I'll go first."

"By all means," said Dr. Bairstow. "Door."

Producing a gun, Major Guthrie covered the doorway, angling the gun up, down, around, leaving no area unchecked.

Dr. Bairstow stood quietly, leaning on his stick, apparently unconcerned. "You might want to check the toilet. Yes, that door there. Don't bother with the lockers—there really is no room even for life's essentials, let alone a concealed miscreant."

"I'm sure you're right, sir," said Guthrie politely, and proceeded to subject the toilet, every locker, and even the area under the console to ruthless scrutiny. Finally, and with some reluctance, he holstered his gun and stood aside.

"If you would be so good," murmured Dr. Bairstow, ushering his passengers in through the door.

Somewhat reluctantly, one step at a time, his guests entered, gazing about them. Their faces gave nothing away, but then they had been government officials for a very long time. They were almost certainly the descendents of a long line of government officials. Cartwheeling with excitement had probably been bred out of them round about the 14th century.

To the right of the door, a console with an incomprehensible array of read-outs, flashing lights, dials, and switches sat beneath a large, wall-mounted screen, currently showing only a view of an empty car park in the gathering dusk.

Bunches of cables ran up the walls to disappear into a tiled ceiling. Two excruciatingly uncomfortable-looking chairs were screwed to the floor in front of the console. A row of lockers ran along the back wall, and in the far corner, a narrow door led into the toilet.

The tiny space smelled of stale people, chemicals, hot electrics, damp carpet, and cabbage.

"I have room for one passenger to sit alongside me in relative comfort," said Dr. Bairstow. "Perhaps, madam, you would like to take advantage of our meagre facilities. I'm sure I don't have to impress upon you the importance of not touching anything."

Somewhat gingerly, Mrs. Green seated herself and looked around.

"It's a little bit . . ."

"Cramped?"

"Yes, but that wasn't what I meant."

"Ah. You mean the smell."

She smiled slightly. "Well, I didn't want to be rude . . ."

"Yes, my profound apologies, but it is a complete mystery to us. We have no idea whence the cabbage smell emanates. We have, in the past, constructed new pods and the next day we are overwhelmed by the aroma of cabbage. One of the great unsolved mysteries of the universe, I'm afraid. You will soon grow accustomed."

As he was speaking, his hands were moving over the console. Lights flashed. "Computer."

The computer chirped acknowledgement.

His passengers, as one man, looked apprehensively towards the door.

Dr. Bairstow said, in what he liked to think of as reassuring tones, "Please do not be alarmed. In the unlikely event of anything going wrong, we will certainly never know anything about it."

Mrs. Green gripped the console with both hands.

"There really is no need to hold so tightly. I am rather good at this. Computer, initiate jump."

The world went white.

INSIDE THE POD, COMPLETE silence reigned.

"You can open your eyes, now," said Dr. Bairstow in some amusement.

Four considerably shaken people opened their eyes.

Major Guthrie said hoarsely, "Did something happen? We didn't move."

"I told you I was rather good at this. Allow me to activate the screen."

Four people stared speechlessly at the screen.

Thousands of tiny figures moved purposefully around a vast landscape. In silence. Cannons fired puffs of silent white smoke. Charging horses thundered silently across the screen. Chaos reigned quietly.

"Dear . . . God," said Mr. Brown, unable to tear his eyes away.

Mr. Black, however, was made of sterner stuff. "I don't believe it. I don't believe we've moved at all. This is just some holo projection and . . ."

Dr. Bairstow said, "Door."

The door opened, letting in the sights, sounds, and smells of one of the major battles of the nineteenth century. Thousands of voices rose over the sound of cannon fire. The thunder of hooves caused the ground to shake. The sulphurous smell of gunpowder hung in the air.

As if in a dream, arm outstretched like a blind man, Mr. Brown moved slowly towards the open door.

"Everyone please remain where you are," said Major Guthrie sharply, drawing his weapon.

Dr. Bairstow closed the door and rose from his seat. "Major, I must ask you to surrender your weapon."

"I'm afraid I'm quite unable to do that, sir."

"I accept your instinct and training make it difficult for you to comply, but one of our cardinal rules is that no harm must ever come to a contemporary at our hands. I cannot emphasise the importance of that rule too strongly. If your life is in danger you may take steps to protect yourself with pepper spray, or a stun gun of some kind, but you must understand that killing a contemporary can have the gravest consequences. Please

remember it is well known that the act of observing changes
that which is being observed. We always, therefore, try to keep
our interaction with contemporaries to an absolute minimum.
Our primary function is to observe, record, and document.
Nothing else. Therefore, Major, I must ask you, in the interests
of everyone's safety, to surrender your gun to me, please."

He held out his hand as he spoke.

Still Major Guthrie hesitated. "My priority, sir, is the safety
of my employers."

"As is mine. The people here are the potential source of my
funding. I would be very distressed if anything should happen
to them and I had to begin again."

Unseen, Mrs. Green smiled faintly.

Dr. Bairstow continued. "Major, I understand your reluctance, but if you attempt to shoot a contemporary, then History
will act to defend itself and you will be dead before such a thing
can happen. And possibly your employers will be as well. And
if you shoot *me* you will, all of you, be here for the rest of your
lives because only I can operate this pod. So, again, Major—
your gun, please."

Reluctantly, Major Guthrie removed the clip, broke open
the gun, and passed it over.

"Thank you, Major. I appreciate your good faith. As you can
see, I shall simply place it here in this locker for safety. You can
access it at any time. I trust you not to do so. And now, with the
assistance of Mr. Black, shall we endeavour to make sense of
what is occurring here today?"

He indicated the left-hand seat as he spoke and after only
the briefest pause, Mr. Black took his place.

"You can angle the cameras, and zoom in and pan out by
toggling these control keys here."

Mr. Black visibly swallowed and then, tentatively at first,
but with growing confidence, began to range the camera back
and forth, making some notes on a pad of paper that Dr. Bair-

stow found for him. Eventually, he cleared his throat and said, in an artificially high voice, "Napoleon Bonaparte has escaped from Elba and, in another attempt to make France the most powerful nation in Europe, he has resumed war against the European powers."

He stopped, cleared his throat again, and continued. "A coalition is formed, consisting of Britain, Prussia, the Netherlands, Hanover, Nassau, and Brunswick, under the joint command of Field Marshals Wellington and Blücher."

He stared at the screen for a while. Dr. Bairstow, who had spent some time studying this event thoroughly and who could have enlightened him, remained silent.

"I believe, yes . . . I believe we are witnessing . . . yes . . . there . . ." he pointed at the screen. "That's the 92nd—the Gordon Highlanders. General Pack ordered them to charge, but they'd already lost nearly half their strength in a prior engagement at Quatre Bras. They've fielded less than three hundred men today."

They watched in silence as the Highlanders moved up, four lines deep, to close with the enemy some thirty yards away, advancing into a hail of French fire.

Mr. Black said quietly, "There's rather a difference between reading the reports that say they were badly knocked about and actually seeing that happen in front of one's eyes. Things are rather bloody down there, aren't they? You can see, they're falling apart in some disorder. Poor devils . . . they're certainly taking a bashing."

There was silence in the pod. The Highlanders were indeed taking a bashing. On the screen, without a sound, men hurled themselves at their enemies, bayonets fixed, mouths open in silent screams, advancing without hesitation into a barrage of fire. Tiny puffs of smoke bloomed and it was as if they had run into a wall. Simultaneously, the front row flung up their arms and fell. Then the second row. All in complete silence.

Everywhere the eye looked, men were dropping to the ground
and not getting up again. Huge holes opened up in the lines as
soldiers fell by the score. Desperately, the Highlanders struggled on but, inevitably, the moment came when they could go
no further.

Dr. Bairstow, who had stepped back to make room, was
watching them all very carefully, waiting for the moment when
it would dawn on them, as it must, that these were not pages
in a History book, or even prints on an office wall. These were
real people—struggling, striving, and dying. Here was fear and
pain and mutilation and death.

Under heavy fire, the Highlanders were retreating over the
bodies of the fallen.

"And not a moment too soon," murmured Mr. Black.

More French forces burst through the hedge behind which
they had been concealed and fell upon them. Caught in a deadly
crossfire, their attempt to retreat in good order was abandoned.
Officers screamed their orders. Sustaining even heavier losses,
the Highlanders were routed.

Silence filled the pod. Three people could not look away.
Mrs. Green gripped the edge of the console.

"I had no idea," whispered Mr. Brown. "This is . . . unbelievable."

"I knew Wellington described the battle as 'a damned close-
run thing'," said Mr. Black, seemingly unable to tear his eyes
away, "but I had no idea they came so close to defeat. Look, the
entire centre is beginning to give way. This is a disaster. Is there
some way I can get a close up? Focus on that part of the battle?"

"Allow me," said Dr. Bairstow, leaning over his shoulder.

Without warning, faces filled the screen. Real faces, running with blood. Eyes white in smoke-blackened faces. Mouths
open, although whether in ferocity or terror was hard to see.
Three people jerked back. Someone drew in their breath with
a sharp hiss.

"Re-form. Re-form your lines, for God's sake," croaked Mr. Brown.

"They will," said Mr. Black. "This is the 92nd. The Highlanders. They have been ordered to hold and hold they will. The few that are left." He stared at the slaughter on the screen.

"Surely," whispered Mrs. Green. "They cannot withstand much more. They must give way."

Mr. Brown stared at the screen. "If the farmhouse at La Haye Sainte falls . . ."

"You know that it will not," murmured Dr. Bairstow.

"How can you say that, man? Look at them. They're being cut to pieces. There can surely be no way back from . . ."

Unseen bugles sounded.

"What's happening?" said Mr. Brown.

"There! There! See! General Picton's men are on the move. Here we go. My God, this is it. I can hardly believe . . . Look. Look there."

From behind the top of the rise, there appeared a row of heads.

The heads became men.

Who, in turn, became mounted men.

The Scots Greys were on the move.

This was no desperate charge. There was no headlong gallop to engage the enemy. The ground was too broken, too uneven. Mud, bodies, even crops rendered a charge impractical.

The Scots Greys advanced at a walk, swords drawn, passing quietly through the still-retreating Highlanders. The horses, snorting with the smell of blood in their nostrils, picked their way over the fallen, held in hard by their riders.

Voices shouted new commands. The Highlanders rallied. Turning to face the enemy once more, they settled their bonnets firmly over their eyes and brought up their weapons. There were so few of them left that they could, legitimately, have fallen back to nurse their wounds. They did not.

Every Highlander who could seized a stirrup with one hand
and took a tight grip on his rifle with the other. More bugles
sounded and the pod was filled with voices shouting, "Scotland
Forever!"

The scarlet-coated Scots Greys picked up the pace to a fast
walk, emerging through the dust and smoke to confront the
enemy like a vision from hell.

The French 45th Regiment of the Line, still struggling to
reform their square, looked up to see their death approaching.
An unstoppable wave of giant white horses, all bared teeth and
iron hooves, bearing down upon them. Each horse was blood-
ied to the knees, eyes wild with battle fury and ridden by an
enormous, red-coated man, sword drawn and murder in his
eyes.

Still clinging to the stirrups, the remnants of the Highlanders re-entered the fray. Not at a flat-out gallop as so often
depicted, but at a walk. Slow, stately, and unstoppable, they
bore down on the frantically struggling French forces.

In vain did the French officers scream new orders. There
was no time. The enemy was already upon them. In despera-
tion, many of them ran about, physically pushing their men
into place. A regimental square, once formed, is well-nigh
invincible to cavalry. A square in disorder is a sitting target.

The Scots Greys rode them down, forcing their way into the
very heart of the French ranks. Men disappeared under horses'
hooves. Those who by some miracle had managed to remain
on their feet were cut down in an instant. The cavalry had a
huge advantage over the infantry. Even standing on tiptoe and
lunging with their bayonets at full thrust, the infantry could not
reach the riders. Confused and milling around in complete disorder, they were hacked to pieces by the Scots Guards' sabres
and trampled into the ground by their horses.

It was over within minutes. The entire square was destroyed.

On the screen, a lone rider broke into a canter, pulling away from his comrades.

"There!" cried Mr. Black. "Look! That must be Charles Ewart. Quick! Quick! I want to see."

Dr. Bairstow adjusted the controls and the cameras zoomed in. A sergeant brandishing a sabre was urging his horse through the French lines, hacking about him like a lunatic. Soldiers fell away on both sides.

"He's after their Eagle. They'll make him an officer for this. Go on, man. Go on."

A tiny group of men encircled the battle standard, defending it to the death.

One brave Frenchman closed in and a slash from Ewart took him through the head.

From nowhere, a lancer flung his lance at the red-coated sergeant who parried it with his sword, all the time urging his horse towards the Eagle.

"Look out!"

Another French soldier coolly knelt, took aim, and fired. At that range, he could not miss, but he somehow did. His bad aim cost him his life. Before he could reload, Ewart was upon him. Struggling to his feet, the French soldier stood his ground, stabbing wildly with his bayonet. His thrust was parried by Ewart, who, in one movement, cut him down and reached out for the battle standard.

"Go on, man. Go on."

With his horse's momentum carrying him forwards, Ewart dropped his reins, stood in his stirrups, and seized the standard with one hand, thrusting at the bearer with the other. The man fell backwards. The Eagle was won.

A mighty roar went up as, sword in one hand and brandishing the captured Eagle in the other, Ewart turned and galloped back towards his own lines.

Inside the pod, three people suddenly realised they had been holding their breath.

"Look," said Mrs. Green suddenly, "this isn't right, surely? What is happening?"

The tides of fortune can turn in the blink of an eye and now it was the turn of the Scots Greys to find themselves in trouble.

They watched the screen as the troopers, now free from obstacles, picked up speed and charged headlong towards General Durutte's infantry, who, unlike their unfortunate colleagues in the 45th, had had the time to form their square. Disorganised and out of control, the Scots Guards swept ineffectively around the outside, unable to penetrate the square and incurring heavy losses. Men and horses crashed to the ground under a hail of gunfire.

Mr. Black pointed. "Their commander, Colonel Hamilton, will urge them on to engage the French artillery. See, there they go."

In silence, they watched a small group peel away and thunder up the facing slope to engage a field battery of French cannon. Their success, however, was their undoing.

Mr. Black sighed. "As Wellington himself said, 'The British cavalry never knows when to stop,' and he was right. Watch."

On the screen, the Scots Greys, their horses blown, and unable to rally, were taking heavy fire. The French cavalry, in a frenzy of revenge and retribution, fell upon them. The fighting was vicious and bloody. Colonel Hamilton was seen briefly, wounded in both arms and holding the reins in his teeth, attempting to lead his men back to safety. The French cavalry, "The 4th Lancers, I think, but I am not sure," murmured Mr. Black, closed in.

Dr. Bairstow, his objective gained, turned the cameras away, pulling back from the slaughter and muting the sound. Once again, tiny figures silently filled the screen.

"The Scots Greys were three hundred and ninety men strong," said Mr. Black, quietly. "One hundred and two men died. Another ninety-eight were wounded."

"True," said Dr. Bairstow, "but by engaging the infantry and forcing them to turn to receive their attack, they caused them to be exposed to the Royal Dragoons who will rout them. Yes, things fell apart, but the centre held. And now will begin the attack on La Haye Sainte."

Again, the screen was filled with cotton-wool puffs of cannon smoke. Occasionally, the pod trembled.

"Should we raise our shields?" asked Mr. Brown, anxiously.

Dr. Bairstow withdrew his gaze from the screen and regarded him with polite incomprehension. "I beg your pardon?"

"Our shields. We do have shields, don't we?"

"I must confess I'm not entirely sure to what you are referring. Do you perhaps mean some kind of force field?"

"Exactly."

"Something that would prevent us being blown to pieces by stray cannon shot?"

"Yes, that's it."

"No, we don't have anything like that."

"We don't? But what happens if we're hit? What keeps us safe?"

Dr. Bairstow shrugged. "A combination of sturdy construction, a very carefully calculated landing site, and the erratic protection of the god of historians."

"I wonder," said Mr. Brown, diffidently. "Would it be possible to go outside?"

Mr. Black and Mrs. Green turned astonished eyes upon him.

Dr. Bairstow smile faintly. "Not that I wish to appear selfish in any way, sir, but should anything happen to you then my

chances of getting this project off the ground would be severely
jeopardised."

Mr. Brown, who against all the laws of nature appeared
to have shed at least twenty years in the last twenty minutes,
grinned like a naughty boy. "My dear sir, to paraphrase, I invite
you to consider the implications to your project of *not* letting us
out for a better look."

"Mr. Brown, I suspect you may be a closet historian."

Another bombardment shook the pod and Mrs. Green, still
watching the screen, pointed. "Look. Who are they? Are they
French? They're coming this way."

Three figures appeared out of nowhere. They were running
very fast as explosions were peppering the ground all around
them. They appeared to be wearing modern body armour and
helmets. One of them, either in an attempt to avoid the bombardment or through disorientation, was zigzagging wildly.
The other two seemed to be attempting to keep him on track.
They were heading for the pod.

"Who are they?"

Dr. Bairstow sighed. "I suppose it was inevitable."

They watched as the three figures ran, ducking and weav-
ing, to the pod. Someone thumped on the door.

"Could you let us in, please?"

"They're very polite. Who are they? What do we do?"

Dr. Bairstow smiled faintly. "They're historians and I sug-
gest we let them in before they have the door off its hinges."

Two men and one woman tumbled into the pod. Which
was now distinctly overcrowded.

"Bloody bollocking hell," said the woman, pulling off a helmet, and displaying the worst case of helmet hair ever. "That
last bombardment started early. I'm going to have a word or
two with the professor when we get back."

"Good afternoon."

The three newcomers froze, staring alternately at the original occupants and then at each other in some consternation.

"Quite," said Dr. Bairstow. "I am not familiar with any of you—yet—but your discretion would be appreciated."

"Of course . . . sir."

"Report."

"Er . . . Maxwell and Bashford, sir. Historians. Markham providing security."

Dr. Bairstow passed her some water. "How interesting. You bring security guards with you on assignments?"

She passed the water to Bashford. "We have to, sir. God knows what they'd get up to if we left them behind on their own."

Markham grinned amiably. "Don't you believe it, sir. No one in their right minds would let the History Department out by themselves." He took a large swig of water and wiped his mouth on his sleeve. "That's better. Thank you very much."

Dr. Bairstow regarded the third member of the trio with some concern. "Mr. . . . Bashford appears to have incurred some sort of injury. Shrapnel?"

"He fell over, sir. And it's Bashford. He could concuss himself on a ball of cotton wool. Frankly, if he spends much more time in a semi-conscious stupor then . . . the Boss . . . is going to stop paying him altogether."

Markham, who had been beaming at a stony-faced Major Guthrie, said suddenly, "Don't see why he shouldn't, actually. He barely pays *me*. Why should I suffer alone?"

Dr. Bairstow said gently, "Really? That seems most unfair. Why would that be?"

"Bloody Deductions from Wages to Pay for Damages Incurred forms, sir. Bane of my life. And a completely necessary and fair system of reimbursement, of course, as I frequently maintain."

"Deductions from Wages forms," said Dr. Bairstow quietly. "How very . . . innovative. And are they frequently implemented?"

"Distressingly frequently, sir."

"Well stop bloody breaking things, then," said Bashford, blinking fuzzily at him.

"I don't. It's not my fault that . . ."

Dr. Bairstow cleared his throat, interrupting what was threatening to become a vigorous, though possibly irrelevant, debate.

"Can we assume that you are here for the same purpose as we are?"

"Er . . ."

"You may speak freely."

"Recording and documenting, sir, yes."

"And not dying?"

She wiped her face. "Well, no thanks to Professor Rapson, sir. We were told we'd have more than enough time after the Scots Greys' charge to get into position to watch Marshall Ney having a pop at La Haye Sainte. As it turned out, however, not quite. We're pretty sure the professor doesn't measure time in quite the same way as everyone else." She took another swallow of water. "Anyway, thanks for the respite, sir. We should be getting a shift on. We're supposed to be covering Wellington's infantry forming squares in preparation for the attack."

"Yes," said Bashford, unexpectedly proving he wasn't as dopey as he looked. "The artillery is in place and we don't want the others getting all the good stuff. Time to go."

"Just as a matter of interest, how many of you are there?"

"Um, well, including the Security Section and all the techies we had to bring in case we broke something, um, seventeen or eighteen, I think. There's a lot of ground to cover out there."

"Don't forget Professor Rapson and Dr. Dowson, Max."

"Both of whom I intend to have a word with later on. About nineteen or twenty, then."

Mr. Black turned from the screen in astonishment. "Twenty people? You brought *twenty people?*"

"We did, yes. And there's probably a lot more around that we don't know about. It's a big day today, you know. There's upwards of a hundred thousand people down there. I'd be surprised if a good number of them weren't from—"

Dr. Bairstow made a warning gesture.

"Weren't colleagues in some form or another."

"And the Time Police, of course, making sure we don't bugger things up," said Markham, cheerfully.

"Speaking of which . . ." said Bashford, picking up his helmet.

"Yes, we must go. Point Bashford in the right direction, will you?"

"No need. I think he operates on some sort of autopilot."

"I heard that," he said indignantly.

"Just as a matter of interest, sir, why are *you* here?"

"We have been observing the Stirrup Charge of the Scots Greys."

She regarded their civilian clothing with some astonishment. "You mean you all thought you'd just stroll into a pod and pop off to Waterloo?"

"That would be correct, yes," said Dr. Bairstow and those who knew him well might have caught an unusually mischievous note in his voice.

Maxwell grinned hugely. "You do know that's a massive breach of regulations, don't you, sir? I shall have no choice but to report it on my return. There is every possibility you may never hear the last of this."

"I very much hope that will turn out to be the case. Would I be wasting my breath if I told you to take care?"

They nodded, innocence oozing from every pore.

"Well, don't let us keep you," said Dr. Bairstow gently.

"Very considerate of you—our boss is a stickler for punctuality."

"I am very glad to hear it."

She smiled and they shook hands. "It's been an honour and a privilege, sir."

The landscape outside was suddenly peppered with explosions.

"I shouldn't hang around if I were you. It's going to be quite lively here in a few minutes."

"Consider us gone, sir."

And with a brief flurry of activity—they were.

Dr. Bairstow watched them go, a rare smile on his lips. Reaching down, he adjusted a control on the console.

In the distance, a faint voice could be heard instructing Bashford to put on his helmet for God's sake before his head fell off.

Back in the pod, Mr. Black turned to Dr. Bairstow. "What a very odd bunch."

"Did you think so?"

"And they were historians?"

"I believe so."

"Not what I was expecting."

"They very rarely are."

ON THEIR RETURN, HIS passengers stared at the screen. A cold, dark London day was drawing to a close. The rain came down harder.

Mrs. Green stirred. "Somehow this seems . . ."

"Less real?"

She nodded, not taking her eyes from the screen.

"A common phenomenon. Somewhat similar to exiting a cinema, I always think. Please, take as much time as you need to reorient yourselves. In the meantime, we must undertake a small procedure. Please do not be alarmed."

The interior of the pod lit with a cold, blue glow. Mrs. Green shivered.

"What was that?" demanded Major Guthrie, sharply.

"Decontamination. Not strictly necessary, since you did not leave the pod, but you did interact with those who had. Merely a safety precaution."

Mr. Brown sighed.

"The Stirrup Charge. It did happen after all."

"Yes, it did."

"But not quite as we thought."

"We frequently find that although things do happen, they don't happen quite as we expected them to. However, the important thing here is not that it happened, but that you, Mr. Black, now *know* that it happened. You may find that you look at your prints with new eyes."

"I think, from now on, I shall look at everything with new eyes."

"Then the day has not been wasted."

"I hope those young people made it safely to wherever they were going."

"Oh, I'm sure they will. Have. Did. And now, if you are quite ready, I shall open the door."

Major Guthrie collected his gun. "Thank you sir, a most interesting experience."

Mr. Brown and Mr. Black stood in the doorway, looking out into the darkening evening.

"Are you ready, Mrs. Green?"

"One moment, if you please, I would like to speak with Dr. Bairstow. Please do not let me keep you."

Mr. Black turned back for a moment, almost as if he was about to say something, and then the two of them, together with Major Guthrie, exited the pod and set off across the car park.

Mrs. Green stopped at the door and looked back at Dr. Bairstow who was shutting things down.

He paused and said quietly, "Is there a problem? You seem . . . upset."

She seemed to be groping for words. "I did not expect it to be so . . ."

"What? Magnificent? Tragic? Wasteful? Horrifying? Spectacular?"

"Yes. No. That such courage, so many good qualities—courage, spirit, and dedication—should be wasted on something as futile as war."

"You are perfectly correct, madam, but those qualities are not used solely for war. And even field marshals are human. Have you never heard the story of the Duke of Wellington and the toad?"

She managed to laugh a little. "No, I've never heard the story of Wellington and the toad."

"Well, it tells us that the Iron Duke was walking along the road one day when he came across a small boy in tears. Rather to his own surprise, I suspect, he stopped and enquired what was the matter. The little boy, not knowing to whom he was talking, told him that he was going away to school the next day and was worried that no one would look after his toad properly. The Duke offered to take the toad under his own care. A week or so later, while at school, the boy received a message which read, '*Field Marshal the Duke of Wellington presents his compliments and has the pleasure to inform you that your toad is well.*'"

Now she laughed.

"And even those considered villains do not invariably display villainous qualities. Napoleon himself was moved to tears by the sight of a soldier's dog standing guard over his dead master. He frequently said he was haunted by the memory for the rest of his life."

She sighed. "War is such a dreadful waste."

"Can I assume you lost someone in the recent civil unrest?"

"Most of my family. Everyone, except for my youngest son."

"My sympathies for your loss."

She said in sudden anger. "They call it civil unrest because it sounds better than civil war." She took a deep breath. "I'm sorry. I am usually more controlled than this."

Dr. Bairstow smiled sadly. "I said before that the act of observing changes that which is observed. It is also true to say that the observer does not remain unchanged, either. You look very pale. May I fetch you some water?"

She sipped it slowly. "It's always all about war, isn't it?"

"Not at all. Yes, we observe battlefields—they are generally important events—but it's not all about that. We will investigate coronations, social conditions, industrial events, legends—the list is quite long. I'm sorry today's demonstration was not to your taste."

"Oh no, no. It was . . ." she paused.

"Horrible?"

"I was going to say fascinating."

"Horribly fascinating then."

She laughed.

"What would you like to see, Mrs. Green? With all of History out there . . . If you could choose—what would you choose?"

She thought for a moment. "Actually, it's not so far from what we saw today. I'd like to see the Duchess of Richmond's ball in Brussels. When the cream of European society was gathered together and Wellington received the news that Napoleon had outwitted him. To see his face. And the faces of those around him. Excited young boys off to war. Sweethearts saying goodbye and trying to be brave. Mothers hiding their tears and fears. Fathers—proud and afraid at the same time—so yes, still Waterloo, but the other side of Waterloo." She looked at him shyly. "I always think History is more about people than events, don't you?"

"Yes—and no. Yes, we study the events but it is people who are the cause of those events. It always comes down to cause and effect."

They both fell silent, not looking at each other.

"Would you—perhaps one day—would you like me to. . . ?"
he paused and visibly squared his shoulders. "Mrs. Green—
you *shall* go to the ball."

She laughed. "Very well. I shall look forward to it."

"It won't be for a while, I'm afraid. There is much for me
to do."

She smiled. "I can wait."

"Not for too long, I hope."

"No, I hope not. And Mrs. Green is not my real name, you
know."

He affected astonishment. "Really?"

"And I suspect Bairstow is not yours."

"My name is Edward."

"Angela."

BACK AT BRITANNIC ENTERPRISES, three hugely important
civil servants, one young major, and the future Director of St.
Mary's were being ruthlessly ministered to by Mr. Strong who
was fussing gently with teacups and messages.

"Let me see, sir. Section Four rang. Normal service
will recommence at 1800 hours tonight. The PM has been
informed. And I've passed that other matter over to Section
Two, sir. It did appear to require immediate but discreet attention and I considered them the best able to deal with the job. I
trust all this is acceptable?"

"Thank you, Mr. Strong. All perfectly acceptable as usual."

Dr. Bairstow, stirring his tea, watched all this with quiet
attention. Standing to take his leave, he took advantage of Mr.
Strong helping him with his overcoat to request a quiet word
with him.

"Of course, sir. My shift ends in twenty minutes."

"I shall wait outside for you."

"You don't want to hang around in the cold, sir. I'll meet
you in The Flying Duck."

The Flying Duck was easily located, situated as it was in the shadow of Battersea Power Station. Inside was steamy and warm. The evening trade had not yet begun and Dr. Bairstow was easily able to find a quiet corner table. He ordered two pints and waited patiently.

But not for long. Mr. Strong shrugged off a shabby mac and sat down. Seen up close, he displayed all the traditional signs of pride and poverty. His shirt spotless and the cuffs frayed. His shoes ancient and well-polished. His jacket had one or two small holes in the sleeve, which had been very carefully mended. He wore a military tie. His hair was neat and brushed. It was easy to picture him in some cold, damp lodging somewhere, carefully laying out his shabby clothes every night, brushing his shoes, trimming his moustache, all ready for the next day's work. Clinging to old standards because they were all he had left.

Conscious that the silence had gone on too long, Dr. Bairstow sought for an opening to the conversation.

"The Flying Duck? I had not realised that was an actual name. I thought it was just an expression."

"Well, I don't know about that, sir, but I do know you heard it around here a lot a couple of years ago. Especially in connection with the old government, if you get my drift."

"I do indeed. Of course, this was the site of the famous Battersea Barricades. Were you present at the time?"

"I certainly was, sir. Did my bit on the East Wall."

"I understand the fighting was particularly heavy there."

"You got that right, sir. Saw a lot of friends fall, I did."

"Tell me, would I be right in thinking the East Wall was commanded by Theresa Mack?"

"That's right, sir. Stood shoulder to shoulder with her at the end. Don't mind telling you, I thought my last hour had come. But it hadn't. Not yet, anyway."

"Do you know where I can find Miss Mack?"

"Mrs., sir. Mrs. Mack. Went back to Cardiff, I believe."

"Interesting. Now, Mr. Strong, you must be wondering why I have asked you here. I have a proposition for you."

He spoke for some time while Mr. Strong sat quietly, sipping his pint, and listening. At the end, without saying anything, he picked up both glasses and went to the bar. Returning, he put two glasses on the table and seated himself again.

Neither man spoke for some time. Dr. Bairstow sat waiting.

Eventually, Mr. Strong sighed quietly and returned from wherever he had been. A light shone in his eyes that had not been there before. He said quietly, "I'd have to give a month's notice, of course."

Dr. Bairstow lifted his glass and silently toasted him. He left Mr. Strong snugly ensconced in his corner with a third pint in front of him and made his way through the cold streets back to the pod. Once there, he pulled out his notebook and reviewed the list of seven names contained therein. Key personnel, all of them. To be hunted down—he mentally crossed out "hunted down" and substituted "located"—and persuaded to join him. Some would be easier than others, but he had the first.

One.

AND YET ANOTHER MEETING. One in a series of many as Dr. Bairstow inched his way towards achieving his aims. As always, the office and its occupants seemed unchanged and unchanging. An acute observer, however, might have noticed that Mrs. Green had a new hairstyle.

Dr. Bairstow, while aware that by normal government standards, events were proceeding at the speed of light, could not help just the occasional twinge of what, in a lesser man, could be classed as impatience. Today, however, was different. There was a definite feeling that, after the jump to Waterloo, a corner had been turned.

"Dr. Bairstow, arising from our last meeting, we have given some thought as to where you and your organisation should be situated. After a great deal of discussion, we would like to offer you a choice of properties we feel would be appropriate for your needs."

Dr. Bairstow arranged his features into something that might, in the dark, resemble an expression of anticipation. "A choice? How exciting."

"We have here," Mr. Black passed over a folder, "a disused castle in Scotland. Very remote. Security would not be an issue. Or here," another folder was pushed across the table, "St. Mary's Priory, just outside of Rushford. A little dilapidated, but easily reclaimable. Or," he produced a third folder, "a modern warehouse complex just outside of Barnstaple, although that would need extensive refurbishment to be suitable for your purposes."

Dr. Bairstow made no move to pick up the folders. "While each property has its own merits, I believe St. Mary's Priory can offer me exactly what I need."

Mr. Brown blinked. "Don't you want to inspect any of these properties before making a decision?"

"Thank you, but no. I have been familiar with St. Mary's for some years now."

"Ah. Yes, of course. I should warn you however, the premises are in a state of some disrepair."

Dr. Bairstow sighed. "They always are, sir. They always are."

ON HIS WAY OUT, Dr. Bairstow requested the pleasure of a few words with the major. In private.

"If you would care to step into my office, sir . . ."

Major Guthrie opened a door to yet another small, dusty room and offered his guest a chair.

Dr. Bairstow settled himself. "Please do not construe this as any sort of criticism, but you're very young to be a major."

"Promotion by attrition, sir. There weren't many of us left at the end."

"So I have heard." He regarded his stick for a moment and then said, "Well, Major, at long last, it looks as if my unit will have a home."

"Congratulations, sir. It's been a long time coming."

"It has indeed, but I think I am now well on my way, and arising out of that, I wonder if you might like to consider alternative employment."

"Another office job, sir?"

"Oh dear me, no. Rest assured this would easily be as hazardous as anything to which you have been accustomed. Unit security will form part of your duties, but your main function will be to prevent a group of gifted, but not always very sensible, young people from killing themselves, levelling their immediate surroundings, and destroying the fabric of space and time as we know it. There will be days when you are not sure whether to shoot them or yourself. I beg that you will do neither. You will frequently operate away from the unit and must rely on your own judgment and abilities to see you through. As will everyone around you. Rely on you, I mean. The responsibilities will be enormous and the pay in no way commensurate with them."

"How incommensurate?"

"Meagre."

"How meagre is meagre?"

"More meagre than you have been accustomed to."

"I'm a serving officer in His Majesty's Forces, sir. You'd be amazed how familiar I am with meagre."

Dr. Bairstow smiled, but said nothing.

"This is about what happened the other day, isn't it, sir? When we went off to Waterloo?"

"It is. I am, I think, very close to securing my funding but one of the many conditions, I am sure, will relate to security. I hope to allay any fears by being able to assure the authorities that all security issues are in your capable hands. I have seen your files, Major, and your achievements are impressive. I have no hesitation, therefore, in making you this offer."

"And my current employers?"

"Your current employers will, I think, be reassured that security issues will be handled by one whom they know to be trustworthy."

"Well, I'll confess, Dr. Bairstow that while peace is very pleasant . . ."

"It's not very exciting. Major, if excitement is what you're after, I believe I may have the very thing."

"Could I choose my own team?"

"Almost certainly. Do you have anyone in mind?"

"One or two, yes. Including that young man you met the other day."

"Mr. . . . Markham?"

"You would not object?"

"Is there any reason why I should?"

"Perhaps you should read his file first."

He unlocked a filing cabinet and passed over a folder.

Dr. Bairstow read quietly. "A most unfortunate start to a young life."

"He's just beginning to find his way, I think."

"He certainly found his way rather quickly through officer school."

"The blaze was soon contained, sir. And it was rather an ingenious solution to the problem in hand. And as he himself argued, who knew the flames would spread so quickly?"

"Well, we both saw him the other day, large as life and twice as dirty, so we must assume, therefore, that I say yes."

"He was part of the team I brought with me when I was transferred to London and I would like to keep him with me."

Dr. Bairstow nodded. "I believe I can provide an environment in which he can thrive. I should perhaps warn you

both, however, that I am very much a 'one strike and you're
out' employer. You will find that while I am prepared to walk
through fire for my people, I have no hesitation, should they
cross me, in using their bodies to feed the fire through which I
should be walking."

Major Guthrie closed his eyes briefly. "Please don't mention fire and Markham in the same sentence."

Dr. Bairstow smiled politely and returned the file. "Well?"

"Count me in, sir."

Two.

ONE MONTH LATER, A coach drew up outside the locked gates of
St. Mary's Priory. After a while, the driver turned off the engine
and waited patiently while everyone blamed everyone else for
not having the keys.

Dr. Bairstow sat quietly in the front seat while Major Guthrie's small team milled around outside the bus. As far as he
could ascertain on such short acquaintance, their names were
Weller, Ritter, Markham, Murdoch, Evans, and Randall. They
represented the entire spectrum of shapes, sizes, and colours,
from the big rumbling giant imaginatively named Big Dave
Murdoch, to the small, scruffy individual at the back who, at
a nod from Guthrie, bent over to inspect the padlock. In a dis-
turbingly short space of time, he had pulled the chain free and
handed it to the major.

"Sorry sir. Came off in my hand."

They climbed noisily back into the bus. Carefully blank
faced, Major Guthrie handed both chain and padlock to Dr.
Bairstow who accepted them without comment.

St. Mary's Priory was a long, low building, not more than
three storeys high at its tallest point. Small windows caught the
sunlight as the coach zigzagged slowly up the potholed drive.
The remains of formal gardens could still be seen. To one side,

a reed-smothered lake hosted an impressive number of swans who had no idea what was about to hit them.

Markham said, for the first and last time in his life, that he liked swans.

Tall chimneys rose from a shallow roof and the whole building was smothered in Virginia Creeper, just beginning to show new green leaves in the spring sunshine.

From the back of the bus, Markham could be heard enthusiastically comparing the building to a haunted house and enquiring whether there was a ghost.

Alighting carefully, Dr. Bairstow stood quietly looking around. A man gazing at the unfamiliarly familiar. He was recalled by creaking hinges and a dragging noise as finally, with some effort and bad language, the front doors were persuaded to open.

Markham, surging forwards, was restrained by Major Guthrie. "After you, Dr. Bairstow."

Slowly, Dr. Bairstow mounted the shallow steps, paused for a moment, and then stepped from sunshine into shadow.

He was conscious of a familiar smell. Damp stone, dust, stale air, and old wood. He tilted his head as if listening and just momentarily, he caught the sound of footsteps clattering on a wooden staircase, voices raised in amiable dispute, a door slamming and somewhere unseen, a small explosion: an echo from the future perhaps.

Becoming aware of the silence around him, he turned.

"Well, gentlemen. Welcome to St. Mary's. This is the Great Hall. The kitchens and dining room will be down there. The Library through there. These rooms off to the left will be the Wardrobe Department. R&D is up the stairs and over to the right. Please find yourselves somewhere to put your gear and let us begin."

"I'll put the kettle on," said Markham.

EXACTLY SEVEN DAYS LATER, Dr. Bairstow was facing a minor uprising. A small space had been cleared in the dining room, a table set up, and Markham was serving an optimistically named chicken stew.

Murdoch prodded his carefully. "I'm almost certain this sort of thing is banned under the Geneva Convention."

Randall was heard to enquire whether something had escaped from Quatermass and The Pit.

"It's nutritious," said Markham indignantly.

"It's grey. No food should be grey."

"I think mine just twitched," said Evans. "Should I stun it, do you think?"

"It's cheap," said Markham, marshalling his secondary arguments.

"I'm sure it's delicious," said Dr. Bairstow. He took a dubious forkful, chewed valiantly for some considerable time, and swallowed. Six pairs of eyes watched him closely.

Delicately patting his mouth with a piece of kitchen roll, he rummaged in his wallet, eventually pulling out a credit card, which he handed to Major Guthrie.

"Please ascertain the whereabouts of the nearest establishment prepared to deliver here and place an order with all speed."

"Hey," protested Markham. "I slaved for nearly twenty minutes over this."

Dr. Bairstow did not shudder. "And we are all deeply appreciative of your efforts. However, Major Guthrie advises me that while your enthusiasm is admirable, your talents are better employed in other parts of the building."

"But—" wailed Markham, loyal to his culinary creation.

Randall passed over his dish. As did Ritter and Evans. Murdoch might possibly have followed suit, but his dish appeared to have welded itself to the table.

"You eat it then," said Evans.

Markham surveyed the dishes before him, many of which were forming a crust.

He sighed. "Chicken and sweetcorn soup with a side order of pancake rolls. Beef and green peppers in oyster sauce. Sweet and sour pork balls. Egg fried rice and a double helping of prawn crackers. For my second course . . ."

EMERGING FROM THE TRAIN station, Dr. Bairstow stopped and looked around him. It was said that the first stirrings of resistance had been born on the night they threw the Fascists out of Cardiff, and there seemed no doubt that the city still bore the scars of that and subsequent fighting. Unlike in London, however, there were no building sites, no scaffolding, and no signs of regeneration. He saw rows of tents pitched wherever enough rubble had been cleared. There were no shops. Just a number of public washing and cooking facilities. He remembered the newspaper headline, "Where did all the money go?" Not to Cardiff, that was obvious.

Consulting his map, he set off.

Thirty minutes walking brought him to a narrow street in Cathays. Possibly due to the high student population, this area had been particularly badly damaged. Most of the paving stones had been removed. Craters rendered the road undriveable. Some of the houses had no roofs and a number of canvas tarpaulins flapped in the wind.

Walking carefully along the right-hand side of the street, he counted the numbers on the front doors, stopping at one particular house about half way down. There, he knocked and waited.

The door was opened by a small woman with bright hair and tired eyes.

"Yes?"

"I'm looking for Mrs. Theresa Mack."

"And you are?"

"My name is Edward Bairstow and I have come a very long way to speak to her."

"From London?"

"That was part of my journey, yes."

She sighed. "You'd better come in."

The front door opened straight into the living room.

There was no TV. No fire. No smell of cooking. One small lamp burned beside an armchair. An open book lay facedown on the chair. A similar armchair was placed on the other side of the empty fireplace. A small table and two chairs stood under the window. A framed photograph of a young couple was the only decoration in the room.

Dr. Bairstow paused beside the table, looked at the photograph, and said softly, "I understand you are married."

"Widowed," she said curtly. "Please sit down."

"I'm sorry to hear that. Was it in the recent fighting?"

"At the Barricades, yes. He survived Cardiff and Monmouth and then fell right at the very end, in London. Almost as the surrender was announced. I could even hear the faint cheering far away over the bridge as the shot rang out. Five minutes later and everyone was shouting, 'Cease fire!' and 'Hooray!' but by then, of course, it was far too late."

A long silence fell and eventually Dr. Bairstow said, "I've just come from there."

"Have they rebuilt yet? I suppose priority goes to London."

"They have made a start, yes, but there's not been a great deal of progress."

"There never is. Have you seen the state of Cardiff?"

"My walk from the station offered me ample opportunity to do so."

"So why are you here?"

"I find myself in need of your expertise."

"I'm too old for all that now. The fight's gone out of me."

"I take leave to doubt that. However, it is your former expertise that interests me at the moment."

"What—catering?"

"Yes. I am currently establishing a small organisation and we have been catering for ourselves. Our efforts have not been as successful as I could have wished. My records show that you enjoyed considerable success in that field."

"Your records? Who are you? Show me some ID."

"Alas, I am unable to do so. I have none."

She regarded him narrowly. "Do you work for the government?"

Just for a moment, he allowed himself a small gleam of amusement. "Actually I may have just persuaded them to work for me. They do, however, supply my funding—via a third party."

She looked at him across the cold fireplace. It occurred to him the room was very quiet. Not even the ticking of a clock.

"Who are you?"

"I told you. My name is Edward Bairstow and while I am reluctant to paraphrase Winston Churchill in any way, I can offer you nothing except extremely hard work, difficult working conditions, and an occasionally hazardous environment."

Receiving no indication of her response to this statement, he continued.

"I am setting up an organisation, the details of which I cannot yet discuss with you. The unit will be situated in England. The work will be of a top-secret nature and my employees will require regular and frequent feeding. You would have complete control over your department. I do not believe in micro-managing. It will be chaotic. Food will be required at all hours of the day and night. And large quantities of it, too. Miracles will be demanded of you on a daily basis. You probably won't be paid regularly. There may be periods when you will not be paid at all."

"Can I engage my own staff?"

"Within budgetary constraints, yes."

"Will *they* be paid?"

"Probably not."

She sat for a while in silence. Dr. Bairstow, possibly a little more tired by his walk from the station than he was prepared to admit, also sat quietly.

"You can't tell me what you do?"

"No, I can't do that at the moment. But I can tell you what I won't do. I won't ever preside over an organisation that wants to put together a working party to investigate the possibility of setting up a steering group dedicated to considering the makeup of a proposed committee. In my own small way, I too am rebuilding, and I want people who will get things done. Are you one of those people?"

Her chin came up.

"When?"

"As soon as possible."

"Wait here."

She reappeared moments later with a small suitcase. Crossing to the table, she picked up the photograph and her book and carefully packed them away.

"I'm ready."

They let themselves out of the front door. She locked it behind her and posted the keys back through the letterbox.

"Let's go."

The two figures walked slowly down the street into the gathering night.

"Three."

"What's that?"

"I beg your pardon. Just thinking aloud."

AND YET ANOTHER LONG train journey. North, this time. Evicting, by sheer personality, a young man sitting in the seats clearly set aside for those physically unable to stand all the way to York, Dr. Bairstow made himself comfortable and contemplated his strategy. A complete waste of time as it turned out.

Catching a local train he alighted at Thirsk and made his way across the Market Place, around the Clock Tower, and out towards the university—St. James's campus.

Spring was springing as fast as it could go. Tubs of nodding daffodils stood on every street corner. A warm wind blew. For once, it wasn't raining.

The St. James's buildings had sustained considerable damage. The Main Hall stood roofless. Every window was boarded up. To his right, the Barbeck Library was just a shell. Dr. Bairstow stood at the entrance to the quadrangle, looking about him. An observer might have said he was remembering.

A college porter appeared from a doorway. "Help you, sir?"

"I am here to see either Dr. Dowson or Professor Rapson. Or both. Whichever is easier."

The porter nodded back the way he had just come. "Up the stairs and to your left, sir. You might want to proceed with caution."

Thanking him, Dr. Bairstow climbed the ancient staircase.

In contrast to the rest of the building, which reflected the grave silence of academia, the corridor at the top of the stairs was witnessing a great deal of activity. A line of gossiping students stood along one panelled wall, all with identical expressions of sheepishness and clutching bottles containing a familiar golden fluid.

Any doubts Dr. Bairstow might have had over whether or not he was in the right place were immediately dispelled. At the exact moment he opened his mouth to make a polite enquiry of the nearest bottle-clutching student, there was a small, damp explosion and a cloud of evil-smelling, acrid smoke billowed from a doorway. Dr. Bairstow closed his mouth, and waited for events to unfold.

A door on the other side of the corridor was hurled open with some force. The students, obviously familiar with the signs and mindful that there was bound to be a pub open somewhere, made themselves scarce.

A small, round man, spectacles balanced precariously on the end of his nose, bounced out into the corridor, waving his arms to dispel the evil vapours, and plunged into the fray.

"Andrew, you old fool, I warned you. Didn't I warn you?" He turned his head, addressing someone unseen. "Mr. Cameron, please telephone the Chancellor's office for me and remind them—again—of my urgent requests to be rehoused. No one should be expected to have to work opposite . . . Andrew, what are you doing now? I demand you stop that at once. You'll blow us all to kingdom come."

A furious pounding could be heard.

A voice said excitedly, "I think I know where I went wrong."

"You always say that."

"Well, it's usually true, Octavius. I think this time I used a little too much urine and not enough toadstool."

"For God's sake, Andrew, it's like a bloody witch's den in here. What *is* this? And *this*? And don't tell me what *this* is because I don't want to know."

A quiet voice said patiently, "It's touchwood, Occy. You soak it in urine—lots of urine—pound the mixture into a kind of felt, and it smoulders. Portable fire. The Vikings used it a lot.

"You are not a Viking. And the 21st century has gifted us with matches. And this did not smoulder. It exploded."

"Yes, I think possibly the fault lies with poor quality urine. I blame the students, you know. It's probably about 90 percent alcohol. Really, when you think about it, an explosion was quite inevitable. I wonder if I could persuade them to stop drinking for a week or two?"

"Andrew, I sometimes think you've lost all touch with reality."

"Well really, that's a little unkind. Actually, while you're here, Occy, I wonder if you'd be kind enough to donate . . ."

At this moment, Dr. Bairstow judged it politic to intervene.

Taking a spotless handkerchief from his pocket, he attached it to one end of his stick and gently waved it around the doorway.

"Gentlemen, may I enter?"

"Oh for heaven's sake, Andrew, you've blown up a civilian. Come in, sir. Are you hurt?"

"Not in any way, I assure you. May I enter?"

"Yes, of course. Andrew, please find the gentleman a chair."

A tall and very thin man with Einstein hair, Professor Rapson looked vaguely around as if perhaps a chair could be found dangling from the ceiling. His hair was in disarray and the front of his white coat was speckled with something that should probably not be too closely examined.

"I am looking for Professor Rapson."

"Oh. Yes. That's me. How do you do?" He began to move around the room, picking up shattered equipment and uttering small, distressed sounds. Pools of fluid dripped unhappily to the floor.

"Andrew, what are you doing?"

"I'm looking for the rest of the student donations and they don't appear to have survived."

"Well thank God for that. Come and sit down for a moment, there's a good chap. You have a guest."

"No, you don't understand. That was the last of . . . Oh, well, never mind, there are many more of them waiting outside."

"Alas, I fear that is no longer the case," interrupted Dr. Bairstow.

"Oh dear. Now what shall I do? I don't suppose, Occy . . ."

"Absolutely not!"

He turned hopefully to Dr. Bairstow. "I wonder, sir, if I could trouble you . . ."

There was a short pause. "I'm afraid not."

"Oh well, I'll just have to save up again, I suppose."

He drooped dejectedly over the remains of a complicated glass retort.

Silence fell. And showed no signs of getting up again.

Since both of them appeared to have forgotten his presence, Dr. Bairstow felt compelled to speak.

"I am looking for Professor Andrew Rapson and Dr. Octavius Dowson. I suspect that I have found them."

"You have indeed, sir. How can we assist you?"

"Gentlemen, I have travelled here today to ask you, personally, whether you would be interested in joining my project. I cannot enter into any great detail at the moment, suffice to say that the work will be hazardous, noisy, a little disorganised, and extremely secret."

It was as if a switch had been flicked. Both men stopped what they were doing and turned to fix him with stares of laser-like intensity. The two bickering academics might never have existed.

"Why us?"

"The University of Thirsk was the centre of resistance in this part of the country and, from reports I have read, the two of you were at the centre of the centre of resistance. The university suffered greatly because of its stand against the Fascist forces. I have in mind a scheme that will benefit everyone—me, you, and the university."

Professor Rapson folded his arms. "Does the Chancellor know about this?"

"She does. There have been extensive discussions."

Dr. Dowson smiled gently. "I imagine she couldn't wait to be rid of us."

"Actually, no. She is greatly reluctant to lose either of you but she concedes the importance of my work and recognises your value to it."

"You haven't told us yet what your project is."

"No, I haven't."

"Or where it is."

"I'm afraid I can't tell you that, either. But it will be in this country."

"What will we be doing?

"I'm not yet at liberty to divulge that information."

"Can you give us any details at all?"

"Not really, no."

"So, just to sum up—you want us to work on an unknown project in an unknown location?"

"That is correct."

"And the work is hazardous . . . ?"

"And noisy and disorganised."

They looked at each other. "Anything else we should know?"

"Regular wages will probably not happen."

"Well in that case . . ." They looked at each other and then back to Dr. Bairstow, nodding enthusiastically. "We accept."

"Good." Dr. Bairstow rose to his feet and retrieved his handkerchief. "I will contact you both shortly. Allow me to give you my card."

Dr. Dowson turned it over. "It's just your name."

"That is correct. Gentlemen, I will be in touch."

He turned and made his way back through the smoke and down the stairs. Pausing at the bottom to draw on his gloves, he groped for his notebook, made two ticks, and permitted himself a satisfied smile.

"Four *and* five. Excellent progress."

TIME PASSED—AND WHO would know that better than the occupants of St. Mary's?

The food improved immeasurably. Although as Mr. Randall remarked, Mrs. Mack could serve up a dead dog sandwich and it would still be a huge improvement on Markham's efforts. A slight scuffle followed this statement.

A steady stream of vehicles wove their way around the pot-
holes, seeking to deliver their cargo under Mr. Strong's directions. Structural work began and was progressing well until
the Society for the Protection of Historical Buildings turned up
with their paperwork and put a stop to all that.

The library slowly began to take shape. It was Dr. Bairstow's opinion that the library might have taken shape a little less slowly if Dr. Dowson could refrain from exclaiming
in excitement and sitting down, task forgotten, to read some
long-forgotten treasure.

Professor Rapson, for no good reason that anyone could
see, had attempted the construction of an automated mango-
nel. The combination of a scale model and an old lawn mower
engine proved too much for the internal walls of his labora-
tory, one of which collapsed under the bombardment. He was
accused of attempting to demolish St. Mary's even before the
cement had dried and, having been compelled to evacuate
while the ceiling was propped up and other safety measures
implemented, he retired, protesting, to assist Dr. Dowson in
the Library. The sounds of heated academic debate soon echoed
around the building. As Major Guthrie said, however, it kept
them both occupied and out of the way.

Living conditions remained somewhat spartan. St. Mary's,
while continuing to absorb money at an astonishing rate, had
very little to spare for creature comforts.

Dr. Bairstow awoke late one night to hear vigorous whispering under his window. A moment later, a vehicle coughed
into life and drove away. Silence fell. Dr. Bairstow turned over
and closed his eyes again.

The next morning, two tables, half-a-dozen chairs, and a
sofa appeared to have mysteriously materialised overnight. The
next night saw the acquisition of three single beds. On the night
after that, St. Mary's appeared to have enjoyed a visit from the

wardrobe fairy. With some regret, Dr. Bairstow requested the presence of Mr. Markham at his earliest convenience.

He bounced into Dr. Bairstow's office, wearing his usual sunny smile, and clutching a diver's helmet in one hand and a lump hammer in the other. With true heroism, Dr. Bairstow forbore to ask.

"Good morning, sir. You wanted me."

"Good morning, Mr. Markham. There appear to be quantities of furniture appearing all over my unit."

"Yes sir."

"The paperwork for which I cannot trace."

"No sir."

"Might I enquire as to the origins of this unexpected bounty?"

"Of course, sir."

Silence.

"Please consider my request as an instruction to explain the origins of this unexpected bounty."

"Sorry sir. The municipal tip."

"I'm afraid I don't quite follow."

"They've got some great stuff there, sir. And it's our duty to recycle," he added, virtue (among other things) oozing from every pore.

"But, and correct me if I am wrong, the purpose of the municipal tip—wherever that might be—is for people to dispose of unwanted, worn out, and possibly infested household items?"

"No, spot on, sir. Well done."

"I have two areas of concern, Mr. Markham. The first is the almost certainly illegal removal of these household items and the consequences should you be apprehended; and second, the varied and no doubt difficult to eradicate wildlife living within it."

"Not a problem sir. Already dealt with. Professor Rapson has come up with some sort of spray and . . ."

Dr. Bairstow held up a hand. "Please say no more."

"OK. Was there anything else sir?"

"If I could just refer you back to my previous comment concerning the illegal removal of . . ."

"Of stuff no one wants, sir. It's recycling. St. Mary's is going green."

"Of that I have no doubt, although possibly we are not referring to the same thing."

Mr. Markham assumed an expression of stricken concern. Lifting anxious eyes to Dr. Bairstow, he said piteously, "We're not doing any harm, sir."

Dr. Bairstow contemplated the guileless face before him. "While I am certain this works with elderly ladies, magistrates, and for all I know, Major Guthrie, it cuts no ice with me."

Markham resumed his normal expression. "No sir. Do you want us to stop?"

Dr. Bairstow shuffled some files from one mountainous pile to another. "I beg your pardon. I am sometimes afflicted with a little deafness. I did not hear your last question."

"I did not utter it, sir."

"I am so glad we understand each other."

St. Mary's first all-staff briefing was generally reckoned to be a bit of a landmark. Especially when it was made clear that an all-staff briefing was just that. A briefing for *all* staff.

"We are all members of this unit. Decisions are made, actions taken, and policies agreed. Everyone is affected and everyone is involved. Physical absence from the unit, serious illness and, in some instances, death, are the only excuses I am prepared to consider and only then if they are accompanied by the relevant paperwork. Mr. Markham and Mr. Randall, please would you present my compliments to the admin and kitchen staff and ask them if they would be good enough to join us. Thank you."

Some minutes later, with a larger audience, he continued.

"As you know, we operate under the auspices of the University of Thirsk, and tomorrow, their new Chancellor, Dr. Evelyn Chalfont, will be paying us a visit."

He paused, shifted his weight slightly, and continued. "I would be grateful if, just for once, the first impression of this unit could be a favourable one.

"Mr. Strong, I know the grounds will be immaculate. Mrs. Mack, I understand you have already begun preparations for a special luncheon and Mrs. Enderby is to give a tour of the Wardrobe Department."

He said no more and passed immediately to another topic, but not before he had caught Major Guthrie's eye. No words were exchanged but it was clearly understood that Mr. Markham and Professor Rapson, if not actually locked in the basement for the duration, would almost certainly be under twenty-four-hour supervision, because nothing must be allowed to interfere with St. Mary's presentation of itself as a sober, slightly dull establishment dedicated to the pursuit of historical research.

At eleven thirty on the day in question, a battered Mini, painted in pink and yellow, and coughing smoke from every orifice, ground to a halt outside the front door of St. Mary's. The driver's door creaked open, disgorging an astonishingly young, dark-haired woman, carrying a watering can.

Mr. Strong bustled forwards. "Good morning, Madam Chancellor."

She seemed somewhat flustered. "Oh, good morning. It's Mr. Strong, isn't it?"

"That is correct, ma'am. May I relieve you of your implement?"

"Oh, yes. Thank you very much. I wonder, when it's cooled down a little, could you splash in some more water? Sadly, she drinks faster than a politician when someone else is picking up the tab. Is Edward around?"

Dr. Bairstow appeared.

"Ah Edward. Good morning. As you can see, I made it. You said I wouldn't and I did. Pay up."

Dr. Bairstow regarded the small heap of metal currently lowering property values all over the parish.

"Good heavens, Evelyn. You appear to have driven here in a slice of Battenberg cake."

"I don't know what you mean," she said, defensively. "It goes like a bomb."

"Not the happiest simile in this context. Can I offer you some coffee?"

"God, yes."

She plunged up the steps and entered St. Mary's.

Seated comfortably in Dr. Bairstow's office, she stirred her coffee and smiled at him. Dr. Bairstow found he could not help smiling back.

"Madam Chancellor . . ."

"Evelyn . . ."

"Evelyn. Please do not construe this as any form of criticism, but surely the need to disarm your political opponents with a display of irresponsible student behaviour is over now. You could perfectly easily have been driven here in your official car, surrounded by the Senior Faculty, and enjoyed the status commensurate with that of Chancellor of the University of Thirsk."

"Don't talk to me about the Senior Faculty. Bunch of self-serving, political failures. You know the saying, 'Those who can—do. Those who can't—teach.' And those who never had any idea what it was in the first place are members of my Senior Faculty. Sorry, Edward, but this is in the nature of a day out for me. You surely wouldn't deprive me of all the fun of getting back and finding what the bastards have been up to while my back's been turned."

He stirred his coffee. "I was aware that yours was a somewhat controversial appointment, but are things really that bad?"

"There are those who feel that organising the resistance actually renders me not only unsuitable for this position, but positively dangerous. Never mind that Thirsk was the rallying point for all those opposing the regime. Never mind that we inspired and protected and defended and . . ." She stopped. "Well, you know what I mean."

"I do indeed. I'm just astonished that your opponents watched you in action for all those years and still think they possess the ability to take you down. That you couldn't deal with them with one hand behind your back while chairing the Finance Committee at the same time."

She laughed. "You must know that it's far easier to deal with the enemy shooting at you from the front than the shadowy bastards trying to knife you in the back."

"I feel certain you are more than capable of dealing with these . . . er . . . shadowy bastards."

"They're not going to cause me any problems. I know I'm a controversial appointment, but I think the feeling was new beginnings etc. Besides, some of those shadowy bastards weren't quite as . . . unambiguous . . . in their loyalties as they could have been. I know it and they know I know it. I'll have them out. It's only a matter of time." She grinned mischievously. "Perhaps Professor Rapson could brew me something untraceable. How is he, by the way?"

"Thriving."

"And Dr. Dowson?"

"The same."

"That's good. They wouldn't have liked the new regime at all and after their magnificent efforts during the uprising, they both deserved better. I'm glad you've taken them. In which particular attic have you locked Professor Rapson for the day?"

"Madam Chancellor, I am shocked you would believe me capable of such an action."

"Sorry. He's in the basement, then."

"Of course. May I refill your cup?"

"And what of you, Edward? With your funding finally secured, you have surely surmounted your highest hurdle. If you have ever had a holiday then I have yet to hear of it. Surely a few days off now would not do any harm?"

Dr. Bairstow stared thoughtfully at his cup. "I have, in fact, been toying with just such an idea. You are right. Some time ago, I made a promise to someone and I should act upon it. A few days away would be . . . very pleasant."

"Excellent. I shall say no more. So, what do you have for me to see today?"

THE VISIT WENT WELL. The Chancellor was eager to be pleased. St. Mary's was eager to please. Mrs. Enderby's tour of the Wardrobe Department was particularly well received and, possibly wanting to end the visit on this positive note, Dr. Bairstow escorted the Chancellor back to her car.

Mr. Strong approached, complete with watering can.

"I hope we haven't taken any liberties, ma'am, but a few of us took a quick look under the bonnet and you shouldn't have any problems from now on. Particularly with the small smoke canister you appear to have concealed behind the carburettor. We were a little puzzled as to its purpose, ma'am, especially as the rest of the engine is so well maintained.

She sparkled with mischief. "My secret is out. I hope you don't want your money back, Edward. Now, I must go. Thank you so much, everyone. A delightful day."

"Our pleasure, Madam Chancellor. Perhaps you would allow Mr. Strong to hand you your watering can."

He watched the tiny car fling itself down the drive, scrape through the gates with barely an inch to spare, and roar away.

"Ah, Mr. Murdoch."

A passing Murdoch, who could have sworn there was no way Dr. Bairstow could ever have known he was behind him, ground to a perplexed halt.

"Mr. Murdoch, perhaps you can enlighten me as to why Professor Rapson has requisitioned twenty gallons of milk and twenty jars of honey?"

Murdoch blinked. Whether in genuine innocence or as a delaying tactic was impossible to say. His big face glowed with innocence and a desire to be of assistance. "Sorry sir?"

"Milk? Honey?"

Mr. Murdoch appeared to give the matter some thought. "Perhaps a breakfast party, sir." Then, possibly feeling that more was required of him, "With a biblical theme?"

Dr. Bairstow's look of blank incomprehension was a reminder—as if one was needed—that there were occasions when humour at St. Mary's could be a bit of a double-edged weapon.

Murdoch regrouped himself into a vision of beaming good-will. "No idea, sir. How badly do you want to know? Would you like me to investigate?"

"I'm not sure the answer will make any meaningful contribution to my peace of mind, Mr. Murdoch, but I thank you nevertheless for your offer."

THAT ST. MARY'S WAS becoming an entity in its own right was apparent by the ever-increasing amounts of time Dr. Bairstow was spending behind a paper-piled desk. It was noted by Markham, sinking his nose into what he considered a well-deserved pint, that the bigger the piles the shorter his temper. This statement was not disputed.

With the amount of work to be done, Dr. Bairstow might have been forgiven for postponing a small promise made more than two years ago. That he had not forgotten, however, was proved by a conversation he had with Mrs. Enderby, head of Wardrobe, who listened placidly to his instructions, took notes, and enquired if the lady had a favourite colour.

Dr. Bairstow smiled. "I think green would be most appropriate. A light green."

She nodded and gathered up her notes. "I shall have it ready for you by the end of the week, Dr. Bairstow," and she left the room.

Dr. Bairstow sat very still for a few minutes, and then sighed, picked up his pen, pulled out a blank mission file, and began to calculate coordinates and plan an assignment.

Exactly as Mrs. Enderby had promised, five days later, a ball gown of sea-green silk hung on the back of his door, carefully swathed in a garment bag. Occasionally he raised his head and looked at it, smiled a little, and then continued with his work.

When he finally had everything arranged to his satisfaction, he reached for the telephone and dialled a number.

It was, perhaps, fortunate that he was alone.

Gently replacing the receiver, he paused for a few moments, his face expressionless, and then dialled a second number.

"Redhouse Nursing Home."

"I wonder if I could speak to Mrs. Green, please."

"I'm sorry, sir. There is no one here by that name."

"I should perhaps have said Mrs. Bessant? Angela Bessant?"

There was a pause so long that the next words did not come as a surprise.

"I'm sorry sir, Mrs. Bessant died last week."

Dr. Bairstow very carefully aligned his files with the edge of his desk.

"That must have been very . . . sudden."

"It was, sir. I don't think any of us, least of all Mrs. Bessant, had any idea how little time she had left."

"I understand her son served abroad. Was he with her when . . . ?"

"No sir. Unfortunately, he wasn't able to get here in time."

"Did she . . . I wonder, did she ask for anyone?"

"Are you . . . Dr. . . . . Bairstow?"

He cleared his throat. "I am, yes."

"She spoke of you several times, sir. She said that every time she smelled cabbage she thought of you. Would that be right?"

He cleared his throat again. "Yes, it would."

"We didn't have any contact details, sir, and the lady wasn't always coherent. I'm sorry, but we couldn't find you."

The silence lengthened.

"I'm afraid, sir, I took rather a liberty. She was becoming agitated and when it became apparent that she wasn't—that she didn't have very long, when she kept asking, I told her you were just downstairs, signing in. She smiled, and said, 'I knew he would come.' And then really, sir, she just—fell asleep."

"I see. That was a kind thought. Thank you, nurse."

"Is there anything I can do for you, sir?"

"Thank you. No."

Very carefully, concentrating on his hands, he replaced the receiver and sat motionless for some time.

Long shadows moved silently across the carpet.

Rising stiffly to his feet, he unzipped the garment bag. The sea-green silk shimmered gently in the half-light. Reaching out, he touched the material with only the very tips of his fingers. Just for an instant.

Hearing a movement in the outer office, he called, "Yes?"

Randall stuck his head around the door. "Just picking up the post, sir. Was there anything?"

With a sudden decisive movement, Dr. Bairstow zipped up the garment bag.

"Would you be good enough to return this costume to Mrs. Enderby with my thanks. Unfortunately, it is no longer required."

"Of course sir."

He disappeared and his footsteps could be heard clattering off down the corridor.

Dr. Bairstow returned to his desk, closed the mission file, and marked it for incineration.

Mrs. Green would not be going to the ball.

THE NIGHT WAS VERY dark and still, even inside St. Mary's. Just for once, the building was silent. Dr. Bairstow sat at his desk, staring at the bottle and glass in front of him. He had not moved for some considerable time.

Everyone has a private face. The one worn when the struggle becomes too much. When the possibility of success seems a very long away. The private face that no one ever sees.

He stirred and reached for the bottle again and as he did so, someone tapped at the door.

The private face fled. He squared his shoulders. "Come in."

The door opened to reveal a tall, elegant woman of indeterminate age. She wore her dark hair in a neat French pleat. Her black suit was impeccably tailored. Standing quietly in the doorway, she waited.

They looked at each other for a very long time until Dr. Bairstow sat back in his chair, smiled a little, and said, "Good evening. If you have come in answer to the advertisement for a PA, I haven't placed it yet."

"No. I have come in answer to a need."

She pulled the visitor's chair around to the other side of the desk. "I think I shall always feel more comfortable on this side."

"You may not get the opportunity." He topped up his glass again.

She clasped her hands. "Something has occurred?"

"Actually, no. Nothing has occurred. I left it too late and now it's—too late. Now . . . nothing will ever occur."

She said nothing.

He gestured. "I had not realised until today how much of myself I've put into St. Mary's. How much it demands of me. And will always demand of me. And it's still not completed. Nor anywhere near."

"I do not think that completion is the issue here."

"Are you here as my PA?"

"No, not yet."

"Why not?" He looked around at the disordered room, the mounds of files, cubes and data sticks. "At least one of us should do something useful."

She dismissed the tottering piles of paperwork with a wave of her hand. "You are lonely."

He smiled bitterly into his glass. "Even the very loneliest person does not like to have this pointed out."

She ignored him. "You have no one. You are out of your own time. You are alone. Your task is Herculean. It would be very natural for you sometimes to feel overwhelmed and Leon Farrell, the one person who might have some understanding of your loss today, is not yet here. You are completely and utterly alone."

"I do hope your purpose here tonight is not to provide support and encouragement because . . ." He made an effort. "Why are you here?"

"To provide support and encouragement."

"Can I refer you to my previous statement?"

She said nothing.

He played with his glass. "I think they may have chosen the wrong person."

"You volunteered for this task and they chose exactly the right person."

He stared out of the window into the dark. "She reminded me of someone I knew a long time ago in the future and then today I learned her name. Her real name."

"Yes, they were related."

"I sometimes wonder if I am not cursed."

She did not reply.

"Is it so beyond the bounds of possibility that one day I would find someone and she would not die?"

"You will not always be alone."

He drained his glass. "Why haven't you come in answer to the advert?"

"Well, you haven't placed it yet."

"I can't imagine that that would ever stop you."

She smiled. "You will have a number of assistants before me."

"Why?"

"All the better for you to appreciate my talents when I do arrive."

He sighed, turning the empty glass around on his desk.

She leaned forwards and switched on his desk light. Shadows fled. Standing up, she turned to the window and drew the curtains, shutting out the dark.

Her voice cut the air like a sword. "You will surround yourself with bright and brilliant people. The building will echo to the sound of ideas, discussions, and the occasional small explosion. There will be triumph and disaster in equal measure. There will be outstanding bravery and heart-stopping betrayal. There will be love and loss. There will be devotion to duty and to each other. There will be treachery and defeat. There will be tragedy and death. You will lead and inspire and protect. And once they walk through these doors, no one in this unit will ever be alone again."

She moved towards the door.

"Will you always be here?"

Her voice came from a great distance. "No, I will not. But I will always be here when St. Mary's needs me."

The door closed and Dr. Bairstow was alone again.

He sat for a while, lost in thought, and then pulled his chair forwards, placed the bottle and glass in his bottom drawer, opened a file at random, and began to work.

CORNERED OUTSIDE R&D AND not having the speed for a quick getaway, Dr. Bairstow smiled benignly on the two representatives of the Forces of Darkness, or the Society for the Preservation of Historical Buildings, as they probably preferred to be known.

"I have agreed the amendments to the new staff block. I have agreed that the hangar should be situated behind the main building so that the original façade may remain unspoiled. Please present me with today's list of unreasonable demands, all of which will, apparently, have been designed to prevent my project ever coming to fruition."

An earnest young man whose cardigan had obviously been knitted by a loving mother, pushed his spectacles further up his nose and said nervously, "Well, to be honest Dr. Bairstow, there is one area that causes Miss Spindle and me particular concern."

Miss Spindle, clutching an armful of folders, gazed adoringly up at him.

"Only one?" Dr. Bairstow said.

The young man shifted his weight and mentally girded his loins. "Our understanding is that this will eventually be an educational establishment."

"An eventuality that seems to recede further and further into the distant future with every passing day."

"Sir?"

"A research facility, yes. Under the auspices of the University of Thirsk."

"Well, I have to ask, sir . . ."

"Yes?"

"Blast doors?"

"Purely a precautionary measure. Nothing to alarm you in any way."

"A precautionary measure against what?"

"Anything that could go wrong."

"What could possibly go so wrong you need a set of blast doors? Are you splitting the atom?"

"Good heavens, no. Well, not on purpose, certainly."

Dr. Bairstow paused for a reaction from the representatives of an organisation famed for its lack of humour. After a while, it became apparent their reputation would remain intact.

"Actually, they are there to protect the old building. We will have a fully functioning R&D department and their function is—well, you could say, practical history. I don't know if you're aware of Greek fire? Or the ballistic properties of a trebuchet? The blast doors are here solely to protect this fine old building from anything untoward that may occur as the academic mind marches unstoppably forwards in its quest for knowledge."

He paused, leaned on his stick, and smiled benevolently at them again.

They stepped back.

"But according to the plans, R&D will be lodged in the main building."

"That is correct."

"So—they will also occupy this space as well?"

"R&D personnel will certainly be present on many occasions."

"But the structure is massive. It's practically an aircraft hangar. What on earth could possibly require this amount of space?"

"My dear sir, have you ever tried to reconstruct the Battle of Hastings? You cannot possibly expect me to fit the entire Saxon fyrd into an area the size of a small bedroom."

"You will be fighting battles inside the building?"

"Only if it's wet outside."

They stared at each other, adrift in a fog of mutual incomprehension. In the future, Dr. Bairstow was frequently heard to remark that any light-hearted frivolity he might possibly once have possessed had been leeched from his soul by prolonged contact with the Society for the Preservation of Historical Buildings and any complaints should be addressed to them. In triplicate. With full supporting documentation, together with the appropriate plans, diagrams, and projections all countersigned, dated, and stamped with official approval.

He tried again. "Not if we cannot reach some sort of compromise today, no. As I understand your function, it is to provide advice and information relevant to renovating a listed building. It is not to question the function to which that building should be put."

"Well, actually . . ." began the young man, who was pretty sure it was.

"The appropriate permissions have been acquired and the plans approved. There really is no more to discuss."

"But . . ."

"I thought I had made it perfectly clear. This project must be completed by the date specified. A great deal hangs on this. I am sure you must be as committed to . . ."

He pushed open a door as he spoke and stopped dead on the threshold.

Contrary to the rest of R&D, which was almost permanently buried in miscellaneous clutter, this room was empty. Or rather, almost empty. At this moment and in this company, Dr. Bairstow would have given a great deal of the money he did not possess for this room to be empty. Unfortunately, it was not.

Messrs Markham, Ritter, Weller, and Evans, naked apart from inexpertly tied tea towels disguised as loincloths, stood motionless in each corner, apparently smothered from head to toe in a mixture of honey and slightly sour milk.

The gently bred Miss Spindle, who had for years been strangely susceptible to men who wore astonishing knitwear, now began to perceive her horizons had been unnecessarily narrow and moved forward for a clearer view.

Professor Rapson himself cut a magnificent figure, reclining on a gilded chaise-longue in the middle of the room. He wore a long black wig and a golden tunic and was, as far as Dr. Bairstow dared ascertain, honey free.

Dr. Dowson, wearing a beekeeper's mask, which was, mercifully, muffling his complaints, was busy decanting what looked like several thousand bluebottles into the room. "Are you ready?"

With a gesture similar to Ramses unleashing his forces at the Battle of Kadesh, Professor Rapson indicated that he was indeed ready. An anticipatory buzzing filled the room. Most of it from the flies.

Released from captivity, they zipped around for a few moments, presumably getting their bearings, and then, apart from one or two specimens who had fallen to the floor in excitement and were now on their backs waving their legs in the air, every bluebottle in the room settled on Professor Rapson.

Dr. Bairstow gently closed the door and ushered his bemused guests down the corridor.

"What on earth . . . ?"

"Human flypaper," said Dr. Bairstow in tones which gave them to understand they now had all the information they needed to know exactly what was going on.

"I'm sorry?"

"Human flypaper. One of the pharaohs—I'm sorry I can't offhand recall which one—in an effort to keep the flies off his sacred self, covered his slaves in a mixture of honey and milk and stationed them around his palace."

"But it didn't work. Did it? I mean . . . that poor man . . . he was covered . . ."

"I expect it was his aftershave," said Dr. Bairstow, taking full advantage of their momentary confusion. "If you could just sign here, please . . . and here . . . and here. Thank you so much."

MUCH OF THE STRUCTURAL work was completed and St. Mary's was, allegedly, weatherproof. Miscellaneous articles of furniture continued to mushroom. Literally, in some cases. Mismatched curtains adorned dusty windows. The acquisition of enough chairs for everyone to be able to sit simultaneously was celebrated by the first St. Mary's All Comers Yodelling Contest, in which a blushing Mrs. Enderby was persuaded to present the prizes, although, as Major Guthrie commented afterwards to Dr. Bairstow, the standard had not been high.

The young man from SPOHB, sporting his most exciting knitwear, asked Miss Spindle for her hand in marriage and was politely but firmly rejected. It was subsequently discovered that she had cut her hair, acquired contact lenses, left SPOHB, and taken up a position with a male modelling agency.

ST. MARY'S CONTINUED TO take care of itself until, one day, Ritter and Evans erupted in a simultaneous rash, Markham fell out of a tree and landed on his head, and Dr. Dowson developed a chesty cough. Since St. Mary's entire medical expertise consisted of two aspirin and an early night, Dr. Bairstow perceived the time had come to expand St. Mary's meagre health facilities.

Boarding yet another train, he made his way southeast, to a small town not noted for its prosperity. Alighting in a bitter wind, he turned up his coat collar, sought directions from an individual who was a stranger to the area, and set off in what he hoped was the right direction. Ten minutes later, he found himself outside the hospital, where they disclaimed all knowledge and directed him to the free clinic. Taking a seat in the crowded, noisy waiting room, he obeyed instructions and waited.

And waited.

And waited. But he was prepared to be patient.

A curtain swept back on its rings and a doctor emerged, followed by a woman towing a very fat boy, rather like a small moon on a string.

The doctor, a tall woman with her dark hair bound up in a red and white scarf and sporting a T-shirt bearing the legend *Does Not Play Well With Others*, finished writing and handed the mother a piece of paper.

"Nothing serious. Certainly nothing that ceasing to stuff his fat face on chocolate and crisps all day won't cure. Five pieces of fruit and vegetables a day will sort him out. Plenty of exercise, too."

"But he doesn't like . . ."

"I don't care what he does and doesn't like. Continue on this course and you'll be looking at morbid obesity, diabetes, heart trouble, high blood pressure, undescended testicles, and complete unattractiveness to the opposite sex. You . . ." she addressed herself to the fat boy. "Put down the computer games and get yourself outside. Fresh air won't kill you. Not enough exercise will."

"But he doesn't . . ." wailed the woman.

The doctor shrugged. "OK then. Suit yourself. Dead by thirty. Probably best if he doesn't start watching any long-running TV series. Your choice. Next."

Dr. Bairstow rose to his feet. "Dr. Foster?"

"Yes? And?"

"I wonder if might have a word."

She surveyed the crowded room. "You are joking."

"No. Never."

She stared at him for a moment. "Two minutes."

"More than adequate."

She jerked her head towards the cubicle and made to follow him inside. Pausing suddenly, she surveyed those still waiting and shouted, "Hey! You! Yes, you at the back! I know why you're here. I've told you before—you have a congenital weakness in your hands and if you continue punching your wife you will do yourself irreparable damage. I'm not prepared to waste my time treating you if you're just ignoring everything I say." She rummaged in her jeans pocket. "I need you to sign this piece of paper saying that if you end up paralysed it's all your own fault for continuing to beat up your wife against medical advice, and this clinic is not in any way responsible."

Heads turned, seeking the subject of these remarkable statements. At the back, a man rose hastily to his feet and tried to slip away.

"No, don't go. Not until you've signed this. Alternatively, of course, you could just stop hitting your wife. Why not give it a go? You'll find your hands will stop hurting and she'll probably appreciate it too."

The doors swung shut behind him.

Dr. Bairstow could not help enquiring, "Was that entirely wise, do you think? I cannot help but feel his wife might suffer considerably at their next encounter."

"There won't be one. His wife is in the next cubicle having her eye stitched up. Again. We needed to get rid of him so she can slip out the back way and off to the shelter. They're waiting for her. What do you want?"

"I want you and I've travelled a very long way to find you. No, don't speak, please. I've read your career history and it's impressive. Your attitude—that's the one that occasionally gets you into a little difficulty—is exactly what I am looking for. I need a doctor who can impose herself upon a group of over-excited and over-educated idiots, and be able to cope with the undoubtedly imaginative ways with which they will try to kill themselves and everyone around them."

"Are we talking about a loony-bin?"

"An astonishingly accurate statement, but no."

She stared at him. "I don't do compassion."

"I'm very glad to hear that."

"Or sympathy."

"That is excellent news. Do you do swift and effective treatment? Can you save lives on a daily basis? Are you able to improvise? Think creatively? Keep your head amid chaos?"

"Who *are* you?"

"My name is Dr. Bairstow. You are Dr. Helen Foster and I would like to offer you the position of Chief Medical Officer."

"No."

"Allow me to give you my card."

"No."

"I have written my telephone number on the back."

"I said no. Are you deaf?"

"Well, if you take up my offer, then we shall be able to find out."

"I do good work here."

"I don't doubt it, but I am offering you the opportunity to do great work with me. The combination of your skillset and attitude renders you unique. Please, I beg you, at least consider the offer."

She stared at him for a while, her dark eyes assessing what she saw. She opened her mouth to speak, and as she did so, two men, locked together, tumbled from another cubicle, crashed to the floor, and began to roll around, flailing and kicking. Trolleys toppled over, shedding bowls and implements everywhere. A number of security personnel appeared and manhandled them out of the door.

"Well," she said, "at least I wouldn't have to put up with this sort of thing ten times a day."

Something in his silence made her turn to look at him. "Would I?"

"Well not ten times a day, of course . . ."

She opened her mouth, but he was already pushing his way through the double doors and down the steps.

Six.

MORE TIME WORE ON. More people assembled at St. Mary's. The structure jokingly known as Hawking Hangar inched its way towards completion.

Dr. Bairstow, exhibiting signs of what might, in a lesser man, be classed as anxiety, was frequently seen to be consulting some sort of schedule. The word "deadline" was on everyone's lips. Tempers frayed. Some snapped altogether and after an exciting session between the newly arrived technical staff and the Security Section, in which views and punches were liberally exchanged, Major Guthrie requested a word with Dr. Bairstow.

"With your permission, sir, and before someone is seriously injured, I'd like to provide some sort of safe outlet for these . . . difficult moments."

"An excellent idea, Major. How about cricket? Exciting, dramatic, and yet requiring skill, coordination, and a sense of fair play—exactly what is required."

"What an excellent idea, sir," said Major Guthrie carefully, "but given the numbers involved and the inadvisability of arming them with bats and pointed sticks, I think football might provide a more effective channel for high spirits."

Dr. Bairstow seemed doubtful. "Well, if you say so. I personally always found that half-a-dozen overs after lunch could cure most ills but possibly, in view of the number of casualties currently inhabiting Sick Bay, football will provide a more effective means of venting the violently homicidal urges demonstrated today."

"I quite agree, sir. Was there anything else?"

"I'm afraid so, Major. Walk with me to Hawking, if you please."

Together, they surveyed the coils of cabling, junction boxes, sacks of concrete, cement mixers, and all the other miscellaneous equipment of a building uncompleted.

"I am sorry, Major, but, for reasons I cannot yet explain, it is imperative this area of St. Mary's is completed by Friday night."

"I have to say, sir, there is very little likelihood of us achieving that deadline."

"That is what I am afraid of."

"Is it at all possible to prioritise, sir?"

Dr. Bairstow stood deep in thought. "An excellent idea, Major. Come with me."

He turned and left the hangar and they stood at the foot of Sick Bay stairs. To their right, the unfinished hangar. To their left, the recently completed long corridor led back to the main building. Ahead of them stretched a short corridor, with various doors opening off it.

Dr. Bairstow limped to the end and halted outside a door.

Major Guthrie consulted his plans. "This room is designated as a paint store, sir." He pushed open the door, revealing a small square room, at present empty except for copious amounts of dust.

Dr. Bairstow stood thoughtfully.

"Sir?"

"Actually, I think this may be for the best after all, Major."

"Sir?"

"Find the foreman, if you would be so good. I want electrical sockets and cable points set up in the back corner there. Ask him to pull his people off everything else. If the work can be completed before five o'clock on Friday night there will be a substantial cash bonus in it for him and his team that we probably won't need to trouble his employers with."

"How substantial, sir?"

"Extremely substantial. On the rare occasions I have to resort to bribery, I like to make a good job of it."

BY FIVE O'CLOCK ON Friday night, the seemingly impossible had been achieved.

Half a dozen exhausted, dusty, hollow-eyed workers had worked the clock round, completed their task, enjoyed a drink at Dr. Bairstow's expense, trousered an unspecified but gratifyingly large amount of cash, and departed for the weekend.

St. Mary's heaved a sigh of relief and put its feet up in the bar, where Dr. Bairstow's unprecedented generosity had provided for them also. It seemed safe to assume they would be there for the foreseeable future.

The rest of the building was very silent as Dr. Bairstow limped carefully down the stairs, through the Hall, and down the long corridor. There, he paused for a while, listening, but other than the echoes of voices raised in song and high spirits, there was nothing but the sounds of a building bedding itself down for the night. Wood creaked. A tiny piece of plaster fell from the ceiling. The smell of wet concrete was very strong.

Standing outside the door to the paint store, Dr. Bairstow checked his watch for the hundredth time and waited. His face gave nothing away.

He checked his watch again.

Somewhere, another piece of plaster fell.

Dr. Bairstow consulted his watch again. The second hand, glowing green in the semi-darkness, swept on.

He shifted his weight a little.

Silence settled all around him. As if the world waited.

And then, the paint-store door creaked slowly open.

Dr. Bairstow drew himself up.

A dark shadow stood silhouetted against a darker room.

"Leon Farrell, sir, reporting for duty."

"Good evening, Leon. You appear to be late."

"Good evening, Edward. You appear to be standing in the dark."

"My dear chap, if you knew the cost of electricity in this time . . ."

He stepped forwards as he spoke and the two men shook hands.

"Leon, it has been a very long time."

They remained clasping hands for a while, although no words were spoken. At last, they fell back and looked at each other.

"How are you, Leon?"

"Not so very different from the last time we met. But looking forward to a new beginning."

"No regrets?"

"At leaving behind my old life? None at all. How about you?"

"Like you, no regrets. A new start for both of us."

"So, how are you, Edward?"

"Exhilarated. Frustrated. Enthusiastic. Excited. Exhausted. Impatient for completion."

"Not long now."

"I hope not. This way."

They turned into the dimly lit long corridor and turned to look at each other properly.

"Leon, you haven't changed at all."

"Well, that's because I haven't. I just waited a few minutes and then jumped after you." He paused. "I'll say this just once, Edward. You look tired."

"I am tired. The years have been long and there was never anyone else to—"

"Well, there is now." Leon Farrell stopped to stare out of a window into the dusk. "So, this is England. What is it like? Is it very bad?"

Dr. Bairstow nodded. "Yes, yes it is. Much worse than the records had led us to believe. Oh, I'm not talking about the physical rebuilding of a nation; I'm talking about the people. Lost, bewildered, without hope. Can there be anything worse than winning one of the greatest struggles in their nation's history and then not having the strength of purpose or the money to build on that. I tell you, Leon, when I saw what it was like, I nearly jumped straight home and requested we postpone for twenty years."

"But you didn't."

"No, I didn't. It occurred to me that in some small way, I could make a contribution. Rebuilding St. Mary's has provided jobs and purpose. Building pods will provide more. I am slowly recruiting admin staff. I have a few historians already lined up and if you could see the sudden hope in their eyes. To go in an instant from counting oneself lucky to be working in a factory for less than minimum wage to finding oneself with a job, a purpose—and what a purpose."

He stopped suddenly and Leon Farrell turned away to examine the long corridor and its bare walls with every sign of interest.

Presently, he said, "So when do I start building pods?"

"Well, Number Two is here already. I would be grateful if you could keep yours quietly tucked away for the time being."

Farrell nodded.

"I'd like another three pods as soon as you can assemble them."

"Three?"

"An enormous amount of money has been invested and I'm being pressed for results—which I am eager to provide."

"If you want three pods then I'm going to need some staff."

"If you can make it as far as the bar, then I can introduce you to your recently arrived team, and especially to a rather large but gifted young man named Dieter, fresh from the Institute of Engineering at Marienstrasse, where, I understand, they spoke very highly of him."

"That sounds good."

"The bar or the gifted young man?"

They walked slowly down the long corridor.

Later that night, Dr. Bairstow was to make another and final tick in his notebook

Seven.

MORE TIME PASSED.

To the great alarm of SPOHB, St. Mary's expanded. Dr. Bairstow's attempts to reassure them by pointing out that for every expansion there was an equal and opposite contraction, usually caused by something else falling down or blowing up, and that he personally felt that the removal of the hideous Victorian clock tower considerably improved the appearance of this fine old building, however helpfully intentioned, were not well received. A bombardment of reproachful memos and the threat of legal action followed. Dr. Bairstow compromised by promising to instruct Professor Rapson to take more care in future.

Mr. Markham, competing in the bicycle jousting tournament, took a nasty tumble over his own handlebars and opened his eyes to find the new nurse, a vision of blonde loveliness, regarding him with a distinct lack of sympathy. Asked what his name was and if he knew what day of the week it was, he found himself unable to answer either question, and was instantly admitted to the new paint-smelling Sick Bay.

When it subsequently became apparent that this temporary loss of faculties was not in any way due to the injury to his head, but rather to his heart, the vision of blonde loveliness heartlessly evicted him from Sick Bay with threats of violence and astonishingly bad language.

The Very First Assignment—to observe Julius Caesar's landing on the south coast of Britain in August 55 BC—was generally felt to have been a mixed success. On the one hand, very little of the landing was actually observed—on the other, everyone survived.

Emerging from their pod on this inaugural event, Dr. Bairstow, together with historians Lower and Baverstock, discovered themselves to have inadvertently landed on the shoreline, approximately midpoint between the Roman legions on one hand and a bunch of very miffed Brits on the other. Finding themselves being regarded with equal hostility by everyone present, they beat a hasty retreat. Fighting their way through a hail of projectiles raining down impartially from both sides, they eventually gained the safety of their pod where Baverstock was heard to enquire, "Dare we hope, sir, that any future perambulations will be accomplished in a more sedate manner?"

Dr. Bairstow's response, "By all means if that makes you feel more comfortable," was deemed to be perfectly acceptable, and they returned in triumph to enjoy, as Mr. Markham had phrased it—The St. Mary's Inaugural Bash.

AND THEN, ONE MILD autumn day . . .

For the umpteenth time that day, Dr. Bairstow got to his feet and limped to his office window. Again, he carefully checked his watch against the old clock in the corner. An observer might have said he was nervous.

The sight that met his eyes was very different from the one that had greeted him on the day of his arrival. The drive was now smooth and pothole free. Rose beds had been planted by the terrace. The South Lawn, under Mr. Strong's obsessive care, rolled gently down to the lake where several swans serenely floated. Dr. Bairstow frowned. Last week they had been pink. It would appear that, as per his instructions, some attempts had been made to remedy the situation because today they were blue.

Averting his gaze, he lifted his eyes to the woods surrounding St. Mary's and beyond them to the moors, whose bracken was already beginning to turn flaming red and gold under the sunny blue sky.

Outwardly peaceful and still, St. Mary's dreamed the day away. As did Dr. Bairstow, snatching a brief moment from his crowded desk to relive old memories and old achievements. He leaned more heavily on his stick and smiled into the past.

Waiting . . .

A small movement brought his attention back to the present. A taxi had pulled up outside the gates and was turning around, possibly for a quick getaway. St. Mary's had acquired a certain reputation . . .

His attention sharpened. A small figure had climbed out and was paying off the driver.

Turning, she stood at the gates. He watched her speak into the intercom. The gates opened. She did not enter for a moment, but stood for some time, taking it all in. She wore a cheap, dark suit and carried nothing in her hands. Her short, spiky hair was exactly the same colour as the autumn bracken on the moors.

Mistakenly concluding that for the most part, St. Mary's seemed harmless enough, she stepped through the gates, and began to walk slowly up the drive. The gates closed silently behind her. She did not look back.

Dr. Bairstow smiled gently to himself, nodded, turned from the window, and limped to his desk.

Picking up the telephone, he said, "Leon, I thought you might like to know. She's here."

THE GREAT ST. MARY'S DAY OUT

AUTHOR'S NOTE

*W*ELL, NOW I'VE REALLY done it. It's hard to count the number of liberties I've taken with this one. Shakespeare. *Hamlet*. Elizabethan theatre. The Globe. Dr. Bairstow's sensibilities. You name it, I've twisted it all to suit my story. If you have an interest in any of the above areas, you might want to skip this one.

The story was originally to be entitled "The Great St. Mary's Day Out", but half way through, I rather thought I preferred, "The Man Who Dropped Shakespeare." That got knocked on the head—rather like Shakespeare himself—so back I went to "The Great St. Mary's Day Out."

I'm afraid it rather appealed to my warped sense of humour to have everyone skidding off the rails as fast as they can go and, just for once, Max is the one sticking to the job and completing the assignment. I mean, it was a foregone conclusion that something horrible was going to happen to Professor Rapson. I did briefly consider letting him be carried away to the New World, but he's such fun that I couldn't part with him in the end. I did rather like the idea of Mrs. Mack and Dr. Bairstow initiating a street brawl and then having to account for their actions to Max.

Markham, of course, having saved the day, is up to his neck in trouble again, but it wouldn't be a St. Mary's story without him facing Dr. Bairstow across his desk and vainly trying to account for his actions.

And who'd have thought I'd ever manage to get the words "Dr. Bairstow" and "selfie" in the same sentence!

THE GREAT ST. MARY'S DAY OUT

I WALKED MATTHEW AROUND St. Mary's because a few things needed to be made clear.

"All right, people. This is a baby. A small human. His name is Matthew and he is not to be floated across the lake in a Moses basket just to see if it could have happened. Nor is he to be stuffed into a warming pan and smuggled into someone's bed. He is not to be dangled off a balcony and presented to the Welsh people as a non-English-speaking Prince of Wales. Permission to include him in any of the imaginative events currently being planned by the History Department is to be sought from his father, Chief Farrell, and good luck to anyone trying that. He is not to be used as a paperweight. Or ballast. Or a draught excluder. Everyone clear?"

You have to tell people these things. Especially at St. Mary's.

IT WAS A GOLDEN time for me. In every sense of the word. Autumn wasn't giving in to winter without a fight. The trees glowed in the late sunshine—gold, russet, red, and orange. In a week, the leaves would begin to fall and Mr. Strong, our caretaker, would gather them up for burning, bringing the sharp smell of bonfires on the breeze.

The three of us, Leon, Matthew, and I, were back at St. Mary's. Without ever having left, actually. Dr. Bairstow had requested we remain here while the vexing question of Clive Ronan was resolved. For our own safety. I wasn't bothered and Leon was in full "Anyone Messing With My Family Will Regret It" mode, and we lived happily in a small suite of rooms up in the attic, so no one could be disturbed by a crying baby.

In fact, he rarely cried—which, as Leon said, just went to show our son was a born historian and already completely failing to live up to popular expectations. He was a happy baby, placidly accepting being passed from person to person, smiling up at whoever happened to have custody of him at the time. He had his favourites, of course. He adored Mrs. Enderby, Head of the Wardrobe Department. It was mutual: she was always running him up dinky little clothes to wear. Peterson claimed Matthew was easily the best-dressed person in the place, but since that place also contained Bashford, Markham, and Professor Rapson—who frequently had to be sartorially checked over before he ventured out in public—this wasn't the achievement it seemed.

Matthew's second favourite, astonishingly, was the multi-hued Miss Lingoss from R&D. He would gaze, big-eyed, at whatever hair colour and style she had adopted that particular day, and she, black-leather clad and embellished with chains and safety pins, would beam back at him.

Leon went back to work shortly after Matthew was born, and I wafted around the place for three or four months, playing with Matthew, painting, and generally getting on people's nerves. The usual maternity-leave activities. I was determined to make the most of things before I went back to work.

My return happened a little more quickly than I had expected. But in a good way.

OCCASIONALLY, VERY OCCASIONALLY, THE Boss finds some money tucked away somewhere and gives us a bit of a treat.

Rumour has it that he deposited a penny in an obscure foreign bank some ten centuries ago, and is quietly reaping the benefits today. Unlikely, but in our job, we've learned never to rule anything out.

However he found the money, find it he did, and suddenly he was calling an all-staff briefing in the Great Hall, and announcing a forthcoming assignment, which would be open to anyone who cared to avail themselves of the opportunity.

Standing on the half-landing, with shafts of sunlight highlighting the last defiant remains of his hair, he began to bring up a series of images on the screen.

"June, 1601." He paused, surveying the rows of upturned faces before him.

Silence greeted his remark. If he has a weakness, it's that he's a bit of a showman, and he does tend to dole out information in tiny dollops. We've learned not to play along.

"London," he said, piling on the narrative tension.

He began to flick through various images, inching painfully along the information highway before finally arriving at his destination.

"Ladies and gentlemen—the Globe Theatre."

Oh, wow! A chance to see the Globe Theatre. The real Globe Theatre, I mean. Not the very excellent replica we see today, but the actual Globe itself. Shakespeare's Globe. Performing Shakespeare's plays. In a contemporary setting. By contemporary actors. Watched by a contemporary audience. You get the drift.

But which play? 1601? I racked my brains—but not for long.

"We shall, I hope, be attending a performance of *Hamlet, Prince of Denmark,* with . . ."

Sensing he was building up to his big finish, a stir ran around the Great Hall.

". . . with William Shakespeare himself taking the role of the Ghost."

An even more stunned silence greeted this remark. He paused, leaning on his stick, well pleased with the sensation he had created. And rightly so. We would be seeing *Hamlet*—the famous production starring Richard Burbage as the dithering Dane . . . and with Shakespeare himself as the Ghost. This was just . . . I groped for a word more amazing than amazing, failed to find one, and resurfaced to find Markham and Peterson gabbling with excitement. And they weren't the only ones.

"Participation is voluntary," continued Dr. Bairstow, cutting across us, because we're a bit of a gobby bunch sometimes, and if he waited for the noise to die down then we'd all be there forever. "So, if those wishing to participate in this treat could give their names to Dr. Maxwell by close of today, please. Report to Mrs. Enderby for costume fittings, collect your background research tapes from Dr. Dowson, read up on the play itself, and report to Hawking Hangar at 11:00 two weeks from today. Any questions?"

I really don't know why he bothers with that last bit. He was already halfway up the stairs and picking up speed. Popular opinion has it that once every couple of years Thirsk University compels him to attend a series of seminars on Modern Management, through which he sits, unspeaking and rigid with disapproval, until their nerve fails them and they return him to us, possibly even less modern than he was before he set out. However, since he can't bear to waste the money, he forces himself to implement one or two very minor changes every year, such as remembering to command us to sit down—especially if we've been wounded—or asking if anyone has any questions. It is always clearly understood that no one ever will. Have any questions, I mean. He did once utter the memorable phrase, "Please remember my door is always open," and it would be hard to say who had been most traumatised by this remarkable statement.

However, as usual, there were no questions and we were left to discuss what amounted to a work outing amongst ourselves.

"I'm not going," said Bashford, firmly. "I suffered enough at school. Long boring afternoons reading endless verse. Even the flies on the ceiling died in self-defence."

"Me neither," said Clerk. "Couldn't stand it at school; hated it on TV; see no reason why it should be any better in the rain, sitting on seats designed to numb your bum in seconds. Not my idea of a holiday."

"Philistines," I said, turning to Markham. "What about you?"

"Are you serious?" he said, his eyes shining and his hair even spikier with excitement. "Course I'm going. Who wouldn't?"

Peterson stared at him. "*You* like Shakespeare?"

"Oh, yeah," he said with enthusiasm. "*Hamlet's* not my favourite, of course. I prefer *A Midsummer Night's Dream* or *The Tempest*, but that bit where he stabs Polonius in the arras . . ."

He mimed stabbing Polonius in the arras.

"When did you ever read *Hamlet*?" demanded Peterson.

"At school. Didn't you? And I've seen several versions of the play. Not live, of course. Can't afford it on my wages." We all looked nervously over our shoulders, but Dr. Bairstow really had gone. "Olivier, Tennant, Branagh, all the greats, and now I'll get to see Burbage. And Shakespeare himself. Although as the Ghost he'll probably be all muffled up so I won't be able to see his face at all, but even so . . . I must see if Hunter wants to go as well," and he disappeared.

"He never fails to astound me," said Leon, watching him elbow his way through crowds of chattering people.

"Nor me," I said. I pulled Leon to one side and lowered my voice. "Did you ever discover his marital status?"

Not so long ago, we—Leon, Markham, and I—had been having a perfectly normal conversation about whether Peterson would survive his proposal of marriage to Dr. Foster, or whether the worryingly long silence from her office was due to her having murdered and possibly eaten him, when Markham had suddenly let slip that he himself was married. To Nurse Hunter. They'd been married for years. He said. We didn't know whether it was true or whether he was just winding us up and, so far, all our efforts to pin him to the wall and beat the truth out of him had been unsuccessful.

Leon shook his head. "These are deep waters in which I'm not prepared to swim. He said he was married so he probably is. Even he couldn't get that wrong. Let's just leave it at that, shall we?"

I smiled in what I thought was a winning manner. "You could ask Hunter."

He remained unmoved. "Or *you* could ask Hunter."

"Or we could get Peterson to ask Hunter."

He grinned. "These days, I'd be astonished if Peterson even knows what day of the week it is."

"I know. Who'd have thought she would say yes?"

"Do you think people are following our good example?"

"I'm surprised they don't regard us as a horrible warning."

He looked down at me. "I thought you quite liked being married."

"Yes," I said, considering. "Some days it's not too bad."

He folded his arms. "That's it? That's all you've got? 'Some days it's not too bad'?"

"I thought you would prefer that to 'Some days it's really not good at all.' Anyway, can we please stop talking about matrimony? Will you be taking part in this cultural jaunt?"

We don't both go on the same jumps—that was the deal. We'd shaken hands on it. Because if anything horrible ever happened—and it usually does—then our baby son would be an orphan.

He shook his head. "Not if you want to go."

"Do you want to toss for it?"

"No. You take this one. I'll have first refusal on the next."

"Deal."

We shook on this too.

PEOPLE WERE IN AND out of my office all day. I got no work done at all.

"Nothing new there then," said my assistant, Rosie Lee.

I regarded her coldly. "Why are you here?"

"I work here."

"Really? When did that happen?"

"If you were ever here, you'd be able to answer that question yourself."

I decided to ignore this. "Could you get me the King Alfred file, please?"

She regarded me with some hostility. I hastened to make things easier for her.

"A file is a collection of documents. In a blue folder. Blue for the History Department." I plucked at my blue jumpsuit to make my point.

The hostile stare did not waver.

"And it will have Alfred the Great and the file reference in the top right hand . . ."

"Just like that one on your desk there?"

". . . corner, just like this one on my desk here."

I picked up the file and opened it.

She stood up. "Comfort break."

"Make my tea first. You know the rules."

She sighed loudly. "If we had union representation here then I wouldn't have to do this."

"If we had union representation here then you'd never have been employed in the first place."

She banged the kettle down. "I should be paid what I'm worth."

"You'd better hope you never are. Where's my tea?"

She changed the subject. "So who's going then?"

I scrabbled through my bits of paper. "A mixed bunch. Dr. Bairstow, of course, which is nice because he doesn't get out much. Peterson, Markham, Guthrie, North, Sykes, Atherton, Mrs. Enderby—costume research, she says—Mrs. Mack, because she wants to check out what people are eating, Evans, Keller, Professor Rapson, and Dr. Dowson—obviously because the 17th century isn't a time in which they've blown something up yet and they want to rectify that situation as soon as possible—and Lingoss."

She stared at me. "Aren't you going? I was hoping to be rid of you for a whole day."

"And me. I shall be leaving you a list of tasks to accomplish during my absence, although I don't know why—it's not as if you accomplish any tasks during my presence. And I shall be locking up the chocolate biscuits, of course."

My mug of tea was banged down in front of me with quite unnecessary force.

SINCE CLERK WASN'T GOING on this one, I was the designated driver. Or mission controller if you want to give me my correct title. Which no one ever did. I had to endure many enquiries as to whether I could remember what to do.

We assembled outside TB2—our big transport pod. I'd calculated that we'd need at least four smaller pods to fit all of us in and that many would make us conspicuous. Besides, with so many inexperienced people on the assignment, I preferred us to jump together. I didn't want anyone being left behind if we had to leave in a hurry, and all the evidence to date suggested that we would.

I ran my eye over the group. We were dressed as lower middle-class citizens. Unimportant but relatively prosperous. Our clothing was dark and respectable, but the material was as good as the Sumptuary Laws allowed. This was an age where clothing defined social status—and vice versa. Peterson had suggested Markham wear a small sack.

I wore a linen chemise, high at the neck, with a dark brown woollen dress over the top, belted at the memory of my waist. My bum roll gave me that authentic wide-hipped Tudor look, although strictly speaking, the bum roll might not have been necessary. I'd covered my hair with a coif and looked every inch the respectable Tudor matron. All the women wore variations on the same theme in shades of brown and russet. The men wore linen shirts and doublets with leather or woollen sleeveless jerkins over the top, trousers to their knees and shoes and stockings. And beards. Well, as much beard as they'd managed to assemble in a little under a fortnight. Which in some cases wasn't very much at all. There had been general mocking and ridicule.

Bearing in mind the length of the performance, I was carrying a broad-weave wicker basket containing bread, cheese, a small pasty, two apples, a flask of water, and a toilet roll. I'd covered all the contents with a heavy cloak in which I had secreted a bar of chocolate the size of Plynlimon.

"It's June," said Peterson, in amusement, looking at my cloak.

"June can be very chilly at this time of year."

WE LANDED IN BANKSIDE, at the back of the Bear Garden, which, mercifully, appeared to be closed for the day. The Bear Garden was synonymous with noise, confusion, turmoil, and unruly behaviour. Hence the expression—noisy as a Bear Garden. According to Leon, it's only a matter of time before Bear Garden is deleted and St. Mary's inserted instead. I wondered if perhaps they didn't open on Globe performance days—too much competition. Whatever the reason, the massive wooden structure—actually very similar in shape to the Globe—was silent today.

We walked quickly past. Southwark is not a respectable area, being full of taverns, bear pits, whorehouses, and the like. And the Globe, of course—actors being considered the dregs of society and best kept outside the city walls.

The day was overcast, with heavy clouds, but warm enough. "Hope it's not going to rain," said Markham, glancing up at the sky.

I had split us into three groups of five. Not feeling that either Miss Sykes or Dr. Bairstow were yet ready to spend several hours in each other's company, I'd lumped her in with the other two weirdos, Dr. Dowson and Professor Rapson, with Keller from Security and sensible, steady Atherton to keep them in order.

The next group—the Respectable Team as I'd named them in my head—consisted of Dr. Bairstow, Miss North, Mrs. Enderby, and Mrs. Mack. It was hard to see how any of that lot could topple off the rails, so they had only Major Guthrie to keep them in line.

I'd spent a great deal of time trying to achieve this happy mix of departments—"happy" being a more appropriate word than "balanced." And more accurate, too.

My group consisted of Peterson and me—historians—Evans and Markham—security—and Miss Lingoss, whose purple hair was currently being restrained by copious amounts of hair gel and an industrial-strength wimple.

We had a few hours to kill before the performance started. Dr. Bairstow doled out the spending money with all the reluctance of Scrooge handing a penny to a starving orphan in a snowstorm, and the other two teams disappeared. The Weirdos were off to the docks because Professor Rapson was passing through one of his nautical phases and wanted to check out the ships moored below London Bridge. Under Elizabeth, England was a powerful maritime nation. Sir Francis Drake had circumnavigated the world, English ships were trading everywhere, and piracy was the career of choice for many adventurous young men.

The Respectable Team were off to investigate the markets. Mesdames Mack and Enderby were practically frothing at the mouth in anticipation of investigating Tudor food and haberdashery. It seemed safe to assume that in the company of Major Guthrie and Dr. Bairstow, nothing much could go wrong there, either.

Our beat was Borough High Street and London Bridge.

"Max and I have been here before," said Peterson to the others. "We'll show you around if you like."

We emerged into the crowded, noisy high street and looked around.

Peterson inhaled deeply. "Don't you just love the smell of History in the morning?"

I stood for a moment, lost in the past. Yes, even more in the past than 1601, because Peterson was right—we'd been here before, back in the 14th century, and almost nothing had changed. Some of the houses fronting Borough High Street were larger and more modern, but not many. The road was still more than ankle deep in dust, old vegetables, rotting straw, animal shit, human shit, and some evil-smelling, greyish pink tubes that smelled so bad that even a passing dog left them alone. People still yelled at each other at the tops of their voices. Women shouldered their way through the throng with baskets over their arms. A goose-girl struggled to keep her flock together. Occasionally a dust-covered rider on a lathered horse would force his way towards the bridge, possibly carrying a message for the Queen. One nearly knocked us over and Peterson pulled us back against the wall out of the way.

We brushed off the dust of his passing. "Hey," said Peterson, staring over my shoulder, "St. Thomas's Hospital is just down there. Remember?"

"How could I ever forget?"

"I got bubonic plague."

"Yes, I remember."

"And then I peed on you."

"Yes, I remember that too."

"We should erect a plaque."

"In that case, there should be one on Westminster Abbey too, because you peed on me there, as well."

He smiled at me fondly. "Nothing but the best for you, Max."

We wandered along Borough High Street, down towards London Bridge.

"It doesn't actually look that different from the last time," said Tim, staring about him.

"How would you know? You were unconscious for most of it."

"Self-defence. I took one look at you aiming that knife at my privates and chose unconsciousness."

"You fainted, you wuss."

"He should be so lucky," said Markham. "I remember going to Egypt with her once. One minute everything's fine and the next minute she's ripping off my clothes and chucking me in the Nile."

"For your own good," I said, indignantly.

"Yeah, well, don't get any ideas today.

"This was a voluntary assignment. You didn't have to come."

"Like two historians and her . . ." he nodded his head at Miss Lingoss, "are likely to get more than ten feet without needing the help of the Security Section."

"He does get agitated these days," said Peterson, thoughtfully. "Do you think married life is getting him down?"

We waited hopefully.

"What gets me down," said Markham, heatedly, "is being out in the field with you three without a battalion of marines, a couple of tank regiments, and air cover to back me up."

Time to change the subject.

"Anyway," said Peterson, looking up and down the street, "the buildings are much the same, the church is still here. The Tabard is still up there. Shame we missed Chaucer."

"Well, if you hadn't contracted the plague then we wouldn't have, would we?"

"Are you ever going to let that drop?"

"I wonder what happened to Brother Anselm."

Brother Anselm was the monk who had given us shelter while Peterson recovered from what he still referred to as his "slight twinge of bubonic plague." I remembered his bright, bird-like gaze and his gentle kindness.

Peterson smiled at his own memory and then said, "I'm sure he spent his days busily and happily and reaped his just reward in the end."

"I hope so."

We walked down to the river, which was heaving with boats. In these days, the streets were so narrow and badly paved that the Thames was *the* major thoroughfare. Water boatmen ferried people around in wherries or skiffs. Up and down as well as from one side to another. Their boats ranged in size from flimsy-looking coracle-style craft to substantial boats that could take up to ten people. They were all doing a roaring trade because London still only had the one bridge and that was packed with people as well. It was obviously easier and quicker to move by river.

Heavily laden barges fought against the current as they ferried their commercial cargoes upstream. Occasionally, a horn would blast as someone important sought to force their way up or down river. There didn't seem to be a traffic system of any kind. Boats milled about in all directions. Boatmen roared abuse at each other and even their passengers exchanged insults and less than polite instructions to get out of the way.

The bigger boats were moored south of London Bridge. I stared downriver at the forest of masts, black against the sky.

"Is that *the* London Bridge?" said Evans, in awe. "Are those houses on it? Do people actually live on the bridge?"

"They do," said Peterson. "And it's not only houses, either. There's a chapel, shops, a mill, even a gatehouse complete with drawbridge. May I draw your attention to the severed heads displayed up there?"

"Cool," said Lingoss, squinting for a better view and we all stared at the massive structure that was London Bridge, with its nineteen gothic arches and seven-storey buildings, many of which overhung the river. Useful for a quick pee, I suppose. You just hung your bum out of the window.

"It's very top heavy," said Evans. "Why doesn't it fall down?"

"Well, bits of it do occasionally," said Peterson, "and there's always rows about the upkeep. Hence the nursery rhyme."

"What nursery rhyme?"

He grinned. "You know the one. 'London Bridge is Falling Down.' Great lumps of it are always dropping off and in 1281, Queen Eleanor, not a popular woman anyway, was accused of diverting money set aside for the upkeep of the bridge to her own personal use. Hence the 'My fair lady' bit at the end."

"Is that what it means? My mum used to sing me that. And 'Ring o' Ring o' Roses'."

"Oh yes," I said. "The Great Plague of 1665. 'The pocket full of posies' or flowers, was supposed to keep the plague away, and the 'Atishoo, atishoo, we all fall down' bit relates to the people dropping dead in the streets."

Evans stared at us. "You're kidding me."

"I kid you not. And I bet you played 'Oranges and Lemons' when you were a kid. The song follows the route of condemned

criminals as they're marched through the streets to their execution. It names the churches on the way and ends with 'Here
comes the chopper to chop off your head.'"

"Stop," said Evans, looking quite shocked. Our security
team is a sensitive bunch.

"Or," said Lingoss, entering into the spirit of things, "'Mary,
Mary, quite contrary,' is Bloody Mary, torturing the Protestants.
The garden was the graveyard, the silver bells were the thumb-
screws, and the cockleshells apparently described the instru-
ments they attached to the male genitalia."

"Are you sure?" said Markham. "Because I always thought
the rhyme was about Mary Stuart—the Queen of Scots, and
the pretty maids related to her ladies in waiting. You know, the
four Marys."

Peterson chipped in. "Well, I heard it was about . . ."

"No. Shut up all of you," said Evans." I'm not standing
here in the 17th century listening to two historians, a certifi-
able madwoman, and him . . ." he nodded towards Markham,
"arguing about genitals and executions. I need a drink."

"Excellent idea," said Peterson. "Let's go to the Tabard."

"Finally," I said. "It's only taken two hundred years."

WE STOOD IN THE corner of a packed courtyard. Markham,
Peterson and Evans knocked back three tankards of small ale.
The more intelligent sex drank from their water flasks. We
spent an hour or so just watching the people go by, speculating
on their identities and relationships, and enjoying ourselves so
much that we were nearly late for the performance. Fortunately,
since the streets were crowded, a lot of people were hurrying in
the same direction, so we allowed ourselves to be carried along.
The flag flew overhead, denoting there was to be a performance
that day. And we would be there. I felt a shiver of excitement.
Yes, I'd enjoyed my maternity leave, but until this moment, I
hadn't realised how much I'd missed my old life.

The Globe reared up in front of us, a big building by the standards of the day. After a dispute over the lease of their former theatre, the two Burbage brothers, Richard and Cuthbert, leased a plot of land on this side of the river, here in Southwark. They demolished their building, appropriately known as the Theatre, carried the timbers across the river, and rebuilt it, renaming it the Globe. Shakespeare himself bought a share in the building. Completed in 1599, it was a tremendous success, staging many of his plays until, during a performance of *Henry VIII*, a canon would misfire and the place would burn to the ground in a horrifyingly short time. It would be rebuilt and continue successfully until 1642, when the Puritans, as part of their mission to suck all the joy out of life, ordered its closure. It was demolished shortly afterwards.

There were people everywhere. *Hamlet* was obviously a very popular play. "I hope we can get in," I said, looking at the pushing crowds.

"They'll squeeze us in somehow," said Peterson, ushering us towards the entrance. "They can't afford to lose box-office receipts."

Our seating order had already been discussed. The posh people—Dr. Bairstow, Mrs. Enderby, Mrs. Mack, Sykes, North, and Major Guthrie were to be up in the gallery on the cushioned seats. At 6d per head. Or 6d per bottom, of course. Just to confuse things—a d is a penny. It's from the Latin *denarius*. Anyway, for them the grand total was a massive three shillings. Having probably put himself well over budget, Dr. Bairstow had given the rest of us to understand that we would be down in the Yard with the peasants. Or stinkards as they were known on hot days.

Having had our pennies doled out to us—I don't know what he'd had to do to obtain authentic Elizabethan currency from our employers, the University of Thirsk, but obtain it he had—we stood in line. Admission to the Yard was only a penny, which in those days was still not cheap.

With a great flourish, Peterson, our designated banker, slipped two ha'pennies, two pennies, and a tuppence into the box—hence the term, box office—and we were in.

We elbowed our way to a position close to the stage and looked around us for the others. At first, I thought I was just missing them in the crowd. I turned again. And again. No—we were the only team here.

I checked out the galleries, while Peterson, specially selected for his height, peered over people's heads, vainly looking for our colleagues.

"Can you see them anywhere?" I asked hopefully.

He shook his head. "Nope. No sign."

Great. The assignment barely begun and ten people missing already.

"It's like one of those Agatha Christie stories," said Lingoss cheerfully, "where everyone gets picked off one by one."

I refused to panic. Remembering the crush around the theatre, I was convinced they'd still be outside, trying to get in. Even I couldn't lose ten people. Especially when those ten people included the Director, the Head of Security, the Head of Wardrobe, the Kitchen Supremo, the Head of R&D, the Librarian, and possibly worst of all, Miss North, who is related to most of the aristocrats in the country. She counts four MPs within her immediate family circle, but to do her justice, never lets it hold her back.

On the other hand, the theatre was filling up fast and there was still no sign of the other teams.

I opened my com. "Dr. Bairstow?"

There was a short pause before he responded. "Ah, Dr. Maxwell. We appear to be experiencing some difficulty, but I believe Major Guthrie has everything in hand." He sounded breathless.

"Sir?"

"A very minor street altercation. Nothing of any great concern. Behind you, Mrs. Mack!"

The link was severed.

I stared at Peterson in dismay. If the Respectable Team were in trouble, in what world-ending cataclysm could Sykes and the other Weirdos possibly be involved?

With some misgivings, I began again. "Miss Sykes?"

"Oh, hello Max."

I did not make the mistake of assuming this cheerful greeting meant all was well. She'd be Hello Maxing me as the Apocalypse bore down upon us. In fact, there are those at St. Mary's who feel that Sykes herself might be the Apocalypse.

"Where are you?"

"Still at the docks."

"Why aren't you here at the theatre?"

Well, we're not too sure how it happened, but the professor wandered on to a ship bound for the New World and now they won't let him off."

"What? Why?"

"I think they think he's their passenger and they're due to sail. You know, tides and everything."

"Do *not* let that ship sail."

"Don't worry—we're on it."

"You'd better not be."

"No sorry, I meant we're on the situation—not the ship. Although we are."

"I'm sending assistance." I closed the link and turned to Peterson, who was grinning.

"On my way," he said.

"You too," said Markham to Evans.

"Your instructions are clear. Get Professor Rapson off that boat . . ."

"Ship," murmured Peterson.

". . . without bloodshed or major damage to property."

They pushed their way through the crowd, leaving Markham, Lingoss, and me.

"And then there were three," said Lingoss in a sinister voice. "Who'll be the next to go, do you think?"

Actually, it was Markham, although we didn't know that yet.

I took lots of deep breaths, which didn't work at all, and considered the situation. Dr. Bairstow and his team were embroiled in some sort of riot. Professor Rapson was possibly on his way to an American colony that had done nothing to deserve such a misfortune. I had no major fears for Dr. Bairstow's team. They had Dr. Bairstow and Major Guthrie. And should that front line crumble, they had Mrs. Mack, former urban terrorist, on their side. They'd be fine.

For a moment I considered joining Sykes in her mission to separate the professor from his involuntary Atlantic cruise, but Peterson would sort things out. And Dr. Bairstow had made it clear that my priority was to record the play. Personal interest aside, that was why we were here and returning without footage was not an option. Dr. Bairstow would frown at me, so whatever was going on outside, my job was to stay in the theatre. At my post. Mission controller going down with the ship. That sort of thing.

If the worst came to the worst—and it would because it always did—I could send Lingoss and Markham back for reinforcements. Counting on my fingers, I could muster Clerk, Bashford, Prentiss, Cox. . . . Was that it? Unless I started pulling out kitchen and R&D staff, yes it was. And Rosie Lee, of course. No—no century deserved Rosie Lee.

I opened my com again.

"Dr. Bairstow? Report, please."

"Ah, Max. Good afternoon again."

"Sir, are you able to talk?"

Something shattered in the background.

"Yes, of course. What is your problem?"

"Actually sir, I was about to enquire whether you required assistance."

"I don't believe so. Mrs. Mack appears to be coping admirably."

Mrs. Mack had led the resistance at the Battersea Barricades. She'd fought alongside her husband. She'd made it. He hadn't—falling to enemy fire only minutes before the ceasefire sounded. She was entitled to a chestful of medals that she never wore.

I felt the role of Dr. Bairstow descend upon me. "Perhaps you could indicate where the problem lies, sir."

"It would appear that someone made the mistake of trying to pick Mrs. Mack's pocket."

"What an idiot. Is he still alive?"

"Hard to tell. It would seem however, that he operated as part of a team, all of whom took exception to him being smacked between the eyes with a hastily snatched-up skillet. There has been a vigorous discussion over Mrs. Mack's unwillingness to assume the role of victim, and a market stall was inadvertently overturned. The sudden appearance of a group of somewhat rough looking fellows whose job it is, apparently, to maintain order within the market precincts, has provided enough distraction for us to be able to slip away. We hope to regroup outside and join you shortly."

I felt a sudden anxiety. He wasn't a young man. I struggled to express my concern in a tactful manner and failed. "Are you all right, sir?"

"Oh yes," he said, sounding remarkably cheerful for him. "It's just like old times. I feel quite refreshed."

"Is Major Guthrie still with you?"

"In body, yes. In spirit, probably not all of him."

"Sir?

"A slight blow to the head. Nothing major."

He paused for me to appreciate his little joke.

He doesn't make that many—you can see why—and I had to take a moment to grope for a suitable response.

While I struggled for words, he said, "I believe I have made your instructions quite clear, Dr. Maxwell. Your duty is to continue with this assignment. That is a direct order. We'll never have another opportunity to do this."

With deep, deep misgivings, I said, "Yes, sir," closed the link, and got on with my end of things.

THE PLACE WAS PACKED. Nearly every seat was taken in the galleries and they were still cramming them into the Yard. Markham, Lingoss, and I linked arms and hung on to each other as the people around us jostled for the best positions.

The noise was overwhelming. The smell even worse. Without even trying, I could smell people, onions, tobacco, urine—because not everyone could be bothered to pop outside to relieve themselves—ale, and a nasty, stale chip-fat smell from the cheap oil they used for the torches. Hanging over everything was the smell of the nearby river. Two or three braziers had been set around the edges of the stage. I suspected someone had looked up at the overcast sky and planned ahead.

The man next to me was smoking a long-stemmed pipe, puffing clouds of smoke around both his head and mine. He wasn't the only one. Tobacco was the latest craze and on this still day, the whole stage was wreathed in a blue fug of smoke.

Lingoss discreetly recorded the galleries and the posh people sitting therein. Theatres were popular with the nobility and Queen Elizabeth. Whom, sadly, we wouldn't see today because when she wanted to watch a performance, the players went to her. We'd replay Lingoss's footage when we returned home to try to identify anyone important here today. Not too easy with the ladies, most of whom were masked. Apparently, it's perfectly OK to have your bosoms on display, but not your face.

I concentrated on the stage which projected out into the Yard. The black curtain informed us we were about to witness

a tragedy. The curtain was flanked by two tall pillars, cleverly
painted to look like marble.

The Globe could hold several thousand people—a lot for
such a small area—and every single one of them appeared to
be conversing at the top of their voice. Or gambling. Or playing
cards. Prossies wandered through the crowds, blatantly tout-
ing for trade. I stood quietly among the thieves, apprentices,
food-sellers, my colleagues, cutpurses, and all the other scum
of the earth, everyone noisy and boisterous, and all looking forward to the afternoon's entertainment. The cobbles underfoot
were rough and slippery. God knows what I was standing in.
I hung on to Markham to avoid being knocked off my feet.
Attending an Elizabethan drama appeared to require a great
deal of stamina and strength.

I called up Peterson. "What's happening?"

"Can't talk. Running."

"To or from?"

The link went dead.

Shit. Shit, shit, shit.

I took more deep breaths. Dr. Bairstow dealt with this sort
of thing all the time. No wonder he had no hair. I made a mental
note to try to be more . . . conventionally . . . behaved in future.
Out of consideration for the few wisps remaining around the
back of his head.

Beside me, Markham and Lingoss, apparently not caring that
the god of historians was pissing all over our chips again, were
yelling excitedly at each other over the noise. Lingoss had Peterson's recorder discreetly palmed, all ready to begin. I considered
splitting us up. Lingoss on one side of the stage, me on the other.
To make sure we didn't miss anything. Lingoss had been a trainee
historian until she left the programme to join the nutters in R&D.
Where, I might as well say, she fitted right in. On the other hand,
we were down to one security guard. We were better off staying
together. It was going to be a long afternoon.

I closed my mind to whatever was going on outside the theatre—those were events I could do nothing about—and concentrated on the task in hand. *Hamlet*. We were going to see
Hamlet. And William Shakespeare himself.

I grinned. Yeah—I love my job.

I DIDN'T THINK, GIVEN the chaotic surroundings that the actors
would be punctual, but they were. Three long blasts of a trum-
pet announced the performance was about to begin. Of course,
they wouldn't want to hang around. *Hamlet* was four hours
long. The nights were short in June, but although the Globe
was open to the sky, the sides were high. The sun would soon
disappear and the whole place would be plunged into shadowy
gloom. It would grow cold. Yes, there were torches and braziers, but even so, compared with today's pampered theatre-go-
ers, Elizabethan audiences were a tough crowd. In every sense.

The crowd fell nearly silent. There was a huge sense of
anticipation.

I can't begin to describe how it felt to stand among people who didn't know the story. Who didn't know how the play
would end. Who hadn't had to sit at school, sleepy with boredom, as the class takes it in turns to read Shakespeare's lines,
droning on and on, fulfilling the education authorities' apparent ambition to render Shakespeare as boring as possible. The
people here had never watched one of those trendy TV productions where the play is—for some reason known only to the
director—set in a modern South American dictatorship, or a
Victorian cotton mill.

There was no scenery and few props. There was just the play
itself. Everything was left to the imagination. The costumes,
though, were magnificent, blazing with colour and fake jewels.
If the sun had been shining, they would have been dazzling.
Even on this dull day, they were brilliant. The stones in the
costumes sparkled and flashed in the light from the braziers.

The actors were good. They were better than good. They were amazing. I don't know why I was surprised. I can only assume that I'd thought, given the lack of scenery and the smallness of the stage, that the performance would be . . . well . . . unsophisticated, and it wasn't. Far from it.

The story progressed at a tremendous rate and the theatre crackled with energy. The actors were never still, continually moving around the stage. All of us, wherever we were, standing or seated, were made to feel included in the drama. To feel a part of what was going on. It was a very personal, intimate performance. They strode around the stage, cloaks swirling, taking the story to the farthest reaches of the theatre, their voices perfectly audible over the continual hum of those watching who, themselves, were never still.

I don't know about anyone else, but I was right there with them. I was there at Elsinore, on a dark winter's night, standing on the battlements as the frightened guards discussed the mysterious appearance of the spectral apparition, building up to the moment of the Ghost's entrance. Played by William Shakespeare himself.

And then, suddenly, there he was, appearing mysteriously from the back of the stage, dark and unmoving. The audience gasped. Like everyone else, I craned to see his face, lost in the shadows of his deep hood. I hopped with frustration. I hoped Lingoss, taller than me, was getting better shots. If everything had gone according to plan, there would have been historians at strategic points all around the theatre, capturing every moment, every line, every gesture, but they, of course, were all off irresponsibly sailing away to the New World or recklessly starting a riot in the market. You just can't get the staff these days.

Unlike the rest of the glittering cast, the Ghost was enveloped in voluminous draperies of grey, under which was just the hint of a breastplate, to denote his armour. I don't know what sort of material they'd used for his cloak, but even the slightest movement caused it to flutter away from his body, giving the appearance of wavering transparency. On this dull day, the effect was excellent. Mrs. Enderby would be thrilled. Or would have been had she actually been here.

I was right there again when Horatio brought Hamlet to see the Ghost for himself. I watched the two of them exit, pause to signify a new scene, and then reappear almost immediately.

The crowd shuddered with delicious horror at the Ghost's words of murder and incest, and if Markham had got any closer he would have been up on the stage with them.

The story thundered on. The Ghost admitted he was Hamlet's father and charged him to avenge his murder. All around me, people were nodding in agreement. This was accepted ghostly behaviour. The themes of the play were recognisable in any age. Murder and revenge.

I began to calm down a little. We were getting some great shots. Peterson and Sykes would sort out Professor Rapson. The combination of Dr. Bairstow and Major Guthrie was unbeatable and, even should the unthinkable happen and they fail, there was always Mrs. Mack. And actually, now I came to think of it, I wouldn't cross Mrs. Enderby, either. She has a nasty repertoire of hard stares. And then there was Miss North. The universe had been smoothing her family's path to success for centuries. She was definitely not one to let anyone or anything stand between her and her goal. They'd be fine.

We'd be fine.

Everything would be fine.

And right at that very moment, Shakespeare burst into flames.

My first thought was that we were witnessing a case of spontaneous human combustion and how disappointed Professor Rapson would be to have missed it, and then common sense kicked in.

I'd been so involved in the various St. Mary's crises—to say nothing of the play—that I hadn't notice the wind was getting up, sending dark clouds moving atmospherically across the sky. With a dramatic gesture of departure that sent his draperies flying out around him, the Ghost had flung out his arm. The movement, together with a sudden gust of wind, picked up the gauzy material of his cloak and blew it across one of the braziers. The next minute, Shakespeare—oh my God, *the* Shakespeare—was alight.

For a moment, everyone stood, frozen. Someone screamed. We stood on the brink of mass panic. The theatre was made entirely of wood. Fire exits hadn't been invented yet. A mass stampede would probably kill more people than any fire.

But not today. Before anyone else could move, Markham had vaulted up onto the stage and cannoned into Shakespeare, knocking him to the ground. I just had time to think—oh my God, that's *Shakespeare*, for God's sake be careful with him— when he began to roll him over, beating out the flames with his bare hands. The classic Stop, Drop, and Roll. We're good at that. Markham can do it in his sleep. I scrabbled in my basket, pulled out my cloak, and tossed it up to him. He used it to envelop the Ghost and an instant later, the flames were out.

The crowd applauded wildly. I don't know if they thought it was part of the play. Someone shouted something I didn't catch, and the pair of them, Markham and Shakespeare, must have been lying on a trapdoor because, suddenly, they both disappeared from view.

"And then there were two," intoned Lingoss.

And with that unerring instinct for knowing exactly when his staff are cantering along the catastrophe curve towards disaster, Dr. Bairstow spoke in my ear.

"Good afternoon, Dr. Maxwell."

"Oh, hello sir. How is your riot progressing?"

"A most satisfactory resolution, thank you. We expect to be with you very soon. How is the play?"

I stared at the spot where I'd last seen Markham and Shakespeare. "I'm sorry sir, I can't hear you very well. There's a lot of noise here. I'll try again in a minute."

I closed the link on him. In itself a capital offence.

"Bloody hell," said Lingoss beside me. "Did you just hang up on the Boss?"

"Of course not," I said, unconvincingly and inaccurately. "Carry on recording, please Miss Lingoss."

I wasn't the only one promoting the whole "show must go on" scenario. Hamlet himself, taking one or two deep breaths, turned to Marcellus and Horatio, themselves realistically pale and shocked—as well they might be since their foremost playwright and actor/shareholder had just gone up in flames—and the play continued.

"I hope to God he's all right," said Lingoss, anxiously, and I was pretty sure she wasn't talking about Markham. "This is bloody Bill the Bard, you know." Just in case I'd forgotten.

"We'll know in a minute," I said. "The Ghost speaks again very soon."

And indeed, we were approaching that moment. Hamlet, having entreated his friends to silence, instructs them to swear an oath on his sword. They pause, uncertain and afraid, and, according to the play, the unearthly voice of the Ghost filters up, supposedly from the underworld, but in this case from below the stage, commanding them to swear.

There was a long silence. No voice from anywhere, never mind the underworld.

"Shit," said Lingoss, and then . . .

"Swear," boomed an unearthly voice, resonant with the terrors of Hell.

Lingoss stiffened. "I know that voice."

"Swear," intoned the voice sepulchrally, throbbing with all the despair and grief and sorrow and desolation of a lost soul. And with a bit of a Bristol accent.

"We all know that voice," I said, through clenched teeth.

"Swear by his sword," commanded the eldritch voice, rising in tone and pitch and finishing on a strangulated note that even a banshee with its balls trapped in a vice couldn't have achieved. All around the stage people stepped back, and on the stage itself, Hamlet's companions completed the scene with almost indecent haste.

"Oh my God," said Lingoss to me, agitated, but still recording I was pleased to note. "What did he think he was doing?"

The scene ended and the actors swept from the stage.

Time to find out.

I opened my com and taking advantage of the milling crowd said quietly, "Mr. Markham. Report."

"It's fine. Everything's fine."

This is St. Mary's speak for "Everything's gone tits up, but I'm trying to sort things out so leave me alone to get on with it."

"Do you require any assistance?"

"No. No. Everything's fine."

I stared at the stage as if I could see through the wood.

Dr. Bairstow's voice sounded in my ear. "Dr. Maxwell, we appear to have lost contact."

"Really, sir?"

"Report, please."

In situations like this—the ones where I'm not quite sure what's going on—it is important to report as fully and clearly as possible without actually saying anything at all.

"It's fine," I said, borrowing from the master. "Everything's fine."

There was a short, disbelieving silence and then he closed the link.

"Just act normally," said Markham, in my ear again. "Every-thing's fine."

"Stop saying that."

"Well it is."

Where are you?

"I'm carrying Shakespeare out from under the stage."

"Oh my God, is he badly burned?"

"No, not at all. His costume is, but he's fine."

I was puzzled. "So why are you carrying him?"

"He's just a little bit limp at the moment."

"He'd better not be. The Ghost appears again later on."

"That won't be a problem."

I stopped. Did that mean that Shakespeare would have recovered by then? Or that someone was available to carry on? I wish people would report more clearly.

"Was that you just now?"

Silence.

I ground my teeth again. "Was it?"

"I'm not sure what the correct answer is to that one, so I'm not saying anything. Anyway, I can't talk now—I'm heaving a living legend around and I need to concentrate on what I'm doing."

I took a moment. This was Markham. Himself a living leg-end, but for completely the wrong reasons. On the other hand, he usually managed to emerge from whatever crisis he had embroiled himself in more or less unscathed. I should let him get on with it.

"Do whatever you think necessary," I said, mentally cross-ing my fingers.

"Okey dokey," he said cheerfully and, if Major Guthrie had heard him say that, he'd suffer for it big time later on.

Guiltily, I remembered my other crisis. The one that didn't involve the world's most famous writer going up in flames.

"Miss Sykes, report."

"Oh, hello Max."

As always, she sounded delighted to hear from me. I wasn't fooled for an instant. Who did she think invented that voice?

"Report."

"Well, there's good and there's bad. The original passenger has turned up and is accusing the professor of stealing his berth. He's quite indignant about it. The captain and his first mate aren't actually on the ship at the moment. Popular opinion has it they're out rogering as many barmaids as they can find in preparation for the long voyage ahead, but the rest of the crew are accusing the professor of trying to stow away. Which I gather is quite a serious crime, although since he's been marching around the deck talking to all the sailors, demanding to know how everything works, and showing them new knots he's invented, there hasn't been a lot of stowing going on. I can't honestly see how they'll make the charge stick. Can I just ask—what's keelhauling?"

Without thinking, I said, "A vicious form of maritime punishment mentioned as early as 800 BC, involving dragging the offender under the keel of a boat. Survival is rare—death being due either to drowning, or having clothes, skin, arms, legs, et cetera, ripped off by the barnacles growing on the ship's bottom. Please use every effort to ensure that does not happen to the professor." I played out possible scenarios in my head. "Or Dr. Dowson, either."

"I'll do my best," she said, cheerfully, "but I'm just a girl. No one's taking any notice of me."

"You underestimate your abilities, Miss Sykes."

"True. And the second mate appears to be extremely fond of the miracle fluid known as rum. I'm sure I can persuade him to let us all go. Everyone's quaffing away, including the real passenger for the New World—and a right miserable bugger he looks. I can feel the War of Independence coming on just by looking at him."

She broke off and I heard an unearthly cry.

"What the hell?"

"Just a couple of passing seagulls who just popped in, had a quick quaff, and are now unable to get airborne again. How are things with you?"

"Absolutely fine," I said, through gritted teeth.

"Oh dear. Never mind."

LONG EXPERIENCE ENABLED ME to identify the exact moment Dr. Bairstow and his party assumed their seats in the gallery. The faint commotion caused by him staring at people long enough for them to move up and make room for him was lost in the general hubbub around me, but I knew he was there.

I ground my teeth, ignored his penetrating stare, and turned back to the stage.

The play was resuming. Scenes came and went. I can only assume that players set fire to themselves all the time, because no one seemed in the slightest bit perturbed. Actors swirled around the stage. Hamlet went not so quietly mad. Glittering costumes mingled with glittering words. The smoke from braziers and a hundred pipes made my eyes sting. I shifted from foot to foot, half discomfort, half anxiety. What was happening? Why hadn't Markham returned? Were they still under the stage? How badly was Shakespeare injured? Was Markham being held responsible? Right now, not ten feet away, Shakespeare could be breathing his last.

I broke my self-imposed rule.

"Markham. Talk to me. Are you being cut into tiny pieces?"

"No, I'm having a beer."

Of course he bloody was. Any concern I might have felt took wings and flew away.

"What about Shakespeare? He's on again in Act Three."

"He's not going to make it."

"He must."

"He can't. He can't even focus, let alone stand up."

"Is there an understudy?"

A long silence. "No."

I gave him my version of an even longer silence.

"You're sure?"

"Yep."

"You're absolutely sure?"

"Well, there's a young lad here, but he plays Gertrude as well, and they're on at the same time."

I sighed. Heavily. I was doing that a lot this afternoon. Some holiday this was turning out to be. "Have you still got my cloak?"

"It's here. Stop panicking."

"You've got my chocolate."

There was an oddly long pause. "Not any longer."

"Is it melted?"

Another oddly long pause.

"Yes."

I could feel Dr. Bairstow's potential wrath hanging over me like the Sword of Damocles. Should I recall Markham? There must surely be an understudy somewhere in this theatre.

He took the matter out of my hands. "There's nothing you can do, Max. Just relax and enjoy the show."

I might as well. Everyone else was. All around me, people were buying pies, arguing with their friends, rolling the dice, or booking a prostitute. I felt quite angry on the actors' behalf. Didn't people know what was happening here? How important this moment was? And here they all were, carrying on as if the whole thing was simply some sort of massive social event, designed for nothing more than to see and be seen.

Until that moment. That magical moment.

Hamlet, wrapped in a cloak and his own thoughts, strode to the edge of the stage, and paused, staring at his own feet. Standing motionless, he stared. And stared. Gradually, the noise of the crowd died away as everyone turned to watch. The background noises were hushed. Prossies went unrented. I swear, even outside, the clatter of cartwheels on cobbles, the shouts, the everyday noises all fell away. For all I know, even mighty Father Thames paused in anticipation. Complete silence fell, and still Hamlet stared at his feet, unmoving. The silence stretched to an impossible length. People began to look at each other in puzzlement.

"Oh my God," whispered Lingoss. "He's forgotten his lines."

No, he hadn't.

Slowly, he lifted his head and swept his gaze over the upturned faces around him. No one moved. No one spoke. The whole world waited.

"To be, or not to be,
That is the question."

A kind of sigh rippled around the Yard—and the galleries, too. I felt my heart thump in my chest. I had an overwhelming desire to burst into tears.

He completed the soliloquy, every word taking flight and soaring to the heavens above. Like golden birds. When he finished, there was a moment of respectful silence and then the sound of tumultuous, rapturous applause. Even the people in the galleries stamped their feet. I clapped until my hands hurt, tears running down my cheeks.

Burbage stood, head lowered for a moment, and then he placed his hand on his heart, bowed deeply just once, swept his cloak around him in a grand gesture and the play continued.

There have been some wonderful moments in my life and that was well up with the best of them. I wiped my face on my sleeve, realised I'd completely forgotten my aching legs and feet, slapped another memory stick into my recorder and carried on.

UNTIL TWO SCENES LATER and the return of the Ghost who, this time, appeared in his nightgown. I wondered if the part had called for this or whether they were improvising after his original costume had gone up in flames. Whatever the reason, it's become traditional. If you've ever wondered why, in Act III Scene IV, after appearing heavily cloaked and in his armour, the Ghost turns up in his nightgown, it's because he set fire to himself in a previous scene. Beside me, Lingoss stiffened and said in a strangled whisper, "Max . . ."

Because without his all-concealing cloak this was, at last, our opportunity to see Shakespeare himself, to compare the real man to the very few portraits of him. To be able to say, once and for all—this is the face of William Shakespeare. My palms were sticky. I checked my recorder for the umpteenth time. This was it.

Except that it wasn't. It wasn't Shakespeare, I mean. This Ghost was a good half a head shorter than the previous version, and bore a startling resemblance to Mr. Markham.

"*Shit*," said Lingoss, which pretty much summed it all up. "What is he *doing*?"

Why does everyone always think I know what's going on?

I could feel Dr. Bairstow's eyes boring into the back of my head. I refused to look around, concentrating instead on formulating plans to spend the rest of my life in this century.

Back on the stage, Hamlet has killed Polonius in front of his mother and, even more emotional than usual—which is saying a lot—is trying to show her the Ghost, terrifying her even further. She flees around the stage, as Hamlet, increasingly desperate and increasingly mad, tries to seize her hands and force her to confront a spectre she cannot believe exists.

All this was happening at the front of the stage. So far, the Ghost had wisely stayed well back, a silent and motionless figure. For some reason, the effect was far more sinister than if he had gallivanted around the stage waving his arms and wailing. Which, I admit, had been my second fear. My first fear, of course, being what Dr. Bairstow was going to say when all this was over. However, back to the plot.

The Ghost was about to speak.

I held my breath.

In a voice resonating with sadness and despair, he spoke.

"Do not forget. This visitation
Is but to whet thy almost blunted purpose.
But look, amazement on thy mother sits."

As well it might since the young lad playing the queen had suddenly found himself being addressed by a complete stranger.

"O step between her and her fighting soul.
Conceit in weakest bodies strongest works.
Speak to her, Hamlet."

To no avail. Gertrude cannot see the Ghost. After a final moment of silent anguish, conveyed, according to the Markham School of Acting, by him clutching at his bosom with both hands, the Ghost drifts away, never, thank God, to be seen again.

A polite round of applause accompanied his exit.

I realised I'd been holding my breath.

"Hey, Max."

Don't ever tell Peterson I'd completely forgotten about him.

"Tim? Where are you? What's happening?"

You're supposed to say "Report." It doesn't always happen.

"Bit of a full-scale war here. I'm pulling everyone out."

I could hear a woman shrieking.

I asked who that was, because he does have a tendency to get himself involved with difficult women.

"Now we know why the original passenger was so keen to get to the New World, Max. His wife and seventeen children have just turned up. She's hanging around his neck like a dead albatross. The kids are screaming. He's alternately trying to pretend he's never seen any of them before and shouting at the crew to cast off. The crew are laughing their heads off. It's all happening. Hang on, she's wants me to . . . No, I will not hold the baby. No. Let go of me. Get off. For God's sake, madam, will you kindly desist. Thank you. Max, stop laughing."

"It's good training for when you're married."

"I should live that long. Look out, Atherton, she's heading your way. Watch out for that baby. It's leaking at both ends. Sorry Max—have to go. Speak to you later."

It was all right for Peterson. He only had an angry, ship's crew, two uncontrollable academics, Psycho Psykes, and an enraged wife and her seventeen children to contend with. I didn't have to turn around to know that Dr. Bairstow was glaring balefully at the back of my head.

"Dr. Maxwell."

"Oh, hello, sir," I said cheerfully, grasping the bull by his horns. "Everything all right up there?"

"*We* are all present and correct, yes."

"Jolly good," I said, ignoring the implication that my team wasn't, and moved slightly to my left to get a better shot of Hamlet ranting about something to someone.

"Is there something you want to tell me?"

"I don't think so sir. Everything seems to be under control here."

"We shall speak later," he promised and closed his link.

THE PLAY CRUISED SMOOTHLY on—which was more than I was doing—the final scene especially providing a body count high enough to compare favourably with that of a modern day block-buster. The final tally:

The Queen—poisoned by the king, her husband.

Ophelia—drowned.

Polonius—stabbed through the arras by Hamlet.

Rosencrantz and Guildenstern—both beheaded by the English.

Laertes—stabbed and poisoned by Hamlet.

Claudius—stabbed and poisoned by Hamlet.

And Hamlet himself—goes mad and then, continuing the established theme—stabbed and poisoned by Laertes.

A dark day for Denmark.

I was on the verge of calling Peterson. His silence was either a very good thing or a very bad thing—but if he needed assistance he would call me. Or so I told myself.

The players took their bows with Markham, obviously aware that the sands of his life were running out, trying to stand at the back and look inconspicuous—something that was never going to happen in any century.

And then it was time to go.

I TURNED AWAY FROM the stage and, not without misgivings, opened my com. "Tim, what's happening?

"All present and correct. Well, mostly correct. A few bumps and bruises."

"You've been fighting?"

"Only a little. Most of the damage was done when Keller tripped over a coil of rope and brought a couple of sailors down with him. They were at some pains to point out they weren't those sort of boys and we had to run for it."

"Bloody hell, where are you now?"

"In the Tabard. We gave up on Shakespeare. Some days you can have too much drama. We've pooled our pennies instead, and there's a lake of ale on the table in front of us. What's happening with you?"

"Shakespeare set fire to himself and Markham made his stage debut."

He whistled. "OK, you win. Much more disastrous than a couple of bloody noses and a crushed codpiece. How about Dr. Bairstow?"

"Up in the gallery."

"Isn't there a song about that?"

"How much beer have you actually had?"

"Hardly any at all," he said unconvincingly. "So what are you up to, then?"

"I, along with Miss Lingoss, whose behaviour has been exemplary, I might add . . ." We both paused to savour this unaccustomed phrase, ". . . have been concentrating on the real assignment. Which is more than can be said for the rest of this bloody unit."

I closed the link. All right, harsh words, but what would you have said?

IT TOOK US OVER an hour to get out of the theatre. No one seemed in any hurry to leave. There was food, drink, and company. Why would anyone want to be anywhere else? The actors jumped down off the stage and mingled with the crowd, slapping backs and cadging drinks. I looked for Shakespeare. A brief glimpse, even at this late stage, might go a long way towards placating Dr. Bairstow, but I couldn't see him anywhere. Sometimes I think the god of historians' job description needs upgrading. Along with the actual god of historians.

Markham, grinning like an idiot, pushed his way through the crowd, pausing only to extricate himself from a not so young but very affectionate lady, who seemed to think physical contact of any kind constituted some sort of binding contract. We watched his struggles without sympathy and ignored his pathetic appeals for help.

Eventually, he emerged beside me, restored to what, for him, passed as normal, and bubbling with excitement. He passed me the sorry remains of my cloak.

"Max, did you see me?"

"Sorry, what?"

"Did you see me?"

"When?"

"I was on stage. I was the Ghost. Did you see me?"

"You were the Ghost?"

"Yes. Did you see me?"

"No, sorry. Must have missed that bit."

"What?"

"Problem with my recorder. Maybe Lingoss got you."

He turned to Lingoss. "Did you get me?"

Lingoss was shouldering her pack. "Get what?"

"Me. On stage. I was the Ghost. I saved the day."

"When?"

"Just now," he said, hopping up and down with frustration. "I was the Ghost. In the play. The one you've just seen. Today."

"Oh, I'm sorry. My feet were killing me. These cobbles are murder to stand on for so long. I took a break and sat down. Must have missed it. Try Max."

He turned back to me. "You *must* have seen me."

"What are you talking about? I'm seeing you now."

"No, not now. Then."

"When?"

"When I was on the stage."

"What stage?"

We could probably have gone on like this all day, but at this point, he realised we were winding him up.

"You're right," he said, casually, taking his pack from Lingoss. "No big deal."

Turning away, and the very picture of guilty furtiveness—although to be fair, that is his normal expression a lot of the time—he slipped something into his pack.

"What was that?" I said, because we're not allowed to pick up souvenirs and he knew it.

"Nothing," he said nonchalantly, thus confirming my worst fears. "Shall we go? Don't want to be late at the rendezvous point."

I held out my hand. "Give it to me."

"What?" he said, grinning and getting his own back.

"The thing you just slipped into your pack."

"What pack?"

"The one that will be referred to as Exhibit A when I'm being tried for your murder."

He grinned and pulled out a recorder, waggling his eyebrows at us.

We stared at it, oblivious of the people pushing past us on their way out.

I said hoarsely, "What did you get?"

"No idea. Exciting, isn't it?"

I nodded at the recorder. "Put that away. Very carefully. Miss Lingoss?"

"Yes, Max."

"Your duty is clear. Should anything happen to Mr. Markham between here and St. Mary's, your one and only function is to save that recorder at all costs."

"Hey," protested Markham.

"Understood," said Lingoss.

THE FIRST PERSON I saw outside was Peterson, unscathed and unperturbed. Beside him, Miss Sykes peered about her with bright-eyed curiosity. Professor Rapson and Dr. Dowson stood nearby with Atherton and Evans stationed one on each side, ready to head them off at the pass should they stray, or intercede should they come to blows. Every single one of them looked as if butter wouldn't melt in their mouths. And all of them reeked of rum.

Peterson patted the pouch holding his recorder. "We've got some really good stuff here. You?"

This casual reference to my recording marathon did not endear him to me in any way.

"Meh," I said. "Just the usual stuff. Shakespeare, Burbage, deathless prose—same old, same old."

He opened his mouth to respond, but at that moment, Dr. Bairstow hove into view, his team trailing behind him, with Major Guthrie bringing up the rear and a definite contender in the Best Black Eye of the Year competition.

The curfew wasn't until nine o'clock but the sun had long since disappeared. I flung my scorched and burned cloak around my shoulders, ignored Mrs. Enderby's reproachful stare, performed a quick head count, and ordered everyone back to the pod.

Dr. Bairstow said very little as we made our way back through the darkening streets. Southwark was, if anything, even livelier in the evening than during the day. Shouts and laughter could be heard through open doors and windows. Some torches and lanterns were being lit, but most streets and narrow alleyways were in deep shadow, and they really weren't places where we wanted to be.

Snatches of conversation drifted back to me.

"It's a kind of a cross between a clove and hitch. I shall call it the clit."

"Couldn't think of anything else to do than shove it down the front of my trousers . . ."

"And then Mrs. Mack fetched him an almighty wallop . . ."

"Scurvy, of course, which is why Americans refer to us as Limeys. Interesting isn't it that in these times one could journey to and from America far more easily than in our time today . . ."

I stood at the bottom of the ramp and counted them all into the pod, congratulated myself on not having lost anyone, and ruthlessly pulled rank to be first into the toilet. The bloody play was four hours long, for crying out loud, and while everyone else might have been happy to splash against the wall, I wasn't. Lingoss, herself obviously not a happy wall-splasher either, was hard on my heels.

I gave the word, the world went white, and still Dr. Bairstow said nothing.

WE LANDED WITH BARELY a bump. I made everyone stand still for decontamination, watching carefully as the cold blue light played over us all. Everyone was still babbling away about their own afternoon. The only person saying nothing was Dr. Bairstow. It was very unnerving.

The ramp came down. Leon entered, smiled for me alone, bent over the console, and began to shut things down.

I don't know why I thought we might get away with it. We never had before. Just as he was leaving TB2, Dr. Bairstow turned and spoke at last.

"As soon as you have finished in Sick Bay, Doctors Maxwell, Peterson, and Mr. Markham, please report to me in my office."

I sighed.

WE CREPT INTO SICK Bay and tried to hang around at the back of the queue—there were many people to process and I think our plan was to get lost in the crowd—but Helen Foster hoicked us to the head of the queue, threw us through the scanner, and pronounced us fit for purpose. Well, no less fit for purpose than we were before, she said, and to get out of here now because she was very busy and had better things to do than hospitalise Markham for a couple of really very minor burns so stop waving them around Markham because no one was interested, and there was no point in Peterson hanging about because she was far too busy to talk to him at the moment, and why was Maxwell still here?

We know when we're not wanted.

We trailed to Dr. Bairstow's office, hoping for divine intervention on the way, but we'd obviously used up our quota for the day, arriving at his door completely unengulfed by catastrophe. As Markham said gloomily, for a bunch of people overtaken by disaster far more often than was good for them, where was a good crisis when you needed one?

"Actually," I said, "I don't know why I'm standing around like a criminal. While everyone around me was stowing away on ships or brawling in the market or bursting into flames, I was the one who continued with the mission."

"That's a very good point, Max," said Peterson. "And I saved the New World from Professor Rapson."

"Another good point. Lead with that."

We both looked at Markham. "I'm the The Man Who Saved Shakespeare," he said, and we could hear the capital letters.

"Leave this to me," I said, and they indicated their enthusiastic willingness to do that very thing.

We waited quietly until the Boss turned up, fresh and smart in clean clothes while we were still in our tatty Tudor gear. We followed him into his office, Markham taking care to display his burns prominently.

There's an accepted routine for this sort of thing. Dr. Bairstow sits in silent majesty and the offenders—that's almost always the three of us, me, Peterson, and Markham with a varying supporting cast—issue the standard blanket denial, offer up an unconvincing explanation, attempt to justify our actions, accept our reprimand, and hasten to the bar to nurse our wounds and our pride and have a well-deserved drink.

But maybe not today.

Dr. Bairstow sat behind his desk. He didn't have enough hair to look dishevelled. He could stand in a Force Eight gale and literally not turn a hair, but he did have a certain battered look about him. His lip was split and a rather impressive bruise was forming under his left eye. I opened my mouth to make a bid for the moral high ground, but he beat me to it.

"Why is it that after every assignment I look up to see you three standing in front of me?" Which since he'd particularly requested the pleasure of our company seemed a little unfair.

We indicated our own mystification.

"So," he said, "and I'm sure you will correct me if I go astray, Professor Rapson inadvisedly boards a boat . . ."

"Ship," murmured Peterson.

". . . bound for the New World. An altercation ensues and your solution, Dr. Peterson, is to ply everyone present with cheap rum, which delays the sailing sufficiently to give the original passenger's wife and family time to intercept the boat . . ."

"Ship."

". . . remove said passenger and restore him to the bosom of his apparently enormous family."

"His enormous *grateful* family, sir."

"I gather that under the mellowing influence of a great deal of alcohol, moves to keelhaul Professor Rapson were circumvented."

"I think they were more of a threat than a promise and . . ."

"Where was Miss Sykes during all this? And don't tell me she wasn't there?"

"Miss Sykes heroically undertook to induce the second mate to release the professor."

"He was in the brig?"

"Not as such, sir. He was actually sitting on a coil of rope demonstrating the er . . . the um . . . his new knot to an admiring crowd."

"And Mr. Keller? What was the Security Section's role in this?"

"Mr. Keller suffered a slight loss of balance—no sea legs, sir—inadvertently falling on a couple of seamen. It was later agreed that his actions had been misinterpreted and there was general mirth and merriment over the misunderstanding."

Peterson beamed at Dr. Bairstow. Who turned his attention to me.

"And you Dr. Maxwell?"

"I recorded the entire production sir," I said firmly, feeling that not enough attention was being paid to the one person who had fulfilled her part of the assignment. "All bladder-straining four hours of it, together with footage of the audience, paying particular attention to the galleries."

I placed my and Lingoss's recorders on the desk in front of him and stepped back, oozing virtuousness and eagerness to please. Both Peterson and Markham refused to catch my eye.

He turned his beaky nose towards Markham.

"So, Mr. Markham, it would seem that when I eventually take a moment from assisting my colleagues in the execution of their duties at the street market and request an update on the assignment, I find that, for some reason, William Shakespeare is engulfed in flames and that you have appropriated his role for yourself."

I thought he was slightly overstating events but refrained from saying so. Markham could usually look after himself.

"Well, Mr. Markham?"

"It all happened so suddenly, sir. One minute the Ghost is denouncing his brother and his queen and exhorting Hamlet to seek revenge and the next minute he's a raging inferno."

Another one slightly overstating events. I stood back to let the two of them tough it out.

"William Shakespeare was on fire?"

"Not all of him, sir. Only his clothes."

"And you extinguished the flames and possibly saved his life."

"I did, sir," he said, casually moving his burns to an even more prominent position and wincing with bravely concealed pain.

"You interfered with History. Are you aware of our Standing Orders?"

"Very much so, sir. Major Guthrie quotes them at me on a regular basis, but I didn't interfere, sir. We have no reports of William Shakespeare being injured or disfigured in a fire. In fact, he lives for many years and goes on to write even more plays. You could say sir, that it was necessary for me to interfere so that History *wasn't* changed."

He had a point. History is like a living organism and it will always protect itself. If it thinks, even for one moment, that someone or something is about to alter events that have already taken place, then the offending virus—or historian as we prefer to be known—is wiped out without a second thought. The fact that our Mr. Markham still lived and breathed was evidence that—just for once—he was completely blameless.

Dr. Bairstow shifted in his chair. "To use a word in keeping with the situation—what exactly was your *role* in all of this?"

Markham assumed his hurt expression—the one resembling an abandoned puppy in a snowstorm. "Well, sir, if you mean did I actually set Shakespeare on fire then no, I didn't. The *part* I *played*—to continue your brilliant example, sir," he said, slathering on the butter, "consisted simply of *acting* to assess the situation, identifying the appropriate measures to be taken, *staging* the Stop, Drop, and Roll *programme*, and assisting the stricken Shakespeare to *exit* to an area under the stage so that I could *perform* any further assistance."

"Which consisted of appropriating the role of Ghost."

Markham beamed again and nodded.

"But what of the understudy? How in God's name did you ever induce him to allow you to do such a thing?"

"I . . . um . . . I offered him something in exchange."

My mind boggled. I couldn't, offhand, think of anything Markham could have had that the understudy would have wanted. We're not allowed to take anything with us. And then—of course—my chocolate. He'd bartered my bar of chocolate. The one hidden in my cloak. True, by that point it might have been a little battered and melted, but even so . . . I took a moment to imagine the impact of a brick-sized bar of fruit and nut on someone who'd never in their life tasted anything like it. The Ghost was not a major role. Only half-a-dozen lines—in exchange for a giant slab of the stuff? Of course he'd allowed it.

"What could you possibly possess that would induce him to do such a thing?"

I stiffened. While taking my own lunch was perfectly acceptable, a great block of as yet undiscovered chocolate was almost certainly not. What would Markham say?

I needn't have worried.

Contriving to look even more abandoned than ever, Markham smiled reassuringly. "The object concerned was completely biodegradable sir. Nothing to worry about at all."

"Astonishingly, this blithe assurance does nothing to lessen my anxiety."

"Your groundless anxiety, sir." He beamed in what he probably thought was a comforting manner.

"So you are telling me that the Ghost's unearthly utterances from beneath the stage and his final but very public appearance in Act Three—all that was you?"

I could see Markham considering possible answers, rejecting them all and settling for the uninflammatory truth.

"If you mean my inspired recreation of a restless soul in torment, unable to rest in peace, languishing in the depths of anguish and despair, and desperate to convey his message from beyond the grave then yes, all that was me, sir."

Dr. Bairstow began to align the files on his desk. Never a good sign.

"I find myself quite bewildered, Mr. Markham. It would seem that, thanks to your admittedly timely intervention, while the damage to his clothing was fairly major, the damage to Shakespeare himself was so minor as to be non-existent. I am anxious, therefore, to learn the compelling reasons for your subsequent appropriation of the role of the Ghost, which thereby deprived the audience—and me—of the pleasure of watching the greatest playwright the world has ever known perform his own lines."

Wow. He was really annoyed. All the signs were there. Long sentences. Polysyllabic words. Faultless grammar. Perfect

punctuation. Dr. Bairstow was—not to put too fine a point on
it—right royally pissed at Markham.

Who shifted his feet, uneasily. "Well, it wasn't so much the
fire that did the damage, sir. The thing is, I might have dropped
him."

The files were now aligned with ominously millimetric precision. "You *dropped* Shakespeare?"

"Only slightly, sir."

"Do you mean you only dropped part of him, or that you
dropped all of him, but not from a great height?"

"Both, sir. There was a step which, in the agitation of the
moment, I didn't notice, and he went down with a bit of a
crash."

Running out of files, Dr. Bairstow gripped the edge of his
desk. "You knocked Shakespeare unconscious? And do not say
'Not all of him.'"

Obviously not feeling able to comply, Markham said nothing.

"Answer me."

"Well, I didn't, sir. Knock all of him unconscious, I mean.
He was just a bit wobbly and the bit was coming up where he's
supposed to intone, 'Swear,' in horrid tones from underneath
the stage, and even after an *interval* to recover, he really was all
over the place, so *acting* in a *prompt* and timely manner, I did it.
And no one noticed. And the show must go on, sir," he added,
laying on the jam as well as the butter. "And then he threw up.
All over himself, sir, and you have to admit it would have been
a bit of a disaster if he'd done that on the stage. I'm not sure
they'd invented ectoplasm in the 1600s."

"Charles Richet, 1905," murmured Peterson, electing to
join the conversation just in time to make things worse.

Everyone, even Dr. Bairstow, turned to stare at him.

"What?" Peterson demanded, defensively. "Helen was
researching anaphylaxis and his name came up."

I'm not sure if he was attempting to deflect Dr. Bairstow's wrath or not. Whichever it was, it didn't work. Charles Richet was dismissed as irrelevant in the scheme of things. Just as Dr. Bairstow leaned over his desk for the kill, however, Markham pulled out his recorder, gently placed it on the desk, and stepped back.

It's not often you see Dr. Bairstow struggle. I could sympathise. Anyone who deals with Markham would be familiar with this situation. Wearing his Director hat, the Boss would want to know what Markham thought he was doing with a recorder. Wearing his historian hat, he would want to know if there was anything interesting on it.

He pulled himself together.

"What is that?"

"It's a recorder, sir. You know, the History Department uses them."

Once again, the beaky nose turned his way and we waited for him to be blasted from the face of the earth. Apparently unaware he had only seconds left in this world, Markham innocently picked up the recorder and began to fiddle with it, talking all the while.

"I don't know what I've got, of course. It was dark under the stage, and even when I'd got him out and around the back, he was still a bit bleary and in no state to continue, so I took advantage of the opportunity to fulfil a lifelong ambition and ensure that the show did go on."

He was still casually fiddling with the recorder. He could drop it at any moment. I was nearly having a heart attack and I'm pretty sure even Dr. Bairstow was holding his breath. "I've always wanted to go on the stage sir, and after my performance today, I reckon my agent is going to need some publicity shots, so I thought I'd take a quick selfie."

I waited for Dr. Bairstow to demand to know who had bastardised the English language to the extent that "selfie" was even a word.

JODI TAYLOR

He did not. He took a deep breath and held out his hand for the recorder.

Markham smiled sunnily at him and handed it over.

He hadn't been able to record but there was a series of still images, most of which were either too dark or were obviously of his elbow. At least, I hoped it was his elbow. Some of Markham's outlying areas can be a little unruly and sometimes you don't know quite which bit of him you're dealing with.

But there, towards the end, were three images.

The first showed a man sitting down, head resting back against a wall, eyes closed. He might have been unconscious or just resting his eyes. The light hadn't been good, but we could make out a long chin, receding hair, the distinctively high forehead, and a thin nose.

"That's just after I got him off the stage," said Markham. "He was in shock, I think. I just sat him down and waited for someone to come and check him over. Someone called to us and Shakespeare said he was OK. Although not in quite those words. Anyway, he obviously wanted to watch the play and see how it was going, so I helped him up. I was OK, but he was a bit taller than me and I think he forgot to crouch. He banged his head on something, staggered a bit, fell down a step, and banged his head again.

"I shouted as loudly as I dared, but no one came. He wasn't out cold, but he certainly wasn't functioning properly, so I took a chance." He flicked to the next image. A long pale face stared in bemusement, while Markham, arm around his shoulders, beamed up at the camera. Given the circumstances, a remarkably clear image.

It was the third image, however, that was the money shot.

A full face, looking directly at us, slightly smiling. And it was him. Definitely, recognisably, undeniably Shakespeare.

Markham said nothing because there wasn't anything anyone could say. Not even Dr. Bairstow.

To sum up, not only had we great footage of 17th-century London Bridge, of Southwark, the Tabard, the docks, a Tudor ship, the market, the Globe and its audience, their production of *Hamlet*, the man himself playing one of his own parts, we had *the* definitive identifying image of William Shakespeare. Bloody hell, we're good. We're St. Mary's and we really are the dog's bollocks.

I was willing to bet Dr. Bairstow was in agreement, although he would almost certainly drop down dead rather than admit it. He and Markham were old adversaries, however, and there was an established procedure to work through. They stared at each other across his desk and prepared to enjoy themselves.

"If I thought for one moment, Mr. Markham, that it would get you out of my unit, I would sign you up for Equity myself."

"That's extremely generous of you, sir, but I couldn't possibly leave St. Mary's to lurch along without me."

"And yet I believe we would survive."

And now he was an *injured* abandoned puppy in a snowstorm. "Without me, sir?"

"Even without you, Mr. Markham. I am certain I could not live with myself should St. Mary's turn out to be an insurmountable obstacle to your glittering career on stage and screen."

"Well, thank you, sir. I have to say I couldn't have done any of it without you, as indeed I shall say in my Oscar acceptance speech."

"I applaud your loyalty."

"I'm not one to forget my humble beginnings, sir."

"I am gratified to hear it and greatly look forward to viewing the imprint of your body in the famous Hollywood Walk of Fame."

"I think you'll find, sir, it's only hand and footprints. Not a whole body cast."

"That is unfortunate. Frequent practice does, however, enable me to live with such disappointments. Please do not allow me to detain you, Mr. Markham. I wouldn't want to get between you and the silver screen."

"That's very kind of you, sir."

"Not at all. Before you leave us for fame and fortune, however, I believe Major Guthrie wants a quick word about your communication protocols."

"My what sir?"

I believe he wishes to focus on your explanation of that well-known Shakespearian phrase 'Okey dokey'."

"Ah. I can explain . . ."

The door opened and Major Guthrie appeared. The small pack of frozen peas he was clutching to a very large black eye was in no way obscuring the awfulness of his frown.

"Do come in," said Dr. Bairstow affably. "Mr. Markham is ready for his close-up now, Mr. DeMille."

MY NAME IS MARKHAM

AUTHOR'S NOTE

SOME STORIES ARE A joy to write. They just fall out of my pen. *What Could Possibly Go Wrong?* was one—apart from losing the twenty-thousand words relating to the princes in the Tower, which I still can't find—*The Nothing Girl* was another, and so was "My Name is Markham."

It's the first story I've ever written as a man—if you know what I mean—and I did have a few doubts. Jane Austen never wrote a scene in which a woman wasn't present because she didn't know how men spoke to each other when they were alone and I've always thought I couldn't do better than to follow her example.

However, the usual phrases and images were clogging up my brain so I thought I'd give the first few paragraphs a go and see what happened.

I couldn't stop—yes, I know, that's a phrase usually only applied to eating chocolate or staring at Matt Damon—but the story practically wrote itself. Although it is actually quite hard to write about sodden, smoky England when you're sitting downwind of two whirling electric fans because it's over forty degrees outside. There were times when I quite envied our hero as he splashed through the cool, damp Somerset countryside.

The one thing about this story is that it goes to show that authors know nothing, because I had killed off Markham in the original version of *Just One Damned Thing*. In that story, Max rescued him from the Cretaceous, along with a very young boy named Matthew Ellis, who was originally one of Ronan's men, left behind in the panic because he'd been blinded in the explosion.

He and Markham were in Sick Bay when Ronan attacked St. Mary's, full of plans for revenge and retribution, and Markham died bravely, vainly trying to protect young Ellis.

I can't remember now why I didn't stick with that—I think the story was just so long that the scene was cut and Markham was reprieved.

Not for long, though. He's shot at the end of the book and I was going to leave him bleeding into the sand. However—and I really don't know what this says about me—I had a sudden picture of him sitting naked at a table wearing nothing but a large wound dressing and playing cards with Nurse Hunter, who had herself barely appeared so far.

In one second he was transformed from expendable character to one of the major players, complete with girlfriends, backstory, and a clear path ahead of him. He's been one of my favourite characters ever since.

He was comparatively cooperative for this story and I could hear his little voice chirping away in my head. (My publisher says I'm not to mention the voices in my head because it makes people nervous and considerably hampers their—my publisher's—efforts to pass me off as a reasonably normal human being, so please don't tell anyone.) Anyway, I thought he was quite engaging as he chatted on about everything under the sun while still managing to get the job done and I hope you do too.

MY NAME IS MARKHAM

M Y NAME IS MARKHAM and I am a recovering security
guard.
Maxwell told me to write this report. Actually,
what happened was that I visited her in her office after our last
assignment and she took exception to me criticising a phrase
or two of her report, and the next thing I knew her scratchpad
flew across the room and hit me squarely on the back of the
head and she said if I thought I could do it any better then I
should write the bloody thing myself.
So I have.

IT WAS, BELIEVE IT or not, the day of The First St. Mary's Annual
Children's Christmas Party. We were doing it for charity. Well,
actually we were doing it because Dr. Bairstow had told us to.
I don't know who'd told him to do it. We were all contributing
something.
Professor Rapson, Head of R&D, had put together a rec-
ipe for artificial snow, which had set fire to his workbench,
and the smell of burning rubber was enough to blow your
socks off. Dr. Bairstow had forbidden any further research in
this area.

In the kitchens, Mrs. Mack was up to her armpits in jelly and sausages and cupcakes. Not all in the same mixing bowl, obviously.

Mrs. Enderby from Wardrobe was making costumes for us all. I was supposed to be one of Santa's Little Helpers, but Evans and I were going to be a reindeer. We'd manufactured a costume out of old blankets. We had a battery-driven nose and I had a couple of handfuls of black olives to drop behind us for authentic reindeer poo. Kids love that sort of thing. We were expecting to be the hit of the afternoon.

Dieter, the biggest man in the place, was to be Father Christmas. He could be heard ho ho ho-ing around the building and getting on everyone's nerves.

Hunter was dressing as Tinkerbell. I'm not sure what Tinkerbell has to do with Christmas, but you don't argue with her. Not unless you want a really, really clean colon.

And if you think that's terrifying, try Miss North as a particularly frosty Ice Queen. She'd offended Mrs. Enderby by hiring a magnificent costume especially for the day.

Bashford, Sykes, and Atherton, on behalf of the History Department, were the world's most mismatched elves.

Max was Anna, and Kalinda Black was Elsa. Kalinda Black is tall and blonde and just the sort of person who wouldn't be too careful where she hurls her icicles. I don't know what she does to anyone else, but she frightens the living daylights out of me. I couldn't believe they were going to let her near small children. She's usually at Thirsk, either fighting our corner for funding or apologising for us, depending on what sort of a week we've had, but she'd come back for The Party. St. Mary's was gathering its chicks for Christmas.

Dr. Foster was going as herself. No one argued with that.

The centrepiece of our efforts, however, was the ever-resourceful Miss Lingoss. Thanks to the best efforts of the Technical Section, her towering red and gold mohican was festooned with flashing fairy lights. She looked sensational.

There would be games, prizes, a dinosaur holo, and tons of party food.

Mr. Strong, our caretaker, was making a sleigh for Santa to arrive on.

The whole building was strung with fairy lights, tinsel, and streamers, and we had a giant Christmas tree in the Hall.

We were going to be a sensation and maybe this time, for all the right reasons.

Oh no, we weren't. As you were with the reindeer. Evans and me, practising in what we thought was a deserted part of the building, were caught rehearsing our reindeer dance and working on our poo-dropping technique—by Dr. Bairstow of all people. I mean, how did he even get up all those stairs? You watch him limping his way slowly around the building with all the speed of a striking snail, and one nanosecond later, he's two floors up and giving you a nasty look from the doorway.

We explained, but it was useless. I even showed him the really clever pouch we'd rigged—black olives for the scattering of—and believe it or not, he looked even more unimpressed. For some reason he laid all the blame at my door and I was ordered to report to Maxwell for the last assignment before Christmas.

I mean, what's that all about? I'd reckoned on a nice, gentle run-up to the festive season, including something imaginative with Nurse Hunter and a couple of beers, and the next minute I'm being despatched to the History Department so they can do something horrible to me.

I drew myself up to utter a well-worded protest, but he silently produced a massive wad of Deductions From Wages To Pay For Damages Incurred forms and, right in front of my eyes, slowly tore them in half.

I indicated my willingness to comply with his commands, and raced off before he could change his mind.

I'VE FORGOTTEN TO SAY that, this week, Major Guthrie was away at Thirsk, which left me in charge of the Security Section. His parting instructions had been clear.

"Never mind trying to keep them safe, Mr. Markham, it's never going to happen. I generally think that if 75 percent of them are still on their feet when we get them back to St. Mary's, then it's been a job well done. And if 75 percent of those not on their feet are still conscious, then it's been a resounding success. Personally, I prefer it when they're all limp, white, and unconscious in Sick Bay—especially the redhead—but that's too much to ask for."

"Got it, sir," I said, my mind on Tinkerbell and her tutu.

"Pay attention, Mr. Markham. Should any assignments occur during my absence, your priorities are as follows:

"One—bring them back.

"Two—bring them all back.

"Three—bring them all back alive.

"Four—bring them all back conscious.

"Five—bring them all back undamaged.

"Six—keep an eye on the redhead."

"Yes, sir."

"Good luck, Mr. Markham."

And off he'd gone, leaving me in charge.

And here I was in Maxwell's office, waiting to learn my fate.

When I was a boy, the man up the road had a cat that used to have these funny fits and go for you. It was perfectly normal most of the time, and then suddenly its eyes would go funny, and it would go mad, attacking everything in sight. Other cats, dogs, lorries, etc, whatever it could get its claws into, and the only warning we ever got was that its eyes would go funny. Historians have exactly the same expression. Bright-eyed madness. Which, as with the cat, always means trouble.

Our main function is protecting historians from themselves, each other, hostile contemporaries, meteorological and geological disturbances, social unrest, and just about everything the universe can throw at us, so as you can imagine, historians and trouble go hand in hand. Our other job is to guard the building, but that just entails watching the monitors and eating our own body weight in ham sandwiches while listening to the footie.

So when I walked into Max's office, and she and Peterson grinned at me with their mad cat eyes, I knew things were going to get exciting.

"What ho," said Peterson, cheerfully, his feet up on Max's desk.

"Good afternoon," I said, because I was now in charge of the Security Section and standards have to be maintained.

"A last-minute assignment," said Maxwell. "Are you up for it?"

I don't know about anyone else, but I've found that as the years have passed, I've become older and wiser, and certainly not stupid enough to jump blindly at something offered by the History Department.

"Of course," I said, which wasn't actually what I'd intended to say at all.

Peterson grinned. "Don't you want to know where and when?"

"Does it matter? It'll all pass by in a blur. There'll be a lot of running and panic. Nothing will go as planned, and I'll pick up some ghastly disease that will ruin my Christmas. The question I do want to ask is 'why now?'"

"Why now what?" they said, muddying the issue. I don't think they can help themselves.

"We're gearing up for the kids' Christmas Party this afternoon. What's so urgent it can't wait until after the New Year?"

They exchanged glances.

"There's been bit of a row."

"Really?" I said, interested. "Have I missed something?"

"Not here. At Thirsk."

"They're always having rows. They're academics. Who's hurt this time?"

"No one. Yet."

"So what's the problem?"

"There's been a certain amount of controversy over the cakes."

"What—you mean like who had the last slice when no one was looking?"

"Not quite," said Peterson carefully. "More like whether they were actually burned at all."

"Surely," I said, because they're historians and sometimes I just can't help winding them up, "this is something their catering department should be investigating. I fail to see why we should knock ourselves out because they've had a bit of a culinary crisis."

"Not them, cloth head," said Peterson, rising nicely to the bait. "Alfred."

"Oh, him. Cool."

They stared at me. They're lovely people, historians—a bit dim, of course, and with the life expectancy of a frog in a blender—but they do tend to think they're the only people who know anything about history. And that's history without the stupid capital H. Just ordinary history.

I sighed. Time to dazzle them.

"Alfred the Great. Can't remember the exact dates but late 9th century. Succeeded his brother Aethelred to become king. Led his country in the struggle against the Danes. Attacked at Chippenham and fled with a handful of men to the Somerset Levels. Conducted guerrilla warfare from there. Burned the cakes. Went on to defeat the Danes and negotiate peace. Enlarged the navy. Instituted legal reforms. Promoted schools and education. The only king other than Cnut to be called 'Great.' Was he the one you meant?"

They nodded, temporarily speechless. You don't see that happen often.

"So do I gather academic blood has been shed over the question of the cakes?"

They nodded again.

"And in the interests of festive goodwill we're off to check it out."

They nodded again.

"And, of course, this unseemly haste has absolutely nothing to do with avoiding the preparations for the kids' party and, with luck, the party itself."

They shook their heads. Absolutely not. How could I even think such a thing?

I heaved myself to my feet. "Just think, Max, next year your kid will be lining up for Santa, as well."

There was a funny sort of silence. I don't know why.

"What's the matter?" I said.

She shook herself. "I don't know. Something just walked across my grave."

"Oh, I get that a lot. Sometimes I think I must be buried in a pedestrian precinct somewhere. So—where and when?"

"Get yourself kitted out and we'll meet you in Hawking in one hour."

"Roger dodger," I said and went off to tell Hunter she'd have to start without me.

I SEE I'VE GOT this far and not explained anything.

We work for the Institute of Historical Research at St. Mary's Priory, just outside Rushford. We do time travel. We're

not supposed to say that and historians get right up their own
arses about it, but that's what we do. We're supposed to call it
investigating something or other in contemporary something
else, but it's time travel. We go back to some obscure event
hundreds or thousands of years ago, our historians get excited
about something or other, something horrible happens, we all
have to run for our lives, and the Security Section saves the
day. We're fairly light-hearted about the whole thing, but that's
because: historians haven't got a clue what's happening most
of the time; the Technical Section doesn't care as long as we
don't break anything; and the Security Section is incredibly
brave and resourceful. But mostly we're fairly light-hearted
because we have to be. People die here, and if we ever stopped
and thought carefully about what we do, then we might not do
it at all.

If I was asked though, I would have to say this assignment—Alfred and his cakes—looked reasonably straightforward. Don't confuse that with easy. Nothing is easy when St.
Mary's is involved. But straightforward was good. In, observe,
and out again. Everything should be fine.

I had a tricky ten minutes with Hunter and, since she was
wearing her Tinkerbell costume at the time, I might, if I hadn't
possessed enormous strength of character and determination,
have allowed myself to become distracted. Unfortunately, I
don't possess enormous strength etc, and my distraction nearly
got my face slapped, but that's usually quite a good sign with
Hunter, so I was optimistic that, on my return, we'd be doing
something interesting with her wand.

Mrs. Enderby in Wardrobe had my gear ready and waiting for me. A coarse, brown tunic, some trousers—thank God,
because I've lost count of the number of centuries that have
been gifted with a view of my nether regions—scruffy leather
shoes, and some sort of headgear that seemed to have been
made from a sack and came down over my shoulders.

Typically, Max and Peterson had commandeered much more upmarket costumes. Max wore a dark dress of some kind. No idea what the material was, but you didn't see her twisting and scratching in extreme discomfort. Peterson wore a short tunic and trousers and both of them had far more adequate footwear than that assigned to me. I made a mental note to request union representation again. Anonymously, of course. I'm not bloody stupid, you know.

And another thing; I don't know what 9th-century women wore under their dresses—actually I don't know what most women wear under their dresses in any century, Hunter has some strong views on that sort of thing—but I was prepared to bet that for all her protestations and insistence on historical accuracy, Maxwell was wearing anomalous underwear.

I stowed away a stun gun and pepper spray—purely for defensive purposes because we're really not allowed to injure contemporaries—and stared at myself in the mirror.

"Very nice," said Mrs. Enderby, brightly. "An authentic Anglo-Saxon peasant."

I was looking at Peterson and Maxwell's outfits and they certainly weren't Anglo-Saxon peasants. Just for once, why couldn't I be the lord, or the baron, or the rich merchant, and one or both of them be a member of the oppressed majority?

I might have mentioned this to them as we lined up outside pod Number Eight and it took them ages to stop laughing.

Peterson and I climbed inside to stow our gear, tactfully leaving Max and Chief Farrell a private moment together. I don't know why we bothered. They shook hands briskly and a moment later, she was inside with us. You'd never guess they were married. And with a kid. We don't talk about him a lot.

"Everything all laid in," said Dieter. "A quick in and out and back in time for the party. Ho ho ho."

I was checking the lockers, making sure I had everything I needed to repel whatever the 9th century was going to throw

at us. I knew dinosaurs and mammoths were extinct and the
Black Death hadn't arrived yet, but that wouldn't stop either of
them from discovering something new and innovative to die
from.

"All set?" said Maxwell, not waiting for a response. "Off we
go then. Computer, initiate jump."

"Jump initiated."

And the world went white.

WE STOOD IN THE doorway and looked around. If I was an
historian—and I think everyone at St. Mary's is grateful I'm
not—I'd be describing the scene in detail, listing the types of
trees and generally being intellectual. All I can say is that everything was wet. Really, really wet. It wasn't actually raining at
that moment, but the lull had only a very temporary feel to it.
The ground was soft and wet. The smell of wet earth, stagnant
water, and rotting leaves curled around us.

We had arrived around the beginning of April, 878 AD, and
spring was springing everywhere. Fat green buds were on the
point of bursting into leaf, although they were no greener than
the tree trunks themselves. Moss grew on everything in this
mild, wet climate. I could see new grass peeping through the
thickly rutted mud. But mostly, everything was wet. We were in
a world of wet.

"Bloody hell," said Peterson, pulling his foot free of the
gloopy mud with a sucking sound.

I was convinced we'd come to the wrong place. There was
no way Alfred would ever get a flame going here long enough
to set fire to anything, let alone the cakes. We were only two
steps from the pod and already Maxwell's hem was soaked—
something about which she would be complaining bitterly later
on. I've seen her endure blood, pain, and broken bones, but
she really doesn't do cold and wet. I think her natural habitat is
a hot bath with a mug of tea.

We'd landed on the Isle of Athelney itself. Tactically, it was a good place for a king on the run—surrounded by marshland and swamps. There was a wooden causeway from Lyng to the island itself, but it was heavily guarded at both ends. Professor Rapson had wanted us to take a flat-bottomed punt to help us get around, but we couldn't get it in the pod. And we had tried; well, the professor, Peterson, and I tried. Maxwell said it wouldn't fit and just sat down with her arms folded, and that expression women have when they're right, they know they're right, and the whole world is only seconds away from knowing they're right. All women have it. Even Hunter. I reckon it's a gene thing and they can't help themselves.

WE SET OFF. MY clothes were itchy and smelled funny. Bloody historians always hog the best things for themselves. I'm always the bloody slave. Or the servant. Or the groom. Or whatever. It's only a matter of time before they make me the eunuch. Figuratively speaking. Maxwell's not so bad. She's a woman—or so she maintains—and she usually stays quietly at the back, keeping her head down and her mouth shut. Except for that time in Viriconium when she poked me so hard with her staff that she nearly impaled my bloody kidney. When I remonstrated in the mildest way possible, she told me that many people live a happy and useful life with only one kidney and to stop moaning for God's sake. Actually, Major Guthrie always says he feels a lot happier if she's in front of him, where he can keep an eye on her, and I think he might have a point, so this time, I stayed at the back, ready to spring into action the moment they got themselves into trouble.

I've only ever been to Somerset once and that was some time ago when I took a girlfriend to the Glastonbury Festival and she went all funny and started rolling her eyes around and falling over. We were all convinced she was channelling King Arthur or Merlin or something, but it turned out she just couldn't handle the local scrumpy.

What I'm trying to say is that, with the exception of the Glastonbury Festival which invariably attracts a year's worth of rain on its first day, Somerset is reasonably dry these days. Not so in the 9th century. I forget who was the first of us to fall into a bog, but it didn't matter because ten minutes into the jump we were all soaked and swampy.

There were paths. There must have been, otherwise the entire population would be permanently up to their knees in mud. In the end, I shouldered the two of them aside, cut myself a long pole, and used it to probe the ground ahead of us. There was a short "Why didn't I think of that?" silence and then they fell in behind me.

I have to say that while no one was ever going to get sunburned here, it was a brilliant place for a king to hide out. You'd never get an army in. And I bet anything metal had a life expectancy of about half an hour before it crumbled into rust. And that would be on a dry day. Which apparently, this was.

We meandered around pools of water, soggy trees, and fallen branches. It was as if the entire landscape conspired to make progress as difficult as possible. I watched my feet sink into the soft soil and each footprint fill up with water. Something twitched in the back of my mind and I stopped.

"What?" said Peterson.

"How heavy is a pod?"

"No idea. I've never tried to lift one. I'm standing in a puddle. Is this important?"

"Suppose the pod sinks."

"What do you mean, sinks? It's not the bloody Titanic. Number of icebergs seen today—nil." He stopped and there was a bit of a silence while they had a bit of a think.

"The weight is evenly distributed," said Maxwell, doubtfully. "It might sink a little, but surely not completely."

"How tall is a pod?"

"No idea, but Dieter can stand upright inside them and he's the biggest man I know. So over six-and-a-half feet."

"Seven feet three," said Peterson.

We stared at him.

"A pod is seven feet three inches tall," he said, with his *why don't you know that* expression, and I made plans to make him an honorary security guard so we could co-opt him on to our team for the Saturday night trivia quiz in the pub.

"It's not going to sink seven feet in a couple of hours," said Maxwell, giving me another poke. "It'll be fine."

Another shining example of the triumph of historian optimism over security guard experience.

We smelled the village long before we saw it. Wood smoke, animals—especially pigs—and cooking.

We crawled forwards amongst the trees to check it out, Maxwell tucking her skirt into her belt to keep it out of the mud. We stared at her legs.

"What?"

"Gryffindor rugby socks?" I said, my mind pondering life's injustices. For the purposes of historical accuracy, I'd been rammed into some musty old sack, probably complete with authentic 9th-century fleas bred by Professor Rapson especially for today, and bloody historians are wearing bloody rugby socks.

She wasn't listening. Of course she bloody wasn't. Neither of them were. They—all historians—have this kind of laser-like focus that drives everything else out of their heads. Not that there's room for much in there anyway. If only they could muster the same laser-like focus on staying alive. On the other hand, if they did, I'd be out of a job, so it's probably just as well they don't.

They'd pulled out their recorders and were muttering away. This could go on for hours. I settled myself against a tree trunk so nothing could get behind me and kept an eye out.

The village was a large clearing with some twenty huts of varying sizes. Most of them were round, and thatched with what looked like reeds. I wondered how waterproof they were. Moss grew on the roofs as well. Many huts had one or more lean-tos built against them, sheltering firewood and livestock. I don't know how waterproof the thatch was, but it did seem to me they were more likely to suffer from groundwater than rainwater. They'd made an effort to build above ground level, with each hut constructed on twelve-inch-high stone foundations that provided some sort of elementary damp-proof course. The stones themselves were thick with green slime and moss.

There were no streets, or even paths, but causeways made of brushwood ran across the clearing, from one hut to another, or to the big central stone pit where a large fire crackled, sending up a plume of blue-grey smoke to be lost in the blue-grey sky.

In contrast to the bustle all around him, a solitary figure sat cross-legged near the woodpile. Occasionally he would scramble stiffly to his feet and with great care and precision, place new logs on the fire.

I know the village idiot is a bit of a cliché, but the thing about clichés is that they tend to be true. Every village has at least one—if not many. I suppose when you don't ever have the opportunity to travel far from your birthplace, it's very hard not to marry your cousin. When the same families interbreed over the years, there are always casualties. They're usually cared for by the community in a way that is supposed to happen today and never does, and appropriate jobs are found for them. Firewood gathering. Keeping an eye on the less mobile livestock. And tending the fire, of course, as this one was doing.

He sat on an old log, huddled into his cloak. His head was down and I could see only a thatch of straw-like hair. Under his cloak he wore a faded red tunic that covered his knees. Everything below his knees was caked in dried mud.

And then, as he leaned over to add another log to the fire, the neck of his tunic gaped and I caught a hint of gold around his neck. At once, he pulled up the neck and wrapped his cloak even more closely around himself, but I'd seen it. And so had Maxwell and Peterson.

"Bloody hell," said Max, in quiet excitement. "That's him. That's Alfred. Must be."

No one is ever quite as you expect them to be. I remember those two legendary lovers, Julius Caesar and Cleopatra, and quite honestly, you'd have to go a long way to meet two uglier people than they were. They both of them had massive noses— maybe that's what drew them together in the first place—and Cleopatra had nostrils like the air intakes on a jet turbine. And eyebrows like two giant hairy caterpillars as well. It was a bit of a shock, I can tell you. Max always says that Henry V was the ugliest bloke she's ever seen—and that includes the men at St. Mary's, which I though was a little unkind of her. Despite being unable to clear five foot six inches unless I'm standing on tip-toe, and not being all there in the ear department, I'm not bad looking. And Hunter's always banging on about Chief Farrell's eyes—usually at some quite inappropriate moments, let me tell you—and apparently she's not the only one who thinks that. And Peterson—generally reckoned to be the best-looking bloke in the building—would be fighting off women with a stick, if they weren't all so terrified of Dr. Foster, of course.

I've forgotten where I was. Yes. Alfred. Alfred the Great as he would astoundingly be known. All right, I know I'd just mistaken him for the village idiot, but it's a mistake anyone could have made.

He was staring thoughtfully into the fire. Tradition says he was so busy formulating plans to defeat the Danes that he never noticed the cakes burning right in front of him. This Alfred, however, obviously took his job very seriously indeed, staring unblinking at the lumps of bread dough set out round

316

the fire, and bringing to them the same sort of single-minded concentration he would bring to every task in his life.

He wasn't much taller than me and that's saying something—but where I'm a living example of good things coming in little packages, he, not to overemphasise the point, wasn't. He was skinny—his arms and legs were stick thin. His face was a yellowy-white with swollen, protruding, bloodshot eyes. His skin was bad—not teenage acne, but a really nasty rash which ran down one cheek, under his chin, and down his neck. It looked too inflamed to shave, but I was willing to bet he didn't need to anyway. I think he was around thirty years old, but he still looked a boy. His movements were slow and creaky. I wondered if he had arthritis. If so, he wouldn't want to hang around here—arthritis capital of the world.

"Crohn's disease," muttered Peterson.

I looked at him.

"There's a theory he suffered from Crohn's disease. On top of everything else. He doesn't have an easy life."

Maxwell shrugged. "Some people thrive on adversity. Us, for example. Maybe he's another."

She had a point. We'd covered this in the briefing. Alfred was a fighter. Legend says that at a frighteningly early age he won a book of Saxon poems from his mother by memorising the entire contents. He had been, as we could see, a sickly child, but he stood alongside his brother, King Aethelred, in the year of the nine battles. When the king died, Alfred was named his successor, even though the king had two young sons. No one objected, so he must have proved his worth. His position was weak, though, and he had no option but to sue for peace. He bought off the Danes, who retired to London, presumably to count their money.

Five years later the Danes had a new leader—Guthrum. Again, Alfred negotiated a peace, but Guthrum broke the treaty. He attacked Chippenham where Alfred was staying for Christmas, killing nearly everyone. Alfred and a small band of

followers barely escaped to Athelney. And here he was—at the
lowest point of his life. Defeated, alone, exiled, ill, and with no
immediate hope of a comeback, scrounging food and shelter in
exchange for such service as he could offer.

Even as we watched, he stood up, stretched stiffly, collected
a few more logs from the pile, and carefully laid them across
the fire.

"Don't underestimate what he's doing," said Peterson.
"This is the communal fire. They'll use it for cooking, drying
wood and clothes, and smoking fish and game. This is the fire
from which all other fires are lit. It's never allowed to go out.
Look at the ash bed on it."

He was right. I couldn't spare a lot of attention—I was
watching their backs because they certainly weren't—but I
could see pans of water set to heat up on homemade trivets,
together with pots, skillets, and cauldrons, all carefully arranged
around the fire. On an arrangement of flat hearth stones at his
feet sat about two dozen lumps of what I'd taken to be dough of
some kind, either proving or cooking in the heat.

"They'll sit round this in the evening," said Maxwell. "I'm
betting those huts are cold and damp. They'll stay by the fire
as long as possible, only going inside to sleep or get out of the
rain. They'll use this one to light their small private fires at
night in their own huts."

I looked at their huts. Their cold, damp, chimney-less huts.
No wonder everyone preferred to gather around the fire. Life
was lived outside. You only went inside when the weather was
bad. I imagined life inside one of those small round huts. I
saw them sitting inside, either in the dark or by the light of a
wick burning in some evil-smelling animal fat. Their tiny fire
would produce a disproportionate amount of smoke, all curl-
ing around looking for a way out. I heard the rain dripping
through the roof. Saw the water oozing up through the floor.
Wet clothes. Wet bedding. What a life.

And yet they seemed cheerful enough.

"Well, they don't know any better, do they?" said Maxwell. "They probably think they've got all mod cons here and life is good."

A bit of a disbelieving silence there.

A number of people were trudging along a broad causeway: the men, home from gathering food. Several of them had a fish or two on a line. One had what looked like a brace of rabbits. Others had various waterfowl, swinging by their feet. But all of them carried a bundle of firewood each, and the first thing they did was distribute it. Two thirds of what they carried went on the big communal pile by the fire. Only one third was stacked neatly in their own hut's lean-to for their private use. And yes, all right, that was quite interesting, but Peterson and Maxwell were nearly having orgasms, muttering about communal needs and teamwork and God knows what. I listened with only half an ear—quite appropriate in my case—because a herd of mammoths could have cantered past at that moment and they'd have missed them. They seemed entirely oblivious to the fact that there were people all around the place, and that half a dozen of them could trip over us at any moment, and good luck with explaining we weren't Danes.

I ran an eye around as much as I could see of the landscape, but everything seemed quiet enough. Birds still sang in the trees, which usually means nothing unpleasant is creeping about. Apart from us, of course.

I became aware the two of them were on the move, crawling about picking up sticks and odd bits of wood. I put a stop to this madness by simply grabbing their tunics and hauling them back again.

"Where do you think you're going?"

Maxwell sighed as if she couldn't believe such stupidity. "Down there, of course."

"Are you out of your minds?" I said, and I think we all know the answer to that one. "The whole country's on Dane alert. They'll skewer you as soon as you appear."

"No they won't," said Peterson, who's also no better than he should be. "That's why we're gathering firewood. As a gift. Firewood is a currency. They'll love us. You just wait and see."

There was no arguing with them. The Major always says the main purpose of the History Department is to get themselves into trouble, and the main purpose of the Security Section is to get them back out again. I sighed heavily and followed them, prepared to fulfil my main purpose, and pausing on the way to pick up a bit of wood.

Peterson stared at it. "Is that the best you can do?"

I considered explaining the importance of remaining hands-free in case of trouble, but they wouldn't have understood me. As I said, historians are lovely people but single-minded. Very, very single-minded.

OK. TIME TO SET the record straight. Yes, history is quite interesting. Even without the capital H. And yes, you can tell the History Department I said that. Sadly, the most interesting parts are probably not true. Poor old Teddy Two probably didn't get the red-hot poker up his bum. Robert the Bruce probably didn't interact with the famous spider in the cave. The lights of Cairo probably did not go out the night Lord Caernarvon died. It's a shame, but there you are.

And I can definitely say, without any hesitation whatsoever—King Alfred did not burn the cakes. Because, for a start, I think it was bread—not cakes. But whatever it was—and I might as well carry on saying cakes—he didn't burn them. We did. We burned the cakes. Well, actually, I did.

Yeah. Sorry about that.

I DON'T KNOW IF he ever gets tired of being right. Probably not. But Peterson was right. They didn't love us, but they didn't kill us either, which is usually the best we can hope for. We walked slowly down the causeway and into the clearing. Peterson went first, with his bundle of firewood. Maxwell followed on behind, staggering slightly under her load because, of course, she'd picked up far more than she could comfortably carry and wouldn't admit it. And, finally, came me, the slave, clutching my twig.

A goodwife scattering something to a herd of marauding chickens was the first to catch sight of us, calling something over her shoulder, clattering her wooden bucket against a stone to attract attention, and then standing straight and still outside her hut.

Around the village, heads lifted. The women melted away and men came forward. None of them carried a sword, but one or two conveniently held axes and one, a monster man with muscles to match, carried a hammer. A visiting smith, maybe. They weren't threatening—they were just there, directly in our path, and it was very obvious we weren't going any farther.

I stood quietly at the back, making an excellent job of portraying the hapless slave who really didn't want to be here. Why on earth we couldn't have watched Alfred's culinary catastrophe from up beyond the treeline was a bit of a mystery to me, but who was I to argue?

Peterson said something, bowed slightly and gestured to his load of wood and then to Maxwell. He was probably introducing them in order of social importance. Wood first, then wife. He didn't bother with me at all. One day, I really am going to have to have a word with them about this.

They could see we weren't armed and they didn't seem particularly bothered by my twig. After a bit of muttering, they stepped aside and indicated the fire. So we'd obviously done the right thing with the firewood. And we couldn't just dump our offerings on the pile, either. There were three distinct components, light brushwood, probably used for lighting this and other fires, medium-sized logs in the middle, and really big logs up near the fire. One of those would probably last a whole night. We laid our offerings appropriately and stepped back.

I think the plan was just to sit quietly by the fire as if we were resting travellers, observe what was going on, watch for Alfred igniting the baked goods, and then make ourselves scarce. Of course, quietly never happens. As Max once explained to me, the mere fact of us being there tends to upset the balance of things. History is trying to get rid of us—like an irritating piece of grit in your eye, she said, looking straight at me for some reason—hence hardly anything goes according to plan. I'm pretty sure this is historian speak for it's all gone tits-up again and it's probably our fault, but don't tell Dr. Bairstow.

Anyway, we settled ourselves by the fire. Maxwell spread her wet skirts to dry and they brought us beer. Nice hospitable folk.

We sat and sipped. Well, Peterson and I did. Max held her beaker as if it would twist in her hand and bite her at any moment, so I finished mine and started on hers as well. It wasn't bad.

I know I'm always banging on about them but—when they put their minds to it—our historians are bloody good. They sat quietly by the fire, ostensibly resting from their travels and drying out, but I knew neither of them would have taken their eyes off Alfred, and that at least one of them would be discreetly recording the village and its inhabitants at the same time. The villagers carried on with their working day. Everything was fine.

Alfred stood up again and, using a cloth, began to select hot stones from around the hearth, dropping one into each cauldron of water. To help them boil more quickly, I assumed. While he was on his feet, he checked the little balls of dough, still proving around the fire, turning one or two to better positions. When he'd finished that, he fed the fire again. He was careful and conscientious, obviously taking his responsibilities very seriously, and only when he was satisfied everything was in order did he come to sit alongside us. I could feel Maxwell quivering with excitement and she was a good three feet away.

He greeted us courteously enough. I could see Max and Peterson were having difficulty understanding him, though, and Peterson responded in Latin. That was enough for Alfred and a moment later, they were well away. I've picked up a bit of Latin over the years and could mostly follow what was being said. He was asking for news.

Peterson responded gravely, saying as little as possible and none of it good. I could see Alfred's face cloud with disappointment. His shoulders slumped and he sighed and looked away. He looked so dejected and lonely, and I only meant it as a kindness, but I offered him my beaker of beer. He looked at it for a while and then at me. Properly. Seeing the man and not the servant. He inclined his head and thanked me politely. Suddenly, I could see why, physically frail though he was, men followed him.

Peterson had wandered off to commune with the midden, so I turned to Maxwell and said, "Can you translate for me?"

She nodded.

If Alfred was surprised to be addressed by a servant and a woman, he had the manners not to show it.

I said, "You shouldn't give up. You should never give up. There's a saying: This too will pass. And it will. Everything gets better. Because nothing stays the same. Bad becomes good. Good becomes bad as well—you can't stop that—but you can be ready for it and deal with it when it happens. But this . . ." I gestured around us, "all this—will pass. You should remember that. That's what I did when I was a kid and some things were too bad to think about. I used to tell myself—this will pass. And it always does."

OK. Surprised myself a bit there. I've never actually mentioned my private life to anyone except Hunter, and then only briefly, and no one was more surprised than me when she put her arms around me and cried a little, which nearly set me off as well.

I waited for Maxwell to catch up and then ploughed on.

"When I was a kid, there were bad times, when nothing went right, and I had to do some things I didn't want to. Like you do when you buy off the Danes. Anyway, I got caught. Several times, actually."

I paused again, remembering. The magistrate had been quite a decent old stick. We got to know each other quite well. He always said how grieved he was to see me standing in front of him yet again, and I would point out, quite reasonably, I think, that if the police stopped arresting me then he wouldn't have to, would he?

Anyway, I was caught once too often and they gave me a choice. Detention or the army. I chose the army and things got better. Because all things pass.

I shifted on my uncomfortable log. "What I'm trying to say is that everything passes and you should never give up because bad times always get better. One day, all this will be in your past. There's a story about a bloke hiding in a cave somewhere, watching a spider struggling to spin a web. It keeps trying. It never gives up. And eventually it succeeds. The man learns from the spider. He doesn't give up and neither should you."

I sat back and watched his face while Maxwell repeated all that in Latin.

When she'd finished, there was a bit of a silence and then, without looking at me, she scooted up and she put her hand on mine. Just for a very quick moment. I patted it carefully because she can be a bit unpredictable sometimes and it made me nervous to have her that close.

Anyway, Alfred seemed impressed—although whether by my tale-telling abilities or my prowess with short redheads was hard to say. We sat quietly together watching the flames, and then all hell broke loose and, just for once, none of it was our fault.

A little girl ran past us. She was wearing what I suspected was her mother's dress, cut down to fit, but still much too big. Her face was alight with excitement.

She ran to a hut, fiddled with the latch, and dragged the door open. Her mother—I assumed—busy tipping slop to the pigs, shouted a warning, but too late.

A dog flew out of the door. Not one of the short-legged, curly-tailed mongrels we'd seen sniffing around the place, but a long-legged, silky-haired aristocrat. Obviously someone's pride and joy. Probably the best hunting dog in the village and, just at this moment, in what you might call a very . . . receptive state.

She raced past the little girl, knocking her over into the mud. The little girl began to wail. Her mother dropped the bucket and ran towards her. The pigs were vocal in their disapproval of this action.

For some reason, I tensed. This had all the makings of one of *those* sort of situations.

The dog ran past us, eyes bright, tongue lolling, and obviously feeling extremely friendly towards other dogs.

The first to notice her was some disreputable rat-thing curled up as close to the fire as he dared to get. Unable to believe his luck, he raced towards her as fast as his stumpy little legs would carry him. He was half her size and I couldn't help wondering what he thought he was going to do when he got there, but I needn't have worried. He took a flying leap and hung on for grim death.

Sadly for him, he didn't enjoy himself for long. I suspected that, rather like me, he was quite some way down in the pecking order, and by this time, others had realised what was happening.

More dogs piled on and it got nasty. Fights broke out. One minute we had a lovely, peaceful rural scene and the next minute we were all embroiled in some sort of massive dog punch-up.

A huge, solid mass of yelping, yapping, baying, growling, snapping, snarling dogs was cartwheeling around the place. Things were knocked over. The pig troughs went flying, distributing their contents in a kind of graceful arc. The pig protests increased in volume. Other things toppled. Shrieking chickens fluttered about, tripping people up in their efforts to fly to safer areas. Women picked up screaming kids. Other dogs raced to join in. Cats yowled and fled for the rooftops. Red-faced men shouted and wildly laid about them with sticks.

Somehow, in all the confusion, we got separated. Peterson was over at the midden anyway, Alfred ended up on the other side of the fire, and Maxwell was swept away in the confusion. I don't think she was in any great danger, but I couldn't afford to let anything happen to her. Chief Farrell would stare at me reproachfully. Then Dr. Bairstow would give it a go, and then Major Guthrie would do a bloody sight more than stare. I had to act with decision and competence.

I stood up and fell over a small child.

You would think, wouldn't you, that parents would be more careful with their offspring and not just leave them lying around all over the place.

A woman, backed up against the same fence as Maxwell, swung her bucket at the seething mass of dogs, missed, and fetched Maxwell a great buffet across the chest. She fell backwards over the fence, showing vast amounts of long crimson and gold rugby socks which were, in the absence of the Sky Sports Channel, probably the most exciting thing they'd seen around here for years.

They would almost certainly have caused a stir if everyone's attention hadn't been on the fact that every dog for miles around was desperate to join the fun, convinced he finally had a chance with the snooty bitch who was never allowed out to play.

Maxwell, meanwhile, was on her back in the pigpen—a phrase I really feel isn't used anything like often enough. Remembering I'm supposed to prevent this sort of thing, I went to help her up out of the mud, but as I moved to assist, Peterson caught my arm and held me back, saying softly, "Why not just give it a moment, eh?"

So we stood and watched, and it was bloody funny because every time she managed to pull herself up, an excited dog or two would race past and down she would go again. Only when the language became particularly ripe was I permitted to intervene.

We went to pick her up and strangely, she wasn't in the happiest mood.

"Where were you?"

"I was here," I said, injured. Where did she think I would be?

"And you didn't intervene because. . . ?"

"Well, they might have turned on me. Did you see the teeth on that mastiff?"

"Yes, actually, I did, thanks to you. Did you at any point remember your primary function here?"

"Of course," I said, drawing myself up proudly. "Not to interfere. Not to do anything to change the course of history. Not to . . ." I paused.

"Not to allow historians to be damaged."

"Yeah. I always forget that one."

She opened her mouth but, thankfully, before she could utter, the noise of dogs rose to a crescendo. The excited barking and yapping had turned to yelping. Dogs were scattering in all directions, tails between their legs, crying in pain. We turned to see what had happened.

They'd been scalded. Not badly—but, with a sense of self-preservation historians would do well to emulate—they were disappearing as fast as their stumpy little legs could carry them. Two seconds later, apart from the grinning hussy who had caused all the trouble—and no, this time I don't mean Maxwell—the village was completely dog free.

Nobody was paying them the slightest attention. There had been a disaster.

The area around the fire was swimming in water. Empty cauldrons and pots lay on their side. Whether someone had deliberately thrown the water over the dogs to separate them, or whether the dogs had knocked them over in the mêlée, was not clear. One thing, however, was very clear.

The fire was out.

Everything had stopped dead, the place was a shambles. Some of the fences had been knocked down and the pigs were out. The chickens were on the roof. The carefully stacked wood-pile was overturned. Washing lay in the mud. Buckets and barrels had been overturned and their contents trampled into the mud.

So this was how the cakes were burned, and we'd missed it.

Maxwell was wiping her face and Peterson was being menaced by a very agitated pack of . . . geese, I think. Big, nasty-looking birds anyway. But not swans, I was happy to note. Otherwise I'd be up a tree by now. Not that that would help. St. Mary's swans can climb trees as well. Why they would want to, I don't know, but they can.

Oh no. As you were. This was *not* the day the cakes were burned. Unbelievably, about the only things not damaged in the entire riot were the lumps of dough still sitting serenely at the edge of the ex-fire. I stared at them in disbelief—you'd have thought they would have been the first casualties, but no, there they were. Intact and unburned. Incredible.

All around us, people were distraught. They were running around like ants, and as if that wasn't enough, it had started to rain again. Not hugely, just a gentle drizzle that soaked everything without you actually noticing.

We did what we could to help, setting things upright again, picking the washing out of the mud, and draping it over fences, but they couldn't get the fire going again. Don't get me wrong— they weren't unskilful. Half-a-dozen men were working away with fire steels and pieces of flint, but it just wasn't working. Anglo-Saxon curses filled the air. People were getting wet. The wood was wet. The fire was out. There would be no warmth tonight. No light. No hot meal. No bread.

Men were restacking the all-important log pile. And still no fire. There were plenty of flames being generated, but nothing would catch. Some people were rubbing two sticks between their hands as well, blowing gently on to a handful of dried grass or what looked like sheep's wool. There was plenty of smoke, but no flames. Somewhere, a child began to cry.

I know we're not supposed to interfere. God knows, we've had that drummed into us often enough. And most of us learned our lesson at Troy. You don't interfere. There are consequences.

I stood and watched their increasingly desperate efforts to get the fire going again. I don't know why all the other people didn't try to get under some sort of cover, but they didn't. Those who weren't desperately trying to get a flame stood in tight groups. Watching. Their fire more than just a tool. It was a symbol of something important to them. And it should never be allowed to go out.

I stepped back and stared at the ground.

We're only supposed to record and document. To stand back and watch people living their lives. To watch events unfold and record them. And we do. I've lost count of the coronations, or assassinations, or battles I've witnessed and I don't know why this was any different. This wasn't some major historical event. This was a few people whose lives weren't that great anyway, facing what was, in their world, a disaster. It's hard to believe, I know. Lighting a fire seems such a small thing. But it was everything to these people. Their only source of light, heat, food, and all the rest of it. Their source of life.

The rain began to speed up, coming down faster.

Maxwell and Peterson reappeared, surveying the shambles.

"Did we do this?" I said to Maxwell.

She shook her head. "Not directly, although I might be responsible for the pigs getting out."

"And," said Peterson, thoughtfully, "Alfred hasn't burned the cakes."

We surveyed the lumps of dough sitting innocently amongst the carnage.

"We don't know that," said Maxwell. "We only know he hasn't burned the cakes today."

"Suppose they never get burned. Suppose it should have happened today and now it never will."

We looked at each other and then at Alfred silently helping to re-stack the woodpile, his face tired and sad. And without hope.

I sighed. It was going to have to be me, wasn't it?

"I'll be back," I said, hoping they'd mistake me for Arnie, but I think it went straight over their heads. Not difficult, I suppose. Typical bloody historians—they think they're so smart and yet they never get the cultural references. They certainly didn't get this one.

"OK," said Peterson, vaguely, all his attention on the villagers' attempts to restart the fire. I don't think Maxwell even noticed I was gone.

IT ONLY TOOK ME about half an hour to get to the pod and back. You can certainly cover the ground a lot more quickly when there aren't any historians to slow you down, and I hardly fell into any bogs at all. I knew what I wanted. I banged in the combination, opened the locker door and grabbed what I needed, shoved it all in an old bag, and trotted back again, splashing through watery mud and muddy water, eventually arriving back at the village hot, breathless, and very wet. Well, I'd been wet when I set out. I was soaked to the bloody skin now.

This was going to be difficult. I couldn't just march into the village and let rip. I circled around, eventually finding a little spot that would do nicely, pulled out a fizzer, and shouted, "Fire from the sky. Fire from the sky."

At the same time, I ripped the tab off the fizzer. You're supposed to fire them into the air, but I shot this one into a damp pine tree where it caught on a branch clearly visible to anyone looking, and legged it out of there.

Away through the trees, Maxwell and Peterson, who aren't anywhere near as stupid as they'd like us to believe, were shouting, "Fyra fram heofon! Fyra fram heofon!" Fire from the sky. Fire from the sky. At least, I assume that's what it was. Whatever they were yelling, the cry was taken up and I could hear people crashing through the trees.

It was time to go, so I went.

I circled back around the village. Most of the men had seized some kind of weapon and were charging towards the strange red glow they could see. Well, everyone could see it, actually. It was a distress flare and they're designed to be seen from a great distance and in all sorts of weather conditions.

I hid behind a lean-to, making sure I had a clear line of sight to the fire. Intentionally or otherwise, Max and Peterson were clearing the area around the fire, pointing at the strange red glow away in the trees.

I switched the blaster to full power and waited for it to stop whining. I had to be quick. They'd all be back in a minute. The second the charged light came on, I brought the gun up and fired. A good long, straight blast of white hot flame, directly at the fire. About seven seconds would probably have done it, but I would only get this one chance and I had to make sure, so I gave it fifteen, which, as I did admit to Dr. Bairstow afterwards, might have been a bit of overkill.

All right, so they hadn't been able to get a flame, but that massive ash bed had been there for weeks. Months, maybe and although the top layers might have been a bit soggy, there must have been a good heat still, right at the very bottom.

For a second, nothing happened and then wood and ash exploded in all directions. Everyone ducked and the whole thing went up like a pillar of flame. As Max said afterwards, it was quite biblical. You looked for a fiery chariot. Well, apparently she did, she said. Pieces of burning wood were scattered all over the village. Several pieces landed on thatched roofs where, given the general sogginess of everything in the area, they spluttered and went out.

The point was, however, that the fire was lit. Well, more than lit, actually. We had a bit of a raging inferno on our hands. Livestock bolted. Women screamed. Peterson later admitted he might have screamed himself.

I stowed the blaster up in the lower branches of an old tree, scraped off some moss to leave a fresh scar on the trunk so that I could find it later, and strolled casually into the village with my patented "nothing to do with me" expression.

Men came racing back and there was confusion and consternation and a lot of shouting, but the whole point—as I kept having to say—was that the bloody fire was going again. Everyone would have a hot meal tonight.

Alfred—King Alfred, I suppose I should call him—was one of the few who had failed to run into the woods to check out the big red spitting thing in the tree. He turned and watched me walk towards him, stared at me for a few seconds and then turned back to the fire again. He was quite bright, was Alfred. I gave him the guileless smile. The one that never works on Hunter. Or Dr. Bairstow. Or anyone, now I come to think of it.

It didn't work on him, either. He stared thoughtfully at me and opened his mouth to say something.

I could only think, bugger—busted.

I was marshalling explanations when someone behind me screamed with rage and I was shoved suddenly sideways. I staggered and nearly fell into the bloody fire. Peterson grabbed my arm and pulled me back.

Now what?

Whatever Alfred might or might not have been about to say to me will forever remain unknown. He was under attack. Some ancient, crooked goodwife with a face like leather and no teeth was shrieking curses at him. He was backing off, hands held palms outwards in a placatory manner. He might as well not have bothered. She was incandescent with fury. If the fire hadn't already been lit, then they could certainly have used her as a firelighter. He was trying to say something, but I could have told him he was wasting his breath. The best thing you can do with women is to let them get it off their chests—whatever it is—and then deal with the aftermath, when they eventually wind down.

This one showed no signs of winding down. She looked about a hundred and eight, which meant she was probably around forty and she was as skinny as the broom handle she was waving around in front of him. In front of Alfred, her king. I wondered if I should do something.

To shouts of laughter and encouragement from the villagers, she fetched him an almighty great buffet around the ear that nearly knocked both of them into the middle of next week. I had no idea what she was carrying on about, actually, I was just glad it wasn't me.

"Well, I'll be buggered," said Peterson from behind me. "Will you look at that?"

"What?"

"That."

We all looked at that.

In all the legends of Alfred and the cakes, you get the impression they were just a bit singed. Alfred burnt the cakes it says. The unspoken implication being you could just scrape off the black bits—much as Max does when she makes toast—and carry on as before. Not this time.

These cakes weren't just burned. They were completely incinerated. Pure carbon. A couple of dozen little black nuggets smoked gently on the scorched hearthstones, and she really wasn't happy about it. Not happy at all. Alfred was giving ground, trying to defend himself from the blows raining down upon him. Everyone seemed to think it was extremely funny. Except the goodwife, of course. Alfred dodged around the other side of the fire. Still shrieking, she pursued him.

At this point, even I wouldn't have blamed Alfred if he'd turned and pointed at me. You know—blame the slave. In this case, of course, quite justifiably. But he didn't. He covered his head as best he could and tried to dodge the blows. People were still laughing and shouting advice.

And he'd burned the cakes. The legend was true after all. Well, I'd burned the cakes and he'd got the blame—which makes a change. In my case, it's usually the other way around. Dr. Bairstow often makes quite spirited attempts to blame me for things that happened even before I was born. Or even before they've happened. Like the reindeer thing. . .

Speaking of which. . .

I plucked at Maxwell's sleeve. She nodded. "Yes, we should go. While we still can."

We discreetly gathered up our stuff. No one was paying any attention to us in any way and we quietly left the village. I glanced back. The flames had settled down a little. Pans and cauldrons were being righted and filled with water again. Normal life was resuming.

Alfred, now minus the goodwife, resumed his position, elbows on his knees, watching the fire. Just as I was about to turn away, he looked up at me. For a moment, we looked at each other. He raised a hand—whether in farewell or thanks, I'd never know. I waved back and then turned to follow Max and Peterson, who could be heard falling off the path some way ahead.

I nipped off to retrieve the blaster. The fizzer had fizzed itself to a standstill without igniting the tree in which it was lodged.

We hurried on towards the pod. It would be dark in an hour. Time to go. Job done. Alfred had fulfilled his part of the legend. And I like to think the whole afternoon had cheered him a little. Given him some hope, perhaps.

In seven weeks, around Whitsuntide, he would ride to Ecgbrihtesstan—Egbert's Stone—to rally the men from Somerset and Wiltshire and Hampshire to his banner. They would go on to beat the Danes, Alfred would be king again, and Guthrum would accept defeat and baptism. England would be saved. For the time being.

It was darker in amongst the trees, and, to tell the truth, just a little bit spooky. Mists curled up through them and now, far from echoing with birdsong and sounds of small creatures in the undergrowth, everywhere was completely silent. Something white—an owl, I hoped—drifted soundlessly past at head height.

I stopped and looked back. Apart from a faint glow visible through the trees, there was no sign anyone lived nearby. I could see why Alfred had chosen to hide out here.

We hurried on, splashing our way back to the pod. Which, contrary to historians' dire predictions, had not collided with an iceberg and sunk. A small amount of smelly water washed in with us as we opened the door, but as Peterson said, the smell of old cabbage was so bad that no one would notice anyway.

St. Mary's, in contrast to the dark, damp woods of the 9th century, was lit up like a Christmas tree—appropriately enough.

We decontaminated, tidied ourselves up, and made our way to Sick Bay where Hunter, disappointingly no longer dressed as Tinkerbell and now clutching a scratchpad, didn't hang about.

"Right—which of you is most injured?"

"None of us," said Maxwell. "Can we get a move on?"

"What have you eaten or drunk?"

"Nothing. I'm starving and desperate for a pee. Can we hurry things along, please?"

Hunter thrust a small container. "Fill that."

Max regarded it in silence. "You'd better let me have a couple of those. Or possibly a small bucket."

"Do you have one in blue?" said Peterson, not helping.

I smiled winningly and waited for her to wilt beneath the Markham charm.

Fat chance. She rounded on me. "What are you doing? Stop that. You'll frighten the children."

"They're here already?" I said, panicking a little because you can't just scramble into a reindeer costume. There are antlers and flashing noses and poo distribution systems to set up. To say nothing of keeping my face out of Evans's backside. I needed to get a move on.

"I'll go first," I said, taking the container. "I can't let anything get between me and the back end of a reindeer," and as the words left my mouth I realised they could be open to misinterpretation, but only by people with nasty minds. Which is all of St. Mary's and especially those standing in front of me.

"I'm not going in the scanner after him," said Peterson in pretended horror, stepping back. "He's a pervert. God knows what he'd leave lying around in there."

"Agreed," said Maxwell and the two of them pulled rank and I had to wait. I made myself a cup of tea, because I don't live in a world where nurses make it for me, and called up Evans.

The History Department disappeared eventually, bickering away, and then it was my turn.

Usually, when it's just Hunter and me, these things can take ages because she says she has to be thorough and, believe me, she is. There have been times when I can barely . . . yes, well, never mind about that now. Sometimes, and for God's sake don't tell anyone this, because I don't think anyone's noticed, but sometimes, after everyone's been scanned, Hunter and I—well, you know. Which is why I always made a point of wearing my best CKs, because even though she worships the ground I walk on—or will one day, I'm sure—there are occasions when the old tightie-whities just won't cut it.

This was not going to be one of those occasions, however, because I knew Evans was waiting in the lift with the reindeer outfit, so I patted her on the shoulder, told her I'd see her later, and pushed off. I'd pay for that later, of course, but I was betting she'd be so thrilled by the reindeer routine that she'd just melt into my arms.

WE CHANGED IN THE lift—and that's not as easy as it sounds. We did Evans first, carefully tying on his antlers and manoeuvring his nose into position. Then me, with the poo pouch dangling between my back legs. I think I can confidently say that's the first time that phrase has ever been used in English Literature.

We had a quick practice—Evans flashed his nose a couple of times. It was dazzlingly bright. We might have over-egged the pudding a little. He was quite blind afterwards. I popped a couple of olives in the poo pouch and wiggled my hips. Distribution successful.

"I can't see a bloody thing," muttered Evans, bouncing off a wall.

"They say that flashing makes you blind," I said, to cheer him up, which didn't work at all, and he told me he'd had egg sandwiches for lunch, and I said he'd better not have and what had I said about that, and he said, sorry, he forgot, but it would probably be OK, and there was rather a tense silence between us, broken only by the sound of someone summoning the lift back up to Sick Bay.

"Quick," I said, and we exited in a hurry. The doors closed and we waited.

"Five, four, three, two, one," said Evans.

"WHO THE BLOODY HELL HAS CRAPPED IN THIS LIFT?"

The words reverberated around the building.

Oh, swiving hell. Swive is a word I'd learned in the 17th century and which has been standing me in good stead ever since. I'd thought it would be Hunter in the lift and we'd have a bit of a giggle, only we'd got Dr. Foster instead and believe me, she doesn't giggle. We could hear her stamping down the stairs. The Footsteps of Fear on the Staircase of Misery.

"Run," said Evans, and we did.

IT'S NOT A JOB for the fainthearted, being the back end of a pantomime reindeer. After only a few minutes, I had neck ache, back ache, and knee ache. It was bloody dark in there and I couldn't see a thing. Not that I could have seen much anyway. Evans has a backside the size of a small pony.

We trotted down the long corridor towards the Great Hall where the festivities were scheduled to take place. The plan was that someone would put their hand to their ear and say, "Oh. I think I can hear someone coming. I wonder who that could be?" and Father Christmas would appear.

I mean—seriously? It's hardly Shakespeare, is it? And trust me, I've met him.

And then Dieter—sorry, Father Christmas—would make a spectacular entrance, pulling up in his sleigh. He would ho ho ho his way through the front doors, followed by his entourage of Ice Queens, Fairies, Elves, Santa's Little Helpers, and all the rest of them, into which we would, with skill and cunning, insert ourselves. Small gifts would be distributed and then, in the lull between that and everyone sitting down and gorging themselves on Mrs. Mack's festive offerings, we planned to do our little show.

Naturally, we needed an accomplice to work the music, and after careful consideration as to levels of technical skill— which ruled out the entire History Department—and sense of humour—ditto the Technical Section—we'd selected Miss Lingoss for the honour, on the grounds that anyone with fairy lights in her hair couldn't be all bad, and she'd agreed. To do it I mean.

THE INITIAL COMMENTS WERE not encouraging.

"Oh, look—are Mary and Joseph here? Have they brought their ass?"

There followed a lot of rude banter which, given the festive season and the age of our waiting audience was not, I felt, appropriate.

Evans tried propitiating people with his nose and that didn't work at all.

"You. Reindeer," said Santa, sternly. "Up front—with me."

We sidled delicately into place and prepared to dazzle the room.

"OK, people," said Santa. "This is it."

The doors were flung open and we were on.

It all went horribly wrong. We hadn't practised climbing steps. I couldn't see where I was going. Evans tripped. Then I tripped. We lurched into Santa who staggered into the Great Hall, belatedly trying to retrieve the situation by bellowing, "Ho ho ho. Merry Christmas everyone," at the top of his voice.

Three kids burst into tears there and then, and there were only twelve of them anyway, so that was 25 percent of them crying their eyes out. Wasn't it? Yes, one quarter. Twenty-five percent. And we were only thirty seconds in.

The parents, unsure of what to expect from the nutters at St. Mary's, who had therefore insisted on accompanying their children, bristled and began to gather offspring to their bosoms, prior to a hasty departure.

I'd banged my nose on Evans's bottom (again, not a phrase often used by Jane Austen) and was beginning to have second thoughts about the whole thing—traumatising kids at Christmas just doesn't feel right somehow—when I heard our music. We later discovered that Lingoss—a bright girl, and I'm not just saying that because her head was glowing—in an attempt to stem the stampede, had started our music. Suddenly, we were on.

We opened with me cocking my leg against the Christmas tree—you know, just to give them a flavour of the sophisticated entertainment in store for them.

"Daddy, he's doing a wee on the Christmas tree."

"Hush, dear. Look at the pretty lights."

"Ready?" muttered Evans. "On three . . ."

I know the cancan isn't a particularly festive piece of music, but it is jolly jolly. Someone somewhere started to clap in time to the music and two seconds later everyone had joined in. Except for Dr. Foster—still miffed about the poo in the Sick Bay lift, I suspect—and Dr. Bairstow, who just doesn't do that sort of thing. He's not so much laid back as bolt upright. In fact, he's slightly more vertical than a plumb line.

It was quite an easy routine. One two three kick. Left right left kick. Wiggle the bum. Flash the nose. Trot in a circle and do it again. We thought we'd incorporate a bit of "business." That's a show-biz term by the way. I'm an actor, you know. I've appeared in *Hamlet*. So we sidled up to Bashford, and Evans pretended to sneeze and squirted him with green goo at the same time. The kids loved it.

"Daddy, why is that man all covered in snot?"

"Hush, dear. Look at the pretty lights."

Bashford took it quite well in that he didn't thump either of us. Not there and then, anyway.

And then we sidled back the other way and I sat on Chief Farrell's lap. I was aiming for Psycho Psykes, because she's always up for a laugh, but not being able to see, I missed. Everyone thought it was hilarious. I could hear Max and Kalinda Black shrieking like washerwomen.

Something told me it wouldn't be a good idea to linger long on that lap, so we got up. We did a lot of creeping up behind Peterson, who was amazing. The kids would shout, "Look out—he's behind you," and he would whirl around at just the right moment to miss us. Pure gold, as we in the acting profession say.

Evans flashed his nose like something out of the Blackpool Illuminations and—the big moment—I activated the poo pouch. A hundred olives delivered with pinpoint precision.

"Daddy, he's done a giant poo. Look."

"Hush dear. Look at the pretty lights again."

I don't want to boast, but our big finish was a huge success. Everyone clapped and cheered.

I poked Evans. "Let's get out of here." Because you should always leave them wanting more.

We'd planned a cracking exit—because appearing as a pantomime reindeer is a bit like robbing a bank—you should always have your exit planned. We moonwalked backwards out of the Hall into the Library. Evan's nose went into overdrive and there were olives skidding everywhere. The kids were cheering, trauma forgotten. We were the heroes of the afternoon.

Lingoss closed the door behind us and everything suddenly went quiet. Evans pulled off his head and gasped for breath, and I straightened my creaking back, breathing in the welcome smell of dust, damp and books.

Evans stiffened. "Look out. He's behind you."

I closed my eyes.

"Good afternoon," said Dr. Bairstow.

Oh yes he was.

WE PULLED OURSELVES TOGETHER—a phrase which, when you're the two halves of a reindeer, has a whole new meaning.

"Good afternoon, sir."

I did feel we were on firmish ground here, because he hadn't actually forbidden us to do the reindeer thing. And we had just saved the afternoon. If it wasn't for us, every social worker in Rushfordshire would be converging on St. Mary's at this very moment, accusing us of God knows what. As it was, the guests had had a bit of a giggle, pressies were being distributed, and soon they'd all sit down and stuff themselves stupid. Where was the problem?

It turned out I might have misread the situation slightly. It wasn't Rudolph he wanted to discuss.

"It would appear," he said, "that the legend of Alfred burning the cakes is not completely accurate, after all."

I suddenly remembered. The cakes. I'd completely forgotten about Alfred and the cakes. Had Peterson and Maxwell grassed me up? That's historians for you.

I remained calm, in the best traditions of St. Mary's. "Not quite sir, no. It was bread—not cakes. As I shall say in my report. Which I shall go and write now." I made for the door.

I swear he never moved, but somehow my feet lost momentum and I trailed to a halt. On the other side of the door, everyone was having a lovely time, singing Christmas carols and distributing the presents, while in here, King Herod was gearing up for the Slaughter of the Innocents.

He waited.

I felt compelled to fill the silence. "Not really my fault, sir. And the people were pretty desperate. It was getting dark, and everything was so wet, and they just couldn't get the fire re-lit, and even though it wasn't my fault the fire went out, I did feel we should do something. Obviously, I was very discreet about the whole thing."

"Discretion is not a word I normally associate with your *modus operandi*, Mr. Markham."

"Well, no sir, I take your point, but it was only the one fizzer as a distraction, and then a quick blast while everyone was looking the other way. Job done, sir."

He said nothing.

I sighed. "I'm sorry about the cakes, sir. I only had a few seconds to get the thing re-lit and I'm afraid the cakes were a victim of friendly fire." I beamed at him because that was rather clever. "Get it, sir?"

Apparently he didn't, staring bleakly at me from across the Library. Evans was demonstrating true Security Section loyalty and melting back into the woodwork.

"Not so fast, Mr. Evans," Dr. Bairstow said, without turning his head, and Evans melted back again.

"Was it Maxwell who told you about the cakes, sir?"

"Why no, Mr. Markham. You did. Just now."

Dammit. I'd just fallen for the oldest trick in the book. This is what happens when you spend the afternoon with your head up Evans's bum. Brain-cell failure on a massive scale.

"Well, never mind, sir. Thanks to me, the world has a legend that is both colourful and heartwarming. A story of courage, modesty, and tenacity. Rather like me when you think about it."

He said nothing.

I thought it would be a good idea to change the subject. Move the conversation on a bit.

"Did you enjoy the show, sir?"

"I did indeed Mr. Markham. Most enjoyable."

I breathed a quick sigh of relief. Whenever I find myself on the wrong end of one of his beaky stares, I always find its best to accentuate the positive and here he was, accentuating away all by himself and without any help from me. Crisis averted.

Oh no it wasn't.

"I do believe the little kiddies are clamouring for Rudolph's return and I know, given your close links with the acting profession, you will not wish to disappoint your audience." He paused. "Or me, of course. I must, therefore, beg you to remain in costume for, let us say the remainder of the day, bringing festive cheer and jollification to us all."

Bloody hell. He couldn't do that. There's a whole section of the Geneva Convention dedicated to preventing this sort of cruel and unusual punishment. To say nothing of Employment Law. Or even the Rights of Man.

They'd all be out there, eating and drinking, having a great time, and we'd be stuck here inside this foetid reindeer darkness, with nothing to eat, and worse, nothing to drink. I had a sudden vision of Hunter in her Tinkerbell costume, using her wand for the benefit of someone else. . .

"But sir . . ."

"The show, Mr. Markham, must go on. And on. And on."

And it did. We were in that bloody costume until midnight. Everyone else thought it was hilarious and I suppose it was—for them.

For us, it was a hot, sweaty, blanket-enclosed, alcohol-free, back-breaking hell. To say nothing of the perpetual presence of Evans's enormous backside, of which I'd already seen more than enough.

And, because I just know there's bound to be some sadistic soul out there who will want to know—no, he wasn't kidding about the egg sandwiches.

A PERFECT STORM

AUTHOR'S NOTE

*A*H, THE NEW KID on the block. I've just finished writing this one. I wanted to do something a little different because I think we all forget that they are the Institute of Historical Research and that sometimes this entails sitting down and looking things up in a book, rather than plodding through the mud and blood of History. There was also the matter of a loose end from *Lies, Damned Lies, and History*, when Max sent out all those fundraising leaflets. Surely one of them must bear fruit?

I also wanted to make the point that some people are perfectly capable of endangering life and limb by staying quietly at home. Let's face it, the crew at St. Mary's could take up crochet and, ten minutes later, half of them would have blinded themselves, a good number would have crocheted themselves to their own chairs and Mr. Bashford would be unconscious.

And, of course, once I'd read about fire setting, there was absolutely no chance that was never going to make it into one of the St. Mary's stories.

By the way, huge apologies to everyone in the entertainment industry. I'd like to assure everyone that Mr. Calvin Cutter is a complete figment of my imagination. Angus, on the other hand, used to live next door!

A PERFECT STORM

PROLOGUE

*P*EOPLE THINK THE LIFE of an historian is packed full of excitement, danger, romance, glamour, and lashings of History. And yes, usually it is, although there's often a great deal more excitement, danger and lashings than a normal person might be comfortable with. But since at St. Mary's lack of normality is in our job spec, we generally manage to cope.

And, believe it or not, coming to a spectacularly nasty end somewhere and sometime in the past is not our only function. After all, we are the Institute of Historical Research and part of our job is actually that—research. We assist authors, educational establishments, private citizens, pretty well anyone who writes to us for help, really. We lecture at educational facilities and societies and, occasionally, we advise TV or holo producers on knotty historical problems. We research the historical facts for whatever epic they're planning, bundle it all up, and send it off to them so they can ignore it. Mrs. Enderby provides the details of the costumes to be worn and sometimes the Wardrobe Department is asked to make them as well. She's been nominated for several awards and we're very proud of her, *and* it brings in a modest but much needed income because, according to Dr. Bairstow, you could fund a small city for a year on what it takes to keep St. Mary's up and running for an afternoon. At this moment, we generally nod sympathetically and edge towards the door.

Anyway, the point I'm trying to make is that we, the Institute of Historical Research at St. Mary's Priory, to give us our correct title, do other things besides endangering ourselves getting to grips with History. Sometimes, we can endanger ourselves by remaining quietly at home.

Take last week, for example . . . not only did we not have any current assignments, we hadn't been up and running properly for some time. A very nasty explosion in Hawking had taken out the hangar and most of the pods inside it. Markham, Guthrie, and Leon had been badly injured. And then a rock fell on me in Constantinople—hey, these things happen.

So, given that everything had been very quiet for a very long time while we regrouped and rebuilt, you'd think that the opportunities for anything catastrophic to occur would be few.

Wouldn't you?

MONDAY

*E*VERY DAY BEGINS WITH tea. That's a given. Leon and I take it in turns and that particular Monday morning, it was Leon's. I lay still and listened to him hobbling slowly around our rooms, getting things ready. It takes him ages these days, but he insists on carrying on as normal and I wasn't going to argue. Well, not very much. I always kept my eyes closed and pretended I couldn't hear him making his very slow and painful way across the room. He was recovering, but it was a long process. He was due back at Time Police HQ in a few days for yet another course of treatment, and I would be back to work next week, so we were making the most of these last few days together.

We always took our time and drank our tea in bed. I insisted on it. Not for any sloppy, sentimental reasons, you understand; mostly to give Leon a face-saving moment to rest before heaving himself to his feet to embark on his shower, shit, and shave routine. Sometimes, on his less-good mornings, it nearly breaks my heart, but he won't accept any help, so I just have to grit my teeth and let him get on with it, cheering him on with word and gesture and by comparing his top speed unfavourably to that of continental drift.

We always walked downstairs to breakfast together as well. Very slowly. We do have a heavy goods lift which is used to get the big stuff up and down the building—it had once had an illegal mammoth in it, but it's probably best for everyone if we don't mention that. Leon wouldn't use it even without the smell. Lifts are for wimps, apparently. Real men use stairs.

We split up in the dining room. He said, "See you later," and limped off to the techies' table, and I joined Peterson and Markham. We'd got into the habit of eating together a year or so ago when we'd done something naughty and I'd been suspended and no one else wanted to have anything to do with us. I'd been reinstated, but as Markham pointed out, for some strange reason still no one seemed to want to have anything to do with us. Peterson and I would shake our heads in bafflement.

Peterson surveyed our civilian clothes. "Am I the only one in uniform these days?"

Markham and I carefully inspected him and then each other. "Looks like it," he said cheerfully.

Leon wasn't the only one struggling with severe injuries. Markham had been hurt in the same incident and Major Guthrie was still upstairs in Sick Bay. They let him out for an hour every now and then, and he was improving, but he would never be Head of Security again. That honour would fall to Markham on his own return to duty.

"I'm due my final checkup next week," he said, carefully building himself the world's biggest bacon butty. "So, I'm sending in Max this morning to soften them up. Anyone who's had to deal with her will welcome me with open arms."

"Why are you worrying?" I said. "With your superpowers, surely Nurse Hunter will pass you fit for duty."

"He's never been fit for duty," said Peterson scathing-ly. "Even before he crash landed on Constantinople."

Markham ignored him and, having now constructed an edifice similar in size and shape to the Leaning Tower of Pisa, was attempting to get some portion of it into his mouth.

We watched in silence and then left him to get on with it. There are some things even an historian won't get involved in.

"So, you have a busy day ahead of you today, Max."

I did. I had my final medical to blag my way through, followed by an interview with Dr. Bairstow. "I have to say, it'll be good to get back into my blues."

"If you pass your medical."

I waved a piece of toast in a manner that conveyed my complete confidence that I would sail through it rather in the manner of the good ship *Revenge* taking on the Spanish in 1591. Actually, she was "outgunned, outfought and outnumbered fifty-three to one," but you get the point.

Beside me, by the sound of it, Markham's butty was getting the better of him.

"It's a bit like watching one of those giant pythons eat a goat," complained Peterson. "And then the goat wins."

Markham made a complicated noise indicating he needed to keep his strength up, chewing valiantly until he could say to Peterson, "You still on for this evening?"

"What's happening this evening?" I asked.

He'd taken another bite by then so it was left to Peterson to say, "Pub crawl."

Ah yes, I'd forgotten. To mark our return to normal working—or as close as we could ever get to normal working—St. Mary's was embarking on a traditional pub crawl and tonight was the night. Markham, cheeks bulging like an overworked hamster, beamed at me and tried to speak.

"I'm sorry," I said, getting up. "Watching him could put my recovery back months. I'm off. See you later, guys."

I trotted down the long corridor, just because I could, and took the stairs two at a time, just because I could—and also because I thought it would give me a healthy colour when I arrived—and presented myself in Sick Bay at exactly one minute to nine.

They shoved me into the scanner, peered at various readouts, muttered to each other and then Dr. Stone turned up,

looking younger than ever. I have a theory he's aging backwards. I'm going to bounce in there one day to be confronted
by a foetus with a stethoscope.

"Any pain?" he asked cheerfully.

"Only when I do this."

He stared at me. "Well, don't do it then."

I nodded obediently. He ticked a box, tore off a slip, handed
it to me, and pronounced me fit for duty.

Yay!

Next thing on today's list of Things to Do was Dr. Bairstow.
He wouldn't take kindly to me wandering around in unnecessary civilian clothing, so I changed into my blues, smoothing
the material fondly because it had been a while, rammed in a
couple of extra hairpins for good luck, and shot off to see him.

His desk was ominously empty. It's never cluttered because
he doesn't work like that, but there's usually a file or two on it
somewhere so that he can fiddle with them before unleashing
his next verbal thunderbolt. On the positive side, though, things
had been so quiet recently that I really didn't see how this could
shape up to be quite the blood-chilling, conscience-examining
precursor to disaster it usually was.

I got that wrong.

"Two things this morning, Dr. Maxwell," he said. "Neither
good. Do you have any particular preference as to which disaster should fall upon you first?"

"None, sir," I said cheerfully. I was a recovering invalid. He
wasn't going to give me hard time.

I got that wrong as well.

"Very well. We shall begin with this." He opened a drawer
and laid a manuscript on his desk.

This particular manuscript did not come as any surprise to
me. I had a copy on my own desk.

I pulled out the specs I now have to wear, thanks to the cunning deviousness—deviosity?—of our new doctor, and plonked

them on my nose. They were, as usual, covered in greasy fin-gerprints and, as usual, I thought how much better I could see before the intervention of the medical profession. I'd chosen horn rims because, as I'd said to Peterson, they made me look both intelligent and sexy. He'd patted me on the shoulder and told me he'd always admired my capacity for self-deception, and I was so happy to see this flash of the old Tim Peterson that I'd let it go.

To look at him now you would think he was perfectly nor-mal, but a little while ago he'd lost Helen Foster—my great friend and the love of his life. I wondered if he was dealing with this in the same way he had dealt with the wound to his arm—keeping it all inside and confiding in no one. I wondered if Dr. Bairstow was aware, because strictly speaking, now that he was Deputy Director, Peterson was his responsibility. He must be, surely—Dr. Bairstow is a great deal cleverer than I am. (Don't tell him I said that because he would only respond by saying there are single-celled amoebas and coffee tables who are a great deal cleverer than I am.)

Anyway, I shoved on my specs and picked up the manu-script. The title page read *The Time of My Life* by David Sands.

There were many bookmarks sticking out from the pages. I'm a godless heathen—I turn down the corners. Dr. Bair-stow obviously walks in a state of grace because his corners remained unturned.

"Like stones," I said chattily.

"I beg your pardon?" he said frostily.

"No stone unturned, sir."

"What stone?"

There's always a point when I must make the decision whether to continue winding him up in what is always a vain attempt to distract him from the matter in hand, or to jump straight in.

"So how can I help you this morning, sir?"

"You've seen this?"

"I have indeed, sir. It's very good, don't you think? Our Mr. Sands is making quite a name for himself these days."

"Did nothing particular strike you about his book?"

"Well, it's very different from anything he's done before, sir."

David Sands wrote thrillers. Very good ones. I had them on my own shelves. And I believe Dr. Dowson had purchased a dozen or so copies to put in the library. Rumours that Miss Lee had stood over him while he placed the order were, apparently, completely founded.

"He seems now to have moved from that genre and into the realms of science fiction and written a story concerning . . ." he paused, gathered all his resources, and enunciated distastefully, ". . . time travel."

"Well, people do, sir. It's a very popular genre."

"Have you read it?"

"Yes indeed. He sent me a copy."

"Were you struck by the many similarities to St. Mary's?"

"Not really, sir. His protagonists appear to be a bunch of highly-trained and well-organised scientists who travel up and down the timeline by means of some sort of time-travelling device they wear on their wrists, having all sorts of exciting adventures along the way. It's all very high-tech and efficient. They never end up in the wrong place. No one is ever set on fire. No one is arrested for stealing a loaf of bread. No one ever catches dysentery and no one has inappropriate sex with anyone else. Really, sir, I couldn't see any similarities to St. Mary's at all."

"The organisation is called St. Christopher's."

"Well, that just goes to reinforce my point, sir. St. Christopher is the patron saint of travellers. A very natural choice."

"If this book is published there will be copies of it everywhere."

"Including top of the bestsellers list, sir."

"Questions will be asked."

"What sort of questions?" I said, getting in one of my own.

"Such as how could I allow this to be published?"

"How could you stop it, sir? He doesn't work for St. Mary's any longer."

David Sands had resigned some time ago, along with Gareth Roberts, a small and noticeably beardless Welshman. We—the History Department—had got ourselves into not a little trouble and they'd both stormed out. I'd been present at the time and knew for a fact there had been no question of getting either of them to sign any non-disclosure agreements.

We regarded each other across the vast expanse of his immaculate desk.

He turned to the title page. *"The Time of My Life* by David Sands. With grateful thanks to Dr. Gareth Roberts of the University of Ceredigion for technical advice."

I beamed. "Oh, that's nice, sir. Gareth's got his doctorate."

"That was not the point I was trying to make."

"Sorry, sir." I waited for the point. Sometimes our interviews are rather like the Battle of Kadesh, when the Egyptians took on the Hittites—no clear winner but each side claims victory afterwards. I put my forces on standby and prepared to repel boarders.

He unleashed his front rank. "I do not believe I can allow this to be published."

I brought up my archers. "With respect, sir, I'm not sure you can prevent it."

He flattened them into the dust. "One telephone call should be sufficient."

The remains of my forces fled. Cowardly scum. "But why?"

"I believe it would be in the best interests of St. Mary's. I have nothing against Mr. Sands or his work. Indeed, I have enjoyed his books greatly, but this hits too close to home, Max."

He marshalled his forces for the victory parade and handed me the manuscript. "It might be easier and gentler coming from you." And razed my capital city to the ground. Great. Thanks very much Dr. Bairstow.

I took it reluctantly. This really wasn't in my remit. "But sir . . ."

Too late. He was moving on to the second unpleasant item on the agenda.

He passed a file across the desk

My heart sank. They say your chickens always come home to roost. Well, this one certainly had. As I've already said, some time ago, I'd got us all into serious trouble and, as part of my punishment, the Boss had set me to fundraising for St. Mary's. I'd seeded the entire country with leaflets, adverts, podcasts, Facebook pages, you name it, all advertising St. Mary's and the services we could offer. And, astonishingly, not only had one of those seeds germinated, it had gone on to bear fruit. I strongly doubted, however, that I was the best person to harvest the . . . the . . . oh, sod it—strangled by my own analogy.

"Mr. Calvin Cutter," he pronounced.

"Who?"

"Calvin Cutter, the producer."

Oh. Him. Calvin Cutter is the co-founder and one of the directors of a film company. They make those romantic, historical dramas that are usually shown on Sunday afternoons as an alternative to the football. You know the ones. They always start with a hand turning the pages of a book explaining the plot. Always a signal it's time to get up and clean the toilet.

"Ah," I said, fully intending to pass this on to whoever in the History Department had annoyed me most recently, but that plan was nipped in the bud because, as Dr. Bairstow unreasonably pointed out, it had been my publicity campaign that had started the ball rolling in the first place.

I was determined not to give in without a fight.

"But sir . . ."

"You will accord him every courtesy, Dr. Maxwell. Show him everything he wants to see and accommodate his slightest wish. You may wish to lock Professor Rapson in the basement where he can do no harm. You will impress Mr. Cutter to such an extent that he signs a contract employing us not only to do all the historical research for his next three films, but to design and supply the costumes as well. Do I make myself clear?"

"But sir, they put horns on their Viking helmets."

"Then it will be your responsibility to ensure that that heinous offence is never committed again."

"And blades on Boudicca's chariot wheels."

"May I refer you to my previous statement?"

"And that musical they did on Hildegard of Bingen, when she wandered around with a cleavage bigger than the Valley of the Kings . . ."

"Why are you still here, Dr. Maxwell?"

I sighed and sagged. "When does he arrive?"

"Thursday. Show him around. Give him lunch. Impress him. Get that contract signed. See to it, Dr. Maxwell."

I'M AN HISTORIAN. RISING to the challenge is what I do. I assembled my motley crew—or the History Department as I try to insist they're called—and harangued, bullied, persuaded, entreated, pleaded, commanded, and made shameful use of my recent injuries to get what I wanted. In the end, nearly everyone signed up, mostly, they said, so I would stop talking and go away.

Dr. Dowson offered to show Mr. Cutter around the Library, which was an excellent idea because it would separate him from Professor Rapson who, together with his volatile section, would be confined to R&D for the duration. Dr. Bairstow had made it very clear that nothing—and I stress this, Dr. Maxwell—*nothing* was to prevent Mr. Cutter being so impressed with the qual-

ity of research done at St. Mary's that he would beg us to sign
as many contracts as we liked. Sometimes I think he imposes
slightly unreasonable demands upon his unit, but never let it
be said St. Mary's is unequal to the task before us.

Peterson offered to set up an archery demonstration and
there was a short silence as everyone tried not to remember he
couldn't pull a bow properly any longer. However, I smiled and
thanked him and he nodded.

"Sidesaddle," said Prentiss. "Sykes and I need the hours,
anyway. We'll blag a couple of riding habits from Wardrobe and
show off."

"Both of those are good suggestions. Mrs. Enderby, can
you provide a display of our best and most beautiful costumes.
Along the gallery, I think. Angle it so that it keeps him away
from R&D."

She nodded her complete understanding.

"Historians, clear the Hall of anything we don't want anyone to see. Lay out some of the Troy, Carthage, and Hastings
material—flashy stuff that will give him a good impression of
our work. Anything else?"

"Is he going to be wandering around the building?" asked
Sykes. "What about the repairs in Hawking?"

"Everything locked up. Blast doors down. Absolutely no
admittance. Civilian clothes to be worn that day. No pressure,
but anyone screwing up will be fed, live, to Dr. Bairstow. Any
questions?"

They shook their heads and wandered off.

THE GREAT ST. MARY'S All Repairs Completed At Last Pub
Crawl has passed into legend. And not a good legend. None of
the participants could remember much about it afterwards—I
swear, it was easier to piece together the fall of Troy than get
a clear idea of what happened that night—but mostly it was
memorable because it was the night Bashford met Angus.

Everyone assembled in the Great Hall. For some reason, they had all decided to dress as superheroes. With much posturing and cape swirling, they set off down the drive to meet the minibus that was to take them into town. It was also supposed to bring them back again although that didn't go quite according to plan. I must say thirteen superheroes assembled together are quite an impressive sight. They'd taken a lot of time and trouble with their costumes and I think it's only right that I should list them here:

- *Peterson—Superman. Not quite as muscular as the original, but making a good try as he led his happy band of heroes to their night of adventure.*
- *Markham—The Flash. Small, scarred and overpoweringly red. Like an acne-ridden teenager.*
- *Dieter—The Hulk. A part he was born to play. It had taken two people the best part of the day to paint him green.*
- *Bashford—The Great God Thor complete with giant silver hammer, and currently hiding from Mrs. Mack who was demanding to know who had stolen her entire supply of kitchen foil.*
- *Atherton—General Zod. Mr. Normal. I was relying on him to keep everyone in line. I don't know why I bothered.*
- *Clerk—Darth Vader. He'd been practising The Voice all week, and now he made a stunning entrance, Darth Vader music blaring, and informed a startled Dr. Bairstow that he was his father. He was bundled away before he could shorten his life expectancy even further.*
- *Mr. Strong—Lex Luthor. Wearing a brown and white pinstriped suit and carrying a violin case. It*

turned out later he'd confused Mr. Luthor with Mr. Capone.

- *Lindstrom—Mr. Fantastic. Complete with nine-foot-long elastic arms over which he regularly tripped. I had no idea how they were going to get all of him on the bus and looked forward to seeing them try.*
- *Miss Prentiss—Captain America. She'd stolen a dustbin lid for her shield and painted it with the old-style Stars and Stripes.*
- *Miss Sykes—Hellboy. Enough said.*
- *Evans—Spiderman. He had equipped himself with one of those party spray things to enable him to squirt his web over everyone, but it was confiscated by the minibus driver and he forgot to ask for it back.*
- *Professor Rapson—Professor X because it was easy for him to remember.*
- *Dr. Dowson—Dr. Doom. Ditto.*
- *Miss North had refused to participate, much to everyone's relief, and I was staying behind with Leon. We were having a quiet night in.*

Anyway, we waved them off from the front steps because, as Leon said, we might never see some, any, or all of them, again. No one seemed particularly dismayed by this prospect. That was Monday. Things soon got worse.

TUESDAY
(THE EARLY HOURS)

*T*HEIR RETURN WAS NOWHERE near as epic as their departure.

No one is very clear how it happened but, at some point in the evening, they had all become separated. I'm not sure how you can lose a group of colourfully clad superheroes but they'd managed it, no problem at all.

First to come to grief was the Great God Thor who, displaying the usual historian sense of direction, had somehow got himself lost and was wandering out of Rushford towards Ireland—and ultimately America—when he encountered what turned out to be his lifelong companion, Angus. When questioned afterwards, both appeared equally confused as to the details of their meeting, but it turned out to be a happy accident for the pair of them because, only five minutes later, they encountered a group of lively and slightly inebriated young men who happened to have a number of issues with Thor and his new friend. Things would have gone badly for the Great God had he been alone but, fortunately, Angus slipped naturally into the role of trusty sidekick, standing over the Great God when he tripped over his hammer, and pluckily defending him against all comers. Having seen off their attackers, they happily turned their footsteps in the direction they believed St. Mary's to lie, although by now, the evening's exertions had become a little too much for Angus, who had to be carried home. Mr.

Bashford's injuries were severe enough to need monitoring for forty-eight hours in Sick Bay, in case of concussion, although how they'd be able to tell was a bit of a mystery.

It didn't get any better. Mr. Fantastic and his elastic arms were delivered to St. Mary's in a police car. No charges were brought, but he was instructed to write a letter of apology to a Miss McLelland, who had never before met a superhero with nine-foot-long appendages and had had to be taken into Tesco's and given a glass of water.

Markham won the "Who can come home with the most traffic cones?" competition. He always does. Seven at the first count, equalling the current record (already held by him), which soared to eight after I had the forethought to nip in and remove the one sitting in solitary splendour on Dr. Bairstow's desk with the rude verse attached. The one which began "There was a Director of St. Mary's . . ."

Wherever they'd been and whatever they'd been up to, General Zod, Darth Vader, and Lex Luthor didn't pitch up until after breakfast the next morning with no clear memory of the night before, although they thought there might have been a badger.

Professor X and Dr. Doom mistakenly boarded an overnight delivery van believing it to be the local bus home. On being discovered some miles away and escorted to the train station, they'd been unable to remember the word for Rushford and boarded a train to Redruth instead. They spent the next day zigzagging around the country, eventually arriving, dishevelled but cheerful, around tea-time.

Our revered Deputy Director, just in case anyone was wondering, was brought home in a disgraceful condition by Captain America, Hellboy, and The Hulk, themselves not much better. They experienced some difficulty getting through the front door since the four of them had linked arms—for stability, presumably—and they spent a considerable amount of time bouncing gently off the door frame and staggering backwards before coordinating themselves enough to mount another attempt. A small crowd gathered to watch them making complete arses of themselves. I believe a great deal of money was won and lost on whether they would ever gain entrance and it was very possible they might be there still if Mrs. Partridge—of all people—had not sighed in exasperation and arranged them in single file instead of horizontally, after which, to loud cheers, they successfully navigated the Scylla and Charybdis of the front doors. She gently guided them into the Great Hall, where, good deed done, she abandoned them to find their own way to their beds. Dieter wandered off to talk to his pods. Peterson, apparently on automatic pilot, successfully found his way to his room. Hellboy was subsequently discovered washed, pyjama'd, and serenely slumbering in her own bed. No one had any idea how that had happened. Spiderman, left to his own devices, fell asleep on the bottom stair. It seemed kindest to leave him there so we did.

Dr. Bairstow, passing that way some ten minutes later and very carefully ignoring the latest thing in draught excluders, commented to no one in particular that his unit appeared to be disintegrating around him and limped on his way. His temper was not improved by finding his beloved car in the middle of the Great Hall the next morning.

I remember staring at it with Markham swaying gently beside me.

"How the hell did you get it in here?"

"To be honest, I can't remember."

"What do you remember?"

He peered at me. "Who are you?"

For some people, Tuesday was a very gentle day. Everyone used their indoor voices.

THURSDAY

WE SPENT MOST OF Wednesday preparing for Mr. Calvin Cutter. I chivvied Peterson and Markham mercilessly, even though they both looked like death in trousers, and then on Thursday, just as things seemed to be settling down again, Mr. Calvin Cutter arrived.

I disliked him on sight.

I don't know why, but I was expecting someone tall and artistic, who would toss his silky blond hair and utter, "*Darling* . . .*" with every other sentence.

Calvin Cutter was below average height, flabby around the middle, and had one of those mobile headset things attached to one ear. I don't know why he didn't have it implanted subcutaneously because he was never off it.

I met him in the Boss's office. He was talking on his phone. Dr. Bairstow stood nearby, rigid with outrage at this discourtesy.

"Ah, Dr. Maxwell," he said, ruthlessly cutting across the chattering Mr. Cutter. "May I introduce Mr. Calvin Cutter, co-owner of Cutter Cavendish Films."

"How do you do," I said, also ignoring his phone conversation, and holding out my hand. It would be interesting to see how many conversations he could hold at the same time.

He stared at it vaguely, still talking to someone apparently named Justin. I seized his unresisting paw and shook it vigorously.

"Welcome to St. Mary's."

"What?" he said, breaking off his phone conversation.

"Excellent." I beamed. "I'm glad that difficult point has been covered. I must admit, we didn't expect you to agree so easily."

"What?"

Dr. Bairstow was regarding me with rare approval. I made a mental note to request a pay rise before it evaporated.

"Shall we begin," I said, moving towards the door.

"Wait," he said, startled. "No, not you, Justin. Just a minute, Dr. Umm . . ."

"I thought we could start with Wardrobe," I said, gesturing ahead of me and setting off at a good speed. I really wasn't bothered whether he was with me or not. It wouldn't be the first time I'd been discovered roaming the corridors of St. Mary's having long a conversation with myself.

Mrs. Enderby had done us proud. A History of Costume through the Ages was ranged around three sides of the gallery, not coincidentally blocking the door in and out of R&D.

"We'll start at Saxon and early Norman, Mr. Cutter. Please note the similarities in style. Moving on now to the early Middle Ages. You can see how, over time, the surcoat has evolved and . . ."

He wasn't listening, staring over my shoulder, and yapping away for dear life. I suspected Justin was being difficult. I waited until he had finished, beamed at him again, and said, "Well, that's very generous of you. Don't think we don't appreciate your kind offer."

"What. . . ?"

"You must let me introduce you to Mrs. Enderby, who has charge of all matters pertaining to costume and wardrobe. I believe you are familiar with her work. I think Dr. Bairstow has already forwarded you a list of productions in which St. Mary's has collaborated. Her designs for *The She-Wolf of France* were nominated for an award."

"Shut up, Justin, I'm trying to concentrate here. Just wait a minute, will you?"

Of course, he could try just switching the damn thing off.

"She's just through here," I said, ushering him into Wardrobe, a hive of chattering activity, and where their latest creation, a 17th-century court dress stood in eye-catching pride of place.

I couldn't see her initially, but it seemed safe to assume the pair of legs poking out from underneath the huge skirt was hers. Which, of course, meant that while her nether regions were on show, her top half couldn't be seen. Or see.

She was talking. "And don't talk to me about Cutter Cavendish Productions. Their last picture was a disgrace. Well, not commercially, of course, but they had servant girls in costumes that laced up the back. And their leading man kept wearing those stupid flimsy shirts with the big sleeves. And all those heaving bosoms. They call him Tits and Bums, you know, because he doesn't care about any sort of historical accuracy so long as everyone's bosom is falling out of their bodice and the men's breeches are so tight that if you look hard enough you can see every—well, never mind. The man's an idiot, anyway."

I really thought I'd covered all my bases. Professor Rapson, if not behind locked doors, was as good as. Sykes was on a horse somewhere far, far away. Bashford—who might or might not be concussed—was in Sick Bay. Miss Lingoss was . . . I didn't know where Miss Lingoss was, but she wasn't here, which was the main thing. And Markham was off in the cupboard the Security Section persist in referring to as their nerve centre and well out of harm's way. I never, ever thought it would be Mrs. Enderby, of all people.

I cleared my throat.

There was a kind of frozen silence and the already voluminous skirt bulged even further and then grew still. Very, very slowly, two legs were drawn up inside the fabric.

I'm an historian. I can deal with a crisis. God knows I've had enough practice.

I said brightly, "Has anyone seen Mrs. Enderby this morning?"

Heads shook and her loyal staff assured us, with complete sincerity, that no one had seen Mrs. Enderby that morning. So convincing were they that if I hadn't just seen her taking up residence beneath a 17th-century court dress I would have believed them myself. Someone shyly suggested she might be in Admin, checking over invoices. Someone else suggested she was out on the gallery ensuring our display was perfect. They were incredibly convincing. I resolved never again to believe a word this section uttered. Ever.

"Ah, never mind, we'll catch her later then. Come along, Mr. Cutter."

Back out in the corridor, he peered out of a window.

"What are those big white things out there?"

I peered cautiously because, quite honestly, it could have been anything. "Oh no, it's all right, Mr. Cutter, it's a swan. Several swans in fact."

"In a tree?"

"Um . . ." I wasn't sure what to say. As far as I know, our swans are unique in that they're more often to be found a good thirty feet up a beech tree, rather than swimming serenely across the lake looking picturesque.

"Dear God," he said, giving his ear a good belt again. I'd have been happy to do it for him. "Justin, book me a call to the BBC Wildlife Unit in Bristol."

I had an idea we weren't going to be featuring on Justin's Christmas card list this year.

Mr. Cutter turned to me. "How long have they been doing that?"

"They've always done it," I said, striving to present at least an appearance of casual normality and slight surprise that other people's swans don't do the same.

"This place is totally weird," he said. "Where to next?"

I led him slowly along the corridor, taking care to go the long way around, and bless me, if there wasn't Mrs. Enderby miraculously ahead of us, breathlessly tweaking the folds of an Elizabethan noble's doublet.

"Ah, there you are," I said, rather brilliantly I thought. "They said you might be here. Can I introduce Mr. Cutter from Cutter Cavendish films?"

Mrs. Enderby, seemingly determined to distance herself from their unfortunate initial encounter, smiled widely and in the world's worst Irish brogue said, "A pleasure to meet you, Mr. Cutter. I do so admire your work. Of course, I was a little astonished to see that, in your adaptation of *Emma*, none of the ladies wore headgear. I know such a lapse was widely discussed afterwards in the trade, and we all agreed there must have been overwhelming production reasons for such an oversight." Adding belatedly, "To be sure."

I think it was around about now that I had an inkling of just how badly things were going to go that day.

He stared at her for a moment. She held out her hand. "Enderby. Mavis Enderby. From Dublin."

She was from Welwyn Garden City.

He shook her hand. "How do you do. These are all . . . very pretty."

The temperature plummeted. He had passed beyond the Pale.

Mrs. Enderby is small, round, and endlessly kind. She also fought in the civil uprisings along with Peterson's PA, Mrs. Shaw, and our Kitchen Supremo, Mrs. Mack. Mrs. Mack commanded the famous Battersea Barricades, and these days was as famous for her raspberry crumble as she was feared for the battle ladle she kept under the counter.

I think I remembered Mrs. Shaw telling me that Mrs. Enderby had worked in logistics while she herself had been in code breaking. To hear the two of them speak about that time, you'd think they just made the tea and did the filing, but I knew for a fact they'd been with the rebel forces in Glouces-ter when the Fascists poured out of Cardiff and across the Severn. They'd been overrun in Westgate Street and fallen back to College Green. With the cathedral at their backs and nowhere to go, they'd made their final stand and prevailed. Three weeks later, after the famous victory at the Battersea Barricades, it had all been over. The three of them had fought together again at the less famous Battle of St. Mary's and had pretty much brought the building down. A compassionate and caring guide would probably take Mr. Cutter aside and point out that many of our civilian staff were, in fact, weap-ons of mass destruction. Yeah, I really should do that. For his own good.

I stared at my feet and wondered what to have for lunch.

She said frigidly, "You are too kind," entirely forgetting the brogue, and stepped back, staring glassily over his shoulder.

A rather sticky silence descended. Even Mr. Cutter seemed to realise he'd gone wrong somewhere or other and, while he was endeavouring to bring himself back up to speed, a fat brown chicken walked past, paused to peck at a bit of carpet, and then continued on its way down the gallery.

Mr. Cutter turned to me. "Was that . . ."

"Was that what?" I said helpfully.

He pointed. "There's a bloody chicken over there. Not ten feet away."

Out of the corner of my eye I could see the chicken was on the move again. At the end of the gallery landing it paused briefly, presumably getting its bearings, and then turned right towards Admin—I didn't much fancy its chances in there—and disappeared from view.

We turned around and ostentatiously looked up and down the gallery.

"No," said Mrs. Enderby with simple sincerity, "I can't see a chicken anywhere. Can you, Max?"

"No," I said in tones of concern. "Can I get you a glass of water, Mr. Cutter?"

"It's gone now."

"Of course it has," soothed Mrs. Enderby.

I winked at her and we led him slowly down the line of costumes. To be fair, apart from glancing back over his shoulder a couple of times, he did make an effort. He admired the Tudor and Stuart stuff—and so he should because the costumes were superb. Optimistically, I began to think we might possibly overcome our unfortunate beginning.

We paused outside the door to R&D, currently being guarded by a model of a Scottish Highlander, complete with blood-stained claymore and a dying Redcoat at his feet.

He peered around the tableau. "What's in there?"

I'm famous for my brilliant ideas. Although brilliant is not a word often used to describe them. But some of them have been stonkers and I had one now.

"Records," I said, smoothly, "Going back to the year dot and hugely fascinating. Let me show you . . ."

His nose twitched. He had instincts. Or hay fever.

"No, I don't think so. What, Justin?"

I took advantage of his distraction to beckon to Miss Lee, invariably present at any potential disaster and whispered, "Release Professor Rapson from wherever he's been stored for safekeeping. Tell him he has my permission to set up the Hannibal Barca experiment. He has two hours and he'd better make it good."

Her eyes sparkled. "Can we have war elephants?"

"If you can find a dozen war elephants in the next thirty minutes then yes," I said, knowing full well it takes a decade of paperwork. Minimum.

"Gotcha," she said, and disappeared. Time to get our guest out of the building.

I piloted him outside, hoping he might be interested in something a little less girlie and a little more action related, but it was the same story for Peterson's archery demonstration and Prentiss and Sykes's rather good sidesaddle show. Yes, he watched them, but he talked all the way through. I told myself he was in the entertainment industry. They were supposed to be able to multitask. Just because he wasn't looking or listening, there was no reason to suppose he wasn't taking it all in somehow. By osmosis, perhaps.

If he was taking it in—osmotically or otherwise—we had no clue as to his opinions. He strode briskly back into the building where we showed him carefully selected examples from some of our more spectacular assignments. Mr. Clerk filled him in on the Troy stuff. Mr. Cutter was disappointingly Helen-oriented. The whole thing was about her after all, he said. Why didn't she get a mention? Which of the film industry's leading ladies did we think she most resembled?

He described a dramatic scene—just off the top of his head, of course—in which, heavily disguised in Paris's battle armour, Helen stole away to the Greek camp at the dead of night to intercede with Agamemnon on the Trojans' behalf, and then slept with Odysseus to seal the deal. Naturally, she would encounter great perils all along the way, including, oh, who was that woman with the snakes—Medusa, yes, that was her, and that hydra thing and possibly the minotaur, all of whom she would despatch with ease. My own opinion was that with those sort of skills, the Trojans could just have sent her out into the field by herself and themselves stayed at home drinking tea. We listened politely because Dr. Bairstow insists on good manners and then, thank God, it was time for lunch—something to which, for once, I was not looking forward. Our Mr. Calvin Cutter was rather heavy going.

Mrs. Mack had set aside a quiet table for us. I was just pulling out a chair when a small miracle occurred and Peterson said, "Mind if we join you, Max?" and he and a grinning Markham sat down with us. I gave silent thanks to the god of historians.

I wondered if the best way to keep Cutter off the phone was to get him to talk about himself. The same idea had obviously occurred to Peterson who, with an expression of great interest, requested Mr. Cutter to tell us about his current productions.

"Well," he said, shovelling his food down with no appreciation whatsoever, "just now we're looking for something a little different."

"Really? What sort of different?"

"I'm not sure yet, but I'll know it when I see it."

He cut us off to talk to his ear again. I refused to catch Peterson's eye and concentrated on my food until Mr. Cutter deigned to rejoin us.

"So tell me, Dr. Maxwell . . ." so he had picked up my name, "what are *you* researching at the moment?"

I tried to choose topics that would interest him. "Well, we've just finished with Hastings, as you've just seen. Before that, we looked at the coronation of King George IV, examined the possibility that King John lost the crown jewels in The Wash, and attempted an in-depth survey of an early version of Stonehenge. Over the years, we've studied the battles of Agincourt and Thermopylae. And some time ago, we took a close look at Mary Stuart, her marriage to the Earl of Bothwell, and the circumstances leading up to it."

He stabbed at a chip. "Why?"

"Well, there was some doubt as to the accuracy of . . ."

"No, I mean why do you waste your time with all this dead stuff?"

Well, that was rather rude. Peterson and Markham put down their forks—a St. Mary's manifestation of outright shock. I was made of sterner stuff, but he must have guessed we weren't that impressed because he smiled a surprisingly charming smile.

"I'm sorry. That came out all wrong. What I meant to say is that this stuff is dead and buried. It's finished—done with. And yet, there are all these people here, ferreting away to uncover tiny bits of information which simply aren't relevant any longer. I mean, look at you all. Most of you are young—comparatively," he said, looking at me and not making any friends at all as far as I was concerned. "I'm not going to say, 'Why don't you all get proper jobs?' but I'm certainly thinking it."

I opened my mouth to reply but there was no chance. It was like trying to hold back the Red Sea after Moses had been messing around with it.

"I mean, it's OK if you're applying this knowledge to something relevant or important, like making a holo or a TV programme maybe, but you're all so up your own—I mean the amount of effort you put into tiny details is quite disproportionate to the results. Who cares if Emma Woodhouse wore something on her head or not? Who cares if we show the Greek cavalry with stirrups? How important is all that, really? In the scheme of things?"

I didn't hit him with my Spotted Dick but I came close. I do think, however, something of what I was feeling might have got through to him.

"I didn't mean that the way it sounded." He smiled again. He really did have quite a nice smile. "I know what you think of me and I enjoyed your efforts when I was talking on my phone. I'm sorry—that was rude of me. Having three conversations at once is standard behaviour in my world, but I forget it's not like that here. I mean, this place is so sedate. And serious. Sober. Solid. Settled."

Apparently, he was determined to empty the English language of words beginning with S. He ended with a big finish. "Staid."

At this moment, Miss Lee materialised at my elbow. For once, I was pleased to see her. It was about time she used her powers for good.

"Professor Rapson presents his compliments, ma'am. The fires have been lit. We have vinegar, sour wine, cola, and water."

Peterson looked thoughtful for a moment then caught my eye. I had a twinge of doubt. He was management, after all.

He took advantage of Mr. Cutter conversing with his ear again, to say quietly, "Do I know about this—whatever it is?"

"No, plausible deniability. You are DD after all."

Markham grinned. "Is that his bra size?"

Peterson regarded him coldly. "And your role this afternoon?"

"None of this is anything to do with the Security Section," he said, spooning up the last of his custard. "We're just going to sit back and watch. See you later."

Peterson watched him go, turned back to me, glanced at the still chattering Cutter, and winked. Another flash of the old Tim. I grinned back again.

LUNCH FINISHED, I TOOK Mr. Cutter outside for our St. Mary's extravaganza. Someone had set up benches and tables and chairs. I chose a table in the warm sunshine which should have an excellent view of unfolding events. Acting on previous instructions, Mrs. Mack brought tea. It was interesting to watch the way it was delivered. Peterson got a warm smile because everyone likes Peterson. I was the recipient of a slightly smaller smile because on the one hand I'm a known troublemaker but, on the other, my ability to pack away gargantuan amounts of her chocolate-orange cheesecake meets with her approval. Mr. Cutter received a ferocious scowl, but I guessed her failure to behead him with the tea strainer meant she too had been warned not to damage him before contract signing had occurred.

Barely had we made ourselves comfortable when we were disconcertingly joined by Dr. Bairstow, who mildly enquired what was happening.

"Fire setting, sir."

He said nothing very eloquently.

"I know what you're thinking, sir, but it's a perfectly legitimate experiment. The professor gave the statutory three-days warning last month."

This three-day warning period had been stipulated by Dr. Bairstow himself after the Clock Tower Trauma some years ago, so he had no cause for complaint there. And besides, if things went well—and the law of averages decrees that surely, one day they must—something this spectacular could just tip things in our favour.

And yes, all right, before anyone says, "Fire setting? Professor Rapson? Are you out of your mind? What did you think would happen?" I have two very reasonable excuses. Firstly, this experiment had been on the books for quite some time and, secondly, it really is quite legitimate.

We all know Hannibal crossed the Alps with his war elephants. Obviously, they encountered a hefty rock or two obstructing their path. For those that didn't respond to the traditional pick and shovel, the ancients used fire setting. It's quite simple. You set fire to the rock. I know they're not usually that flammable, but Professor Rapson could ignite a bucket of water, so no difficulties there.

Anyway, having set fire to your rock and got it good and hot, two things could happen. Either the rock fell apart all by itself due to the heat, or—and this is the good bit—you adopted the Hannibal Barca method of rock disposal and tossed vinegar on it and watched it shatter. Apparently, he carved his way across the Alps that way. Pliny bangs on about it somewhere if you want to read up on it. It's very efficient and I believe people used variations of this method until comparatively modern

times. Especially down the mines. The main drawback is the
production of what everyone refers to as "foetid vapours" but
because, here at St. Mary's, Health and Safety is paramount at
all times, we were doing it outdoors. Where absolutely nothing
could possibly go wrong.

And yes, you're right. I wanted to shake Mr. Cutter out of
his anti-history complacency with something spectacular. To
put things in perspective, I had, at one point, considered a spot
of jousting—spectacular *and* exciting—but that's only fun and
games up until the moment when someone loses an eye—as
the French king Henry II discovered to his cost in 1559 and
look at all the trouble that caused. I bet fire setting doesn't look
so bad now, does it?

Anyway, to add a modern twist to things, not only was
the professor using historically accurate vinegar, but we were
also having a go with sour wine—available by the amphora in
ancient times—water, or melted snow as it would have been
then, and cola. Everyone knows the effect cola has on pennies, teeth, and stomach linings—but now we were using it
for a practical purpose. If it performed as well as vinegar, then
maybe they could add fire setting to their advertising campaign.
It could be the real thing.

We have some rather pleasant rock gardens at St. Mary's.
They were laid out about two hundred years ago, when landscape gardening was all the rage. There are a couple of quiet
pools where big, orange goldfish swim serenely from one end
to the other. We don't have any problems with herons: Bashford swears he once saw one dragged under by a couple of
determined koi.

Obviously, we weren't going to have a go at anything in the
rock garden because it was almost certainly the horticultural
equivalent of a listed building. Happily, whichever 18th-century
garden designer had ordered most of the rock in the county
of Westmoreland to be delivered here had got his quantities

wrong, and we had four enormous if superfluous slabs of Westmoreland stone stationed at one end of the car park. No one knows why. They'd sat there for donkey's years. Although if the professor got things right and things went well today—not for very much longer. So, as I pointed out to Dr. Bairstow, this experiment had a practical value as well.

They'd obviously had their fires going for some time. A smouldering framework, stuffed full of burning wood, encased each rock. A massive heat haze hung over the whole area. We were a good way back and I could feel the heat from here.

From the corner of my eye, I could see Dr. Bairstow looking around with an expression of mild anxiety. I didn't blame him. The experiment was taking place next to the car park. We're not idiots, however. The car park had been emptied immediately, I'd given the go ahead and, as a further precaution, Dr. Bairstow's beloved Bentley—which traditionally does not fare well during this sort of thing—was parked a good half mile away in the village. In the Falconburg Arms car park to be precise.

The horses had been removed to a safe distance away in the second paddock. Over the years, they'd displayed enormous reluctance to become involved in anything Professor Rapson related, and at the first sign of anything unusual happening they tended to be off and away, and we would be collecting them from all around Rushfordshire for days afterwards. For some reason, the police always seem to know they're ours. And, as usual, the swans were roosting some thirty feet off the ground, so I was confident we'd covered everything.

Dr. Bairstow sighed, hung his stick off the arm of his chair and, taking advantage of another Cutter dialogue with his ear, said quietly, "Please reassure me that there will be absolutely no risk to Mr. Cutter. I don't think either of you quite appreciate the difficulties involved in persuading a dead person to sign a contract. Quite apart from the practical issues, which are complex and wide-ranging, such documents are extraordinarily difficult to uphold in a court of law. You will, therefore, oblige me by not killing Mr. Cutter until the ink is well and truly dry.

Peterson and I nodded solemnly. "Understood, sir."

Surprisingly, he seemed satisfied by this and turned his attention to me. "In your haste to leave my office this morning, Dr. Maxwell, you forgot this."

He handed me the manuscript I'd deliberately left lying on his desk. Damn and blast!

"Thank you, sir."

"I thought you might be concerned you had lost it," he said, settling back comfortably.

What can you say?

Several St. Mary's personnel, all dressed as brutalised slave labour—i.e. wearing their normal St. Mary's gear—were rushing around with their arms full of wood, stoking the fires. Smoke, flames, and crackling sparks curled into the air. The heat was extraordinary and the addition of any sort of liquid seemed superfluous. Surely the flames alone would be sufficient to shatter the stone.

Apart from all that, the day was lovely. A warm sun shone in a clear blue sky. Mr. Stone, obviously under the same starter's orders as the rest of us, had ensured the grounds looked immaculate. If it wasn't for the St. Mary's personnel, the scene would be idyllic.

Given recent events I was quite happy just to sit in the sunshine and watch other people work, but I had forgotten the short attention span of the entertainment industry.

"So," said Calvin Cutter, apparently not addressing his ear this time, "this is rather slow. What's supposed to happening here?"

"Well," said Peterson leaning forwards and, remembering his audience, kept the explanation short, sharp, and spectacular, using sugar cubes and milk to demonstrate.

Dr. Bairstow gazed on in benign approval.

Peterson paused.

Mr. Cutter did not. "And?"

"And then we shall see what we shall see."

Calvin Cutter looked at us. "Don't you know what will happen?"

"Nope," said Peterson happily.

Dr. Bairstow coughed gently. "We tend to find that the element of uncertainty only adds to the excitement of the proceedings," which came as a complete surprise to Peterson and me who had, on many occasions, been given to understand—quite strongly sometimes—that the element of uncertainty did not feature prominently on his happy list.

"So, you've no idea how this will turn out?"

"None at all. Would you like some tea?"

"No," he said shortly, which I thought was rather rude even for a member of the entertainment industry.

Dr. Bairstow stood.

"Are you leaving us, sir?" I said, trying not to sound too relieved.

"Alas," he said, "Although I have not yet had the opportunity to explore the more remote areas of my in-tray, I am certain that whatever is lurking there will be less explosive than remaining here. Please bear in mind my earlier comments on the difficulties of implementing contracts of dubious provenance, Dr. Maxwell."

"Of course, sir," I said gravely.

"Good afternoon, Mr. Cutter. I'm sure I shall be seeing you later this afternoon. Probably."

He limped away.

We sat some more.

"This is rather slow," said Mr. Cutter again, shifting impatiently. "At this rate, it would have been quicker for them just to have waited for glacial erosion, don't you think?"

Beside me, Peterson twitched. I suspected he was desperate to get stuck in with the rest of the History Department, but as Markham had pointed out, he was DD now. Rank doth not always have its privileges. I, on the other hand, older than I would like to be both in years and experience, was staying well out of it. There was every possibility there would be tears before bedtime and I was determined none of them would be mine.

Clutching a megaphone, Professor Rapson began to mount an ancient pair of stepladders which swayed somewhat precariously.

"Andrew, you old fool, come down at once," shouted Dr. Dowson—albeit from a safe distance. He had dressed for every meteorological contingency imaginable in bright yellow wet-weather gear, green wellies, trousers tied below the knee with string, a hard hat surmounted by a sou'wester, and he was carrying a Roman shield in one hand and a gas mask in the other.

I looked up at the cloudless sky and shook my head. It was probably best not to ask.

With an eldritch shriek, the professor activated his megaphone.

"STAND BACK, OCCY. I'M NOT QUITE SURE HOW THIS IS GOING TO TURN OUT."

Thirty people reeled backwards clutching their ears.

"SORRY . . . sorry," he said, adjusting the volume. "Can you hear me now, Occy?"

"Of course, I can hear you, Andrew. They can hear you in Madagascar. And I am already standing well back. Do you take me for a complete idiot?" Wisely not pausing for a reply, he hastened on. "And come down from that ridiculous contraption. I fail to see how you will be able to assimilate the results of this preposterous episode accurately if you've broken your neck."

"No need for concern, Occy," boomed Professor Rapson, startling birds from the trees for a radius of two miles. Except the swans, of course. "I have everything completely under control."

That he wasn't instantly blasted from his perch only goes to show how very much not up to the job the god of historians is.

The megaphone gave another appalling screech.

"Remember everyone—you are Carthaginian troops on your way to attack Rome. You will also be at risk from avalanches, unpredictable war elephants, and possibly the local tribespeople as well. Try to factor that in."

A small group of people standing nearby obediently lay on the ground—avalanche victims presumably. Several more ran screaming from the scene—"Exit pursued by an elephant," murmured Peterson. Sykes, meanwhile, was dealing with imaginary local tribespeople by shaking her fist and shouting, "Shoo. Shoo. Go home you naughty tribespeople and trouble us no more."

I resolved to have a word with her later.

"Last loads everyone," boomed the professor as the final armfuls were dumped on the fires. The flames roared even higher. People retired to a safe distance. That's a St. Mary's safe distance, obviously, not some girlie safe distance dreamed up by the HSE to drain all the excitement out of life.

"We shall dowse all the rocks simultaneously," the professor continued, "so we can ensure they've all received the same amount of heat for the same amount of time. Dowsers—stand ready."

Four people stepped up, suited and booted in fireproof suits. Well what did you think? We're not complete idiots, you know. A plastic dustbin full of murky-looking fluids and a stirrup pump stood close to each, by now almost incandescent, rock.

"On my mark," boomed the professor.

"What's going on?" said Mr. Cutter, cutting Justin off in mid-flow. "Is this it at last?"

Everyone stood very still. The only sounds were the crackling flames and the occasional snap of burning wood.

"Mark."

Each figure immediately began to pump like a madman and a small river of miscellaneous fluids simultaneously engulfed each rock.

Which, as Peterson said later, might have been a bit of a mistake.

In my ignorance, I thought the rocks would just crack. I thought that Hannibal's men would chuck a gallon or so of vinegar at the obstructive hot rock, then give it a bit of a poke with a sharp implement, that the rock would fall apart, and then everyone would continue on their merry way to bring down Rome. What do I know?

Many, many things happened all at once.

Four vast plumes of steam boiled and hissed into the air to a considerable height, merging into one colossal mushroom shape of doom. The smell was appalling, catching at the back of my throat and making my eyes stream. With a massive crack that hurt my ears, all four rocks exploded simultaneously.

Something zipped past my ear. And then something else clattered onto the table. Something else thudded to the ground beside my chair.

"Everyone down," yelled Peterson.

He grabbed Calvin Cutter and dragged him down under the table.

I'm an historian. I was already there.

"What was that?" said a somewhat muffled voice. We rolled him onto his back so he could breathe.

"Shrapnel," said Peterson shortly, and it was.

Great lumps of flaming rock were flying everywhere. I heard shattering glass somewhere in the distance.

"What the hell. . . ?" said Mr. Cutter, trying to get up. We pulled him back down again.

The fumes were appalling. I could feel my eyes running and the back of my throat felt raw. It hurt to swallow. We rolled Mr. Cutter back onto his face again so he could inhale dirt rather than foetid vapours.

"We should get him out of here," I said, becoming aware of a nasty headache beginning to throb above my eyes.

I peered around. Some people were running away—some had done as we had and taken refuge under the tables as rocks and burning wood rained down upon us. I swear my ears were still ringing.

"It's like the K-T extinction event," said Peterson.

"The what?" said Cutter, coming up for what he mistakenly thought was fresh air.

"You know—the end of the dinosaurs. We could be looking at a nuclear winter by teatime and extinction by lunchtime tomorrow."

I should be so lucky. If anything happened to Calvin Cutter, as far as Dr. Bairstow was concerned, extinction would be the least of my problems.

There was another clatter of stones on the table top over our head and we all huddled back down together. Suddenly, Dr. Dowson's bizarre get-up made a great deal of sense.

Speaking of whom . . . I rolled over. "Professor, are you all right?"

His voice came from not too far away. "Yes, yes, Max, I'm perfectly all right. Thank you for asking."

"Should it have done that?"

"Not really. I think perhaps the rocks may have been defective. I must say, Max, this sort of thing does make you doubt Pliny. I mean, I don't know a lot about elephants but I'm sure they would have found this sort of thing most upsetting. I find it hard to believe they wouldn't have turned tail and fled, don't you?"

"What is he talking about?" demanded Calvin Cutter.

"I feel sick," said someone nearby.

Yes, we needed to get out of here. I needed to get everyone evacuated back inside St. Mary's. Which would make a change. It's usually the other way around. The smell was terrible. We were going to have the Parish Council around again.

Everything was still enveloped in steam.

In the distance, I could hear hoofbeats as the horses galloped past on their way to safety. Asia presumably.

"There go the dinosaurs," announced Peterson, whom I
began to suspect was not taking this seriously at all. "It'll be
the mammals next. I'd keep my head down if I were you, Mr.
Cutter."

Cutter, the silly ass, had somehow acquired David Sands's
manuscript and was using it to protect his head as he peered
over the table top trying to see what was going on. Peterson
yanked him back to safety, but undeterred, he produced a small
palm device and began bashing away at it, generating his own
heat haze of excitement.

"Justin, Justin, you won't believe what's happening to me.
How do you spell ricochet? . . . What? . . . You'll have to speak
up—I'm under some sort of bombardment here . . . Yes, you
heard me. I tell you Justin, these people are bat-crap crazy."

I was about to refute this statement—and with some indig-
nation, too—when all the security alarms went off. The for-
merly peaceful sunny afternoon was rent again with klaxons
and bells. I closed my eyes, but it didn't help.

And here came the cavalry, headed by Markham himself,
pre-empting Dr. Stone's permission to return to work. For all
his talk of none of this being anything to do with them, the
entire Security Section was already togged out in fire-fighting
gear. Some had extinguishers, others those flat paddles with
which they attempted to beat out the flaming grass.

A small group of them broke away to try to round up the
horses before they caused chaos—well, further chaos—by
escaping to the village. Or trying to get into the main building.
Or in the case of the big, dirty brown beast known as Turk,
chasing, catching, and eating Markham, against whom he had
a long-standing grudge.

Peterson grinned at me. "So much more enjoyable when I
know none of this is my fault."

I shot him a reproachful glance. Water off a duck's back.

My com bleeped and Rosie Lee said, "You still alive out there?"

I was touched that she would ask and said so.

"I was concerned something had happened to you," she said. "because you haven't yet signed my timesheet this week. And I wanted to tell you a bloody great meteorite just came through the window and landed in your in-tray."

"Good job I wasn't working at my desk."

"You're never working at your desk."

I ignored that. "Is there much damage?"

"The entire top layer is toast."

"Really? Because right at the very bottom there's a request for pod stats over the last two years. Could that be toast too?"

"I'm under my desk at the moment, trying to find something in my bottom drawer."

"What could be more important than this, for God's sake?"

"Clean underwear."

"You're not wearing clean underwear?"

"Not any longer."

"Listen—lose the pod stats and I'll do my best on behalf of your beloved's manuscript."

"Max! Bad news! The pod stats have just gone up in flames! All two years' worth!"

That's my girl.

I WAS IMPRESSED OUR Mr. Cutter hadn't run a mile. Now, however, Peterson finally allowed him to emerge from under the table.

We waved our arms to dispel the foetid vapours. For all the good it did. Professor Rapson trotted over, a scarf tied around his nose and mouth. "Everything all right here, Max?"

"Yes," I said, turning slowly to get the full effect. It looked as if a small war had occurred. The whole area was covered in pieces of rock, burning wood, and overturned furniture. Some areas of grass were still on fire. A pall of evil-smelling smoke hung over everything.

Peterson was surveying the remains of the ex-rocks. "They certainly went up with a bang, Professor. Was that intentional?"

Professor Rapson pulled me aside and whispered, "Actually, Max, for your ears only, I might have cheated a little."

"What?"

"Well, Miss Lee said you said I had to make it good, so I added a little something extra."

"Don't tell me," I said quickly. "And Dr. Peterson doesn't need to know at all."

He nodded. "Understood."

I just had time to give thanks that however half-arsed a job the god of historians had done today, at least Dr. Bairstow hadn't been around to witness it, when my com beeped and Dr. Bairstow's voice said, "My office, Dr. Maxwell, at your earliest convenience, please, when I look forward to hearing your explanation as to why the History Department has just tried to kill us all."

"Shit," said Peterson—management's invariable response to a crisis. Second only to looking around for someone else to blame, of course.

It dawned on me that Calvin Cutter had been quiet for a very long time which might have been because when I looked round, he wasn't there. I panicked. Surely he hadn't incurred some injury. Nothing that would render him unable or unfit to sign a contract anyway. It would be just my luck if he croaked before signing something vital to our future financial stability.

And, my other responsibility—David Sands's manuscript—what had become of that? I sighed. This wasn't turning out to be one of my better days. And then things got even worse, because Calvin Cutter had retired back under the table and was gazing at the manuscript, apparently lost to everything going on around him.

He sat, silent and still, staring at something probably only film producers could see. I was concerned he might be having some sort of neural event, although there was always the possibility this was a perfectly normal state for those in the entertainment industry. I told myself it might be some form of sleep-sitting to which he and his colleagues might be prone, and that waking him could cause more problems than it solved. At least he'd stopped talking, which, as far as I was concerned, was a huge improvement on before. Peterson and I stood quietly as St. Mary's whirled past us in the traditional aftermath of one of the professor's forays into Practical History and waited for events to unfold.

And unfold they did.

Returning to the real world, Mr. Cutter thumped his ear again. "Justin, give me Marj . . . What do you mean in labour? Labour is something you do—not go into . . . What? No never mind. I'll do it myself."

He addressed himself to his ear again. "Call Marj . . . Marj? Where are you? . . . Why don't I know you're not in the office today? . . . What? But you had it last week . . . Yes, you did. I distinctly remember giving you time off to go to the hospital . . . Well, how many checkups does one foetus need? You should nip this sort of thing in the bud, you know. This constant attention-seeking does not bode well for the future . . . Anyway, enough of that. I need you to draw up contracts for . . . What? . . . What? Who are *you*? . . . No, you're not her sister. She doesn't have a sister. I had her vetted very carefully for potentially demanding family members and close personal relationships. The word sociopath is not the stigma people think . . . *What* sort of sister? . . . Oh . . . Well, now I come to think of it, how did she manage to get herself pregnant in the first place? Put her on . . . Put her back on . . . Marj, as soon as you can—this afternoon will be fine if you're busy now, I want you to draft . . . I don't understand. Why can't you? . . . Well,

how long do you think it will take? . . . Why don't you know?
Are you even married? . . . Three years? You never mentioned
it . . . No, you didn't. Who are you married to? . . . Never heard
of him . . . What *our* SAS? Well, yes, obviously, I've heard of
them. They're in all those films about storming embassies and
. . . Hello . . . Hello . . . Who the hell are you? . . . Oh . . . Right
. . . OK . . . Sorry . . .Yes . . . There's no need for . . . Yes . . .
Right . . . Sorry."

He tapped his ear and turned to us. Peterson and I were
looking everywhere but at each other.

"He seemed a bit unstable for former SAS, but maybe I'm
not the only one who can't get the staff these days." He paused
to readjust his ideas. "Justin, send flowers to St. Brenda's Nursing Home in Bath. Lots of flowers. And chocolates. And one of
those gift voucher things so they can get a pram or something.
Or nappies. Send lots of nappies. And those cute suit things
that babies wear . . . I don't know. Do people still do pink for
boys and blue for girls? . . . Are you sure? Well, send both to
be on the safe side. It'll be one or the other. And fruit. I've
read somewhere that women need a lot of fruit after childbirth.
Send a fruit basket every day. And a card. Give it to Chelsea—
she can forge my signature better than I can. Have it all delivered today. And stick in a note asking her what she's done with
the script for *Fanny Price—The True Story*. And where are the
budget figures for the thing on Bonnie Prince Charlie? And
about the contracts, of course."

"Do you think we could keep him?" murmured Peterson.
"He's rather good value, don't you think?"

WE BUNDLED HIM UPSTAIRS to Dr. Bairstow's office, which was,
mercifully, foetid-vapour free, and finally got him sat down. Mrs.
Partridge placed a cup of tea in front of him which he ignored.
I saw her lips tighten and hastened to thank her because you
really don't want to get on the wrong side of Mrs. Partridge.

I don't think he stopped talking the whole time. I'd never seen him so excited. It was a miracle his ear didn't drop off.

"Hello. Justin. Yes. Write this down. An historical society. Dull as ditch water on the surface. But hiding a secret. They're secret time travellers—changing history for the better. Bringing back the dinosaurs. Which escape and terrorise . . . oh I don't know, how about Edinburgh? We could have them rampaging down Princes Street and destroying the castle. They help Boadicea when she defends London from Julius Caesar. They save Elizabeth I from the Great Fire of London."

"No," I said, feebly.

"Freeing the princes in the Tower when Richard III tries to murder them."

"He probably didn't," I said, even more feebly.

"There'll be a handsome hero."

Peterson preened. On what grounds remained unclear.

"And a beautiful heroine—stacked, of course."

Someone made some sort of noise, but when I stared at them suspiciously, Peterson was staring at his feet and Dr. Bairstow was gazing serenely out of the window.

"She keeps having to be rescued, of course. From Pharaoh's harems. From being burned at the stake. You know the sort of thing. She falls in love with a Viking and brings him back to the modern day. Could he have superpowers? We could start with the *Mayflower* and the brave pilgrims fleeing religious persecution."

"They didn't," I said feebly. "They emigrated because England wasn't strict enough for their . . ."

He wasn't listening. "Well, I don't know—a tunnel, maybe. Or a time rift. They're always popular. Especially in Cardiff. Or," he said, rifling through David Sands's by now quite bedraggled manuscript, "some sort of time-travelling amulet they discover when raiding a secret South American ziggurat. Like in that film with that woman who pouts a lot. That could happen. We'll sort something out. Talk to you later."

I tried again. "But . . ."

The Boss waved me into silence. "An exciting idea, Mr. Cutter. I think you have a winner there. You can rely on St. Mary's to provide you with everything you need." He opened his desk drawer and pulled out a bottle and two glasses. "Shall we sit down and thrash out the details?" He ran an experienced eye over two of his most senior members of staff. "Dr. Peterson, Dr. Maxwell, please do not let us detain you."

We exited slowly and with great dignity—as befitted two senior officers in a top-secret government establishment. Through Mrs. Partridge's office and around the gallery. We descended the stairs wearing our best responsibility-laden expressions, worked our way through the boiling mass of historians in the Hall, out through the front doors, and down the steps into the very nearly fresh air. And then—and only then—were we able to let go at last.

It took some time. Peterson's a giggler and every time I thought I'd got myself back under control he'd catch my eye and off we'd go again. Until finally. . .

"Haven't done that in a long time," he said, straightening up and wiping his eyes.

"No."

"You all right now?"

"I think so. Yes."

"So," he said, smoothing down his hair and striking a noble pose. "Who do you think they'll get to play me?"

I took a deep breath. "Lassie, probably," and stamped off to suss out the damage.

Yeah, Thursday was quite exciting.

Friday, however, was aftermath day.

FRIDAY

THE NEXT MORNING, STRAIGHT after breakfast, Leon and I called in to Sick Bay. Leon had another medical appointment and I wanted to see how Mr. Bashford was doing, still bruised and bloody from his encounter with the deity-bashing young men. As his supervisor, I was supposed to care. Sykes, Markham, and Peterson came along for the ride and, as Sykes said, to see if his compost was mentis.

Leaving Leon in the probably capable hands of Dr. Stone, we wandered into the men's ward.

Bashford was sitting up in bed, propped against his pillows, looking interestingly pale and with a massive bruise on one cheekbone. He had a split lip and both hands were cut and swollen, so he and his trusty sidekick had obviously given a good account of themselves.

Angus, from whom he had tearfully refused to be parted, was sitting happily on his lap, crooning gently. They gazed adoringly at each other.

Have I remembered to say that Angus is a chicken?

It says much for St. Mary's that we'd apparently had a chicken roaming the corridors since Tuesday and, apart from Calvin Cutter, no one appeared to have noticed. Nurse Hunter was giving him vigorously to understand that keeping a chicken on his wardrobe—no, actually keeping a chicken *anywhere* in a medical facility—was unacceptable.

"I have to," he said, tragically. "If Dr. Bairstow finds out . . ."

"You surely don't intend to keep him," I said.

"Her," he said, tickling the back of her neck. She closed her eyes in bliss.

"You can't keep her. We're not allowed pets."

"I don't see why not. When you think of the amount of wildlife Markham has harboured over the years . . . fleas, lice, fungus, tapeworms, every type of bacteria known to man . . ."

"And probably still is," said Hunter nastily, obviously not in a good mood and having a go at everyone in sight.

"Not voluntarily," he said to her. "Trust me, no one *chooses* to have ringworm."

"It's the fact that ringworm so frequently chooses you that is the point of my argument."

"How can you be maundering on about ringworm when there's a bloody great chicken in the room?" he said, indignant over yet another of the world's injustices.

She pointed at her patient, still obliviously chatting to his chicken. "It was Bashford who brought the subject up."

"I can't believe you're siding with a man who has a chicken on his lap."

"After you, anything looks good."

Peterson caught my eye and grinned.

"Where would you keep her?" I asked, feeling someone should address the practicalities.

He'd obviously thought it through. "She likes wardrobes. She can live in mine during the day and sleep on it at night."

"No, she bloody can't," said Sykes with a certain amount of menace. "At least not unless you want to be up there with her."

I suspected he hadn't thought it through quite enough.

It seemed there was going to be a certain amount of blood up the walls and I was just marshalling my conflict-resolution skills when we heard a murmur of voices on the other side of the door. The door handle rattled dramatically. The traditional

St. Mary's sign that Dr. Bairstow was here and we were all doomed.

Bashford scooped up Angus and shoved her under the bedcovers where, surprised but willing, she stamped around, making herself comfortable, and apparently perfectly at home in her new surroundings.

We all turned to face the door.

After all these years, Dr. Bairstow must surely be accustomed to the guilty silence that falls whenever he enters a room. I think he quite likes it. It shows he's doing his job properly.

We stood grouped around the bed, a tableau of caring supervisors and colleagues come to visit the sick. Nothing to find fault with there.

The bedclothes bulged unfortunately as Angus settled herself more comfortably and, having arranged things to her satisfaction, uttered a long, low chicken noise of contentment.

I found I couldn't look.

Bashford, caught between either admitting to the world's most massive groin malfunction, or explaining why he had a chicken in his bed, closed his eyes and pretended he was dead. Which was probably only anticipating events by a few minutes.

Dr. Bairstow—who was, I suspected, perfectly aware of the existence of Angus in his unit, as indeed, he was aware of everything that happened at St. Mary's, and had only stopped in for a little light entertainment at the expense of his staff— stood like the proverbial pillar of salt.

I made sure I stood behind Sykes, who just for once in her life could be useful. Hunter suddenly began to bash away at her scratchpad, Markham was busily tucking into Bashford's grapes, and Peterson was staring thoughtfully out of the window, to all appearances mulling over some tricky temporal conundrum.

"Good morning, Mr. Bashford."

The silence went on until Bashford, realising he'd been abandoned in his hour of need, seized the bedclothes and prepared, somewhat painfully, to get out of bed and, possibly, to flee the country.

The point of Dr. Bairstow's stick pushed him firmly back against his pillows. "I think I speak for all of us, Mr. Bashford, when I say we would be grateful if you could remain exactly where you are."

"But, sir . . ."

I had to get out. Now.

At the same time, Markham said plaintively that his arm hurt.

"I'd better take a look at that," said Hunter instantly, pushing him towards the door.

"I have to . . ." I said, and stopped, suffering a complete inspiration failure.

". . . write my . . ." said Sykes.

". . . report . . ." I finished, and we all bolted for the door, headed by Peterson, showcasing senior management's usual loyalty and commitment in a crisis.

Outside, Dr. Stone, still talking to Leon, looked up, astonished, as we burst through, closing the door thankfully on whatever was about to happen to Bashford.

"What on earth is the matter? Is it Bashford?" He began to move towards the door.

Hunter took a deep breath, but before any of us could reply, the door opened and Dr. Bairstow limped into the reception area with Angus clamped firmly under one arm. Apparently thrilled with this new and enhanced view of the world, she was looking around with bright-eyed interest. In many ways, she reminded me of Sykes.

He limped past us murmuring, "Good morning."

We chorused, "Good morning, Dr. Bairstow," like infant schoolchildren. He called up the lift, the doors opened, and he

stepped inside, Angus bobbing her head happily at this unexpected treat.

The doors closed. They disappeared. It had taken him
approximately eight point seven seconds to resolve the Angus
crisis. Although to what end. . .

"You don't think he's going to eat her, do you?" said Hunter
anxiously.

"No," we said, unconvincingly.

"Dammit," said Sykes, in despair. "Bashford's only conscious for an hour or so each day and now I have to share him
with a bloody chicken."

"Cheer up," said Leon, who was trying not to laugh. "It
could be worse."

"How?"

"He might be conscious all day."

She brightened. "I hadn't thought of that."

Anyway, to cut a long story short, rather to everyone's surprise, and probably as a reward for saving Bashford from serious injury, Angus was allowed to remain at St. Mary's. I believe
Dr. Bairstow made several cruel remarks about raising the level
of intelligence in the History Department. She spends her days
hanging around the stables and her nights on top of Bashford's
wardrobe where she utters a series of crooning noises in his
direction before settling down contentedly.

As far as I know, the two of them are very happy, although
Sykes wouldn't speak to him for a week and Housekeeping
refuse to go anywhere near his room.

I BUNDLED UP EVERYONE'S reports, and signed and initialled
all the paperwork. I was expecting all sorts of grief over—well,
everything, really. Calvin Cutter, the manuscript, Bashford,
Angus, exploding rocks—it was all a bit of a perfect storm.
Anyway, at his command, I presented myself to Dr. Bairstow
that morning. Mrs. Partridge waved me through. I searched

her face for some clue as to his mood, but she was wearing her usual expression. The one that gives me to understand I rank somewhere beneath blue-green algae in the great scheme of things.

"Please do not delay him this morning, Dr. Maxwell. A deputation from the Parish Council will be arriving at eleven o'clock."

Oh God—the rural mafia were on their way.

I took a deep breath and entered. "Good morning, Dr. Bairstow."

He was staring out of his window. "Good morning, Dr. Maxwell. An update, please."

"All the fires were easily extinguished, sir. The car park has been cleared of debris and shrapnel. Everyone's cars have been returned unharmed. The building sustained two broken windows but Mr. Strong reports no structural damage. Dr. Stone reports no major injuries, although Dr. Dowson did sprain his wrist when Professor Rapson fell off his stepladder."

"Clarify."

"He fell on him, sir."

I paused in case he had something to say about that, but no. I carried on. "The horses have returned to the paddock. Mr. Markham has received medical treatment for minor Turk-related injuries."

"Serious?"

"Just a nip, sir."

"I meant for the horse."

"Oh, no sir, I believe Mr. Strong has some sort of antiseptic equine mouthwash for these occasions. Both Markham and Turk are expected to make a full recovery. In other news, sir, Mr. Dieter reports the repairs to Hawking are complete and everything is ready for our next assignment next Monday. And um . . ." I paused and braced myself.

"Yes, Dr. Maxwell?"

"I'm very sorry, sir, I don't know how it happened but, somehow, in all the confusion, Mr. Cutter appears to have walked off with Mr. Sands's manuscript."

He continued to stare out of the window. "Ah well, no great harm done."

I blinked. "But sir, he was talking about making a movie or a holo. About time travel. Based on Mr. Sands's story."

"Yes, I believe he was."

"But won't it be even worse if they make a movie out it than if he publishes the book?"

"Of course not, Dr. Maxwell. When have you ever known a movie to bear even a passing resemblance to the book from which it is adapted? Once the entertainment industry gets its hands on it, the original work will be completely unrecognisable, trust me."

"Oh."

"And given their normal rate of progress, it could be years before it even goes into production. With luck, we will all be dead by then."

"I shall keep my fingers crossed for an early demise, sir."

"I have no doubt that you will be successful, Dr. Maxwell. Thank you, that will be all."

I turned to go and then had a sudden thought. "Oh, by the way, sir, did Mr. Cutter sign the contracts?"

"What? Oh, yes, I believe so."

He believed so? He *believed* so?

"I thought it was a matter of financial life and death, sir."

"Oh no. The cost of repairing Hawking is so astronomical that even the national debt pales into insignificance in comparison. Nothing we could do would even dent it."

"But you said this was important, sir."

"And so it was."

He turned around, his back to the window, face unreadable.

"But not as important or as welcome as the sight of you and Dr. Peterson laughing together again. Thank you, Dr. Maxwell, that will be all."

THE END

THE FIRST BOOK IN THE BESTSELLING BRITISH MADCAP
TIME-TRAVELLING SERIES, SERVED WITH A DASH OF WIT THAT
SEEMS TO BE EVERYONE'S CUP OF TEA.

The first thing you learn on the job at St. Mary's is that one wrong move and history will fight back—sometimes in particularly nasty ways. But, as new recruit Madeleine Maxwell soon discovers, it's not only history they're often fighting.

From eleventh-century London to World War I, from the Cretaceous Period to the destruction of the Great Library at Alexandria, one thing is for sure: wherever the historians at St. Mary's go, chaos is sure to follow in their wake . . .

Just One Damned Thing After Another
The Chronicles of St. Mary's Book One
Jodi Taylor
978-1-59780-868-2
Paperback / $12.99

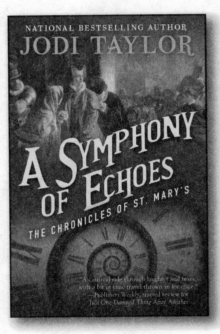

BOOK THREE IN THE BESTSELLING BRITISH MADCAP TIME-TRAVELLING SERIES

In *A Second Chance*, it seems nothing can go right right for Max and the historians. The team jumps to an encounter with a mirror-stealing Isaac Newton only to wind up at the bloody battlefield at Agincourt. Then they discover how a simple fact-finding assignment to witness the ancient and murderous cheese-rolling ceremony in Gloucester can result in CBC—concussion by cheese.

Finally, Max gets to make the long-awaited jump to Bronze Age Troy, but it ends in personal catastrophe. Just when it seems things couldn't get any worse—it's back to the Cretaceous Period to confront an old enemy who has nothing to lose.

A Second Chance
The Chronicles of St. Mary's Book Three
Jodi Taylor
978-1-59780-870-5
Paperback / $12.99

BOOK FOUR IN THE BESTSELLING BRITISH MADCAP TIME-TRAVELLING SERIES

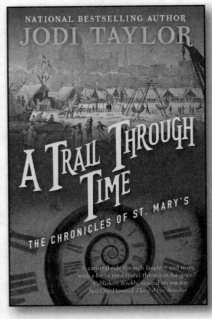

In *A Trail Through Time*, Max and Leon are reunited and looking forward to a peaceful lifetime together. But, sadly, they don't even make it to lunchtime.

The action races from seventeenth century London to Ancient Egypt and from Pompeii to fourteenth century Southwark as they're pursued up and down the timeline, playing a perilous game of hide-and-seek until they're finally forced to take refuge at St. Mary's—where new dangers await them.

Max and company maintain their signature sense of humor throughout, but the final, desperate Battle of St. Mary's is in grim earnest. Overwhelmed, outnumbered, and with the building crashing down around them, how can St. Mary's possibly survive?

A Trail Through Time
The Chronicles of St. Mary's Book Four
Jodi Taylor
978-1-59780-871-2
Paperback / $12.99

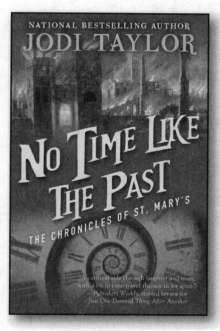

BOOK SIX IN THE BESTSELLING BRITISH MADCAP TIME-TRAVELLING SERIES

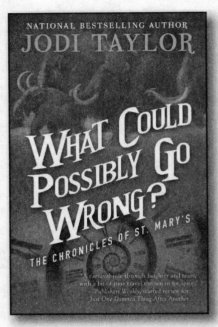

**What Could Possibly
Go Wrong?**
The Chronicles of St. Mary's Book Six
Jodi Taylor
978-1-59780-873-6
Paperback / $12.99

In *What Could Possibly Go Wrong?*, Max is back with a new husband, new job, and a training program for the new recruits that cannot fail.

After having her knee reconstructed, Max has restricted duties. She becomes the Chief Training Officer and takes five fresh trainees through the initiation process. But for Max, the old way of giving trainees extensive theoretical lessons before allowing them to "investigate major historical events in contemporary time" is pointless and doesn't really prove that these recruits have what it takes to be a historian. She decides to toss them right into travelling under "safe conditions."

With Max as the interim Chief Training Officer, the five recruits, Joan of Arc, a baby mammoth, a duplicitous Father of History, a bombed rat, Stone Age hunters, a couple of passing policemen who should have better things to do, and Dick the Turd, it's practically guaranteed that nothing will go according to plan.

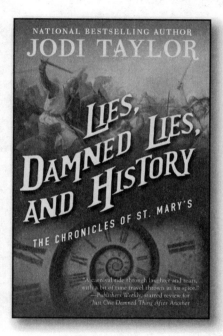

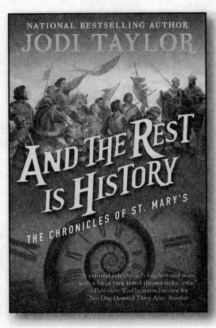

ABOUT THE AUTHOR

JODI TAYLOR (WHO ALSO writes as Isabella Barclay) is, and always has been, a History Nut. Her disinclination to get out of bed for anything after 1485 can only be overcome by massive amounts of chocolate, and sometimes, if it's raining, not even then.

She wanted to write a book about time travel that was a little different, and not having a clue how difficult this would make her book to classify, went ahead and slung in elements of history, adventure, comedy, romance, tragedy, and anything else she could think of. Her advice to booksellers is to buy huge numbers of her books and just put one on every shelf.

The result is the story of the St. Mary's Institute of Historical Research and the nutters who work there.